BEYOND THE LAVENDER FIELDS

also by

ARLEM HAWKS

Georgana's Secret

BEYOND THE LAVENDER FIELDS

ARLEM HAWKS

SHADOW
MOUNTAIN

Interior image: vectorpark/Shutterstock.com

Visit us at shadowmountain.com

This is a work of fiction. Characters and events in this book are products of the author's imagination or are represented fictitiously.

Library of Congress Cataloging-in-Publication Data
Names: Hawks, Arlem, author.
Title: Beyond the lavender fields / Arlem Hawks.
Description: [Salt Lake City] : Shadow Mountain, [2021] | Summary: "In Marseille, on the eve of the French Revolution, a royalist and a revolutionary clash and struggle to navigate their relationship in a society that forces people to choose sides"—Provided by publisher.
Identifiers: LCCN 2021035803 | ISBN 9781629729350 (hardback)
Subjects: LCSH: Eighteenth century, setting. | Marseille (France), setting. | France—History—Revolution, 1789–1799—Fiction. | BISAC: FICTION /Historical / General | LCGFT: Historical fiction. | Romance fiction.
Classification: LCC PS3608.A89348 B49 2021 | DDC 813/.6—dc23
LC record available at https://lccn.loc.gov/2021035803

Printed in the United States of America
Sun Print Solutions, Salt Lake City, UT

10   9   8   7   6   5   4   3   2   1

For Mary Carol, Grandma Carol, Caroline, and Carolyn—

four amazing women who have changed the course of my life.

Thank you for your influence and example.

NAMES

ÉTIENNE (AY-tyen) FAMILY
Aude (ode)
Claire (clair)
Claudine (kloh-DEEN)
Gilles (jeel)
Maxence (max-AHNCE)
Victor (vik-TORE)
Roger (roh-JAY)
Rosalie (roh-zah-LEE)

DAUBIN (doh-BAHN) FAMILY
Angelique (on-jel-EEK)
Émile (ay-MEEL)
Guillaume (gee-YOM)
Marie-Caroline (mah-REE cah-roh-LEEN)

OTHER CHARACTERS
Florence (flore-AHNCE)
Honoré Martel (aw-no-RAY mar-TEL)
Jean Sault (john soht)
Laurent (lore-AWN)

Luc Hamon (luke ah-MOHN)
Moreau (more-OH)
Nicolas Joubert (nik-oh-LAH joo-BAIR)
Père Franchicourt (pair fron-shee-COOR)
Savatier (sah-vah-tee-YAY)
Sylvainne Valois (sil-VEN val-WAH)

PLACES
Belsunce (bel-SUNCE)
Marseille (mar-SAY-ye)
Montpellier (mohn-pel-YAY)
Panier (pah-NYAY)
Le Rossignol (luh ross-in-YOLE)
Saint-Cannat (sahn can-AH)
Saint-Malo (sahn mah-LOH)

FRENCH TERMS

Allemande (all-eh-MAHND): Literally "German." The name of a popular dance thought to have come from Germany.

Allez (ah-LAY): Go.

Aristo (ah-ree-STOH): An aristocrat

Aux armes, citoyens (Ohz arm sit-wah-YUN): To arms, citizens.

Bête (bet): Beast or brute

Bien sûr (byun sur): Of course.

Bonne nuit (bon NWEE): Good night.

Bonsoir (bohn-SWAHR): Good evening.

Bonté divine (bon-TAY dee-VEEN): Literally "divine goodness." Goodness gracious.

Bourgeouis(e)/bourgeouisie (boorj-WAHZ/boorj-wah-ZEE): The middle or merchant class of French society. Included in the Third Estate group of French citizens, meaning they were commoners.

C'est naturel (say nat-ur-EL): Literally "It's natural." Of course.

Cher/chère (shair): Dear

Chèrie (shair-EE): Dear one

Ciel (syel): Heavens.

Comédie-Française (coh-MAY-dee fron-SEZ): A famous Parisian theater group founded in the 1600s that is still around today

Coquin (koh-KUHN): Little devil. Little rascal.

Diantre (dee-ON-truh): Literally "the devil." Good heavens.

Farandole (fah-ron-DOL): A line dance used at revolutionary gatherings

Grandmère (grahn-MAIR): Grandmother

Jacobin (Jack-oh-BUN): A member of the Jacobin Club, which was one of the most influential political factions in the French Revolution. The Jacobins were against the monarchy and responsible for the Reign of Terror that lasted from 1793 to 1794.

Je t'aime (juh-TEM): I love you.

La patrie (lah paht-REE): The fatherland

Livre (LEE-vruh): Pound. The unit of money used prior to the franc becoming the official monetary unit in 1795

Ma fille (mah FEE-ye): My daughter

Maman (ma-MAW): Mama

Merci (mair-SEE): Thank you.

Mère (mair): Mother

Mon ami (mohn ah-MEE): My friend

Mon amour (mohn ah-MOOR): My love

Mon fils (mohn FEES): My son

Mon frère (mohn frair): My brother

Oui (wee): Yes.

Parbleu (par-BLUH): Egad!

Père (pair): Father

Que diable (kuh dee-AB-luh): What the devil!

Révolutionnaire (rev-oh-loo-shun-AIR): A revolutionary. Someone who sided with the revolution.

Royaliste (ro-yahl-EEST): Royalist. Someone who supported the king.

Rue (rew): Road

Sacrebleu (sah-kruh-BLUH): Literally "Sacred blue." Oh my gosh.

Sans-culotte (son cew-LOHT): Literally "without breeches." Breeches (as well as wigs and other fancy clothes) became a symbol of the upper class early in the French Revolution. This antiroyalist group was strict about wearing only long trousers. This group was made largely of lower-class Frenchmen, and they were one of the most violent groups of the period, taking part in many of the riots and public executions. Another of their symbols was the red liberty cap.

Savonnerie (sav-on-eh-ree): Soap factory

Sur le Pont d'Avignon (sur luh pohn da-vee-NYON): "On the Bridge of Avignon." An old and very popular French tune.

Tartuffe (tar-TOOF): A play by Molière

CHAPTER 1

May 1792
Marseille, Provence, France

Gilles Étienne shifted in his chair and leaned closer to the ledger before him. Most days he relished political debates, but this evening he had too much to finish before his Jacobin meeting. He resisted the temptation to join in the argument between his fellow soap-factory clerks.

"The monarchy has nothing but love for France," the new clerk said as he marched toward the door.

Gilles faltered in his writing, an errant mark from his quill defacing the page. Ignorant *royaliste*. The monarchy had brought only pain and suffering to their country. Gilles wound his fingers through his mess of dark curls. His employer, Monsieur Daubin, needed these numbers tomorrow morning, but the quarrel behind him rang through the office with increasing volume, nearly drowning out the sound of a carriage passing outside the factory.

The other clerk snorted. "Frenchmen have enjoyed more freedom in the three years since the start of the revolution than they've seen in centuries, perhaps millennia." Out of the corner of his eye, Gilles spied the young man pulling a red cap, a symbol of the revolution, out of his pocket. It was a bold move since, as far as they could tell, the owner of the *savonnerie* aligned himself with the *royalistes*. "Come, Étienne. Surely as a Jacobin you will not stand for such ridiculous treason to reach your ears."

"Mostly I wish for only silence to reach my ears," Gilles mumbled. An ocean breeze, so faint only a practiced nose could pick it out, skipped through the open office window and tried to draw away his attention. He'd gladly left the sea behind two years previous, but disputes with unyielding monarchists almost made him wish to flee to the deck of a ship at full sail. Almost.

"Leave him be," the *royaliste* clerk said. "Étienne knows he has no real evidence against the king."

Gilles ground his teeth to keep from launching himself into the argument. He had many reasons the king deserved to be removed, starting with the extravagance allowed to the queen. But disputing with someone whose mind was already made up would not put more money in Gilles's pocket.

"Or he simply wants to make sure he is in the *monsieur*'s favor," the *révolutionnaire* spat.

There was truth in that. Staying in Monsieur Daubin's good graces meant earning a few extra *livres* here and there. Every addition to his wage put him one step closer to joining his second oldest brother at the prestigious medical school in Montpellier.

Footsteps on the stairs halted the argument. "Until Monday, *messieurs*," Gilles called cheerily as his companions hurried out the door to his right. *Sacrebleu.* They could be so tiresome.

He went back to the numbers before him, which were not adding up as he expected them to. Perhaps one of his fellow clerks had made a mistake in calculating somewhere.

Creaking in the corridor announced an intruder on his solitude. Gilles extracted his fingers from his hair and straightened. Monsieur Daubin, no doubt. Few employees stayed late at the *savonnerie.*

"Gilles," hissed a voice too intense to be the *monsieur*'s. Émile, Monsieur Daubin's oldest son, poked his head through the doorway of the clerks' office, an impish gleam in his eyes. Though he was a year older than Gilles, some days Émile did not act it. Neither did Maxence—Émile's friend and Gilles's brother—and he was two years older.

Gilles chuckled and stuck his pen back in the inkwell. "I did not know you were due home. Is Max with you?" The two often traveled back together from Montpellier.

"He expected you to be at home by now, so he continued on." Émile's grin hadn't dimmed. "There's someone you should see in my father's office."

A patron? Gilles leaped from his chair and snatched up his jacket. "Did you see who it was?" Monsieur Daubin did not have an appointment scheduled so late in the evening. Not one he had told Gilles about. Had the minister come to inquire about his order? "Was it an older gentleman? Tall and thin?"

Émile leaned against the doorpost and folded his arms. "Tall and thin, yes. But most certainly not a gentleman."

Gilles paused in pulling on his jacket. "A lady?" What lady would come to the *savonnerie*? Most women preferred Daubin's quiet shop in the Noailles district for purchasing their soaps and perfumes.

"A young one. And well dressed."

"Waiting for your father?"

Émile shrugged. "She said she has business with him." Something about his nonchalance made Gilles raise an eyebrow. He was playing at something.

Émile nodded behind him. "You should see."

Gilles glanced at his incomplete work. Monsieur Daubin would not get angry about the unfinished business, not after he had sent Gilles all about Marseille on various errands earlier in the day. He closed the ledger, capped his ink, and pushed himself out of his chair. With writing utensils stowed and the desk cleared, he turned to a smirking Émile.

"My father might will this factory to you, if you aren't careful." He caught Gilles's shoulder, eyes narrowing conspiratorially. "I have a wager."

Aïe. Not that.

"Kiss that girl in there, and I'll give you twenty-five *livres.* Unless you are too frightened."

Why did he and Maxence enjoy this game so much? Not that Gilles didn't like kissing girls—he liked it too well—his conscience just had a stronger hold than either his brother's or their friend's. And the look Émile gave him indicated that he expected a challenge.

But twenty-five *livres* . . .

"Why do you not kiss her yourself, if you think her worth it?" Gilles asked.

Émile's eyes glinted. "I think you have the better chance."

"Of course I do. Women love darkly handsome mariners more than they like pale university students." Émile's complexion and hair were lighter than most *Marseillais,* even though the rest of the Daubin family looked like they fit in the Mediterranean port city.

"You hardly have the appearance of a sailor anymore," Émile said. "Two years in an office changes a man."

Gilles did not like to think on the changes. Every time his father returned, he pointed out how soft Gilles was becoming.

"Are you going to make an effort? Or shall I go find your brother to do the job properly?"

"Does she need to be kissed so badly?" Émile was being strangely persistent.

His friend snorted. "Every woman needs to be kissed. Especially this one, by the looks of her."

But they did not all wish to, Gilles had found. He paused in the doorway, face to face with Émile. "And what happens if I fail?" He could not afford to hand over twenty-five *livres*.

"You must keep me company at a welcoming dinner for my sister next week." Émile wrinkled his nose, looking like Gilles's six-year-old niece rather than a twenty-three-year-old university student.

"The married one?"

Émile's look of disgust deepened. "I wish it were. No, the unmarried one."

"Do you dread the dinner or the arrival of your sister?" Though he'd never met Marie-Caroline Daubin, Gilles had heard much groaning over Émile's backward-thinking sister, who was Maxence's age.

"Both equally." Émile's voice lowered. "We shouldn't be hosting extravagant dinners with the country in such a state. It's unpatriotic nonsense, and if it would not offend my mother, I would not attend." Then his devilish grin returned. "Do we have a deal?" He held out his hand.

Gilles hesitated only a moment before grasping it. Émile thumped him on the shoulder. "*Allez, mon ami.* Go catch your lady or face the terror of dinner."

With a final glance at the window, through which he could see the cloudless sky beginning to fade into evening, Gilles stole from the room. This was idiocy. A high-class young lady would not be willing to kiss him. Even though social hierarchy was a thing of history, many still held to their status like a boy clinging to the rigging on his first journey across a ship's yard.

He would not push the matter. If she were a flirt, he'd take the easy prize. But he'd rather face Émile's feudal-minded sister than be caught by Monsieur Daubin in his own office trying to coax a reluctant patron into a moment of amusement.

Gilles crept slowly up to the office door, keeping his shoes quiet against the floor. For a moment he longed for the encouragement of the reviving Mediterranean air, rather than the heaviness within the *savonnerie*.

Be Maxence. His brother rarely lost these games. Gilles pulled himself up to his full height, but even straightened he could not compare to his brother's much taller stature.

The young woman, garbed in a brilliant indigo riding habit, stood before the large desk on the far side of the room with her back to the door. A few long, brown curls hung from her coiffure and curved around her neck to rest atop her shoulder. A little tune tripped through the office, and it took him several moments of listening to her humming before he recognized it. *Sur le pont d'Avignon*, an old song about dancing on the bridge in Avignon.

Gilles cleared his throat, cutting off the humming, and nodded a bow when she turned. "Might I assist you, *mademoiselle?*" He lifted his head and caught a pair of piercing, dark eyes. Her hands rested on his employer's desk as though she owned it.

"I am only waiting, *merci*."

"May I fetch something for you while you wait?" Gilles took a few casual steps into the room. She held her head high, lips pressed together as she studied him. He let a warm smile swell gradually across his mouth.

"I think not, but I thank you all the same," she finally said.

"Perhaps I can keep you company while you wait for Monsieur Daubin." He stopped beside her at the desk.

Her eyes traveled from his tousled hair to his worn shoes, then back to his face. For a moment his resolve wavered. No doubt she had already dismissed him as an insolent employee. Her brow arched, almost as if she saw through his pleasant words. "I am not the sort who needs constant attention. I assure you, I will be perfectly at ease on my own."

Gilles leaned back against the edge of the desk, not daring to peek at the doorway to see if Émile was watching. "I am Monsieur Daubin's head clerk. He did not tell me he had an appointment this evening. Let alone one with such a beautiful customer." He set his hands against the wood, just far enough away from her white-gloved fingers that their nearness might have been an accident. Would Émile settle for a kiss on the hand? He hadn't specified, though usually their games only counted kissing the lips.

Gilles swallowed, his mouth suddenly dry. If he ever found the chance, he would enjoy kissing those full, soft-looking lips.

The *mademoiselle* took a marked step to the side, but her fingers trailed along the desk as they swept away from him. Was she toying with him?

"What business do you have with the *monsieur*?" he managed. "Perhaps I can help."

Gold buttons marched up the front of her jacket, leading to her throat and the tiny white cockade, small enough one might have mistaken it for a flower, pinned at the top of her cravat. On close examination, he could not mistake the looped ribbons.

White. The color of the monarchy.

A *royaliste*, then. How she'd managed to wear such a symbol openly in the streets and not get harassed, he'd never know. Perhaps he would let Émile have his victory. If this young woman were a blatant supporter of Louis XVI and his bumbled monarchy, he'd rather lose Émile's wager than kiss her.

"Nothing with which you can help, I am afraid." She walked with clipped footsteps to the window behind the desk, out of his reach.

Gilles followed her, coming to stand by her side as she gazed out the window. What was her business? She'd practically made the office her home without invitation. Had Monsieur Daubin decided to throw his efforts into the counterrevolution? Perhaps she was a messenger.

The young woman rested her hand against one of the glass panes. Over the rooftops of the buildings across the street, fingers of sunlight reached around chimneys and through alleyways as the sun dipped toward the horizon. There were a few hours of light yet, but the streets below had begun to dim.

"I forgot how much I do love this place," she murmured.

"The *savonnerie*?"

The quip earned him a glare. "Of course not. I meant this city."

Gilles planted his hands on the sill, but she paid him no mind. "Have you been away long?" he asked.

"I have been living just outside Paris these two years."

A messenger from Paris? All the factions of the revolution, including *royaliste* groups, had leadership in that city.

"I was not impatient to return," she continued, "but Marseille is already reminding me of her merits."

"Is she?" Gilles inched closer, fingers gliding in the direction of hers until they barely touched. The longer he watched those lips, the more satisfying the thought of making a conquest of this *royaliste* became. It was only a kiss, and yet his pulse raced at an alarming speed he hadn't experienced since his first kiss. She carried herself with more poise and confidence than he usually saw in the girls he kissed. If she'd just come from Paris and the moralless aristocracy in that city, perhaps he had a better chance of succeeding in his wager than he'd thought.

"Though her abundance of overeager young men and shameless flirts, I did not miss in the slightest." She seized his arm by the sleeve of his jacket. Gilles flinched at the unexpected touch, but her grip held strong as she swung his hand back to his side of the windowsill. "What is your name, that I may commend you to your employer?"

His face heated, which he wouldn't have had much trouble hiding two years ago when he'd stepped off the gangplank of *le Rossignol* for the last time. But after extended days at the factory, his tanned skin had long since faded.

A gruff voice at the door turned both of their heads. "Ah, Étienne. Still here?" Monsieur Daubin entered, face buried in a stack of papers. He tossed his modest wig onto the desk and rubbed his balding head as he read.

The young woman whirled to face Gilles, this time with an icy stare as her eyes swept the length of him. "Étienne?"

"*Oui*, Gilles Étienne." He took a step back, for once unnerved at a young woman surveying him. "Have we met?"

Monsieur Daubin looked up from his documents. "You're here? What is this?"

The young woman threw one last glare at Gilles, and he felt as though she'd seen through to his very soul. Clearly she did not like what she saw. Her skirts whipped past him as she sauntered over to Monsieur Daubin.

And kissed him on the cheek.

Gilles's eyebrows shot up as his employer hugged her to him, planting a kiss on the top of her hair. Her muffled response did not carry. Who was this girl? Gilles thought he knew Monsieur Daubin well after two years of seeing not only to his business but also to his personal matters.

"I expected to see your brother here, not you," Monsieur Daubin said, releasing her and returning to his papers.

"I came with him. Maman was hovering, and I needed some relief."

Gilles went cold. Her brother?

The soap maker perked up. "Émile is here? Why did he not come to me?" He tossed the papers on his desk. Gilles had taught himself to immediately arrange his employer's papers, but the realization suddenly dawning clouded his mind.

No . . . Émile wouldn't.

Monsieur Daubin made for the door, motioning to Gilles in the corner. "You may send him for tea if you wish." He disappeared into the corridor.

"Thank you, Papa."

Gilles wanted to drop his head to his hands. Of course Émile would amuse himself by making Gilles look the fool. He was probably cackling in a corner of the soap factory at the good joke of making his friend try to kiss his older sister.

Her shoes echoed against the office's wood floor as she strode forward. She stopped before Gilles, the hem of her petticoat lapping against his shoes. She turned her face to him, and if he hadn't been frozen in place, he would have found her lips an easy target. But she wasn't a willing tavern girl, and he was her father's clerk.

"I do not want to kiss you," she said. "Not now. Not ever."

"Kiss me?" Gilles sputtered, face aflame. She knew. How did she know? "Pardon, *mademoiselle*, but I never—"

"I know what sort of boys my brother's friends are." Mademoiselle Daubin spun on her heel and swished over to her father's chair. She sat, then pulled out a piece of paper from the writing box Gilles had positioned there that morning. After pulling off her gloves, she waved absently toward the door. "You may go."

As though she were the queen, sitting in her finery at the Tuileries Palace. The *révolutionnaire* within him bristled at her orders, but he kept his mouth closed as he sprinted from the office. Though he had tried valiantly to forget every last thing he had learned from life aboard his father's ship, one memory rang clear in his mind: A stiff wind whipping at their caps, every sail extended and straining, sea spray pelting the deck. His father watching a company of British East Indiamen shrinking into the horizon. *You must learn to recognize which battles you can win, and which you must flee*, his *père* had said. *It is not cowardice to be wise. A brave fool who goes after the prize when he knows he cannot win is still a fool.*

Yet as Gilles fled the office as fast as he dared, somehow he felt both the coward and the fool.

CHAPTER 2

19 May 1792
Savonnerie Daubin
Marseille

My dearest cousin Sylvainne,

I have arrived safely, and Marseille has already given me a greeting so true to its character I cannot help but shake my head. I'd forgotten what loose manners this city upheld. But what should I have expected with the Jacobins grasping tightly to its government?

Maman succumbed to weeping the moment of my arrival, and it was as though I was seven years old again. She's hardly left my side since I arrived this afternoon. I had to convince Émile to let me ride with him to the savonnerie so I wouldn't go mad. But I should have stayed with my mother. It serves me right for trusting my brother not to make a scene.

If my aunt is listening to you read this aloud, please stop here. For what I have next to say, she would not approve of.

Do you remember when last you visited Marseille, we attended a public ball just after Émile began his studies at Montpellier? I'm sure you cannot have forgotten, since Émile dared his friend Maxence Étienne to kiss you in the course of the evening. I did not expect to repeat the experience on my arrival. Unfortunately, my brother has not outgrown his childish games.

As I waited in my father's office for him to finish his business, I was set upon by Gilles Étienne, Maxence's brother, who must be at least two years younger than myself. From the moment he entered the room, I knew his aim. The sultry look in his brown eyes, the toss of his wild hair—for a moment I thought he was Maxence, as I had never met Gilles. But the poor young man has not his brother's height—he is hardly taller than I—nor does he have the same distinctive sharp features that you found so pleasing on the older brother. I will own he has a nicer smile than Maxence. Not so calculating. Indeed, I might have considered him handsome if I didn't know what he meant to do.

The attractiveness of Gilles Étienne's smile, however, did not in-dicate a lack of stupidity. That he or Émile or any other young man would think the average young lady idiot enough to kiss someone on the first meeting belies a deficiency of sense that should have excluded them all from studying medicine. What the professors teach them at Montpellier, I cannot guess, but it is not to have a thinking mind.

Lest you worry over my well-being, I easily put the puppy in his place, and he fled the room with his tail between his legs. I hope the humiliation of the experience taught him to show a greater measure of respect in his interactions with women, but if he is anything like my younger brother or his older brother, the hope is vain. Why must men with supposed intellect assume every woman a glance and a kiss away from being in love with them?

But no matter. It is what women have dealt with since the dawn of time. If only you were near, Sylvie, so that I may share my frus-trations in person and not rely on the tiresome pen. How I miss our *quiet evenings with your mother and father in Fontainebleau. Do not let my brother Guillaume falter in his studies. Even at seventeen, he is too much like Émile. Maman hates him being so far away, but I think it best. I could not have two younger brothers like Émile without turning into a veritable Lyssa of ancient Greece.*

Give my love and gratitude to my aunt and uncle for allowing me to stay so long and for taking on Guillaume's education as well. Our family is greatly in your debt.

Affectueusement,

Marie-Caroline

Imbecile.

Gilles tromped down the stairs, pulling at the collar of his shirt. Flirting with his employer's daughter. Was twenty-five *livres* really worth all this? If she urged her father to give him the sack, where would he go? Monsieur Daubin was a respected member of the *bourgeoisie* in Marseille. A clerk let go for trying to get too familiar with an employer's daughter would not be welcome in any of the other *savonneries*, let alone the other factories that made their home in the Saint-Lazare district.

It had been a dirty trick. Gilles should have seen through it, just like Mademoiselle Daubin had seen through his own ruse. He clamped his hat onto his head and swung open the door. Instead of one step closer to medical school, he could be ten leaps further away by this time tomorrow. The *Savonnerie* Daubin sign, with its sprigs of painted lavender cascading down the wood board, rocked lazily. Its chortling creak taunted his stupidity. Maxence would have sought out Émile immediately, for a word or a fist, but Gilles couldn't bring himself to face their friend. He needed to go home and bury his shame in his book.

He ducked his head and set his course for the Panier Quarter and home. Most factory workers had cleared the streets. Several clerks and personal secretaries floated about, finishing up their employers' work or escaping a day of too many tasks.

He wondered what his mother and Florence had concocted for dinner. Something simple, he hoped. And dinner would be all the better if Maman had not invited any old friends she'd met in the market.

"Étienne!"

Gilles jerked to a stop. His friend Honoré Martel pushed off the wall he had been leaning against and stalked over. "What has taken you so long to leave the factory?" the slim man, a couple years younger than Gilles, asked.

"I . . ." *Was trying to kiss Daubin's daughter and got thoroughly reprimanded.*

Martel shook his head. "We must hurry. The meeting will start soon."

The meeting! He'd forgotten it was Saturday.

"Oh, come," Gilles quipped. "We are always the first to the meetings. Once in a while the others deserve the honor."

His friend ignored him and set off on egret-like legs toward the confiscated church where their Jacobin club met to discuss the revolution. Gilles had to run to catch up. Let Émile and Maxence enjoy their ridiculous games. He would find his own amusements from now on.

"I saw Monsieur Daubin's son while waiting," Martel said. "As much as I dislike his father, Émile is a good man and a fine patriot."

Except when he decided to play games on innocent friends.

"Monsieur Daubin is not a bad sort. He is fair with his employees and dedicated to his family."

Martel huffed. "He is a monarchist."

"He has not declared it to be so." At least not openly. Monsieur Daubin was a shrewd businessman, to be sure, and his trade in soaps and perfumes had suffered with the decline of the aristocracy. But he had not openly supported one side or the other, beyond grumbling about the Jacobins trying to overthrow stability and reason.

"Daubin hardly pays a fair wage to his workers but lives as fine as any *aristo* himself. You cannot tell me he sides with the *révolution-naires*."

It did not help Martel's attitude that Daubin had turned him down for a position. But Gilles held his tongue on that count. "He pays more than most soap makers." But then he also earned more. Those buttons marching up his daughter's pristine jacket bordered on extravagant.

Martel's lip curled. "I cannot believe you would defend Daubin."

Neither did Gilles. Deep down, he knew Monsieur Daubin was no *révolutionnaire*. While the soap maker remained silent on the subject, Émile had been more than candid about his parents' views. "We should not accuse without proof, *non?*" Gilles said with a shrug. "Acting on unfounded accusations can only lead to chaos."

"Sometimes chaos is the only way to make change."

They turned onto the *rue* Sainte-Barbe, heading ever closer to the harbor. Nearing the ocean always quickened Gilles's breath, though he'd tried to suppress such excitement the past two years. It was as if in his core, he knew he belonged to the sea. Generations of mariners before him had engraved the paths of ocean currents into their bones and infused its waters into their blood, passing the inhuman pull to each rising generation. Try as he might, he could not run from it. The sea had written its vast expanse into his soul.

"There is one thing for which I will give Daubin credit," Martel said. "He has produced one exceptional Frenchman and one exquisite daughter."

A flush crept up Gilles's neck once more. "His daughter?"

"Did you not see her?" Martel threw back his head. "She was a goddess. Even with the filthy white cockade she wore."

Of course Martel would notice the cockade. "Yes, I saw her," Gilles muttered.

"I am certain," his friend went on, "with the right guidance, and rescued from her father's damaging influence, she could be swayed to more enlightened beliefs."

Not likely. The fierceness with which she'd turned those brown eyes on Gilles left little doubt as to her intentions of letting a man sway her.

Martel's toothy smile took on a nasty glint. "What I wouldn't do to—"

Gilles's stomach soured. "Has Sault returned yet?" It flew from his mouth before he could think. He had heard Martel launch into those sorts of conversations about girls too many times before. The thought of hearing Mademoiselle Daubin spoken of in such filthy tones made him squirm. The way she carried herself, the way she spoke—it demanded more respect than Martel's crass imaginings.

They came upon a *boulangerie*, where the baker's daughters always greeted them on their way to club meetings. The perfect distraction from that conversation. Two blushing faces peeked out from behind the shutters amid a cloud of giggles.

Gilles winked and nodded to them, earning a chorus of delighted shrieks quickly muted by the slam of shutters. He'd kissed one of them, he did not recall which, last month. It had been the barest of touches, but he did not admit that detail to Maxence and Émile as he collected his earnings. The girl had been too eager.

"*Bonsoir, mes amies!*" he called. Shrill chatter followed his salutation. They were pretty enough girls, the sort who happened upon cafés just as groups of young men were exiting in order to flirt, but he had no real interest in them beyond an evening greeting or a fleeting kiss to win a dare.

Hands fluttered through the slats in the shutters. The tittering and indistinct whispers continued even after the men had passed.

"You changed the subject rather quickly. What is it, Étienne?" Martel gave him a sidelong glance. "You usually enjoy a little banter when women are involved."

He did. Many a long evening, he had sat through stories and laughter with Maxence and his friends. Exaggerated tales of escapades with young women, not all of them fit for polite company. Gilles did not contribute to those conversations—he had nothing of interest to share—but he'd listened. He'd guffawed.

But now Mademoiselle Daubin's face glared disapprovingly in his vision, as though she stood on the street before him.

"I was only curious if Sault would be there, as we have been without our leader for nearly a month." He tried to shake the phantom of her from his mind.

The Church of Saint-Cannat came into view, a few Jacobins filtering through the wooden door. Gilles fished out his watch. Two minutes until six o'clock. No wonder Martel was on edge. Gilles mounted the steps, letting his friend greet their fellow club members.

It was time to think on more important matters than his bruised pride, such as stoking the fires of liberty throughout the region of Provence. He shoved his watch back in his pocket. The stinging rebuke of a *royaliste* had no place in this conquered edifice turned school of revolution. If only he could banish the look in her eyes and that tantalizing curve of her lips from his mind.

CHAPTER 3

Someday Gilles's father would buy Maman a better house in a nicer quarter of the city. He'd earned enough from selling off ships he'd captured that he should have done so by now. Gilles pulled on the creaky door at the back of the house that led from the alleyway into the kitchen. If he tread softly, perhaps he could ascertain whether Maman had any guests to dinner. The events of the day left his stomach growling, but his mind craved the quiet of his bedroom.

He eased the door closed and stood for a moment in the darkness as his eyes adjusted. A small trickle of light slipped through the kitchen entrance, too faint to come from the dining room. No guests, then. Not even his oldest brother, Victor, who often came for dinner with his wife and daughters.

Wisps of smoke lingered in the stale kitchen air, evidence of someone recently dousing the fire. He made for the table, hoping anything left over from the meal hadn't gone too cold. Had Maman waited for him, forgetting, as he had, that the Jacobin meeting was tonight?

His shin struck metal, and pain shot across his lower leg as he tripped forward. Dishes clinked. Gilles caught himself on the edge of the table. Water sloshed out from the washbasin he'd stumbled over, soaking his shoes.

"*Ciel!*" he hissed, lowering his head to the table as he waited for the throbbing in his shin to ease. Florence, the woman his mother had hired to help with cooking, hadn't emptied the wash water before going home.

Footsteps pattered through the dining room, and a candle appeared at the doorway, illuminating his mother's and Florence's wide-eyed faces.

"Oh, Gilles!" Maman rushed forward, but he waved her off with a grumble.

He straightened and shook out his leg. Blasted washbasin.

Florence set the candle on the table, her face pale. So she hadn't left yet. "*Désolée, monsieur!* Are you injured? I will fetch you some dinner. That will cure it. I did not complete the washing; he arrived just as we were finishing . . ." She continued her prattle while scurrying about the dark kitchen.

"Is Maxence here?" Gilles asked, leaning against the table. How could a stupid washbasin hurt so much? Granted, he deserved it after acting the *bête* with Mademoiselle Daubin.

Maman pointed to the ceiling and sighed. "He went upstairs complaining of a headache." The little lines around her mouth, which had made their appearance gradually over the last two years, deepened in her frown.

Gilles's eyes narrowed. A warning tickled the back of his mind. Maxence hadn't retired with an excuse like that for some time. A masculine voice rumbled in from the drawing room like thunder off the sea, and Gilles gritted his teeth. That was not the voice of his brother.

"I think I have a headache as well," Gilles said. He should have expected *le Rossignol*'s arrival, but sometimes he pretended the ship did not exist.

Maman caught his arm. "Son, you cannot keep avoiding him each time he is in port."

He did not brush her off as Maxence no doubt had done. Of course Maxence meant no disrespect, but sometimes his emotions overcame him to the point he could not see the hurt on Maman's face when he stormed away.

Gilles put a hand over hers but avoided looking at her.

"He is in a fine mood tonight," his mother said. "Go speak with him." She wasn't talking about Max.

"He is always in a fine mood." Gilles had rarely seen the man in the sitting room in anything except a fine mood. But a fine mood did nothing to prevent the bating. "I am too tired to spar with him just now." He had Émile to thank for that.

"Please?"

Gilles made the mistake of glancing down at her hopeful face. Was she really asking so much? He had lived in close quarters with the man for ten years of his life. What was one evening, for the sake of his mother?

Florence brought him a plate of cheese and bread, and a bowl of soup that Gilles hoped he could stomach. He nodded his thanks. "Very well. I will talk to him for a short while. But I must study tonight."

Maman's lips turned upward, and she rubbed his arm. "Yes, you must attend to your studies." She kissed his cheek. "*Merci*. Come, Florence. We must finish cleaning this kitchen."

Gilles squared his shoulders and stalked into the salon. A lone figure sat in an armchair, his shoes sprawled across a footstool. The fire flickering in the hearth caught the circle of gold clinging to his ear and the several days' worth of stubble that heightened his sharp features.

Gilles cleared his throat. "*Bonsoir*, Père." He moved quickly to the sofa and sat, then balanced the plate of food on his lap. Digging vigorously into the bread, he felt rather than saw his *père*'s crooked grin.

"That is some greeting for your father. You'd think I'd been gone for the day, rather than months." Tall and lanky, he did not have the stocky mariner's build Gilles and his oldest brother inherited from their mother's side. Their father cropped his dark hair tight against his scalp, the way many *aristos* and *bourgeois* cut their natural hair so that they could wear the wigs that were quickly losing favor in the eyes of the public. But Père had never worn a wig. He preferred a seaman's cap.

"Has it been months?" Gilles asked. "I would have sworn it had not been more than a few weeks." After their last voyage together, any appearance made by his father was too soon.

Père chuckled softly, stirring up memories of long, damp nights on the lower deck filled with stories and song. He laced his fingers and looped them around one knee as he studied Gilles. "Do they not let you out of that office during the day? You are as pale as a *navette*."

Gilles took a large bite of bread so that he did not have to immediately respond. Since Gilles was a boy, Père had made fun of the fact that Gilles disliked the dry, boat-shaped *navette* biscuits.

"Are you a doctor now? Is that why you have grown so sullen and silent since giving up the sea to become a *marin de l'eau douce*?"

A mariner of calm waters. A landlubber. Gilles bridled at the taunt. He hadn't ended his six years at sea because of fear. "Why can you not come to terms with your son wishing to be a doctor?" Gilles asked. Two years of goading—as if that would make him change his mind and return to life on *le Rossignol*.

Père shrugged. "I already have one son trying to be a doctor. I have no use for two."

"And your oldest son is already a mariner. Why do you need two of those?"

His father leaned back and crossed his ankles on the footstool. "Victor does not sail with me." Père's uncle, who owned the shipping company, had given Victor command of his own vessel a few years ago. It brought a much better income for a husband and father of two little girls. "You do not need this fancy schooling to become a doctor," his father went on. "You can learn all you need from my surgeon."

Gilles's blood boiled. His father enjoyed these disputes far too much, which was one of many reasons Gilles kept his distance from Père, as though he carried the plague.

"Do you even have a surgeon?" Gilles set the plate beside him on the sofa, his food half finished. His stomach had clenched too tightly to try to fill it.

Père shrugged, just as Gilles had expected. He hadn't found a good surgeon after Gilles's last voyage, and no one questioned why. Who wanted to sail with a captain who cared so little for his crew? "You could be my surgeon."

Gilles snorted. He had nowhere near the needed credentials to care for the health of an entire crew, even the small crew of a brig. Would the recklessness ever cease? He'd had a pitifully small amount of training thanks to his father.

"Oh, come. It is not so crazy an idea." Père took his feet from the stool and leaned forward, elbows on his knees. "You've read more books than any university-educated doctor I've met. Do not discount your abilities, *mon fils*. You have a good mind, and no professor at that school will teach you anything you do not already know."

Books could not stand in for a real teacher and training from one of the oldest schools of medicine in the world. They had wound through this argument every time his father returned home during the last two years. That enraging smile still marred Père's face, and Gilles set his jaw to keep from saying anything more. He pushed himself to his feet.

"Surely life in the fresh air trumps sitting in a chair keeping track of a gluttonous pig's fortune," his father said.

Gilles's fists clenched by his sides. "That gluttonous pig is one of your patrons." Defending Daubin twice in one day. He wouldn't have guessed.

"He hasn't chartered an Étienne ship in years." Père tossed up his hands. "Before the revolution, my contraband tobacco was good enough for him. Now he won't so much as look at one of the family's ships."

Gilles understood Daubin's change of heart completely. Old age kept his great-uncle from maintaining the order and discipline among his captains the Étiennes had once been known for. Daubin did not want to risk compromising his goods. "I would rather work for a gluttonous pig than for a pirate."

For the first time that evening, a look of displeasure clouded his father's glinting eyes. "I have a letter of marque."

"One that is not recognized by the current government."

Gilles bridled at Père's laughter. "They do not know what they are about. We'll have a dozen new governments before the dust settles," his father said.

Gilles strode to the door. He'd had enough. "I did not take you for a monarchist."

"I did not take you for Maxence."

Gilles halted and glanced at his father. Better to follow in the footsteps of an aspiring physician than in the wake of a smuggler and thieving privateer with an expired license. Maxence had influenced him in ways that would make him a better man. Hadn't he?

Not in Mademoiselle Daubin's eyes.

"Perhaps I should have followed Maxence's example and left the sailing life early. You do not hound him to return to your crew." At least not anymore.

Père pressed his hands against his knees and stood. "Maxence was never a mariner. Even in my most hopeful moments, I could not convince myself he had a future at sea." He wagged his finger at Gilles. "You, *mon fils*, could anticipate each swell, sense a storm before it showed its face, feel the slightest variance in our course. You were born for the sea. Come back. Be my second."

His second-in-command? Once Gilles had desired the position, when he'd watched Victor work in the coveted role alongside their father. Gilles had set his sights on the same honor, but that dream had shattered after his last voyage. He wanted nothing to do with a life so cutthroat it tainted one's loyalty to friends.

"Both your second and your surgeon, so you do not have to pay as many crew members?" Gilles shook his head. Anything for a bigger share in prizes. "I am trying to forget my years at sea, not return to them. I wish they had never happened."

The corner of Père's mouth twisted upward. "The sea made you the man you are. You cannot run from it."

"We are building a new nation here," Gilles said. "A place where a man is not shackled to the traditions of his past."

"Except when it suits him."

Gilles held his father's stare. A challenge sparked in the man's eyes, while the eerie glow of the fire undulated across his skin. It did not suit Gilles to hold onto anything from his past. That was why he had charted his course for the field of medicine, where he could help his countrymen rather than stealing from foreigners.

Gilles turned his back on Père, catching a glimpse of his mother standing in the opposite doorway, hidden in the shadows, her eyes on the floor. How much of the argument had she heard? Everything said tonight they had contended about before. And yet her downcast face seared into his mind.

"Gilles."

He would not have reacted to his father's call, but he saw a flash of gold out of the corner of his eye. It spun through the air between them, and Gilles snatched it, trapping the token in his fist without looking at it. A warm hoop of metal. An earring like Père's, perhaps? Plenty of captains wore them. Did he think a token of camaraderie would persuade him to reconsider?

Gilles shoved it into the pocket of his waistcoat. Père would be sorely disappointed. Nothing could make Gilles set foot on *le Rossignol*'s deck again. Ahead of him was the school at Montpellier and a life of service that mattered. He practically ran for the stairs, trying to relax his tense jaw before he broke a tooth. So much for being able to study tonight.

I did not seal the letter yet, and so I am writing a few more lines. There is room, and I am at a loss.

I'd forgotten my brother and father's battles. Their contention seems to have increased since I've been away. I mentioned the government's response to the issues in the grain market, and Émile's teasing attitude (which he's had since the incident with the Étienne boy) fled. He and Papa were instantly at arms, my father denouncing the failing economy and Émile those Frenchmen too cowardly to fight for a new government. I am surprised it did not come to blows. Maman sat in shock, staring helplessly between the two.

Émile left a moment ago, Maman thinks to the Étiennes' home. I thought I hated the shouting, but the unearthly silence is worse.

She tells me that more often than not, Émile and Maxence remove to cafés for most of the night when they visit, especially if both my father and the Étiennes' father are at home. Though the captain is not a royaliste, she tells me. Something else has turned the son against the father in that family.

I wish they had not called me back. At least in Paris I could imagine the revolution as a grand, national battle between age-old tradition and misguided innovation. Here, I see that it has infiltrated the one refuge I dreamed untouched by change. If the wave of revolution has corroded the very heart of this family, can I hope it will not destroy anything and everything it touches?

M. C.

Gilles sat cross-legged on his bed, his volume of *Traité des maladies chirurgicales* cradled in his lap. But rather than ingesting Chopart's knowledge about maladies of the head, Gilles's eyes grazed over the words without his understanding them.

Two clashes in one day—one with Mademoiselle Daubin and one with Père—and in both he had come out looking the fool. Though he couldn't banish the first from memory, he wouldn't give the one with his father much thought—except for Maman's dejection after the quarrel. She only wanted all her loved ones together, unharmed, and at peace. When had that happened last? Gilles had gone to sea at fourteen, then Maxence had given up the mariner's life a year later, launching them both into their current wary relationship with Père.

Seven years of this tension in her home. How had Maman lived with it?

Gilles leaned back on his elbows. The new tallow candle his mother had placed in the holder beside his bed cast uncanny shadows about the dark room. Sounds from the street outside his window had mostly quieted, though in the Panier Quarter noise was common until quite late. His watch, sitting beside the simple but well-made candlestick, read ten o'clock. The Panier had quieted early tonight, especially given that tomorrow was a Sunday.

Not that Sundays held much importance anymore besides being a day without work. Since the new government had seized property from the Catholic Church and banished all nonconforming priests from their parishes, few *Marseillais* bothered to attend. Even Maman, who used to go to mass on her own each week, gave up after the new government-appointed clergymen took over.

Gilles closed his book and tossed it onto the bed. He would arise early to study tomorrow before breakfast. An hour of well-rested, focused study would do him more good than hours of distracted reading.

He rose from the bed. Below him in his brother's room, he could hear Émile's and Maxence's voices mingled with the occasional clink of glass. Though their tones had been agitated when Émile had first arrived, they turned calm and jovial as the evening wore on. Gilles imagined they did this every night in Montpellier, when they were not out in cafés. Sometimes he joined them, but after the run-in with Émile's sister this morning, Gilles wanted to keep his distance.

He rolled his head back and scrunched his eyes shut. What a fool. Girls had refused him before. Why did this instance refuse to leave his mind? Perhaps because she was his employer's daughter? He would not discover until Monday whether his idiocy affected his standing with Monsieur Daubin.

Gilles pulled himself off his bed and wrapped his linen banyan around him. He did not need the extra covering for warmth in his top-floor bedroom during the late spring and summer months, but the ground floor tended to chill after dark. After snuffing the candle, he let himself out of the bedroom and down the stairs, taking care when passing Maxence's room, though their brash laughter covered any sound he might have made. Were they laughing at his blundering mess from earlier? Gilles set his lips and pushed on to the kitchen.

The fire in the parlor had died down, and his father's shadow that had overtaken the chair earlier in the evening had disappeared. Only a glimmer of light from the kitchen shone through the cramped dining room.

Maman sat on the bench beside the kitchen table, a tiny candle illuminating the mound of shirts and trousers beside her and the dying fire in the hearth. The candle was the same size as the one that had been in his room yesterday. She must have switched it so he wouldn't run out of light while he studied.

A basin of water stood at her feet, and a needle glinted in the faint light as she worked. Mending and cleaning his father's things, no doubt. "Gilles?" She did not turn from her task.

He entered and sat on the bench opposite her. She clipped a line of his father's clumsy stitches with little scissors, then set about resewing the seam. "It is late to be mending," Gilles noted. He laid his arms on the table and rested his chin on them.

"I might as well be useful if I am not sleeping."

"You are the most useful woman in Marseille. And when you are upset, you are the most useful woman in France."

The corners of her lips softened, and she finally looked at him. "You and your brother could flatter the barnacles off a ship's hull. If only you put that talent to good use."

Gilles cocked his head. "Good use? We put it to very good use."

"Chasing the baker's daughters for kisses is not good use, you silly *coquin*."

He winced. And especially not the daughters of soap makers.

His mother ended the seam, then clipped the tail of the thread. "I wonder at your being able to find a wife with your current methods."

"It is fortunate for me that I am not in the market for a wife just yet." He widened his eyes innocently. "You do not wish me to marry now, do you, Maman?"

She reached out and swatted his face with the sleeve of the shirt she worked on. "You are far from ready for that responsibility. I only wish you and your brother would leave the poor girls alone."

Gilles pulled away, laughing. "It is simply for amusement." That's what Maxence always said. A few *livres* and a bit of fun. Though Gilles couldn't say this evening's game had ended pleasantly.

Maman mumbled something he couldn't decipher. Holding the needle between her lips, she pulled a length of thread from the spool and cut it at her desired length. Then she held the needle toward the flame, eyes nearly crossing as she rethreaded it.

"Besides," Gilles cleared his throat, "when I am ready, it means I will have a long list of girls from which to pick." One of them had to be filled with the same determination and loyalty as Maman. He just had to find her.

She harrumphed and stabbed her needle into another tear. For a captain, his father did not do well at looking after his clothes. "I do not think those girls should be included on your list of potential mates."

"*Surtout pas!* Some of them do not kiss well at all. I shall leave them off the list." He waited for her laugh at his joke. She always caved to his teasing eventually.

Maman's frown only deepened, and she attacked the repair with increased vigor. She stood abruptly, tossing the shirt to the table. "Would you like some *chocolat?*"

Gilles glanced at the remains of the fire. "Shall I stoke the fire?"

Without responding, she moved to the hearth. She set a piece of wood into the wavering flame, then caught up the bellows and coaxed it into a steady burn.

"Did I anger you?" Gilles asked tentatively.

She pumped the bellows and poked around with the iron until

the fire rose to her satisfaction. Without looking at him, she made for the cellar.

A third person angry with him today. He wasn't used to this. Gilles slid the discarded shirt over to his side of the table and sought out the needle. He'd mended his father's shirts when on board his ship. Père had little patience for mending. Now Maman took out all his hasty work and remended his clothes every time he came home.

Gilles eyed his mother's careful stitches, then began his own where she had left off. They did not come out as straight as those of Maman, but one could only tell on close examination. He hadn't mended something in years. On land, this was women's work.

His mother's footsteps announced her return. They were not terse as Mademoiselle Daubin's on the office floor earlier that evening, but soft, resigned. Milk lapped against the sides of the copper kettle she carried. She eased it onto the crane and swung it over the fire, which hissed and crackled against the cool sides of the kettle.

"Why do you do this if he does not care what the mending looks like?" Gilles brushed back a wave of curls that had fallen over his brow.

Jars rattled behind him as she brought out the container of liquid chocolate. "Because he does care. He ignores his own mending because he cannot do it well himself, but he likes to look nice as well as any of you." She poured some of the chocolate into the chocolate pot and set it beside him on the table. Then she returned to the fire to stir the milk. "And that is not the only thing you boys inherited from him."

Gilles paused his stitching and waited. But Maman did not go on. Once the milk began to bubble, she used a tea cloth to carefully pull the kettle from the fire. She added the scalded milk to the chocolate pot, then used a stirrer to mix it.

"What else did we inherit from Père?" Gilles stuck the needle into the cloth of his father's shirt and dropped his work to his lap.

Maman set two cups in the middle of the table. She poured the thick, frothy drink into the cups before setting the chocolate pot aside. Gilles did not take his until his mother had sat and pulled her cup toward her. He copied her, breathing in the rich steam swirling off the chocolate before bringing it to his lips.

After a long sip, his mother sighed. "Your father was a shameless flirt as well. And still is." She stared into her cup, a gentle smile on her face. "But he has one thing I wish you and Maxence would learn."

Gilles took another drink. What could their father possibly do better than he or Maxence, besides sail a ship? He was loud, intrusive, and all too eager to start a fight. "And what is that?"

Maman met his eyes. "Respect."

Gilles sputtered. "Respect? I assure you, respect is not something I lack. If you saw me at my work, you would—"

His mother put a hand over his. "That is not the respect I mean. I know you are respectful at the *savonnerie*, and that is why Monsieur Daubin trusts you so."

"How, then, is Père better than I am?" His father did not respect anyone at his work. Gilles saw that firsthand. Père demanded respect, to be sure, but respecting another person?

"Your father has always valued women. His mother, his sisters, me. We were not pieces in a game, things to be caught and tallied like a hunting prize."

Gilles swallowed against the bitter taste lining his mouth. He did not think it was from the chocolate. Though she spoke gently, her rebuke rang clear through the kitchen. The fire crackled in the hearth. He watched it, not meeting her eyes.

That was not how it really went with Maxence's games. The girls were always willing participants. Well, usually.

"We do not treat the girls like animals," Gilles insisted.

"Oh?" She set her chocolate aside and took another needle from her sewing kit. "Is that how Mademoiselle Daubin felt this evening, or did she feel like a doe you were stalking in the forest?"

Gilles flushed. He took a rapid drink of his chocolate, but the cinnamon and nutmeg she'd added caught in his throat and set him coughing. If the *mademoiselle* had felt like a hunted animal, she was a tigress, not a doe.

"How did you . . ." His throat tickled, and he started coughing again.

"I heard Émile boasting of it when they went upstairs." Maman examined another tear, this time in a pair of breeches. "I know you and Maxence like to have your fun and that you did not get much of it in your youth while sailing with your father. I wish he had been home more often to show you his respect for me."

Gilles flinched. "We respect you, Maman."

She leaned across the table to pat his face. "Yes, you do. And so does Victor. Even Maxence, in his own way. But I think you forget that I am a woman. Do not the others of my sex deserve respect as well, or am I the exception because I bore and raised you?"

Gilles couldn't look her in the eye. Was it different? The girls he and his brother chased were much younger and sillier than his mother. They played the game as much as he and Maxence did. Mademoiselle Daubin excluded, they *liked* it. How, then, were his actions disrespectful?

"I love you, *mon fils.*" She smoothed his hair out of his face, then slid off the bench.

"*Je t'aime*, Maman," Gilles murmured.

"Douse the fire before you go to bed." And then she left. He listened to her move across the dining room and up the creaking stairs.

Even if she was wrong about most of the girls, Maman had reason on her side in one case. He had known from the start Mademoiselle Daubin was not open to such games, and he should have backed off earlier. Perhaps an apology was in order. His stomach sank at the prospect. Max would harass him mercilessly if he found out Gilles wanted to beg her pardon.

The contents of his waistcoat pocket pressed against his side. He fished out his father's gift from under his banyan and held it up to the waning candle. It wasn't an earring at all. He should have known that from its weight. The firelight caught the ridges of little words etched into the simple gold ring. *Jamais en vain.* Never in vain.

It was Grandmère's ring, which his father always wore on his little finger. Gilles smoothed his thumb over the calligraphy. The *poésie* ring had passed through several generations of his father's family. Why had Père given this to him, and why now? Was he trying to tell Gilles all those years at sea had been worth it?

He shook his head but slipped the ring onto his little finger. Though he'd loved the sea and the men he'd befriended, he would never count those years as anything but a waste. They made him a stronger man, nothing else. And he could have pulled that strength from any other line of work. Père might have tricked Maman into thinking he was respectful, the best of gentlemen, but he did not fool Gilles or Maxence. If Père respected women as she claimed, then why did he not respect his own men? It was all an act. His way of flirting to keep her singing his praises.

Gilles moved a stool beside the fire. He would apologize to Mademoiselle Daubin and show, at least to himself and his mother, that he was the better man. He poked at the flames, sending them popping and snapping indignantly. Though he stared into the light, he saw only that young lady's intense eyes—eyes he would have to look into as he bumbled through an apology.

Heaven help him.

CHAPTER 4

Gilles stood at the edge of the cauldron watching the soupy, green-brown mixture roil inside. To his right and left, identical cauldrons, all with a diameter longer than a man was tall, sat in a long line. Two workers watched each cauldron, occasionally using long sticks to stir the oil and soda.

In his ledger, he noted the date next to the cauldron number. Another batch of soap begun. How many more batches would he oversee before he quit the *savonnerie* forever?

"Excellent work, Luc." Gilles closed his ledger.

The man, who had a red cap sticking out of the waistband of his trousers, pushed against his handle to scrape the deep bottom of the cauldron with the paddle end of the stirrer. Faint voices came from the basement, where other workers stoked the fires below each massive cauldron.

"Someday we will not be slaves to this," Luc muttered. Sweat glistened on his face.

"There will always be a market for soap, I'm afraid." Gilles leaned against the waist-high brick wall that encircled the cauldron and put his pencil behind his ear. He rolled the sleeves of his shirt up to his elbows. Even in winter, one rarely needed a coat in the factory. At those times, Gilles wore his coat from the office and immediately shed it when he walked through the workroom doors. With the approaching summer, temperatures within the *savonnerie* marched toward stifling, and he'd simply left his jacket on its peg near his desk.

Luc grunted. "Not this fine *aristo* soap."

There was truth in that. Gilles lifted a shoulder. Even if the aristocracy completely crumbled, as Luc's *sans-culottes* desired, the *bourgeoisie* wasn't leaving. Anyone in the same circles as the Daubins would not give up their fine soaps happily. He did not mention this to Luc, however. Though both on the side of revolution, the *sans-culottes* and Jacobins had widely differing views on how to achieve it. Gilles preferred the enlightened reasoning of the Club to the violence, destruction, and anarchy displayed by the lower-classed *sans-culottes*, but more and more the Jacobins were forced to rely on their hot-headed counterparts to create needed change.

The worker's eyes narrowed. "Who is that?"

Gilles glanced over his shoulder. Through the steam rolling off the cauldrons, a wave of white advanced into the factory. A straw hat fitted with violets and a matching ribbon appeared through the soap mists as she approached.

He straightened, tucking the ledger under his arm, and smoothed his waistcoat. What was she doing here? He hadn't counted on speaking to her now, but perhaps the fates had smiled on him. An apology in a quiet corner of the factory was much better than trying to find a moment during tomorrow evening's dinner.

"*Mademoiselle*, I did not expect to see you here." Gilles hurried forward, locking his most charming grin into place.

Mademoiselle Daubin's austere expression did not change as he approached. "I am once again looking for my father." Today she wore one of the gauzy chemise dresses that had curiously come into favor among the wealthier class. Once seen as scandalously unstructured—almost revealing—when the queen had worn it for a portrait, the loose, gathered gown was now touted for its divergence from the rigid extravagance of the old aristocracy. While the Jacobin in him wanted to dislike the style, the man in him could not help but admit it looked well on her.

Gilles bowed. "It is a pleasure to meet you again. I fear your father might have left for the *parfumerie* already since he was scheduled to be there at noon, but I will help you search for him if you like." He offered her his arm before realizing it was rather lacking in sleeve.

She glanced at it and sniffed. "I still do not want to kiss you," she said under her breath, turning away with her head high.

Gilles blinked and scanned the factory to see if anyone had heard. The men went about their duties without interruption. She was not one for subtlety, it would seem. He cleared his throat. "*Bien sûr.* I wished to speak with you about that. Will you walk with me?"

Luc and some of the others watched them, and Gilles was glad for the heat of the factory to mask the warmth creeping into his ears. Mademoiselle Daubin walked on. Gilles swiped his shirtsleeves down, fighting to button them while keeping hold of the ledger under his arm and matching her pace. "I can send someone to fetch your father, if you like."

"If my father is not here, I will meet him at the *parfumerie.*" She surveyed the workroom, with its tall ceilings and rising steam. They reached the end of the line of cauldrons, and she paused at the last. The workers tending it had broken their methodical mixing to drink water. She grabbed the end of one of their stirrers and passed it from one hand to the other, examining it as though she had never seen one before. Gilles stepped closer to her, and she flinched away, lip curled. "I said I did not want your—"

He held up a hand. "I wish to apologize."

Her dark brows rose. "Apologize?"

"I acted poorly. Last week, in the office. I never should have tried to kiss you, and I am sorry." Her hard stare bored into him like cutting lines through a fresh batch of soap. Gilles fidgeted. Should he wait for her to respond? Change the subject? Excuse himself to find her father? She traced her hands down the handle of the stirrer, worn smooth with use. Then she grasped it and pulled, as the workers were doing around them. The pole wavered in her hands, moving much slower than the employees'.

"Is that what you say to all the girls?"

"What girls?" Gilles asked. She was going to flip the muddy-looking paste all over her pristine dress if she wasn't careful, and while he would be hard pressed not to laugh heartily at the scene, he'd put himself in enough trouble with her last week.

"All the other girls you kiss in your little games."

He opened his mouth to protest. None of the other girls took such offense at the thought of kissing him.

"Or do you apologize because I am your employer's daughter, and you only hope to keep your position?"

"Certainly not." He shook his head quickly. Of course, over the past seven days he had frequently feared he would be reprimanded, but that had not pushed him to this apology. He hadn't thought much on what she might say in response, only that for some reason he wished to be in her good favor. He would have taken gratitude or a sweet smile. "I was speaking with my mother—"

She tilted her head, a condescending smirk on her lips. "Ah, you are asking forgiveness because Maman instructed you to do so. What a good boy."

Gilles groaned inwardly. Did she not see his sincerity? He forced a grin and winked. "I always listen to my mother."

The workers assigned to this cauldron moved back toward them. He took hold of the handle just above her hand, stilling the stirrer. "You must take caution, *mademoiselle*. This is where we combine the olive oil and soda to prepare it for soap making. The mixture is getting quite hot from the fires below it, and I would hate for you to burn yourself or ruin your gown."

She instantly released the handle and stepped away. Gilles nodded to the workers and handed the pole back to them. When he turned to Mademoiselle Daubin, she had her arms folded across her chest.

"The paste is not hot."

Gilles shrugged. "It could be."

"It isn't. The fires were lit this morning and the materials just poured in. We have some time before the paste reaches temperature."

Well, yes. She was right on that account.

"And, I will have you know, I have five methods to rid clothing of soap-paste stains. I've stood at the cauldrons stirring them with my father since before you were born, so do not try to impress me with your two years of knowledge in soap making, *s'il vous plaît*."

Then perhaps she would help him rid his clothes of the stains after he dove into the paste to avoid her withering glare.

"I do not know what sorts of girls you chase after, but if they are anything like the ones my brother fancies for his escapades, allow me to assure you, I am not one of those girls."

Time to tack this ship and flee. Once again he found himself in a fight he could not win with this lady. He only hoped the Daubins had invited enough guests to tomorrow evening's dinner that he would be able to easily avoid another confrontation. Gilles rubbed his brow with his sleeve. How had it grown so hot in the factory so quickly? The fire tenders must have added more fuel. "Then, if I may be so bold, what sort are you?" He should not have asked.

Mademoiselle Daubin squared her shoulders. "The sort who does not appreciate when young men assume she has only a handsome face and pretty figure, with no knowledge, conviction, or opinion to make her worthy of being considered a rational human."

Gilles retreated a step. She was accusing him of thinking himself above her. She, a *royaliste*? And for simply trying to explain when she had seemed unfamiliar with the process before them. He chewed the inside of his cheek while she looked down her pleasingly straight and saucily upturned nose at him.

She sauntered back toward the door, inspecting each cauldron as she passed with the same strict expression her father wore during his examinations. Gilles shuffled behind her, making the last marks in his ledger to finish the initial notations for this batch. Had she learned this superiority during her time in Paris? Émile did not exude supremacy wherever he went. He did not care whether he spent time with a mariner's son or a duke's, so long as he had a yearning for revolution.

As they arrived at the door, the fresh breeze dispelled some of the thick air from the workroom. Gilles sucked it in to cool his frustration.

A rat skittered around the corner of the door. As one, Gilles and Mademoiselle Daubin shied away, nearly knocking into each other as the creature vanished into a shadowy corner. She did not immediately retreat from the closeness. The glare from the bright sunlight outside haloed her straw hat as she met his gaze. When she spoke, her voice had lost some of the brash tone. "Thank you."

"For . . ."

"For your apology."

And here he thought it had offended her.

"My brother and yours, they do not apologize for their actions," she said. Before he could dip into a gracious bow, one of her brows twitched. "Perhaps there is a spark of hope that the little brother will grow up to be the better man."

Then she swept into the bright afternoon, her white dress reflecting the burning sun. Gilles could only chuckle. He did not know what else to do.

Tomorrow night would prove interesting.

25 May 1792
Marseille

Ma chère *Sylvie,*

You'll forgive me for sending a letter before receiving a response from my last one. Maman held a dinner this evening to celebrate my arrival, and once more I long for the society of Fontainebleau. It truly is a perfect location—near enough to Paris to attend the ballet and otherwise partake in its merits, but far enough to enjoy the comforts of the country and not be bothered when the sans-culottes *make mischief. Though I must admit, I have always found it interesting that the Jacobins fear the* sans-culottes *as much as the* royalistes. *I suppose it shows that any ideals can be taken to zealous extremes.*

Of the two families who accepted my mother's invitations, only one arrived—the Poulin family. We received hastily scrawled excuses from the Linville family. Neither Maman nor I could read what Madame Linville wrote, and when she called to inquire after their welfare, they had vanished. The windows were boarded up, servants gone. No trace that anyone had been there for several days. We can only guess where they have gone, but it is not so difficult to determine the cause.

Maman is devastated, as Madame Linville has long been one of her dearest friends. Monsieur Linville used to spend late nights discussing the deplorable state of the country with Papa. He was much more outspoken than Papa in public. More than once he drew the wrath of the crowds, but they kept to smashing in his windows and shouting at his household. Papa says he had been quite vocal of late in his denunciation of the massacres at la glacière *in Avignon last year. I can only imagine the harassment and threats the Linvilles must have suffered before their departure. I wonder if they have stayed on the continent or gone to the Americas.*

Émile was ecstatic, of course, as he hates the Linvilles. Even now he is cursing them as "cowardly émigrés" before his enthusiastic audience, which consists of the Poulins' oldest daughter, who is smitten with him, and the Étienne brothers, who are equally smitten.

Yes, I have the misfortune of spending this evening with the Étiennes yet again, which is why I am writing this letter rather than engaging in the usual post dinner conversation. The young people are gathered in one corner with their drinks, as though sitting in one of their Jacobin cafés, discussing things they know nothing about in serious tones. Mademoiselle Poulin is soaking in every word, never mind that her family does not side with the revolution.

I will say, I did find a small source of pleasure in the evening. I was able to compare the two Étienne brothers, a rather fascinating distraction, especially after an encounter I had with the younger one yesterday at the factory. I had gone to fetch my father after Maman's distress at the Linvilles' departure. And can you believe it, Gilles apologized for his attempt to kiss me in Papa's office Saturday last. Of course, moments later he proceeded to explain in condescending tones the process of soap making, as though I hadn't grown up in a savonnerie. He still takes after his brother far too much for me to ever like him, but his attempt at reconciliation astounded me. Have you ever heard Émile apologize for his boorish bravado?

Gilles follows Maxence and Émile as though they were Greek philosophers with the wisdom of ages. No wonder Émile so easily persuaded him to make a game of trying to kiss me. And though he matches them for brains, if not for wit, I cannot see the younger Étienne among their posse of medical students at Montpellier. The shadow of a swarthy mariner has not completely left him. I better imagine him on the deck of a ship than in a lecture hall. He is too broad through the shoulders to make a good doctor.

And now I am being called away. I shall try to write more tonight. Not that I will have any more interesting news for you, my dear cousin. If you were here, I would make a wager on whether Mademoiselle Poulin leaves this house unkissed tonight.

CHAPTER 5

Mademoiselle Daubin had hardly spoken to Gilles all evening, even with Émile's expert maneuvering to get Gilles seated beside her at dinner. Gilles only hoped Émile would soon tire of the game of throwing them together. Now the young lady sat across the room from them at her writing desk, shooting disapproving glances in his direction.

"The National Assembly is calling for thirty-one new battalions to help with the war," Émile said, sipping his drink. "The time to make up our minds is now."

Mademoiselle Poulin's little mouth formed a perfect "O." She fluttered her fan quickly.

"It is not so easy a decision as you claim," Gilles insisted. Not that he would shirk if called upon, but the decision of marching to war should not be made lightly.

Émile scoffed. "Where is your patriotism, Gilles? If a man is not willing to lay down his life in defense of freedom, he does not deserve it."

Gilles shifted in his seat on the window ledge. Of course he believed that. But human life was hardly an expendable resource.

Mademoiselle Daubin's merry hum, once again *Sur le pont d'Avignon*, floated across the room. No one else paid it any mind, not even the Daubin and Poulin parents in carefree discussion near the hearth. Was she lost in thought and mindlessly humming as she wrote her letter, or was she trying to drown out their discussion of war?

"You had best take care with voicing such opinions, Gilles," Maxence growled, earning him the complete attention of the wide-eyed young lady at his side. Gilles had little doubt his brother would succeed at getting that kiss from her tonight, along with Émile's twelve *livres*. "You do not want to sound like Lafayette."

Émile pretended to gag at the mention of the general.

"It is not traitorous to think of one's family and livelihood," Gilles said, swirling the contents of his glass. His stomach had soured at the talk of the recently declared war on Prussia and Austria, and he had drunk very little.

"Perhaps if a man has a family," Émile said. "But when last I checked, you had neither wife nor child." He shook his head. "Who ever heard of a general so afraid of confrontation as Lafayette is? That man is headed for the *louisette*, mark my words. He must be in league with the royals, if not Austria and Prussia."

"*Louisette*?" Gilles asked. One of the domestics brought in the tea service and set it up beside Madame Daubin. She called to her daughter, who grudgingly put away her pen and blotted her letter. After hastily folding the page, Mademoiselle Daubin stuffed it into her pocket and rose. Who could she be writing to in the middle of an evening held in her honor?

"The *louisette* is an ingenious machine the Assembly has approved for executions," Maxence said. His eyes took on a strange glint Gilles rarely saw. From him, anyhow. Their father always got the same look the moment he decided to chase a merchantman at sea. "I am surprised you have not heard of it. I'm certain I've mentioned it. The device was largely successful when they debuted it last month."

Gilles shook his head. He must have missed Maxence's news.

"A man named Guillotin oversaw its development. It is simply a blade that drops to sever the convict's neck." Maxence brought his hand down sharply against the side table. Glasses resting on the table sloshed at the loud smack, and Mademoiselle Poulin jumped. "No need to bribe the executioner for a clean cut. It is quick, efficient, and humane."

"Barbaric, rather," an even voice said.

The rustle of silk announced Mademoiselle Daubin's arrival. She handed a cup of tea to Mademoiselle Poulin, whose face had taken on a pallid hue at the mention of executions. "Would anyone else like some tea to go with their conversation of *la guillotine*?"

Maxence and Émile shook their heads, and Gilles held up his still-full glass. The young lady did not move to return to the cart for her own cup of tea.

"Have you come to reprimand our lowly Jacobinism and preach *royaliste* truths?" Émile asked.

"*Mais non*," his sister said, pulling over a chair and setting it in the middle of them. She sat regally and arranged the skirts of her lavender and white gown. "Maman insisted I socialize."

"Then tell us, *mademoiselle*," Maxence said, leaning forward, "how regulating executions to give no preference for birth or fortune is barbaric." His leering expression made Gilles glance toward Mademoiselle Daubin. Maxence had met her before. Surely he remembered her sharp tongue. Did he think this would be an easy fight? Gilles had no way to warn him to back down.

"As I am the only one in this party who has seen this new

machine, I can tell you it is shocking. Unless the Assembly plans to execute large numbers of people in a very short amount of time, it is unneeded. To put so much effort into the science of execution is, yes, barbaric."

The young men exchanged knowing glances. A woman's sensibility, and a sheltered woman's sensibility at that. Gilles set his glass beside him on the windowsill. This conversation would only get more interesting with Émile in a fighting mood and his sister always ready to spar.

"You have seen it?" Mademoiselle Poulin squeaked. "In action? Was it very terrible?"

"I only saw it cut the cabbages used for demonstration. But my cousin's maid saw when they executed a highwayman. She said the ease of it was horrific."

"What do you suggest to execute enemies of the state, then?" Gilles asked, too late remembering he had committed to not engage Mademoiselle Daubin in conversation after his sound defeats in previous encounters.

"I do not think it necessary to execute enemies of the state since I do not have confidence in the Assembly's method for determining true traitors." She sat with her hands folded in her lap, as though they were discussing an unclear passage of Rousseau rather than a killing machine.

"I suppose you also look down on studying the science of war," Maxence said. He leaned farther forward, his target for the evening forgotten. "Would you have us kneel before our enemies and offer France to them on a gilded platter?"

"I do not know our enemies care much for what is left of France. They only wish for stability in the region."

"What is left of France?" Émile cried.

Maxence's nostrils flared.

"Yes, what is left of France," Mademoiselle Daubin said. "How do you not see it? France is in tatters. Your glorious revolution has left us no closer to stability than we were before. Have the bread riots stopped? *Pas du tout.* The French people are still hungry. There is constant battle in your National Assembly." She set her attention on Gilles, as though daring him to join the mêlée. "I beg you, tell me how the country has improved since the Third Estate took control."

Gilles was not about to get involved. Maxence's eloquence far outweighed his own. He gripped the sill of the window, hoping Maxence had a good rebuttal. Of course things were better with the common people in charge of the country.

"France is in tatters because she still has an incompetent king," Maxence said, nearly coming out of his chair. "The Jacobins will reweave *la patrie* into a tapestry the likes of which has never been seen in Europe since the fall of Rome. But we must first dispose of a king who could not care less for the people he governs."

"You don't know that," Mademoiselle Daubin said softly.

Gilles snorted. They knew very well. Louis had tried to flee the country. What king with any love for his people would run when they needed him most?

Émile's head lolled back. "Caroline! Hold your tongue, or you could be labeled the next enemy of state."

They called her Caroline? That was odd. Most people with names like hers went by their first, not their second name.

"Ah, *oui.* I forgot you Jacobins prefer your women silent." She waved a hand dismissively, as though she'd forgotten her brother hated sugar in his tea.

Gilles flinched at the barbed jest. She had quite the cynical view of her brother and his friends. "I would not say—" he began, but Maxence overrode him.

"Why is a woman such as yourself so concerned in these matters?"

He now sat back casually in his chair, a sneer on his face, and folded his hands across his smart red waistcoat. Despite his distinctly more fashionable clothing, he reminded Gilles of Père's condescending attitude. Except for the unruly curls, Maxence was a near copy of their father in both looks and mannerisms. "This is a work for men."

Mademoiselle Daubin lazily traced the embroidered flowers on her white skirt with a finger. "That is not what the Jacobins said after the market women stormed Versailles. In fact, I recall your precious Robespierre lauding their efforts, as no man had succeeded in bringing the king's court to Paris yet."

Maxence settled back into his seat, chuckling. "Monsieur Maillard led those women. If he had not been at their head, the entire campaign would have been a disaster. His name will be remembered in history for it, not any of those women's."

"Are you defending revolutionary women, Mademoiselle Daubin?" Gilles asked with a grin. A little teasing would dispel the intensity of the conversation.

Fire snapped in her eyes. "If their male counterparts will not acknowledge them, yes. It is our country as much as it is yours. Why can we not try to shape it as we see fit, no matter our sex?" Her hands had abandoned the floral stitching along her skirt and now gripped the arms of her chair.

Émile returned to his drink. "This sort of unwomanly boldness is exactly the problem with young ladies who refuse every proposal that comes their way. They think they know things, even when they don't. They need husbands to direct them."

His sister burst from her seat, the heels of her leather mules thumping against the wood floor. She clenched her fists. "You are mistaken," she said in a surprisingly calm voice. "I have never refused a proposal, as I have received none."

"Little wonder," Maxence murmured—loud enough to be heard by all—to Mademoiselle Poulin, who tittered behind her fan.

"Max!" Gilles hissed. His gut twisted as he glanced at Mademoiselle Daubin—alone in her beliefs but still unwilling to back down. He may not agree with her views on the government, but the sinking in his heart whispered that many of her points were not without reason. Émile and Maxence were speaking as they always did. Nothing they said was new, and yet tonight their remarks seemed harsher and more unfeeling.

"I could not agree more, *monsieur*," Mademoiselle Poulin piped in, earning her a grin of false gratitude from Maxence. How young she looked beside him. She couldn't be more than eighteen. "The revolution is a man's duty."

"Then I expect all of you to go," Mademoiselle Daubin said, catching each young man's gaze. "Go and form your battalions. Do your duty. Leave the women to clean up your mess, as we always do." Her voice caught, but Gilles could not find tears in her eyes or a flush in her face.

"Do you doubt for a moment that each of us will go?" Maxence asked. Had he moved closer to the Poulin girl? "I am glad we have come to an agreement on our respective duties."

"What young man in the ranks of Jacobins wouldn't gladly give his life for the cause of liberty?" Émile asked.

Some unspoken pain tugged at Mademoiselle Daubin's austere visage, perhaps a memory or an inclination. Or was it a realization that despite her deepest convictions, her way of thinking would never prevail against the power of the Jacobins? Gilles hadn't seen a chink in her armor since they met. Had the possibility of her own brother dying for a tenet she did not believe in cause her to falter?

Gilles swallowed at the sudden tightness in his throat. All evening his skin had been crawling at the thought of the looming decision between saving for university and marching for patriotism. If he was truly committed to the revolution, he should join those defending *la patrie* from the Prussians and Austrians.

"Marie-Caroline?" Madame Daubin called from the sofa near the hearth. "Would you fetch the copy of *le Journal de la Mode et du Goût* you brought back from Paris? I wish to show it to Madame Poulin."

Would Gilles do more for his country by dying or by learning the skills to save lives? Was saving lives through medicine not as noble a pursuit as defending them through war?

"Yes, Maman," Mademoiselle Daubin said. Her footsteps did not clip against the floor with their usual conviction as she slipped through the doorway.

"How do you live with that girl?" Maxence muttered when she'd left and the older party had returned to their conversation.

"I haven't lived with her for two years. Before that . . ." Émile shuddered, then threw Gilles a knowing grin. "You were doomed from the start in our little wager."

Not this again. "Yes, I quickly discovered that," Gilles said. He tugged at his cravat. His seat at the window had grown incredibly warm, notwithstanding his distance from the fire.

"A wager?" Mademoiselle Poulin asked, inching closer to Maxence. She was playing right into his hands. Émile would lose those twelve *livres*, and the young lady would lose her first kiss to a man who did not care one wit about her.

Gilles's gut tightened in a way it never had before when watching his brother play the game. He glanced at the clock on the mantel. Eight thirty. Too early to leave without being rude. What a simpleton he was. If Mademoiselle Poulin was as willing as she seemed, he had no reason for this apprehension.

"Yes, a wager. Gilles thought he could best my sister in a game of wills last week," Émile said, shaking his head. "He was sorely mistaken."

"*I* thought so?" Gilles cried. "I'm quite certain you—"

Maxence reached to thump him on the back amid a peal of laughter but knocked Gilles's glass on the way. It plunged to the floor and shattered across the wood. Gilles whipped his face away from the tinkling of broken glass. Red wine splattered over the brothers. Belatedly, Mademoiselle Poulin shrieked as if a cannon had exploded, punctuated by Maxence's cursing.

"Nicely done, Gilles," Émile said, sipping at his own drink.

As though he'd had anything to do with it. Gilles glanced down at his speckled trousers. For a moment, the red liquid covering his legs was not wine and he stood not on the smooth floor of the Daubins' parlor, but on the sea-battered deck of *le Rossignol*, his clothes covered in blood. A familiar burning ignited in the back of his throat, which he choked down. He thought two years in relative safety would have stilled the impulse. "I'll fetch a domestic," he mumbled, skirting the mess of dagger-like edges and crimson puddles on the floor.

"We'll ring for one," Émile said, but Gilles waved him off. He could find the servant easily enough, and he hurried from the room through a shower of concerned questions from the older set.

Once through the door, Gilles paused and breathed in the coolness of the quiet vestibule. He did not attend many social dinners. Maman's dinners were intimate affairs that only involved debate if Maxence arrived. A few candelabra, scattered about on side tables, lit the front hall. Their flames shimmered off a puff of light purple and white silk on the stair.

Mademoiselle Daubin?

She sat on one of the lower steps and stared unseeingly at the checkered floor tiles. Her arms wrapped loosely around herself, as though she were nearing sleep.

"Are you ill?" Gilles asked in a soft voice so as not to startle her.

She looked up as he cautiously approached. Her dark, velvety curls framed her face, and candlelight flickered in her vacant eyes. "What did you say?"

The shadows of the vestibule did not veil the pallor that had set on her countenance. "You do not look well." He rested his arms on the banister to study her. "Shall I send for a doctor?"

A mirthless smile flitted across her lips. "Three medical students in the house, and no one has the confidence to diagnose what is wrong with me?"

"Only two." But someday he would be the third.

She straightened, and the listlessness dissolved. Whatever memories or thoughts had plagued her seemed to instantly vanish. "I am not ill. And if Émile has renewed his wager, I wish to reaffirm that I do not want to kiss you."

Gilles settled his chin atop his fist. So much for offering concern for her well-being. "If you continue to say that, *mademoiselle*, you might find yourself believing just the opposite." He could tell she wouldn't answer if he asked what was upsetting her. Whatever weak point in her armor Émile's comment had pierced, Mademoiselle Daubin had rapidly repaired it.

"That would be like kissing my younger brother." She wrinkled her nose. "*Non, merci.*"

"We are hardly well enough acquainted for it to be like that."

"If he has taught you everything he knows, it is close enough."

Gilles scoffed. "I am far better at kissing than Émile."

Mademoiselle Daubin rose and straightened her skirts behind her. "Then if you will send me a list of all the girls you've kissed, I will compare it with my brother's list—as I am sure there are plenty of shared conquests—and seek out their opinions on the matter. With valid references, I would reconsider your request."

"Your brother has a list?" Gilles asked, pulling away from the banister. Even he didn't remember the names of all of the girls he'd kissed.

"Of course he doesn't." She turned to ascend the staircase, eyes falling to the hems of his trousers. "Did you just come from battle?"

Gilles winced. The glass! Her strange attitude had distracted him. "There was a small accident with my drink. I was finding the means to clean it up."

The corners of her mouth twitched. Now she really saw him as a younger brother. Heat rose to his face. "You will find our cook and chamber maid in the kitchens, straight down this corridor."

He thanked her and pivoted, wishing to be out of her presence and out of this house. Why did he always come out of these encounters looking a complete fool?

"That was kind of you to come to my defense."

He halted midstep as her voice carried to him. "Your defense?"

"You did not agree with anything I said, and still you reprimanded Maxence when he turned to insults. That took greater character than I have given you credit for."

Gilles shrugged, pulling at the edges of his jacket. "Can we call ourselves good men if we cannot be civil toward our enemies?"

"The Jacobins did not teach you that," she said, taking the rail with a slender hand and lifting the hem of her skirt to climb the stairs.

"No, my mother did."

Her head tilted ever so slightly, and once again she let her gaze wash over him in that disconcerting way that made him feel like a new mariner standing at attention for the morning inspection. Without another word, she glided up the stairs and disappeared around the corner, leaving Gilles to continue his pursuit of cleaning up the mess.

Now I find myself in need of a priest. Oh, Sylvie, I'd hoped the lies would stop when I returned, but they smolder inside as hot as the day they began. I lied again to Émile tonight, in front of his friends. About Nicolas. Where I am to find a priest, I am at a loss. My mother has not attended mass since the Constitution of the Clergy sent all faithful priests into exile. Do not worry on my behalf. If there is a priest still loyal to his vows in this city, I will find him. All is not lost, though hope dwindles by the day. This week in Marseille has only made it clearer that imminent change will not allow us to return to the happy peace we once enjoyed. Secrets, war, and division await. We will have to be strong.

And tonight has made another thing clearer—Gilles Étienne is a stupid boy.

But he has the potential to become a decent man.

How I miss you, ma cousine. *Give my love to the family. May God bless you.*

Affectueusement,

Caroline

CHAPTER 6

Gilles sat at the table in the kitchen, candle lit despite the early-evening light coming through the window. Hair, bone, and skin littered the table around him. He stabbed his needle into goat flesh and pulled it through the opposite side of the wound. When he was a real doctor, he wouldn't have to create wounds and then close them. But for now, the thick hind leg of a goat from the butcher would have to do for practice.

Voices outside the door and footfall on the steps made Gilles pause midsuture. No one had been home when he arrived after work except Florence, who quickly left to fetch something before the shops closed. Charged to watch the fire in her absence, he'd pulled the goat leg from the cellar to strip and cut for drying.

The kitchen door creaked open, and Maman entered with a basket. Florence followed close behind. The young woman chattered enthusiastically as she stepped inside. They both stopped short and stared at the mess over the table. Gilles threw his mother a sheepish smile and shrugged.

"Is it wounded?" Maman asked, setting her basket by the door.

"I just wanted to practice. I was studying sutures last night."

"Ah." She bent down to retrieve a few bottles from under the cloth covering the basket. "And my kitchen just before dinner was the best place and time to do so." Her words came out flat and stern, but a laugh twinkled in her eyes as she moved past him to the cellar door.

Florence sighed. "I am supposed to prepare dinner in this? We'll be eating goat hair with our chicken."

"I'll clean it up as soon as I finish cutting this meat."

She eyed his needle. "You seem to be working in the wrong direction."

Gilles cut the needle from the ligature and removed the stitches he'd made. "I thought you'd be much longer."

Maman returned from the cellar, and Florence helped her tie on an apron. "I saw Madame Daubin and her daughter while buying vinegar," his mother said. "She was happy you came to dinner last week."

"She is a kind woman, if a bit misled." He knew very little about his employer's wife beyond the fact that she came from a lesser *aristo* family. Émile had been furious when the Daubins sent his younger brother to live with their uncle, who was third in line for a *baronnie*. But unlike the *aristos* they railed against in Jacobin meetings, Madame Daubin had not acted above her company at the dinner. She'd treated him with as much respect as her friends, even though he was simply her husband's clerk.

"I invited them to dine with us, but they had previous plans."

His stomach leaped. Thank goodness for that. He could only imagine being stuck in his own dining room under Mademoiselle Daubin's disapproving stare.

Florence handed him a bowl for the goat meat. "How strange to have a *royaliste* family with such a *révolutionnaire* son."

"The Daubins are *royaliste*?" Maman asked him. "I thought you said the *monsieur* would not support one side or the other."

Gilles swept the goat debris to the side to clear room for his butchering. He cursed as the needle rolled off the table and spun to the floor. "He keeps his opinions on the subject mostly to himself, but his daughter is very open that her loyalties lie with the king." That haunted expression she'd worn on the stairs had stayed with him the last four days. He'd told Maman about the fine food and smaller than expected number of guests, but he'd left out the sparring and Maxence's cruel comments. After the dinner, Gilles had been relieved—perhaps for the first time—when his brother returned to Montpellier.

"Mademoiselle Daubin seems a charming young lady."

Charming? He wouldn't use that word. "She's a pretty girl."

Maman's lips pursed as she collected a head of lettuce from her basket. "She has quite the wit. I can see Maxence getting on well with her, whenever he decides to stop chasing girls he never intends to catch."

Again with chasing girls. What had put Maman on that subject? "Only if she did not have such strong feelings toward the monarchy. Maxence would never marry a *royaliste*." Gilles slid his knife along the goat leg, separating the rest of the skin from the meat. "Nor would I," he added in a mutter.

Maxence and Mademoiselle Daubin. A laughable pair. Maman had the best intentions, but she hadn't seen their arguing. No young lady could be further from a well-suited match for his brother. Gilles sliced off strips of meat and plopped them a little too emphatically into the bowl to be salted and dried. *He* was far better suited in disposition to marry Marie-Caroline Daubin than Max. Look at how his brother had hurt her at the dinner party.

Most women had the tendency to cry over every ailment. Except his mother, of course. And Victor's wife, and Grandmére. Something about being mariners' wives seemed to have strengthened them.

While Mademoiselle Daubin did not have that distinction, she seemed more likely to shout than cry over things that upset her. And yet, Maxence's words had stung. Gilles had seen it in her eyes as she sat on the stairs.

He rotated the leg to better pull the remaining flesh off the bone. His brother had said similar, biting things in the past, and Gilles always brushed them off. Maxence wasn't as cruel as his comments let on. Not really. Nor was Mademoiselle Daubin as ill tempered as Émile let on. Only passionate about her hopeless cause.

Gilles cut the meat in silence, stewing over the matter while his mother tore lettuce for a salad and Florence tended the roasting chicken. Over the last two years, they had worked just this way more evenings than he could count, though usually Florence spoke more. He preferred the quiet companionship of these two women with Père and Max away. Part of him wondered why he hadn't married Florence so as to keep things just as they were. Not that he had any feelings for her. Just the feelings of warm camaraderie. Her husband had snatched her up the year before, and who knew how long it would be before she left their employ to raise children? It would be quiet with just him and his mother most evenings.

"Where is Père?" he asked. For a moment he had forgotten his father was in port.

"At the docks," Maman said, not turning around. "He leaves for Naples next week, and *le Rossignol* needs repairs."

A short stay on land, then. Gilles would not complain about that.

Knocking from the front door echoed through the house, and Florence hurried to answer it. She returned just as swiftly. "It's Jean Sault, Monsieur Gilles. I showed him to the sitting room."

Jean Sault! Gilles extricated himself from the bench at the table.

"Who is that?" Maman asked.

"The president of my Jacobin club." How had she forgotten? He rushed to rinse the meat juices from his hands in the basin by the door. Sault had never visited him at home in the months Gilles had been a member.

"*Bonsoir, monsieur,*" Gilles greeted him on entering the room, holding out his hand to shake Sault's. "To what do I owe this honor?"

Sault waved away the pleasantry and grasped Gilles's hand firmly. Nearing forty, the attorney had a grin that made him pass for one of the fiery young patriots in their chapter. "Cooking in the kitchen, Monsieur Étienne?"

Sacrebleu, he'd forgotten his apron. He unbuttoned it and tossed it hastily over a chair.

"I didn't take you as one to enjoy women's work," the older man said.

Never mind that all cooks on ships were men. "I was only cutting meat to be dried for my father's voyage," Gilles said, to which Sault nodded appreciatively. "What do you need of me?"

"I am off to Aix for recruiting purposes on Friday. I wondered if you would open Saint-Cannat for Saturday's meeting."

"Yes, *bien sûr.*" This meant Gilles would not be able to put in extra work at the *savonnerie*, though that was no matter for one day. He'd need to be at the appropriated church as early as possible. It wasn't a great honor, in truth, but as one so new to the cause, Gilles could not help but feel the weight of the president's trust.

Sault handed him the church's key. "Martel will run the meeting. If you could open the church and lock it back up afterward," he said. "I hate to miss the chance of conversing with my brothers, but what better excuse to miss it than to bring more Frenchmen into the light of Jacobin principles? Of liberty from oppression and the empowerment of citizens."

Gilles slipped the key into the pocket of his waistcoat. "It is always my pleasure to serve."

Sault squeezed his shoulder. "Would that every section of the Club from here to Calais could have members as stalwart as you, Étienne. This revolution will rise on the wings of France's courageous youth. You, *mon ami*, will stand between us and the despotism that threatens from within and without."

Gilles nodded in agreement. *Then I expect all of you to go,* Mademoiselle Daubin had said. As though she doubted their conviction. He'd prove he could be as dedicated a Jacobin as she was a *royaliste.*

As Gilles bid farewell to Sault, he wondered whether she would mock or applaud him when he signed his name to the list.

29 May 1792
Marseille

Chére *Sylvie,*

You may rest assured that, despite the revolution's greatest efforts to destroy the church, I have found a loyal priest. What's more, he is the priest who presided over Saint-Cannat when we were members of that parish. I had not seen Père Franchicourt in many years, and though he has aged considerably, he still has the same fire about him that I loved so much as a girl.

As you can imagine, he keeps his presence a secret and holds very private mass in the attic of the house where he hides. Only our cook, the old couple who shelter the priest, and three others attended on Sunday. The owners of the house gave me wary looks when I joined them for the first time, and I can only hope they come to see me as a friend and not a threat.

Confession was much more awkward, as the small attic has no room for a confessional as yours does. So I am determined not to lie the next time a certain subject is broached, if only to avoid confession. Of course I joke, but in all seriousness, my family deserves to know about Nicolas, even with what happened. I should have known better than to dream of happiness in the midst of revolution. Though I pray marriage and proposals do not come up again in the company of Gilles and Maxence Étienne.

The attic was a sorry substitute for a church. Père Franchicourt does not even have a missal from which to read the mass. I wonder if the revolutionaries left the books in the church or if they destroyed those at the same time they marred the chapel. Père Franchicourt said they use it as a meeting place for a Jacobin club. Of all things!

I wish I could visit and see what is left. If we still lived near it, I could not be kept away. What right do the Jacobins have to take these things from us? Have they not done enough by taking our government? No, they are greedy to control every aspect of our lives, lest someone rise to oppose them. Perhaps I will go to Saint-Cannat after all, if only to prove the Jacobins do not have the hold they think they do. Taking back what rightfully belongs to the Church is not really stealing, is it?

I can see your face paling, Sylvie. I shall be on my guard, and no one will suspect. What's more, I do not know how I would even smuggle books out if I did find them. It is a pity pocket hoops went out of style so long ago. I do not think even Maman still has hers from when I was a child. One could smuggle several books out of a church wearing those. While I admire the current trend toward the natural womanly shape, I find it horribly inconvenient for crimes against the revolution.

You must tell me of any news about Monsieur LeGrand. You were silent on that matter in your last letter, and I must know if he has made any more advances. Do you think I've forgotten all about your plight since leaving? Mais non! I have thought about little else since *arriving in Marseille. The most eligible bachelors here are the Étienne brothers. Therefore I have no prospects, and must live vicariously through your happy interludes with that fine gentleman. I beg you to tell me how it progresses. Perhaps I will convince Papa to accompany me up to Fontainebleau if an agreement is made.*

In the meantime, I pray for you and I pray for France. Surely this madness cannot continue forever.

Affectueusement,

Marie-Caroline

Gilles settled back into his pew at Saint-Cannat, a few rows from the front. The hard wood was less comfortable than his chair at the *savonnerie*'s office. Glaring remains of decapitated statues surrounded the chapel. Members of their club like Martel found the sight empowering—testaments to the strength of revolutionary zeal. But the sorry figures only added to Gilles's discomfort. Most meetings he ignored them. Tonight he could not keep his eyes away.

Martel stood before the group of merchants, clerks, and artisans—a sheet of newspaper in his hand and tawny hair slipping out of its tie. "Marseille is the greatest hope this nation has," he said. "But if we do not ensure its citizens stay on the side of truth and rebellion, how are we to succeed?"

An older gentleman motioned for recognition. "Marseille has more spirit than any commune in France." Murmurs of pride rumbled through the gathering. "How can we do more than what we are already doing?"

"Yes, we are strong," another man said. "But so are the counter-revolutionaries. The *royalistes*. They keep quiet now, but they lie in wait for an opportunity to spring."

Gilles caught himself sliding down against the smooth wood of the pew. He pushed himself back up, his foot knocking something under the pew in front of him.

"And if enemies of the state gain control of Marseille's ports, they could starve the whole of France." Martel nodded, looking more like a wizened leader than the youngest man in their section of the Club.

Gilles ducked his head to investigate what he'd kicked. A black leather book lay open and facedown on the floor, a few pages crumpled at the center. He slid it out. Evening light pouring through the high windows above the entrance illuminated an etched cover. He turned it over to find pages and pages of Latin text. Some sort of prayer book. How had this been missed when the church was ransacked after the start of the revolution?

"We need new recruits, and we need them today." Martel circled a bust of an American diplomat whose name Gilles could not recall. They'd set it upon a crate at the front where the bust of Mirabeau, a leader of the revolution, often sat. Their muse of liberty for the evening. "Not tomorrow. Not next week. Today. Someday soon, men will be called up to fight for the freedom of France, and who will protect our home if there are not brothers-at-arms to carry on the duties of the Jacobins in our absence?"

Gilles nearly threw the book back under the pew. As a Jacobin, that should have been his response. But its battered binding and creased leaves gave it the look of a whimpering puppy. It was only a book. And from a religion well on its way to dying in this country. He did not need to tread on one of the last relics of religion in Marseille.

Glancing around, he tucked it between him and the end of the bench, out of sight of the other members. When he locked up the building, he would find a place for it. Then someone else could decide its fate.

"Étienne?"

Gilles straightened and met Martel's quizzical eye. "*Je m'excuse.* What was asked?"

"It was suggested you could accompany me on my campaign to Hautes-Alpes," his friend said.

Hautes-Alpes? That was more than a day's journey. He hesitated. "I . . . I'm certain an arrangement can be made." When had Martel decided to lead a campaign himself? Monsieur Daubin would not like Gilles asking for a week's leave to travel, especially if he was doing so to recruit Jacobin followers.

His mind churned as Martel ended the meeting. With Père departing soon, that would mean abandoning Maman. True, she had Florence during the day. But at night? Max was a day's journey away and therefore not helpful. Père had no qualms leaving her alone for months at a time. It wasn't as though she needed Gilles there, but the proposition left a bad taste in his mouth.

He rose with the others, tucking the book under his arm between his jacket and waistcoat. Men filed out of the dim church and spat at the feet of a defaced saint near the door. Several donned red liberty caps like the ones the *sans-culottes* wore.

Gilles waited until the rest of the club members had exited before shuffling toward Martel, who was moving the plaster bust from the front of the room. He placed it in a row with busts of Rousseau, Mirabeau, and other *révolutionnaire* heroes used to decorate their meetings.

"Thank you for volunteering to go," Martel said, shifting the bust into the perfect line.

Volunteering? Someone else had volunteered him. And Gilles had been too caught up with the silly book to hear who had. "I wished to speak to you on that. How long are we to be gone?" A week would be difficult, but if he worked extra hours before and after, perhaps Daubin would not get so cross.

Martel brushed his hands against his trousers. "Three weeks to a month, I should think. Enough time to establish clubs and get them used to the way of the Jacobins."

Gilles's brows shot up. "A month?"

"No sacrifice is too small for *la patrie*," Martel said with a shrug.

"And . . . and your employer has agreed to this?"

"*Bien sûr*. He knows the importance of these campaigns." He studied Gilles. "Will Daubin allow you to leave?"

They walked down the aisle toward the door. The tome under his arm started to slip, and he squeezed it tighter. It would not do to drop a book of religion in front of Martel while convincing him the campaign scheme would not work for him.

"I do not think I would have a job when I returned," Gilles said. "What's more, I cannot leave my mother."

Martel snorted. "Your mother can survive on her own. You know that." He stopped at the door and crossed his arms. "You must decide whether your work is more important to you than the cause."

If he didn't have the book smashed against his ribs, Gilles would have thrown up his hands. "My work is paying for schooling."

"As is mine," Martel said, "and yet I am leaving."

"I do not hesitate because I want the schooling for myself," Gilles insisted. "I wish to help others. Is there only one way to serve the nation, according to the Jacobins?"

Martel did not answer. After a moment, he spat at the statue's feet. "You are a Jacobin, Étienne. Do what you see fit." He marched off into the evening without any more of a farewell.

Gilles sighed as he watched his friend's spindly frame pass a woman in a brown dress before turning the corner. The revolution needed men with Martel's enthusiasm. And yet, Gilles wondered if too much enthusiasm could ever prove detrimental. He retreated inside, pulling the book from under his arm. His friend was not the most sympathetic of people, even on his amiable days. Martel set a high standard for his own conduct, and he expected every *révolutionnaire* to adhere to it as well. Many days Gilles could not meet the man's standards.

Red panels stretched across the walls at the apse of the church, some of the only ornaments not vandalized. Gilles studied them as he made his way to the altar at the front, which hadn't yet been removed but had lost its cloth. He crouched behind it and slid the book to the back corner of the shelf underneath.

There. No one would find it unless they were looking for it.

Gilles stood and leaned in to blow out the candles sitting atop the altar, when a movement at the door made him pause. Was Martel back to argue?

A cinnamon-colored redingote over a petticoat of the same shade eased through the doorway at the front of the church. The woman Martel had passed outside. She carried a basket, but with the dying light behind her, Gilles could not see her face. She walked quickly up the center aisle, then froze part way to the altar. After a moment's hesitation, the woman turned and walked to one side of the church, her haste suddenly exchanged for a leisurely pace.

"May I help you, *madame?*" Gilles called.

"I am only looking, but I thank you all the same."

He could not mistake the steady, confident voice. One corner of his lips curled upward. Of all people to meet tonight, Mademoiselle Daubin? "This building is closed to visitors beyond members of the Jacobin Club." He hopped down from the dais onto the checkered floor and ambled toward her.

She hesitated, then continued forward with her face turned to the side aisle as though admiring the colonnade. Her hair hid under a white cap without the usual ringlet or two falling down from the coiffure to curve around her long neck. "Has this church been claimed as property of the nation?"

"Yes, of course." Gilles slowed as he approached. The *mademoiselle* was dressed much simpler than usual. She'd almost pass for a shopkeeper's wife.

"For the people of France?" she asked.

What was she playing at? She knew all churches had been taken to be repurposed or sold. At dinner the week before, she'd made a comment about the "travesty" of churches being taken. "Yes, for the people of France."

"Then surely, as a citizen of France, I have every right to be in a place of which I hold partial ownership."

It was more complex than that, but Gilles didn't have the words to make an argument. He bit down a grin. In some ways, she was correct. Gilles halted and dipped his head. "Mademoiselle Daubin, how good it is to see you again."

"I do not wish to kiss you," she said in greeting, brushing past him to continue her perusal of the church. Bottles clinked together in the basket she held over one arm.

So she'd determined to remind him each time they met, had she? Perhaps the more she did it, the easier it would be not to blush at the memory of his humiliation. "I cannot fathom why." Gilles leaned against the side of the nearest pew. "The other Jacobins have gone. No one would see. We could pretend it never happened."

She glanced at him over her shoulder without breaking stride. "You lie. You would go straight to Montpellier to collect your prize from Émile."

Gilles chuckled. He'd be hard-pressed to fool her. "The sweetness of the kiss would be reward enough."

"Then you would be sorely disappointed. My kisses are not sweet."

His eyes narrowed as he watched her progression. What did she mean by that? That she was not good at it? She could not have meant the opposite. She was too much a lady.

Before he could make a quip about her ambiguity, she paused before a statue and gave a cry of disgust. "Why would they do this?" Her hand ran along the battered edges where the saint's face used to be. "I loved this statue," she whispered.

"Some *révolutionnaires* got carried away." Gilles scratched the back of his head, trying to remember if this was one of the statues Martel had helped deface.

"It's savage." Mademoiselle Daubin backed away, still staring at the mutilated saint. She pressed her lips together and moved with more purpose deeper into the church. "You won your revolution. Why not leave the Church alone?"

She thought they'd won. Gilles snickered. The revolution was far from over. "You can hardly blame them, when all their lives they've been oppressed by the First Estate. This defacement was to be expected. The Church benefited at the expense of French commoners."

Her back remained straight and defiant, but what he'd give to see her face. "There were some clergymen of the First Estate who exploited their positions, certainly, but you are a fool if you think all the Jacobin leaders are saints."

"I think they would be offended to be likened to saints."

She wandered to the altar and trailed her fingers along the polished wood as she circled it. Her head moved back and forth, taking in the details of the piece and its dais. "If the Jacobins truly want freedom, why do they keep our religion from us? Plenty of clergy are humble, loyal citizens of France who wish only to serve. But you've labeled them all traitors and ordered their deportation, guilty or not."

He winced at her reference to the National Assembly's most recent edict. All priests who would not give up their association with the Catholic Church and swear fealty to the new government were to be driven from France, whether they were foreigners or not. Martel had exultated about the matter during that evening's meeting. One of Martel's uncles was among these nonjuring clergymen. His friend wanted nothing more than to bring the man to justice.

"Many have been led blindly into their poverty in the name of religion," he said, crossing his arms. "How are we to protect our unknowing citizens if there are enemies in our ranks?"

A spark of defiance—or was it just the candlelight from the altar?—touched her face. "The Church is no enemy of—oh!"

Gilles glanced up to see Mademoiselle Daubin stumble and disappear behind the altar, the contents of her basket rattling. He bolted upright. "Are you hurt?"

"I've only lost a shoe. Do not worry." The large altar muffled her voice.

Still, he shot across the transept of the empty church and up onto the dais. She pushed herself to her feet as he arrived. His proffered hand came moments too late.

"I am well, thank you." She righted her purchases and pulled the cloth that lined her basket more tightly around them. The corners of the napkin would not touch over the bottles despite her fussing. Both were etched with "*vinaigre*" on the sides.

"Are you certain?" Gilles asked, pulling his hand back. "Your ankle is not twisted? You have no pain in your wrists?" She'd disappeared so quickly, she must have fallen hard.

Mademoiselle Daubin cocked her head. "No, Doctor, my ankles and wrists are well, as are my knees and elbows and most of the rest of me, though I have had the slightest case of sniffles the last week. Perhaps you might prescribe a tisane?"

Gilles ducked his head. "My apologies. I was simply concerned."

"Yes, concerned about everyone else's affairs, as a good Jacobin should be." She switched the basket to her other arm and held it away from him as she squeezed between him and the altar. The sleeve of her redingote brushed against his arm. His breath stuttered for the briefest moment as he caught a whiff of her deep perfume. It was gone before he could deduce the scent.

"We are not so heartless as you think, *mademoiselle*."

She met his gaze, fire snapping in her umber eyes. "And we are not so obtuse as you believe, *monsieur*."

Many of the devout *royalistes* he had met were idiotically set in their archaic ways. But here stood one *royaliste* who did not fit that description. She had applauded the efforts of the women's march on Versailles, hadn't she? Even though she disagreed with their actions. Could he bring himself to admit that some supporters of the monarchy were not complete imbeciles? He asked her to delay judgment on his fellows; surely he could offer her the same.

Mademoiselle Daubin rearranged the basket against her hip. "Thank you for allowing me a glimpse at my old sanctuary. I must deliver these purchases to my mother."

"I thought you bought vinegar on Tuesday," he said quickly as she turned away.

She scowled. "Tuesday?"

"Yes, my mother said she saw you and Madame Daubin buying vinegar on Tuesday."

"Ah, *oui*." Her grip tightened on the handle of the basket, her knuckles turning white. "We did meet your mother. *C'est vrai*. She is a very lovely person." A waver crept into her voice. "I would not have guessed she was related to you."

Gilles raised his eyebrows. He'd caught her at something. "You bought vinegar Tuesday, but you needed more on Saturday."

"Our cook dropped the bottles."

"What a mess, I am sure," he said, shaking his head. What was she up to? "Might I escort you home? It is getting late."

"*Non, c'est gentil.* My manservant is waiting at the carriage. I have stayed too long. Good evening, *monsieur.*" She hastened away from him, as though he'd told her the *sans-culottes* were coming. The still-open door lit her flight, and sunset's dying glow cast her shadow long and slender across the floor of the nave. At the threshold she paused, then darted into the darkening dusk.

Gilles turned slowly and wandered over to the candlesticks at the altar. Every encounter he'd had with that lady ended rather strangely. He blew out the first candle, then moved to the next. How odd she'd acted after falling, like a cabin boy trying to cover the fact that he'd upended the captain's coffee pot.

He went down on one knee to examine the floor in the light of the remaining candle. Feeling along the floor with his hand, he found nothing protruding that would have caught her foot. Unless she'd tripped over the corner of the altar, but she'd been too far from that. Gilles rested his chin in his hand and scanned the area once more. Perhaps she had just misstepped.

Time to close the church and return for dinner. He grasped the edge of the altar to pull himself up and glanced once more at the corner where he'd hidden the book.

It was gone.

Gilles bent and felt for the book. Nothing. He could have sworn . . . A grin split across his face as understanding dawned. That little thief! She'd snatched up the book under the guise of an overly dramatic fall. He righted himself and planted his hands on the altar. Quiet laughter bubbled up within him.

He should report her. Theft from the state was nothing amusing. He watched the door, wishing for a moment she would reenter so he could tease her. Had she come here to take something in an act of defiance against *la patrie*?

With a puff of air intensified by his laugh, he blew out the remaining candle on the altar and made his way to snuff out the others scattered around the church. He would not report Mademoiselle Daubin. Plenty of *révolutionnaires* had pillaged this and other churches with more malicious intent. But he would not miss the next opportunity to take the upper hand in his dealings with that frustratingly obstinate *mademoiselle*.

2 June 1792
Marseille

Ma cousine,

I have done it! And under the nose of none other than Gilles Étienne. That in and of itself makes this victory all the ~~sweeter~~ nicer. (Also, I shall never use the word sweet *again.) But heavens above, I have lied once more. If Père Franchicourt is ever found and chased from the country, my soul shall be in grave danger.*

Most of the furniture has been taken from Saint-Cannat, and all images and statues of holy saints desecrated. But heaven smiled on my efforts. As I searched the altar, I found a shelf at the back of it with a little missal someone had overlooked. I feigned tripping and scooped it hurriedly into my basket. As I sought to escape without calling Monsieur Étienne's attention to the book, he pointed out that the bottles I carried had been purchased earlier in the week. I had to run from the church to keep my secret.

But Sylvie, he did not discover my mission, and as I write, the book is sitting on my desk ready to take to Père Franchicourt. I should feel remorse for lying to Gilles about Cook breaking the previous bottles; however, I feel only satisfied pride. I'm sure I will regret it later, but for this moment I thoroughly enjoy the sentiment.

Father has been silent over the course of the week. More so than usual. It cannot stem from politics, since the only recent change has been the call for deportation of the clergy, which he cares little about. He and Émile parted on calm—if not speaking—terms last week, which is decidedly better than how they parted the week before. We do not expect to see my brother in the next month as he continues his studies, which will allow the embers to further cool. I can only conclude something has happened with the savonnerie *or* parfumerie. *Maman does not see anything amiss, but then she rarely inquires. She would rather continue in ignorance than suffer the nervousness.*

You will excuse my return to the subject, but Gilles Étienne does not seem very much like a Jacobin to me. True, he is passionate for the cause of freedom. But there is a kindness and concern about him that Émile and Maxence have lacked for some time. His face when he thought I had fallen was not that of one who saw me as an enemy.

He is still a fool, and his efforts are greatly misguided, but I prefer a kind fool to a rude wit.

Mass is tomorrow. It cannot come too soon. But do you think I shall make it another week without a horrid lie? There is only One who knows.

      Affectueusement,

      Caroline

CHAPTER 7

Monsieur Daubin made his way to the first cauldron with Gilles at his elbow. Gilles stifled a yawn. In the dim morning light of the factory, his employer's face still creased with the weight of yesterday's worry.

The order of salt from Camargue had come late last night, and the soap maker had paced his office, wringing his hands until the shipment arrived. Gilles and the other clerks had stayed much later than usual to document the delivery. Of course Maman had guests to dinner that night, and he had arrived just as Florence cleared the dishes, forcing him to insist the party advance to the parlor without him.

Now the murky paste roiled before them as workers stirred. With the salty brine added, it had begun to separate, the extra fats sinking to the bottom of the enormous pots.

"I cannot keep that girl from the factory," Daubin muttered.

"Pardon?" Gilles glanced at the door and the wave of skirts advancing on it. Monsieur Daubin's daughter. A grin crossed his face. Excellent.

"Will you go keep her occupied?" Monsieur Daubin asked. "Her mother is terrified she will fall into the cauldron."

Gilles had a higher chance of falling into the cauldron than Mademoiselle Daubin, he was sure of it. And if he angered her, he would not put it past her to grab him by the lapels and make certain the deed was done. "You do not want her in the factory at all?"

His employer grunted. "Not if you can help it. *Bonne chance.*"

Gilles hurried to the entrance to intercept the young lady. She did not have the usual stern scowl for him as she slowed and stopped.

"*Bonjour, mademoiselle,*" he said with a bow. "What brings you to the factory this morning?"

She stopped only long enough to curtsy. "Papa said they were salting off the batch." An odd glint touched her eye as she tried to move past him. Satisfaction, perhaps.

He sidestepped to cut her off. "What sort of greeting is this?"

Mademoiselle Daubin raised an eyebrow, hands going to her hips. "I apologize. *Bonjour, monsieur.* How do you do?" She curtsied again, this time sinking nearly to the ground as one would only do in the king's court. Despite the irony of the gesture, she performed it with practiced grace. "Will that suffice?"

"I simply meant you did not insist on your unwillingness to kiss me, and I wondered whether that indicated you had changed your mind on the issue."

With a huff, she brushed by. He'd failed in all of sixty seconds. Gilles caught her arm before she made it too far. "How are you liking your prayer book?" he asked so only she could hear.

Her arm went rigid in his hand, and she froze in the doorway. "Prayer book? Which prayer book? I have many."

"The one that magically appeared in your basket Saturday evening after your terrible fall behind the altar at Saint-Cannat."

She whirled, her normally light olive skin now as white as her dress. "I do not know to what you refer."

"Oh, I think you do know exactly what I am referring to. The little black book you snatched from under the altar and tried to hide under the vinegar bottles. Vinegar bottles, I might add, which were bought several days before your little outing to the church."

Her pale cheeks instantly flushed. She tugged with her arm, but he did not release his hold. "Your father does not wish you to go in there," he said.

"My father? I find that hard to believe. Let go of me."

"In truth it is your mother." He let her sleeve slip through his fingers. "Your mother fears for your safety."

Mademoiselle Daubin's eyes closed tightly. "Yes, of course. And my father asked you to dissuade me from entering."

Gilles shrugged. It was hardly his fault.

"So I am to wait for my father out here with a *révolutionnaire* who wishes to blackmail me for a kiss to earn a few *livres* from my brother." She sighed and turned away.

Blackmail? "I said nothing of—"

"Tell him I will wait in the office. With the door barred this time." She strode toward the side building that held the offices and stores.

"*Attendez, mademoiselle!*" Gilles called, jogging to catch her. "Wait, please."

"Have you gone to your Jacobin friends?" she hissed, not looking at him. "Or is that your plan if you cannot convince me to kiss you?"

He slid ahead of her and blocked the door to the offices. Though the Mediterranean sun had not yet reached its zenith, its rays beat down on him. The days were warming, and this job did not have the benefit of a cool, sharp wind off the sea to dry the sweat beading along his hairline.

"I will not tell a soul," he said, hoping the sincerity he felt showed true on his face.

"I highly doubt that." She took a step back from him, glancing toward the factory. Would she run for that door again?

"You have your reasons for wanting such a book as that. It's not as though it would fetch a good price or contribute to the value of the church when they decide to sell it. Your secret is safe." He flashed her a reassuring smile, but she refused to return it. "And I do not require anything more than simple gratitude."

She reached for the door handle once more. Gilles opened the door before she could take it.

"I am grateful you have decided not to inform your leaders of the incident," she said. "For now."

"You do not trust my word? I will not disclose your secret, *mademoiselle*."

She winced, wrapping her arms around herself. "And what will they do if they find out you have been keeping secrets for a monarchist?"

As none of them knew the book existed, he had little fear of that ever happening. "Is that what we shall always be? Jacobin and monarchist?"

Mademoiselle Daubin nodded toward the factory, where the workers carried on the salting process. "Our country is separating itself, bit by bit, just as that soap. Until those in power decide to stop throwing salt in the mix, I think we are destined to be separated in thought and in heart." She smoothed the slender sleeve of her gaulle dress. "When I say heart, I mean sentiments, of course."

"Of course."

"You cannot tell me your Jacobins will be happy to learn you allowed me to take a missal from the church."

Gilles winked and said, "I think they will forgive me for helping a pretty face." It wasn't entirely true, or those aiding the queen would not have found themselves in such perilous circumstances.

Mademoiselle Daubin's eyes narrowed, all goodwill vanishing. "Is that what I am to you? A pretty face?"

He swallowed against the dryness in his mouth. In all reality, she did have quite a pretty face. Even now with her brows dangerously lowered and nostrils flared. She stormed past, flinging the door open and pushing his arm out of the way.

"No, I did not mean it to—" With a crack, the door slammed shut. He grabbed the handle, but when he pushed on the door it budged very little. He tried again. It was of no use; she'd secured the latch. "*Mademoiselle*, I beg you, please . . ." His voice trailed off at the faint sound of her shoes tapping against the floor, moving farther away.

Gilles slumped against the door and wiped away sweat with the back of his sleeve. Someday, he would have a conversation with her that did not end in her hasty escape.

Gilles blew out a long breath when he finally arrived home that evening. Surprisingly, pots and dishes still rattled from the kitchen, announcing his parents had not begun their dinner. He closed the front door and stood in the dark vestibule until his eyes adjusted to the dimness. Beside the door sat Père's sea chest.

Praise the heavens. He'd forgotten his father was leaving tonight. *Le Rossignol* would sail on the morning tide.

"Gilles, there you are."

Only a few more hours of hearing that voice. His father's shadow crossed the front hall, and Gilles gave him a wide berth while trying to slide past.

"You are home late," Père said. "At sea, you never have to worry about that."

"Yes, because you never leave your work," Gilles grumbled.

"Or your home."

Gilles paused before he could turn the corner and end the conversation. On the corridor wall before him hung a little watercolor his mother had made of a sea at dusk with a tiny ship in the distance. Before joining Père's crew, he'd loved the painting. He had dreamed of being on that ship sailing to wealth and adventure. Now he avoided looking at it, constantly convincing himself he preferred standing with feet firmly planted on the shore, watching *le Rossignol* sail off.

"The sea was never my home," he said quietly, forcing the words. He should have just walked away. Left the interaction where it was. But his earlier arguments with Mademoiselle Daubin had either weakened his resolve not to take the bait or simply given him a desire to win.

"No, you long for the quiet solitude of a cramped office owned by another man."

Gilles clenched his fists and slowly turned around. Would Père ever give up this argument? His father sat on his trunk, hands behind his head as he leaned back against the wall.

"Rather, I like to be home with Maman," Gilles insisted.

"You say that, and yet you plan to leave her as soon as you've saved sufficient funds to attend the university." It wasn't accusatory. His father's words held a laugh as they always did—a calculating, devious laugh.

Gilles pushed his shoulders back. "This from the husband who leaves her for months on end. Let's not play the hypocrite."

Père flourished a hand. "*Touché.*"

This man, who thought he knew so much. He played with lives

according to his fancies and couldn't care less how his decisions affected others, so long as he got his prizes. "The least you could do is provide her a more comfortable home and a larger staff," Gilles snarled. "You think nothing of her or any of the rest of your family."

His father pushed off the wall, straightening. "You should not speak of things you know nothing about."

Gilles had aggravated him. He fought against a smirk that would have mirrored the expression his father usually wore. "Oh, I think I do know something about it. You should see Maman's face when you are gone. You should see how she works her fingers to the bone doing everything herself, when she should have a husband by her side."

Père crossed his arms, still keeping his seat atop the trunk. "You purport to know quite a lot about women."

"More than you do, I would wager."

His father's grin glinted in the dim light of the corridor. It rarely stayed away for long. "Kissing every female fortunate enough to cross your path does not give you adequate experience with the workings of their hearts. Only the workings of their lips."

Gilles exhaled sharply. Père excelled in turning the conversation away from his own faults. "Maman deserves better than you give her." He could go on, but his father would not listen. Perhaps he would ask Florence to bring a tray of dinner upstairs tonight so he wouldn't have to endure more of this. Gilles's pulse raced as though he'd just run from the *savonnerie*. This was the last thing he needed after two grueling days at work. He made to leave, but Père's soft yet penetrating voice froze him in place.

"Just as Mademoiselle Daubin deserves much better than how you treat her."

Gilles took a step back, glaring at his father. "I have been nothing but a . . ." The words caught in his throat.

"Do not say 'a gentleman.'" Père pushed himself to his feet. "I've heard the way you and Maxence talk about that young woman."

The sinking in Gilles's gut would not let him form a protest. He did not join in, but neither had he stopped Maxence or Émile from saying rude things about the latter's monarchist sister.

"I would venture to say that, despite all the company you keep with starry-eyed girls begging to be loved, you do not understand women so well as you think you do, *mon fils.*" Père cut the distance between them and clapped Gilles on the shoulder. Gilles's mind had clouded too much to shrug him off.

"She is loyal to the crown and the Church," Gilles murmured. Her sharp look as she had stormed into the offices bored into his vision despite the darkness of the corridor. She could not stand for his company, and he was beginning to think she was very well justified in that sentiment.

"Does it matter where her loyalties lie?"

Did it not?

"She is a human being, after all," Père said. That was what Maman had told him the night Gilles helped her with mending.

He *did* treat Mademoiselle Daubin as a human. He was sure of it. It was hardly his fault she bristled at his every attempt at kindness. And yet the falling sensation in his gut suggested otherwise.

Behind them, the sounds of his mother and Florence descending with platters and candlesticks drifted in from the dining room along with the scent of fish and spices. The warm glow seeping through the doorway reflected off the single gold hoop in Père's earlobe.

"If I were you, I might reconsider my own life before calling another man a hypocrite," his father said. "But do as you will. My advice has long since ceased to hold any importance to you."

Père strode from the vestibule and entered the dining room with a jovial greeting that was met with enthusiastic returns, leaving Gilles alone and unable to swallow back the bitter taste on his tongue.

That man, he is unbearable. Gilles Étienne, on my father's wishes, escorted me away from the factory this morning. Not only did he tease me about taking the missal—for yes, he did find me out—but made it quite clear he thought me in possession of neither intelligence nor sense. "A pretty face," he called me. Insufferable man.

But perhaps I am just the idiot he described. To think I believed I had fooled him! I was so proud, so triumphant. Did God decide I needed the humbling? Or was it punishment for my continued lies?

Never worry, Sylvie. Gilles has insisted he will not reveal the secret. I think he will be true to his word. Though if he knew I took it not for my personal use but for the use of a nonjuring priest, I think he would not honor his promise.

Are there no good men left in this world? Excepting your Monsieur LeGrand, bien sûr. *I used to think I had the world to choose from. But the arms of revolution are too powerful. One way or the other, they have all become corrupted. Do you remember how I would tease you for reading those old stories of knights and valor? I do not laugh anymore. I wish with all my heart to be spirited away to those fantastic worlds where justice and goodness were not things of debate and where gentlemen proved worthy of the designation.*

CHAPTER 8

Gilles closed his worn copy of Molière's *Tartuffe* and plopped the book on his chest. He sucked in the orchard's fresh, rich air as he stretched. Morning sun peeked through the wide fig leaves that formed a small canopy above where he lay. Months had passed since the last time he stole away to his great-uncle's orchards for a little Sunday reading. He'd forgotten how much he enjoyed it.

He tucked his hands behind his head and followed wasps with his gaze as they wandered through the line of fig and almond trees. While he had no desire to be a fig wasp, sometimes he envied the simplicity of their existence. They did not have to deal with the disapproval of their fellows.

Père had sailed nearly a week ago, but his words from their last encounter in the entry hall still pounded in Gilles's brain. He rubbed his eyes with the heels of his hands. The accusations would not go away. Gilles rolled to his side, letting the book flop onto the blanket he'd brought. His father couldn't be right. Not about him, not about his mother, not about women. How dare he suggest Gilles was anything less than an honorable man?

He snatched off a purple-skinned fruit from the woody part of the tree and sank his teeth into it. The fruit, part of the early breba crop, had less flavor than the main crop would have at the end of the summer, but the taste was still enough to stop his frustrated musings. Its syrupy heart, like perfectly ripe berries drizzled with honey, spread across his lips on his next bite. Tiny seeds crackled under his teeth as he chewed. He would have to return next Sunday, when more of the early fruit had ripened, and he could bring some home for Maman.

A hum of voices cut through the murmur of nearby water. Gilles glanced toward the road and the bridge that crossed the canal. This street was not heavily used by the *Marseillais*, as it led mostly to farmland. Two women walked with purpose in his direction, one in a pale, airy gown and the other in more modest, darker colors. Lavender ribbons rippled from the straw hat of the first woman.

Mademoiselle Daubin? Gilles did not know why he grinned. Hastily he wiped his mouth on his sleeve and rolled to his knees. He shoved his arms into his jacket as he staggered upright, swiping fig branches out of his face. Where was she headed so early on a Sunday? And with the Daubins' cook, of all people.

"*Bonjour, mademoiselle!*" he called, plucking up the blanket and book. He threw the blanket, now covered with bits of orchard debris, over his shoulder, then shoved the book under his arm.

The pair of women halted at the bridge, turning about. Gilles cut through the trees. A stupid grin threatened as he descended the gentle incline that separated the orchards from the road.

"I did not expect to catch you here," he said.

Despite the warm summer glow, the young woman's eyes turned icy on his approach. "We are not fish, *monsieur*."

"You can catch more than fish." He should have taken the warning and fled.

"We are not thieves, either." Mademoiselle Daubin stood straighter.

Beside her, the domestic shifted, eyes darting between her employer's daughter and her employer's clerk.

Gilles bit his lip to hold in a chuckle. Not a thief, she insisted. The *mademoiselle*'s color did not change, but the poor cook's face turned bright as a red mullet fish. Did the older woman know about Mademoiselle Daubin's escapade to Saint-Cannat the previous week? "Why would I ever call a young woman of such high standing a thief?" Gilles asked. Light colors truly did become her. The delicate blue of her dress set off her dark hair and deep brown eyes.

She nodded to her cook. "Continue on and tell my friends that I will arrive shortly, if you please."

The older woman scurried away, glancing over her shoulder as she mounted the bridge before disappearing behind a bend in the road.

"So you are visiting—" Gilles began.

"If you attempt to kiss me, I will ensure you regret it."

Gilles held up his hands and retreated a step. Why did all of their conversations begin this way? "*Mademoiselle*, rest assured that I will never try to kiss you again."

She scoffed and crossed her arms. "You are Émile's friend. I hardly believe that."

"For the rest of my days. I swear it." Perhaps now she would stop with these uncomfortable greetings. "Who are your friends? My father's uncle lives nearby; perhaps I am also acquainted with them."

A swallow rippled down the muscles of her neck. "Oh, I should think not. They do not know very many people who live nearby."

She was lying to him again. Had she gone back to the church and pilfered something else? Her steady gaze held his, and strain as he might, he could not read it. Only her fingers pulling at the tips of her gloves belied her distress.

He leaned closer, dropping his voice despite their solitude. "Have I not proven myself trustworthy?"

Birds called from the trees that lined the road—the only sound that broke the silence as she studied him. "That remains to be seen," she finally said.

"Of course." She did not trust him. Why did that sting like rope tearing across his palms? He'd kept her secret about the book.

She backed up farther. "If you will excuse me, *monsieur*, I must be off."

"I hope with time I will come to earn your trust." He meant the words that tumbled from his mouth. Something about the way she carried herself in conversations, the sincerity of her words and convictions, made him want to gain her confidence.

Her brow raised. "You are a *révolutionnaire*. I am a monarchist. How can that ever be? People who believe as I do, we live in constant fear that your people will decide we are a threat."

Gilles took a slow breath. Many *royalistes* were threats. The king himself was a threat. "Then allow me to escort you to your destination, as a sign of good faith."

"*Non, merci.*"

He cocked his head. "I am to take this as *royaliste* actions?" If she were involved in secret meetings . . . What would he do? He should have reported her for the book. But a meeting of *royalistes* was more serious, and if anyone found out he knew about them, where would the trouble end?

"You may take this simply as a private matter of personal enlightenment," she said. "Please excuse me."

It was his duty as a Jacobin to find out if there really was a secret meeting. But strangely, pure curiosity held greater sway. "I could follow you, you know." The corner of his mouth lifted in a flirty grin that did not affect her steely expression in the slightest.

"That would not bring you any closer to earning my trust."

His father's face in the dark vestibule appeared in his mind before

Gilles could make a coy quip about finding other means. *You do not understand women so well as you think you do.*

Gilles drew in his lips to run his tongue over them and the remnants of fig juice, now sickly sweet. Perhaps Père had reason in this one instance. He hated to accept it, but here she stood, radiantly firm in her convictions, and he hadn't the faintest understanding of the inner workings of Mademoiselle Daubin's mind. How she held to the dying monarchy with such conviction. How she stayed true to a religion that failed so many. How she did not melt under any of his teasings or playful smiles.

"I suppose now you must choose between gaining the trust of a woman with whom you vehemently disagree and investigating the terrible treason she might be off to commit." She rested her hands on her waist, further accentuating its slimness. "I know which one the Jacobin would choose."

Gilles's foot inched back of its own accord. "It may be that you know me as poorly as I know you," he said softly. He would let her go. He shouldn't, but he would. "Might we part as friends?" He continued to back up, putting a safe distance between them.

She still eyed him warily. "If you do not follow me, I will agree to not being enemies."

"I can accept that compromise." He gave a gentle bow, then pivoted and walked away. The blanket over his shoulder rose and fell softly against his back as he made for the Panier district. Strangely he did not feel the tension that usually came after his encounters with Mademoiselle Daubin. He had not made the mistake of implying she was simply a pretty face, as he had the last time they met. His cheeks grew hot at the memory. Imbecile.

He pulled his book out and stretched the arm that had held it against his side for the whole of their conversation. *Tartuffe.* When he'd first read the tale of the hypocritical clergyman and his victims,

Gilles had taken it as a confirmation of the corruption of religion. Now he wondered if it had more to say than just criticism of the church.

The figs and almonds gave way to olive trees as he walked the straight road. He filled his lungs with fresh air, something scarce at his home in the middle of Marseille. After journeying several minutes, he came to a bend in the road and looked back. He could see a straw bonnet and dress the color of a summer sky.

Still watching.

He raised his arm and gave an exaggerated wave, not sure if she could even see it. In a moment her arm lifted to return the gesture, a blue thread caught on a blanket of forest green. He grinned and turned back to his path, whistling a little tune about dancing on the Pont d'Avignon.

The next morning, a rap on the doorframe caused Gilles to look up from his desk. Both his fellow clerks were in the factory, and Monsieur Daubin was breakfasting with his family in his office down the hall. Why his employer breakfasted here and not at home, Gilles could only guess.

But it wasn't Mademoiselle Daubin at the door, as he'd hoped. "Martel?" He rose to greet his friend, who wore a haversack slung over one shoulder. "Are you off this morning?"

"I have only a moment, but I wanted to offer once more for you to join me." His friend's sharp features seemed even more severe today, with his eyebrows drawn low and his mouth pressed so firmly shut when he wasn't talking that it nearly disappeared into the rest of his face.

Gilles opened his mouth to respond, but he did not have words. He'd already told Martel why he couldn't go.

"The Assembly is calling for troops," Martel said, stepping into the room. "Austria and Prussia are beating on our door. Change is afoot, Étienne. We've passed the time for sitting dormant while others do the work of freedom for us. If we do not unite the country, we will fall."

"I would make you late," Gilles said lightly. "I will have to wait for your next recruiting trip."

Martel shook his head. "The longer you put it off, the harder it will be. When will I see you dangling from a rope with the other *royalistes*?"

Gilles tried to laugh, but the sound fell flat in the empty office. "Some of us do not have the privilege of employers willing to save our jobs for us while we traipse about the countryside looking for worthy Frenchmen."

"Fate smiles on those who take action."

Could he never win? Gilles's greatest efforts had still left him lacking as a mariner, as a Jacobin, as a trustworthy friend. Being pulled from so many directions had begun to take its toll. He rubbed a hand over his forehead. What to say to make Martel leave . . .

A softer tap on the door made Gilles's heart flip. "Monsieur Étienne?" The clear, confident voice rejuvenated the oppressive atmosphere of the office.

"*Mademoiselle*," Gilles said, skirting around his friend and bowing to her. "How good it is to see you this morning." And today he truly meant it.

"My father wished for your report on the perfume shipment yesterday," she said. "Who is this?"

Someone he wished were not in the room. "May I introduce my friend, Honoré Martel."

Martel strode forward, hand extended to her and a smirk creasing his features. Mademoiselle Daubin hesitantly laid her hand atop his.

"*Enchanté*," Martel crooned, bowing low over her hand. His fingers tightened around hers, and in an instant his lips rammed against her bare knuckles.

Mademoiselle Daubin tore her hand away, a moist circle on the back of her hand glinting in the light coming through the window. Gilles grimaced with her, flesh crawling beneath his shirtsleeves. Why would Martel do that to someone he'd never met?

His friend straightened, expression unchanged. "I do hope we meet again when I return, *mademoiselle*."

She threw one look at Gilles—he could not decide if she meant her disgust for him or his friend, or perhaps a combination of both—and fled the room. The heels of her shoes clipped sharply against the corridor's floor.

Martel snickered. "She'll be back for more of that." The dangerous smile sent a chill up Gilles's spine. This wasn't how *he* looked when flirting, was it? His throat tightened and his morning meal threatened to reappear as realization struck. He probably looked exactly the same as that in his games, with the overconfident grin and smoldering stare.

"I should think not," he blurted. "Have you not heard Émile? She is not a girl easily won." Not by any man Gilles had met. "What's more, you know she's a monarchist."

"That can easily be changed." Martel waved a hand as though shooing away a mosquito. "What do women really know of politics and the world?"

Gilles had underestimated her in much the same way, and where had it led him? To consenting to keep secrets for a *royaliste* and agreeing that his father was sometimes right.

"Do not lie and tell me you've never dreamed of kissing that," Martel said, readjusting his pack.

Gilles had wanted to touch those full, soft lips with his own since the day he sauntered stupidly into that office and found her humming *Sur le Pont d'Avignon*. But seeing his friend's interactions with Mademoiselle Daubin strengthened his resolve to never try again. "She is a human, not an animal," Gilles said. "The least you can do is speak of her as such."

Martel's sneer at his friend's reprimand only increased the gooseflesh wriggling up Gilles's arms. "You have high regard for a woman as confused as *she*." He spat the word out as if trying to taunt Gilles's conviction.

Gilles slipped his watch quickly from his pocket. "Will you not miss your coach? It is nearly half past nine."

"I look forward to traveling with you as brothers-in-arms one day soon," Martel said, giving Gilles one last, hard look.

"Yes, *bien sûr*." He nodded emphatically, as if that would hasten his friend from the *savonnerie*.

"*Vivre la France*." Martel stuck out his hand, and Gilles reluctantly grasped it. "*Vivre la nation*."

"*Vivre la France*." Gilles followed him to the door. Though Martel towered over him by at least three inches, Gilles had no doubt that with his stockier form he could easily sweep his friend from the building. He refrained, but watched Martel descend every stair and waited until the front door to the office section of the *savonnerie* had closed before moving from his post. "*Bon voyage*," Gilles muttered. He'd never felt so relieved to see his friend leave.

"Good riddance."

Gilles startled at the voice coming from the corner near his employer's office. Mademoiselle Daubin moved to stand beside him at the top of the stairs.

"And I thought Émile had terrible friends," she said. Her lip curled in disgust as she stared at the front door.

He didn't know whether to laugh or cringe at that. Instead he dug into his pocket and pulled out his clean handkerchief, then held it out to her.

"What is this?" She took the folded square, head tilted to one side.

"To wipe off your hand."

Her face softened, and he thought he glimpsed a smile playing on one corner of her mouth. She wiped at the back of her hand, though no doubt the saliva had dried by now.

"I'd give you the shirt off my back if you thought it would help wipe away that kiss," Gilles grumbled, shaking his head. He couldn't account for this unease. He'd seen Honoré Martel, not to mention Maxence and Émile, act in this same manner on numerous occasions. Every time they went to a café, in fact. Was it seeing her repulsion and Martel's lust that triggered this strange reaction? Or did he cringe because for once he saw how his own actions might appear? He did not mean to look that way. He didn't want to.

"Oh, no. I prefer your shirt where it is." He cast her a sidelong glance, and when their eyes met, she let out a quiet laugh.

A laugh? It lit her face with an enticing glow, smoothing away the stern expression she most often wore. "Why do you find that humorous?" Gilles couldn't help grinning as well. "I was in earnest."

"Because the first time we met, you tried to kiss me. And now you are trying to help me remove a kiss."

He shrugged. "If I am to gain your trust, I must do something. Teasing you and trying to keep your gown from getting dirty have done me nothing so far."

"And if by some miracle you someday do gain my trust," she said, the mirth in her voice mellowing, "what will you do with it?"

Gilles pursed his lips. Why did he want to gain her trust so badly? He wanted to prove he wasn't the monster she, his father, and even his mother had suggested he was. But there was something more to it, something he couldn't name. A deep, disconcerting something in his core that he fancied leaving alone just now. "I will wear it as a badge of honor to be trusted by a lady as—"

She huffed and waved him off. "And here I thought we had moved past the idle flattery."

"Idle flattery? *Mademoiselle*, do not discount my sincerity."

"Marie-Caroline?" a voice rumbled through the cracked door of Monsieur Daubin's office.

"I've found him, Papa," she said, walking quickly away. "He will bring the report directly."

Gilles raced for his desk. "You see, Père?" he said under his breath. "I am every bit the gentleman." And even though he could almost hear his father's disbelieving chuckle, neither Père's presence in his mind nor Martel's presence in the office could ruin this morning.

CHAPTER 9

19 June 1792
Marseille

Chère *Sylvie*,

Émile has returned after nearly a month away, and he is as smug and apt to put on airs as ever. I do not know what sort of indoctrination he experiences at Montpellier, but it has rendered him impervious to reason. It is as though he has returned solely to argue with Papa. Classes at the university have not paused that we know of, and yet he told us he is here for the entire week.

I shall not attend mass this week, so as not to alert him. Perhaps if our fine National Assembly had not made all nonjuring priests equivalent to enemies of the state, I would not worry so. But Émile is the sort of révolutionnaire who would gleefully search out a clergyman for deportation just to distinguish himself as a true patriot. I can only hope that our supposed backwardness will drive him mad and he will leave before Sunday morning. I do not need another instance of *practically leading a Jacobin to Père Franchicourt's door, as you will remember from my letter Sunday last.*

As to your question in your previous letter, I insist I have never sought out the company of either Étienne brother, and I wish you to never again suggest that I have. It is inevitable, with Gilles working for my father, that I will see him regularly. And while he is not so monstrous as I thought on first impression, the idea of establishing any sort of preference to his company is preposterous.

You are the only person in the world privy to the knowledge that I do know how it feels to be in love and to form an attachment. I can assure you most passionately that I have formed no attachment and never will form an attachment with a rakish pig who considers stealing kisses from unsuspecting young women a sport to place bets upon. As surprisingly civil and generous as he has been on our last few meetings, I cannot forget our first meeting. Come, Sylvie. You know me better than to assume such things.

I worry for your safety. Even with a staff so loyal to our cause, you take an enormous risk housing the clergymen you do. I don't think Papa would ever allow us to do something so dangerous. He shuns anything that could affect the success of the savonnerie *and* parfumerie. *More so now than before I left for Paris, but it is to be expected. With so many aristocrats fleeing the nation and everyone else parading their humble circumstances, reality or no, who has desire for fine soaps and perfumes these days? I have begun to fear that in the twelvemonth our family's situation will not look the same as it does now.*

Moments after Gilles entered his room, freshly arrived from a workday that seemed neverending, Maxence rapped on the door.

Gilles sank onto his bed and inhaled deeply before calling, "Come in." Maxence had surely heard his footsteps on the stairs, or Gilles would have pretended not to be there. He did not want to see anyone or anything except his bed just now. Luc Hamon, one of the best workers at the *savonnerie*, despite his *sans-culottes* allegiance, had not come to the factory that day, leaving one of the cauldrons shorthanded and sending Monsieur Daubin in a strange panic.

Gilles pulled one arm out of the sleeve of his jacket.

"Keep it on," Maxence said, motioning with his head toward the door. "There's a Jacobin meeting at *la rue du* Thubaneau."

"That isn't my club." Gilles paused in his undressing. "Saint-Cannat meets Saturday evenings."

"There's a missive from Barbaroux. They're reading it at the meeting."

"Barbaroux?" He was a young politician from Marseille, currently serving as a member of the National Assembly in Paris. "Who told you?"

"There are many *Montpellierains* here this week." Maxence's fellow university students, no doubt. Shirking their studies for a bit of revolutionary excitement.

Gilles winced. What was he thinking? That thought could have come straight from . . . He cleared his throat. A *royaliste*. But of course not any specific female *royaliste* with dark eyes and a quizzical stare.

He stuffed his arm back in his jacket sleeve. *La rue du* Thubaneau was a street nearby. Just a little ways past Saint-Cannat and not so far as the *savonnerie*.

"I will go to see what it is about," Gilles said. "Did you tell Maman?"

Maxence smirked. "Why does she need to know? We are grown men."

They were still her sons living in her house. "I will find her quickly, and then we may go." Gilles rose, adjusting the collar of his jacket.

Maman said she would save their dinner, and Gilles hadn't the heart to tell her Maxence would most likely head to a café after the meeting. When they finally left the house, the two brothers walked on in silence through the greying streets. A gull sailed lazily overhead, evidence of their proximity to the harbor. A harbor both Gilles and Maxence avoided at all costs.

"Where was Père sailing this time?" Gilles asked.

Maxence shrugged one shoulder. "Malta?"

If it were Malta, he would be back again soon. Gilles pursed his lips. He did not want to see his father's face again for a long time. Their conversation from the night Père left continued to gnaw at him. His father had been right, but his sympathetic thoughts on women contrasted sharply with his lack of sympathy shown on their last voyage together.

When they arrived at number 11 *rue du* Thubaneau, the main room of the apartment was filled from wall to wall. The gentlemen, more young than old, wore the elegantly simplistic dress that had gained popularity among the *révolutionnaires*. A few wore the red liberty caps of the *sans-culottes*. And there was, of course, not a pair of breeches in the room. Only trousers. Breeches were a symbol of the upper class.

Émile waved them over to the back corner. He enthusiastically shook Maxence's hand, then nodded toward the opposite side of the room. A soft white cap peeked through the shadowy doorway.

"Five *livres*," he whispered.

Maxence scowled. "Ten at least. With this many men around?"

"I gave you twelve for the Poulin girl. This one's not worth that much."

Gilles watched the young woman in the doorway. He couldn't see more than a profile of her face. Was she a servant or the host's relative? His stomach twisted. Weeks ago he would have jumped to his brother's defense and insisted on ten *livres* for the kissing wager. But Mademoiselle Daubin's disapproving glare and Maman's disappointed glance filled his mind. This girl looked near the same age as Mademoiselle Poulin from the dinner party.

"Brothers and friends!" the rotund host called. Conversations quieted through the room. "There is word from Paris."

Gilles pushed himself onto the balls of his feet to see around Maxence. He scanned the room for reactions, but most simply watched the front of the room with impassive faces. A silent thrum of electricity extended through the chamber. Gilles's pulse increased to match it.

"The National Assembly has called on the sons of France to come to her aid. Austria and Prussia knock at our door, threatening to march toward Paris and plunge *la patrie* back into the darkness of despotism." The man drew a folded page from the pocket of his coat. "I have here a copy of a letter sent to the mayor of Marseille from our esteemed brother and fellow *Marseillais*, Charles Barbaroux."

Barbaroux's name rippled through the crowd. The man was barely older than Maxence and had already made a name for himself in Paris as a passionate defender of liberty and steadfast opponent of the king.

The host lifted the letter high, reciting rather than reading. "Send to Paris six hundred men who know how to die."

A jolt shot down Gilles's spine, frigid as a northern sea. Men who knew how to die. Members of the crowd looked to their friends. Some nodded slowly.

Nodded? Gilles shifted, trying to keep his focus on the man at the front. Gilles had faced death. For years he'd run gunpowder from the magazine to the upper deck in his father's sea battles. He'd captained multiple gun crews and, under the direction of Dr. Savatier, patched up sailors clinging to life. Had he softened so much in the two years since leaving the sea that the talk of facing death set him shivering?

"We must work quickly to form a battalion to protect our country," the host said, "before the monarchy has time to block our efforts."

"*Mort au roi*," someone grumbled, just loud enough to be heard. Death to the king.

"As Jacobins and Friends of the Constitution, it is our duty to act." He turned to a young man beside him.

"That is François Mireur," Maxence whispered. "He just finished his medical studies at twenty-two."

Barbaroux and Mireur—two men who had already begun to make a difference in the world, despite their age. Gilles chewed the inside of his cheek. They put Maxence and him to shame. But they hadn't been dragged aboard a ship in their youth and forced into seamanship.

The brown-haired Mireur took a step forward. "*Frères et amis*, our king has refused his support of the Assembly's call to gather twenty thousand volunteers to defend Paris." More grumbling ensued. "Our brave troops are at the border keeping Austria and Prussia at bay, but what will become of us if our enemies break through and march on Paris? What will happen if the enemies within our ranks rise against us? Paris, the National Assembly, all we have fought for these last two years would be lost."

Mireur had a point. Gilles found himself nodding with the others. They could not let that happen. It was no secret Louis XVI wanted Austria to invade and return him to the full power he had once enjoyed. The royals' attempt to flee to a *royaliste* stronghold last year had been the final straw for many Frenchmen, Gilles included.

"We, as citizens of France, must sanction the call to arms." Mireur emphasized his words with a pointed finger. "We, as *Marseillais*, must march on Paris and declare our support of the National Assembly and the constitution. Aristocrats and conspirators have inundated the capital. We must exterminate them!"

A cheer erupted through the group. Gilles did not join in, but the truth of Mireur's words rattled his bones. If they did not all pull together in defense of their country, what would be left? The barren wastelands of the last thousand years spent under the monarchy's thumb.

Maxence leaned over to Émile. "Seven, or I refuse the wager."

Gilles's brows knit. Mireur had called them to arms, and still all Maxence could think about was stupid games? There were more important things to consider.

Émile sighed. "Seven. Agreed." He noticed Gilles watching. "Care to make it a competition?"

The girl still stood in the shadows of the doorway. An urge to go to her itched at Gilles's mind. He shook his head. More than a month had passed since the last time he'd participated in their game. Tonight he did not have the stomach for it.

"Tomorrow evening we will feast in Mireur's honor and herald the start of our preparations," the host said, returning to his place by the younger man's side. "Go to your homes. Consider the task that has been placed before us. Young men, unattached to wife or child, we are counting on you to step forward and pledge your lives to the cause. If we do not find enough among your ranks, the rest will need to fill the deficit."

His mother's dependence on him would not count. Gilles rocked from one foot to the other. He did not fear death. He feared oppression from an evil king. In the months since joining the Jacobins, he had sacrificed little in support of the cause besides attending meetings. If every young man in France held onto his dreams, his career, or his schooling instead of defending their nation, what chance did France have? None.

He drew in a shaky breath. Tonight he would ponder his options. But the tapping at the back of his consciousness suggested he already knew his answer.

"You'll have to act fast," Émile murmured. "She could flee at any moment. I could use the seven *livres* to recover my losses from Mademoiselle Poulin."

"I am already making plans to spend it," Maxence shot back.

Had they heard a word of what their fellow schoolmate had said? Or the letter from their beloved Barbaroux? Before he could think, Gilles slipped away from his brother. He wove through the ocean of enthusiastic listeners, making apologies as he jostled them. Most did not take notice.

When Gilles reached the opposite side of the room, he edged toward the doorway. *"Mademoiselle?"* He bowed his head.

She turned toward him, and Gilles confirmed his suspicions. This girl was at least as young as Mademoiselle Poulin. "Are you enjoying the meeting?" he asked, voice barely audible.

She colored, eyes dropping to the floor. "Of course, *monsieur*. But my father does not know that . . ."

Gilles held up a hand. "I understand." He hesitated. "There are gentlemen in this gathering who do not have your best interest at heart." His gut clenched at the betrayal falling from his mouth. But how could he look his mother in the eye that evening if he allowed Maxence to prance over and catch this young woman unprepared? "I think it best you retire before the crowd begins to leave. For your sake. I do not wish to see you used for someone's fleeting pleasure."

The red in the girl's cheeks heightened. She glanced around the room and then back at Gilles. He waited for her to throw out some witty and sarcastic comment as Mademoiselle Daubin would do. But she curtsied. Her hand touched his arm. "Thank you for your concern, *monsieur.*" She turned wide, admiring eyes on him one last time before disappearing into the rest of the house.

Gilles frowned. He hadn't intended to win the girl over with chivalry. Perhaps he'd only imagined the look of praise. He tried to refocus on the host's announcement about Friday evening's dinner, wondering whether he had truly helped or simply made things equally bad, though in more honorable ways than Maxence would have employed. His conscience, which had so lately been taking the face of Mademoiselle Daubin, had pushed him toward what she believed was right. Unfortunately she had failed to consider the consequences of good deeds.

CHAPTER 10

The blush of evening touched the courtyard where Gilles sat wedged between Maxence and another acquaintance from Montpellier. He hardly had room to move his arms to cut the tantalizing roasted goat, flavored with rosemary and garlic. Nearly eighty men had arrived at the banquet for Mireur, and the host had been forced to move the feast to the courtyard. Even in the open air, they hardly fit around the tables.

"Seven *livres*," Maxence muttered.

Gilles followed his brother's gaze to an upper window, where a face watched through the open panes. He quickly ducked his head and shoved a bite of meat into his mouth. It was the girl from last night.

"She's ogling you." Maxence nudged him with his shoulder. "What did you say to her yesterday? Trying to win the seven *livres* yourself to make up for Marie-Caroline?"

Marie-Caroline? When had Maxence started using Mademoiselle Daubin's Christian name? Gilles knew her far better, and even he did not feel it his right to call her by so familiar a term. He choked down the meat and cleared his throat. "Only that she should take care."

"Snatching her up with the soft approach and undermining your own brother." Émile shook his head across the table, a smirk on his face. "That isn't usually your style."

"We all change our approaches from time to time." Gilles kept his eyes on his plate. For once, he hadn't attempted to reel the girl in. It seemed he had more success when trying not to. He shooed away a fly attempting to share in his feast.

The cacophony of conversations that echoed through the courtyard hushed as a figure rose toward the front. Mireur, ready to plead once again with his countrymen to come to the aid of their nation. Gilles turned on the bench to better see. The young leader gazed into the crowd of revelers, seeming to individually catch each eye.

"*Allons enfants de la patrie, le jour de gloire est arrivé.*" Come, children of the nation, the day of glory has arrived.

Mireur's song rumbled against the stone walls that enclosed the group, silencing any remaining whispers. The hairs on the back of Gilles's neck stood on end. A strange tingling tiptoed up his arms.

"Against us, tyranny's bloody banner is raised." Mireur continued, the simple but striking melody reverberating through Gilles's core. Enemies were on their border, ready to destroy all they loved. All he loved. Maman. Victor and Rosalie. His little nieces, Aude and Claire. Florence. Beside him, Max wore an intense expression showing he thought on the same things. Standing down, staying home, meant opening the doors for harm to come to them.

Mademoiselle Daubin's face also appeared in Gilles's mind. She didn't want saving, especially not by him. But she didn't realize the danger that awaited.

"*Aux armes, citoyens!*" To arms, citizens!

Gilles breathed deeply, but the thundering within him would not slow. How could he let Austria and Prussia tear apart this land? Beside him Maxence nodded. Some listeners sat frozen, fists clenched and eyes unmoving from the lone figure at the front of the courtyard. Others swayed like Maxence, letting the music fill the depths of their souls as the song continued, preaching against tyranny and calling France's young men to stand.

"Form your battalions. Let us march! Let us march! Let an impure blood water our fields."

His own blood pulsed in rhythm with the tune. Montpellier and its medical school would be there when Gilles returned. What good would it do for him to learn the art of saving his neighbors and his family if there were no people left to save? What horrors would those he loved face if he did not stand in their defense?

When the chorus began again, Gilles found himself among the men who leaped from their seats to shout, *"Aux armes, citoyens!"* with the rest of the company. He would go. For Maman, if nothing else. For Victor's family. For the glory of France. He would do something with his life other than raiding and stealing for his own glory as Père did.

Mademoiselle Daubin's voice rang in his head, not quite drowned out by the blaring song around him. *Go and form your battalions. Do your duty. Leave the women to clean up your mess, as we always do.* Gilles brushed it aside. What did that woman know? She played at being a *royaliste* and thought she was doing the nation a favor by clinging to the past. A new age had begun. They could not go back. The sooner she saw that, the better for her and for France.

The notes of Mireur's song rolled through the evening air. Verse after verse cemented in Gilles's heart the determination to join Marseille's national guard. It was the right thing to do. He would not let them down. He couldn't.

The city is in an uproar. No corner of it is safe from talk of the fédérés, as the recruits call themselves. They will set out to join the battalions in Paris in less than two weeks. Of course Émile has volunteered to go. He will not let our family forget the fact, and it has driven Maman to fits of weeping when he is not in the house. Maxence Étienne has also signed, and Émile assures me Gilles will shortly follow their lead.

It will make my world much more peaceful. Papa and Émile will not shout so much, and I shall not be forced to cross swords with Gilles and Maxence during our frequent—and entirely unplanned—meetings. Why, then, my dear Sylvie, does this hollowness swell inside me, like a ballroom devoid of music and light and dancers? It isn't as though I shall miss all the young révolutionnaires.

The fédérés' chosen anthem rings through the city in the silence once filled by church bells. It is stirring, to be sure, and very clearly is the cause for so many men enlisting. And yet, as I listen to its words echoing through the house while Émile prepares to return to Montpellier, I cannot help but whither under the barbarism and intransigence of some of the sentiments. They claim to represent the people of France and fight against those attacking this nation. But will they defend the people of France who do not agree with the course of their revolution? The massacre at Avignon earlier this year would suggest not. Are priests and royalistes this "impure blood" of which their anthem sings? Will it be the blood of my family watering their fields, when we simply wish for a government different from what they propose?

I am sorry to send so gloomy a letter. Perhaps when the fédérés have left, it will be easier to find more things about which to be cheerful.

Affectueusement,

Marie-Caroline

Gilles halted on the steps of Saint-Cannat after his Jacobin meeting. The days were lengthening, which would prove beneficial for him and the other *fédérés*. He sucked in the warm evening air, and not even the hint of a sea breeze could dull his mood. In two weeks, he wouldn't have to worry about that pesky breeze or the constant reminder of his seafaring past.

A few older members of his club passed him on the steps, shaking his hand and thanking him for volunteering to march to defend Paris. He hardly knew them, but their refrains of *"Aux armes, citoyens!"* stilled any apprehension he had. He was doing for them what they could not do—defend their nation and their Club.

One of the setting sun's rays poked through the rooftops to light the front of the church. Marseille had begun its preparation for the glory of summer. Gilles lowered himself to the stair and stretched his legs out before him. Since he would miss the whole of summer, he might as well enjoy this taste of it for a few moments.

Behind him, the doors shut with a low and gentle boom. Keys clanked together. He winced at the scrape of someone winding up to spit, then a splat sounded as the projectile hit its mark. Gilles hadn't bid farewell to Saint-Cannat by spitting on the statue for almost a month now. Not since seeing Mademoiselle Daubin's horror at the desecration of her beloved saints.

Jean Sault descended the stairs until he reached Gilles. "It is a pity our friend Martel will not arrive back in time to leave with the *fédérés*."

Gilles nodded, all the while imagining spindly Martel trying to wield a musket. Perhaps it was better for the man to be where he was. He could do more good converting the people of Provence with his zeal. A fiery passion such as Martel's might find too much fuel among the riot-ready Parisians.

"He will not be happy to have missed the feast for Mireur," Sault went on. "Ah, to have been there myself. Your account of it this evening . . . How could you sit still for a moment?"

"It is a night I will never forget, to be certain." What was this sudden weariness in his limbs? The club president held Gilles's gaze as though waiting for another delicious detail of the thundering performance of Mireur's song, but Gilles could think of nothing more that he hadn't said during the meeting.

"Just think of all the *royalistes* and traitors you will depose in Paris." Sault gave a wistful smile. "If I did not have a duty to my family, I would be at the front of the line of *fédérés*."

"We are mostly going to defend Paris against the Austrians and Prussians, of course." Gilles adjusted his seat. The long day of work had taken a bigger toll today than he'd anticipated. Luc Hamon hadn't arrived to work at the *savonnerie* again, sending word that he and his family had fallen violently ill. His absence had led to much scrambling throughout the day for everyone.

"Any enemies of *la patrie*," Sault corrected him, "from within or without."

"Yes, *bien sûr*." But Gilles hoped they would not have to fight fellow Frenchmen. The thought of leveling a musket at a countryman, no matter his standing in regard to the government, gave him a bitter taste in his mouth. He gnawed on his lip. Did Sault not have a family and dinner to go home to?

"You will make us all very proud, Étienne. You and your comrades. Our foes will be harnessed, and we shall see France rise to the egalitarian splendor she deserves." The man raised his fist. "*Let us march! Let us march! Let an impure blood water our fields.*"

Gilles raised his fist in a silent cheer as Sault bid farewell. The leader set off toward his home, and Gilles slowly let his fist fall to the cement steps. Every time he heard the word *royaliste* these days, Marie-Caroline Daubin's face popped uninvited into his mind. Not that he would be fighting *royalistes* such as she.

Would he?

Though most Jacobins hated to admit it, the *mademoiselle* was right. It had been women who had finally succeeded in dragging the king and queen from Versailles to Paris. Would the *royaliste* women sit in their silk-covered chairs and let the revolution play out, or would they rise up with their pitchforks to demand their own idea of justice and liberty? He could very well imagine Mademoiselle Daubin taking to the streets to support her cause.

Gilles swallowed, suddenly chill despite the sun's embrace. Could he level a musket at those dark eyes? Or watch someone else do it?

A simple brown dress rounded the corner, backlit by the weary sun. Gilles sat up. What was she doing here again?

Mademoiselle Daubin walked briskly along the side of the road, looking very much the same as she had that evening three weeks previous when she'd stolen the prayer book, with a basket over her arm. Only this time she came from the opposite direction, moving east toward her home. She did not look at Saint-Cannat. A young servant trailed along behind her, scuffing his shoes in the dust of the road.

It was lucky for Gilles that Sault had already locked up the church and taken the keys. She wouldn't be able to tempt him to open the building for her. Gilles stood and brushed at his trousers. "*Bonsoir, mademoiselle!*"

She slowed, turning her gaze to the columned façade of the church before lowering it to the steps. After hesitating a moment, she returned his greeting and nodded her head, but continued her pace.

Well, if she did not wish to speak to him, he would not press her. His feet, however, did not understand his brain's instructions to start off in the opposite direction toward home. They hastened him down the steps and across the street.

He would just see how she fared, and then he would turn around. After all, he had not seen her in nearly two weeks. Not since catching her on her way to some meeting she wished kept secret.

Mademoiselle Daubin did not slow her pace, though he could not tell if she was purposefully ignoring him or innocently unaware of his presence. Why had she returned, once again without a carriage?

"What is in your basket this time?" he asked as he fell into step behind her.

She showed no surprise at his voice. "What I have in my basket is no concern of yours." A linen napkin covered the top of it.

"Come. There should be no secrets between countrymen."

"I do not subscribe to such Jacobin notions. My life is my own."

For certain. Gilles leaned in. "Going for more prayer books?"

That brought her to a stop. She flashed him a vehement frown, eyes darting behind her to the servant boy.

Gilles drew his shoulders up to his ears in a silent apology, though the boy did not appear to have noticed.

Mademoiselle Daubin huffed. "Marc, run ahead and tell my mother I will arrive shortly."

The servant's head came up. "*Madame* said I was to keep you in my sight the whole time."

A fine job he had been doing of it, with his eyes on the ground.

She pulled in her lips before speaking. "Tell her that Monsieur Étienne is escorting me home and we shall arrive very soon."

The boy nodded and took off at a faster pace toward the Daubins' fine residence in the Belsunce district to the east.

"You are allowing me to escort you home?" Gilles took his place to her right as she began walking again. "Does this mean that if I offer you my arm, you will not refuse as before?" He extended his forearm to her. She wouldn't take it, of course, but he wanted to see the look of annoyance on her face. Perhaps that would banish these odd feelings that had sprung up when he imagined having to fight *royalistes*.

She eyed his arm.

"I will promise not to ask any more questions about what is in the basket."

Mademoiselle Daubin leveled her chin, then pulled back the covering. "This basket is empty. I have nothing to hide from you."

How strange. "Not even a bottle of previously purchased vinegar."

"Not even that."

Then what was she doing, practically by herself, in the Panier district at sunset? And without a coach of any sort. "You must have had an important task, then. Does it have something to do with the book?"

"I no longer have the book in my possession and would appreciate your not bringing it up again."

Not in her possession? Had her family forced her to get rid of it? Or perhaps she had given the book to someone else?

Gilles lowered his arm just as she slipped her hand around it. The movement left her hand pressed against his side. His breath caught. He swallowed. The lightness of her gloved fingers against his arm should not have sent him panting.

She'd taken his arm. Stubborn, *royaliste* Marie-Caroline Daubin had taken his offered arm. He used all his concentration to take an unaffected breath. "If your errand is not about theft, then what other reason do you have to be in *le Panier* so late?" This was ridiculous. She was holding his arm. Nothing more. And yet he felt as giddy as fifteen-year-old Gilles stealing his first kiss.

Mademoiselle Daubin remained quiet for a moment. The faintest wisp of amber hit his nose as they walked. Was it the rich perfume that sold so well in the shop? Gilles had always favored that one, though he couldn't bring himself to pay so much for a vial to give to his mother.

"I was bringing some food to a family," she finally said. "Papa took the carriage to the lavender fields this afternoon."

Ah, yes. Gilles had forgotten, though he'd seen Monsieur Daubin off himself. "It could not have waited until tomorrow when the carriage was back?"

When dressed in her usual elegant style, a shiny curl always danced across her shoulder when she shook her head, but today all her hair was pinned under her cap and did not move at the gesture. "The father of this family has not been able to work the last two days due to illness, and no one in the family will be working for the next few days at least, until the sickness passes."

They paused in the road to let a coach go by. Mademoiselle Daubin avoided meeting his gaze. "Do I know the family?" he asked.

She pulled them forward after the vehicle passed. "It is the Hamon family. Monsieur Hamon works for my father."

Gilles's eyes narrowed. She went to visit Luc Hamon? "But . . . He is a . . ."

"*Sans-culotte*? Yes." She increased her speed, practically pulling his arm to keep up with her.

"But he hates *royalistes*."

They came upon a church with boarded up windows. The *mademoiselle* tilted her head to take in the intricate stonework that graced the old building's frieze. "At some point we all have to swallow our pride when faced with difficulties. Since your *révolutionnaires* have shackled the churches in this area, and the churches generally take care of the sick and the poor, someone needed to step in with help."

Gilles grunted. "Too many churches swallowed the money they

were given for the poor, padding their own purses. Is it not better for the people of France to care for their own, as you have done?"

"But where were Hamon's comrades who spout these grand ideals?" A sad smile crept onto her face. "As far as I could see, they had not yet come to help Monsieur Hamon's family."

He had no answer for that. In a perfect France, help would have been there, but the revolution had plunged the country into chaos. Someday there would be better order and people would be taken care of. That was what he, Maxence, and Émile were marching for.

They turned onto the neat road on which the Daubins lived. Mademoiselle Daubin's pace slowed. Or perhaps Gilles had imagined it. He did not want their walk to end just yet.

"You are going to Paris, are you not?" Her voice did not hold the accusation he'd come to expect from her.

"Of course."

Her hand slid from around his arm to adjust her basket. Gilles held his arm out, waiting, but she did not return her hand. "Then I wish you the best," she said.

"Surely I will see you again in the next week." Gilles let his arm drop to his side. "You cannot stay away from the *savonnerie.*"

Mademoiselle Daubin lifted a shoulder. "My mother is more protective these days. And I can only imagine that will worsen as Émile's departure approaches. I am her only child at home now, with my sister married and youngest brother still in Fontainebleau."

He counted himself very fortunate that his mother was not so prone to worry. She'd dealt with more farewells than the average wife and mother. Still, as he imagined her standing on the steps to see off two of her three sons, a pang of guilt reverberated through his chest. He blinked, clearing the thought. Maman would not struggle any more this time than she did each time Père or Victor left. Gilles hadn't seen her cry over a departure since the first time he went to sea.

"I hope to see you before we leave."

The white stone house, painted dusty blue by the evening light, loomed above them. Houses across the street blocked most of the sunset.

"We shall see how much *révolutionnaire* zeal I can tolerate between now and then," she said with a tight smile. "Émile returns home tomorrow, and I do not know if sharing a house with him will leave me with enough fortitude to face more than one of you."

"Must we always be Jacobin and *royaliste*?" He stopped at the foot of the stairs leading up to the Daubins' front door.

She curtsied a farewell. "Do you plan to turn your back on the Jacobins? Since I do not plan to change my beliefs on the matter of our government, I think that yes, we must."

"What I meant was, is there any room for friendship in the middle ground?"

She gave a humorless laugh and ascended the first step. "I do not know many monarchists and Jacobins who are still friends. Do you?"

He caught her hand to stop her. "Someday that has to change, doesn't it? If we are to live in peace. Why not now?" Her fingers went rigid in his as he bowed over them. He checked himself before he kissed her knuckles. That would do nothing to help his plight, especially after Martel's display prior to leaving. "I have kept your secret."

Gilles released her hand and backed away. Above them, the door opened and warm light flooded the street. Mademoiselle Daubin ascended the rest of the stairs as her father's rough voice asked after the Hamon family. At the door, she paused and glanced back. A small smile played at the corners of her mouth. Then the door closed behind her.

Gilles quickly retreated into the deepening gloom, shoving his hands into the pockets of his jacket. His flesh still tingled from the light pressure of her touch on his arm, and his heart pattered at the elusive smile she'd thrown him. What would it matter if she accepted his plea for friendship? He would be gone in two weeks. Leaving the women to clean up his mess, as she had put it. Still, he couldn't help wondering if she desired friendship as well. She hadn't refuted his last question.

Despite the bleakness and despair on the horizon, he wandered home with a spring in his step and a whistle on his lips.

CHAPTER 11

In barely a week, Gilles would be gone.

He closed the medical book he'd attempted to read and sat up on his bed. The battalion would have doctors enough with so many *Montpellierains* joining, they wouldn't need his meager knowledge that came from studying under Dr. Savatier on board *le Rossignol* and reading books in his room after work.

Gilles rose and walked to the foot of his bed, where a great trunk lay. He knelt before it, taking in the faded etching on the lid. *Étienne.* Once, this chest had gone to sea with his father, but Père had given it up for a newer, finer trunk. As a boy, Gilles had been so proud to inherit it. He pulled open the lid and slid his book in line with the other medical books that used to make their home atop his mantel. Nearly all his belongings took up residence in this trunk now. Maman would have an easier time cleaning out the room should he . . .

With a sigh, Gilles sat back on his haunches. He'd seen death before. He'd faced death before. But somehow preparing for the possibility now set his head spinning. He hadn't taken time to prepare for it then. At sea, there was a chance of meeting one's end, but no one counted on it, especially when the mission was to transport goods from Marseille across the Mediterranean, not battle despots, traitors, and tyrants. The *fédérés* marched for war and glory.

> *Form your battalions.*
> *Let us march! Let us march!*
> *Let an impure blood water our fields.*

Gilles shivered as the words of Mireur's song tumbled through his mind. Removed from the fire of Mireur's voice and the thrumming excitement filling the courtyard on *rue du* Thubaneau, the lyrics had a chilling edge to them. They'd done their duty to persuade him to leave, but now he found himself wishing they didn't constantly whirl through his consciousness.

He pushed himself to his feet, letting his eyes wander over the collection of medical books. What if he did die at the hands of *royalistes* in Paris or in the advance of the Austrian and Prussian army? He'd spent so many hours examining each page of these books, extracting any knowledge he could. If he died next month, had he wasted those hours? Should he have instead taken more time with his mother?

As he closed the lid, a little glimmer caught his eye in a corner of the trunk. Odd, since he owned very little besides his watch that resembled gold, and the watch was still in his waistcoat pocket. He fished the little gold ring out from the dark corner. His *grandmère's* ring. The one Père had given him on arrival.

Jamais en vain. Never in vain. He ran his thumb over the elegant calligraphy engraved on the ring's surface. Grandmère had died before he reached his tenth birthday, but he still remembered her cheery smile as she wrapped him in bony hugs whenever she came to visit. Was she speaking to him now with this ring, assuring him his efforts would not be wasted?

Jamais en vain.

Gilles slipped the ring onto his littlest finger. It fit snuggly, but not enough to hurt. He drew in a breath, the stifling tension within him slowly releasing at the touch of the cool metal on his skin.

A little giggle tripped up the stairs, and the corners of Gilles's lips shot upward. Maman had invited the best kind of guests to dinner tonight, it appeared. He closed the trunk without another glance at his books and didn't bother to don his jacket. The girls wouldn't mind.

Two puffs of curls, the color of melting chocolate, skipped down the hall and into the sitting room, oblivious of their favorite uncle descending the stairs. Gilles tiptoed the rest of the way down and hid behind the doorframe to observe. The girls sat on the couch, each with a doll in her arms. Well, *sit* was perhaps not the best word for it. Four-year-old Claire had flopped onto the couch on her belly, little shoes dangling above the floor.

Growling and extending his fingers like claws, Gilles pounced into the room. Seven-year-old Aude shrieked and bolted for the opposite door, while Claire gave him a withering glare and continued to walk her doll across the couch cushion. Gilles caught Aude before she could escape.

"Where are you going before you have paid your respects to Oncle Gilles? You know the laws of this house."

"Tyrant!" she cried through a fit of laughter.

"Tyrant? I believe you mean Supreme Uncle, Lord of the House and Protector of Nieces."

His mother appeared at the entrance to the sitting room. "Must you rile them up before dinner?"

Gilles shrugged and offered a sheepish smile.

"You aren't lord of this house," Aude said. "Grandpère is."

Of course she would point that out. How his father had managed to gain the girls' affection, Gilles would never know. Perhaps it was because he always brought them gifts. Gilles let Aude wriggle out of his arms and formed his mouth into a deep frown with a jutting lower lip. "I don't even get a kiss?"

His older niece whipped her head back and forth, curls bouncing. "Your face is scratchy."

Gilles rubbed his cheeks. He'd shaved that morning. Alas, the Étienne men could not escape whiskers before the end of the day. His were not as bad as his father's.

"Papa's face is scratchy, and you still give him kisses," Claire grumbled from the couch.

Aude cocked her head, then scampered over to Gilles and lightly kissed him on both cheeks.

"Dinner is on the table," Maman said, her face softening as she watched her son and granddaughters.

Gilles scooped up Claire, who squawked in protest, and proceeded toward the dining room. He threw her the same pout he'd given Aude. "Do you have kisses for Oncle Gilles?"

Claire huffed and pushed the corners of his mouth up into a smile with her small fingers. "No."

Two rejections from two girls he loved. How very unlucky. At least Claire's scowl was adorable. Mademoiselle Daubin's instilled fear.

Gilles's face heated like the kettle just before it whistled. He did not love Mademoiselle Daubin, of course. What had put that strange thought in his head? He could count her as a friend, perhaps, but love? What a laughable notion, the idea that he, a Jacobin, could love a monarchist. And he didn't, *bien évidemment*. He was only thinking of his love for Claire and the rejections both gave him.

Claire poked his face. "You're turning red, Oncle."

Gilles laughed and set her down at the door to the dining room, then ran a hand over his face. So he wished to kiss Émile's sister. Who wouldn't? She was beautiful. That hardly meant he loved her.

He sat between his mother and Aude, still trying to will a measure of coolness to his skin. Across the table sat his sister-in-law, Rosalie, her face resembling the pale green of the steaming courgettes resting before her. He opened his mouth to ask after her health, but a sharp shake of his mother's head stopped him.

He raised an eyebrow. Rosalie was an even-tempered woman, unlike others of his recent acquaintance. Others who he had no interest in courting and who he wished would leave his thoughts.

Maman gave a silent sigh, then glanced at her daughter-in-law. Rosalie's attention was on her empty plate. His mother caught his eye again and cradled her arms, swinging them gently back and forth, almost as if she were rocking a . . .

Oh. *That* sort of illness. Gilles nodded his understanding. A little one. And Victor had just gone to sea and would not return for a month or more. Poor Rosalie. Perhaps Gilles could take the long way home after work tomorrow and fetch the girls to give her a little peace. It wouldn't be much, though, as he could only do that for the next week. The *fédérés* left on the second of July.

Gilles's stomach sank. He wasn't really abandoning these women; he was going to fight for their protection, but it felt as though he were leaving them to fend for themselves. He hadn't spoken of his leaving to Maman yet. But the distance in her eyes when she watched him told him she'd already guessed. What's more, he had yet to tell his employer. And if he were to go at all, he needed to actually add his name to the lists.

Florence brought in a steaming turret of soup and set it on the table. Rosalie looked at it, taking a deep breath. She swallowed. Then she quickly excused herself from the room.

Little Claire pressed her lips together. "Maman doesn't like to eat anymore."

Florence shook her head sadly as she ladled the soup into bowls. "Poor dear. Perhaps she can stomach some of the bread. I'll take it out to her as soon as I am done here." She continued her musings as she filled everyone's bowl, including a bowl for herself. Her husband must have been working late at the docks that evening, as she did not often eat with the family since her marriage.

"Oncle Maxence will not get Florence's cooking when he goes to Paris," Aude mumbled softly, staring at the soup in front of her. No one else heard her over Florence's talking.

Gilles leaned toward her. "He already doesn't get it often, being at university."

"But doesn't he have someone to cook for him there?"

He reached for the basket of crusty bread and fished out a piece for his niece. "Yes, there is a cook for the house where he stays. And he often goes to cafés for his meals."

"Will there be cafés on the road to Paris?" The worry in her faint voice rattled his core.

"Not many on the road, I'm afraid."

"Oh." She did not touch the bread or the soup. It must have seemed a grave misfortune to a girl of seven to not have good food readily available.

"Not to worry," Gilles said, tapping her shoulder gently with his arm. "There will be many cafés for him in Paris."

The deluge of Florence's chatter cut off as she went to the kitchen for water to make a tisane for Rosalie. He'd miss that incessant sound of her talking when he left with the *fédérés*. And the tap of Claire's spoon against her bowl, which his sister-in-law was not there to hush. His mother's gentle inquiries and observations in the quiet moments between Florence's talking. One of the girls kicking the table leg.

He dipped a chunk of bread into his soup and brought it to his mouth. Sacrifice. It would be worth it. He must keep reminding himself. Their separation wouldn't be forever.

But how long would it take to free the country from the grasp of despotism? How long would Prussia and Austria press in on their eastern border? Despite three years of revolution, France still had so far to climb until she reached stability. When he returned, everything about his family could be different.

A skinny arm looped through his and pulled him close. Aude rested her head against him. "I'm glad you aren't going, Oncle Gilles."

He had to force his bite of bread past a lump that sprang to his throat. Maman's eyes met his, the corners pinched.

"Are you going?" she mouthed.

Gilles's neck stiffened, preventing him from instantly nodding his response. Yes, of course he was going. He had no good reason to stay. At least no better than Maxence or Émile. They'd already signed their names to the lists.

"Do you know why your uncles are going to Paris, *ma petite*?" Maman asked Aude, the barest tremble in her voice.

"To fight the despots."

The corner of Gilles's mouth lifted at hearing the Jacobin cant from his young niece. He doubted she had learned it from Rosalie or Victor, who held a much more moderate view of the revolutionary proceedings. Friends or acquaintances, perhaps.

Instead of smiling at her granddaughter's impressive words, Maman's eyes clouded. The noise from Claire's spoon crescendoed, but his mother returned to her soup as though she did not hear it. Aude stayed attached to his arm. Her shoulders lifted and fell in a sigh.

Gilles's eyes dropped to his dinner, and suddenly he empathized too well with Rosalie. The homey richness threatened to gag him. He swirled the soup around with his spoon through the rest of the meal. Excitement over defending one's country, one's beliefs, was much easier felt when in the swells of like-minded and similarly zealous comrades. In the quiet of home, with thoughts of facing the change ahead, that fervor dimmed.

After seeing Rosalie and the girls safely to their home, Gilles trudged back through the grey streets of the Panier Quarter. He let himself in the door of the house and bolted it behind him. The darkness of the front hall pressed in as he leaned back against the door. He could barely make out the lines of Maman's watercolor of the ship on the wall opposite him.

Two years ago he'd stood just this way after disembarking *le Rossignol* for the last time. He'd leaned against the door, relief flooding him as he closed that chapter in his life. It had been an easy decision to leave life at sea. During the last voyage, Père had refused to make land to find help for his surgeon and longtime friend, Dr. Savatier—Gilles's mentor—who had taken violently ill. Instead Père had ordered them to go after a fat English merchantman who turned out to have sufficient firepower to stave off *le Rossignol*'s attack. Savatier nearly lost his life, not having the medical supplies or anyone more knowledgeable than Gilles to tend to him. And they'd nearly lost the whole ship. The front door of this house had shut out all those hardships Gilles would no longer have to deal with.

But now the door would not hold back his problems. Aude's hopeful face stared back at him through the darkness as though she stood before him.

"So you are off to fight the despots with your brother." Maman's voice carried softly from the corridor. A moment later, the blue shadow of her face appeared around the corner.

"Paris needs us, Maman. France needs us. Austria and Prussia will destroy all we've worked for, and the country with it, if we do not take a stand."

"But . . ." She took another step into the front hall. Florence's singing filtered through the walls from the kitchen. The happy tune did little to dispel the cold that permeated the vestibule. "But are you really going to defend *la patrie*, or are your leaders sending you to defend their Club's hold in the government?"

"The Club *is* France." Gilles rubbed his eyes with his thumb and forefinger.

"I do not think Mademoiselle Daubin would agree."

Gilles pushed off the door. Why was Maman bringing her into this? "Mademoiselle Daubin is as foolish as the next *royaliste*. She doesn't know what's best for her." He crossed his arms. "Has she been trying to convert you to the cause of the monarchy?" It came out harsher than he'd anticipated, but Maman did not retreat.

"I do not want the king restored to his power," she said with quiet firmness. "But when the *fédérés* march on Paris to defend freedom, will they defend the freedom of all? Or just those who believe the things the Jacobins have deemed correct?" She turned back toward the kitchen. "Will my sons be caught up in taking away the choice of others, all for the cause of liberty?"

The breath shot from his lungs as though he'd taken a loose spar to the chest. He'd mulled over those doubts, trying to drive them from his thoughts. Hearing the suspicion from Maman shook those resolutions he'd once considered immovable.

"I support whatever decision you make. I always have, *mon fils*. Make sure you are doing this because you believe it to be right. Not because your brother does or because your friends in the Jacobin club told you to believe it." His mother quit the front hall, leaving her words ringing in the stillness. They spun through his mind at a furious pace until Gilles sank down before the door, unable to banish the piercing fear that he was following the path of hypocrisy.

Gilles balked as he raised his hand to tap on his brother's door. He cleared his throat as silently as he could. Though he'd heard his brother arrive an hour before and should have gone downstairs to help Maxence haul up his trunks, Gilles had remained shut up in his room.

Get on with it. Gilles rapped on the door. He had spent two days of agonizing over this decision, and he was ready to be done with it.

The door swung open to reveal Maxence, hair mussed in a roguish fashion and cravat loose about his neck. Max grinned. "*Mon frère,* I thought you'd gone to bed. Come in." He motioned into the well-lit room, which was draped with various articles of clothing, while stacks of books littered the floor in no understandable order. "My brother by blood, and now my brother-in-arms."

Gilles sighed at the hint of a slur to Max's speech. He'd gone to the alehouse before coming home.

"You are lucky, you know," Maxence said. "You did not have to cart home all your belongings before setting off for Paris."

Gilles kept his feet planted on the opposite side of the threshold. "I wish to speak to you on that subject."

"Our departure?"

"The whole venture." Gilles's eyes dropped to his feet. His shoes had plenty of wear left, though they had long since passed being mistaken for new. They looked tattered next to Maxence's red leather mules, which Gilles had never seen before.

"What venture?"

The dark staircase leading up to his bedroom called to Gilles.

He should have waited until tomorrow. Or until Max broached the subject. If Maman were around, perhaps his brother wouldn't get so angry. Or even if they were in Mademoiselle Daubin's company. Max would be furious, but Gilles would at least have an ally.

An ally. In Marie-Caroline Daubin. A strange notion.

He ran a dry tongue over his lips. "I have decided to remain in Marseille and help build up the Club here."

The floor creaked as Maxence straightened. "You aren't joining the *fédérés*?"

Gilles picked at the sleeve of his shirt, the sleeve Aude had clung to most of dinner. "We can't all go off to follow our convictions and leave Maman on her own."

Max looked away sharply. "Hang Maman."

Gilles bristled, hands curling into fists at his side. How dare he. After all she'd been through, practically raising them on her own with Père at sea.

"France needs you more than Maman." Max wiped a hand across his mouth. "You had no qualms running off on *le Rossignol*. And now you're worried about her being alone? She has Rosalie. The girls." He slapped his palm against the doorframe. "France needs you, Gilles."

"One man is not going to make a difference."

"How many others are making that same craven justification?" He smacked the doorframe again. "The *fédérés* are counting on you. The Club is counting on you. If we do not stand between Paris and her enemies, what will this country come to?"

"Paris's enemies, or the Jacobins'?" Gilles murmured. The revolutionary spirit of that night in *rue du* Thubaneau stirred in his belly.

"What did you say?"

Gilles lifted his head, shaking it. "I was never the best on the gun crews. I think the *fédérés* will hardly miss me." He tried a light shrug, hoping to ease the tension with a dash of nonchalance.

Max snorted. "Never the best? You practically were the gun crew. Père made you a crew captain before you were even an able seaman."

Only because he'd wanted his son in a place of authority on the ship. Gilles could give commands if he had to. "I'm pathetic with a musket."

"You think the *fédérés* won't have cannon? You're exactly what they need." Max growled and pulled at his hair. "Don't do this, *mon frère*."

"What about Maman? Rosalie? The girls? What if there's an attack by sea, or what if the *révolutionnaires* are overrun by the monarchists while we are away?"

Max chuckled, but not in a pleasant way, as he retreated into his room. He moved to a stack of books on his bed and began tossing them one by one to the floor. When he left for Paris, Maman would have to come in to sort this sorry mess.

They did leave women with such messes to clean up, didn't they? Mademoiselle Daubin was right.

"You refused to go recruit for the cause with Martel," Max said after he'd removed every book from his bed. "You refuse to go to Paris to help us maintain peace and liberty. And you call yourself a Jacobin." He spit at the floor, as though he were in one of the student-frequented cafés rather than his bedroom. Without turning back, he began rummaging through his belongings, ignoring his younger brother standing in the doorway.

Gilles expected the conversation to go this way, and still the weight of Maxence's accusations settled unbendingly on his shoulders. "I am no *royaliste*. I wish for freedom and a new France. I simply . . . " He scratched the back of his head. "What will we do in Paris? If the army holds the Prussians and Austrians, I mean."

"What we do here. Advance the cause with every waking breath."

Max threw a cravat over his shoulder, then another. He wouldn't need those on his march.

"But what does that mean? Stir up riots? Beat those who disagree into submission?"

Another cravat. And another. How many did Maxence own? "Whatever is needed." His growl rumbled through the room like thunder across an open sea. It rattled Gilles's bones in the same manner as those chilling storms. Sitting in repurposed churches, he could nod his head about forcing his fellow Frenchmen into seeing the truth of Jacobin teachings. But if they beat their fellow citizens into believing an ideology, was that any better than the monarchy's beating its subjects into the hierarchical ranks of society?

"I left *le Rossignol* to help people, not to hurt them." Gilles's voice hardly carried over Maxence's sifting.

The soles of the new mules clunked sharply against the floor as Max traversed the room, keeping his back to Gilles. "Sometimes a little pain is what is best for them."

"But you cannot force it. Do they not still have the right to choose?" Just as Max had the right to choose anger. Gilles took a step backward. Down the stairs, silence reigned across the ground floor. Maman must have gone to bed already. It wouldn't do to wake her with their arguing.

"You are a coward, Gilles Étienne," Max said over his shoulder.

"It is not cowardice to be wise." Their father's words stampeded out of Gilles's mouth.

His brother finally turned, with lips pulled into a sneer. "You sound like Père. Fitting for someone who cares only about his own safety and gain."

Gilles went rigid. His shoulders squared. His hands balled into fists. "I'm not the one leaving home to prey on those who cannot defend themselves," Gilles said through grinding teeth.

Maxence rushed at the door, banyan flying out behind him. Gilles planted a foot behind him and crouched. What advantage his older brother had in height, Gilles made up for in breadth. They hadn't wrestled in years, but it would be an even fight now.

With a snarl, Max caught himself against the doorframe. Though backlit by the candles in the bedroom, the whites of his eyes contrasted starkly with the shadows of his face. "Then stay and hide behind the women's skirts. And may your impure blood water the fields with that of every other enemy of France."

The door slammed with a resounding crack. Gilles blinked in the black of the corridor. His fingers slowly loosened, and his arms fell to his sides. A numbness settled over his brain—a fog thick enough to scoop up with a pail. Maman, Père, Maxence, Émile, Marie-Caroline, Martel . . . Were any of them right?

He trudged back up the stairs to his empty and silent room. Perhaps no one was, and whatever deity presided over this sorry plight was laughing in the skies at the disaster.

CHAPTER 12

Gilles sighed audibly and brought the utilitarian white cup to his lips. Even in a coffee house that did not allow female patrons, Maxence had found one to ogle. His brother's eyes followed the lone serving girl throughout the crowded room, which was alive with clattering cups, noisy consumers, and revolutionary fervor.

"I thought you said Émile was coming." Not that Gilles really wanted to face their friend, not after the confrontation with Max last night. Snippets of the song Mireur had sung at the feast drifted about the coffee house. Every round of *Aux armes, citoyens!* pushed men to their feet and cups of coffee onto the floor for the poor serving girl to wipe up.

"He will be here. His mother must have held him up at home." Maxence pulled a face as he lifted his cup. "She's been clinging mercilessly to him since Friday. But he will be here."

If Madame Daubin clung to him with enough force that he did not show up this evening, Gilles would not complain. Max had arrived at the *savonnerie* just as Gilles was readying to leave. Most of Max's anger from last night had dissolved into grim determination.

He hadn't told Gilles why he was bringing him to the café, but it did not take a scholar to guess. Max had failed to convince him to join the *fédérés* but hoped their friend could succeed.

Light brown hair sticking out of a crimson liberty cap strolled through the door of the coffee house, and Max jumped to his feet to wave Émile over to their corner table at the back of the room.

Blast. Gilles swirled the bitter drink in his cup, steeling himself for the barrage. Émile would use ardor rather than fury to try to persuade him. And Gilles would come out looking the obstinate fool for denying his Jacobin passion and choosing to stay home.

"Good evening, *mes frères*," Émile said, clapping Maxence on the arm across the table before sitting beside Gilles.

His brothers? When had Émile started calling them that?

Their friend signaled the server for a cup. "You will excuse my tardiness. Women troubles at home."

His long-suffering expression made Gilles want to shake his head. Give him a week on the road with hundreds of dirty, tired men, and Émile would pine for the comforts of home and the company of those women.

"Maxence tells me you have some misgivings about our march." Émile rested a hand on Gilles's shoulder like a wise, old master trying to encourage his pupil. "What has made you consider changing your mind?"

Gilles pushed his hand away. The idiot. Émile was hardly a year older. Perhaps he was trying to act like the leaders of his *Montpellierain* Jacobins. "I am not considering it. I have already changed my mind. I wish to fight for liberty and justice here in Marseille, not the streets of Paris. War will spread throughout the country. I wish to be where I can protect my family."

An odd grin twisted Émile's face. "Ah, *oui*. Your family, past and future." He cast a knowing look across the table, but Max looked as confused as Gilles. "It is a noble sentiment, to be certain. But you are a Jacobin, Gilles. *La patrie* is your family."

"And if Britain jumps into the fray with Austria and Prussia, or the monarchists sheltering all over Provence rise up and attack, I am supposed to rest easy knowing I was defending the National Assembly while my mother and nieces were slaughtered?"

Maxence's head rolled back. "There will not be an attack on Marseille."

"Marseille has had more than its share of bloody clashes between *révolutionnaires* and monarchists," Gilles retorted. "What if the *royalistes* rise up to avenge the massacre of all those priests at Avignon in February?" If one thing could be counted on in this revolution, it was that no one truly knew what would happen next. A violent uprising could form without warning in a matter of hours and change everything.

Émile blew out a long breath. "It is normal—expected, even—for a man to fear impending battle. You need not be ashamed, Gilles."

The muscles in Gilles's stomach seized. He lowered his cup to the table.

"Maxence and I will be by your side. I assure it. This trio of *fédérés* will make France proud. We will crush the despots at home and the tyrants abroad."

"What do you know of war, Émile?" Gilles hissed. Memories flashed across his mind. Mists of sea spray from a near hit chilling faces. The deck painted red with the blood of a comrade. Smoke stinging his eyes and nose as the big guns bucked. Din and desperation. A son of the *bourgeoisie* like Émile, raised in the comfort of monotony, couldn't fathom these things.

"Don't call him a coward when you are the one staying home, Gilles." Maxence glowered over the rim of his cup.

Gilles pushed his drink away. Maman would have dinner ready

soon. He'd take her dining room full of unexpected guests over this company. "Yes, I am the coward. And yet I have fought more battles than either of you."

"I didn't think I would ever hear you boast of that."

A month ago, Gilles would not have thought a glare, other than one from Mademoiselle Daubin, could make him wish to run from the room. But sitting under the heat of his brother's searing disapproval, he saw how wrong he'd been. He did not fear Max, but how had it come to this? They had once been the greatest of friends. Now Max looked on him as though Gilles had declared himself a supporter of the monarchy.

Émile held up both hands. "Gilles does speak the truth. I have little experience in the art of war. But what I lack in skills, I make up for in passion. 'Let me perish myself before the death of liberty.'"

An oft-quoted line from one of Robespierre's speeches in the Assembly. It did not send the fire of revolution through Gilles's veins this time as it had so often in the past. If Émile wanted to perish in the streets of Paris protecting the Jacobins, so be it. Gilles pushed out his chair.

"But I do not think that it is cowardice that holds back our brother Gilles," Émile went on.

"No, he wants to advance his own aspirations," Max said. "Defending his country will affect his plans for university." He snorted, as though schooling were Gilles's most ridiculous excuse yet.

"No, no. Bettering oneself in order to further the cause of *la patrie* is a noble pursuit, if not the most pressing at the moment." The serving girl brought over Émile's cup of coffee, and he gave her a playful grin as she set it before him. Then he turned that grin on Gilles. "But I do not think that is the passion keeping him from joining ranks."

Gilles squirmed. What was Émile suggesting?

"Gilles couldn't even kiss Caroline. How could he have a lover?"

Max folded his arms on the table and cocked his head in the direction of the serving girl. To think that Gilles had ever wanted to be a part of this incessant frivolity.

Émile was imagining things. Gilles nearly laughed. He pulled out his pocketbook to find a coin for his half-finished coffee. The only women who concerned him were Maman, Rosalie, the girls, and Florence. And perhaps one other lady, but of course not in the way Émile implied.

"Will there be anything else, *messieurs*?" the serving girl asked evenly. She clearly hadn't fallen for either man's flirtatious looks.

"Yes, one more thing." Émile kept his gaze on Gilles. "Would you take a tray out to the carriage at the door? I promised I would have one sent."

"Tea? Coffee?"

"Some coffee, if you please."

When the server left, Max raised a brow. "Who is in the carriage?"

Gilles's fingers froze around a coin. Had Émile come with . . .

His friend saucily plucked up his cup and took a drink. He winced at the heat, then licked his lips. "Gilles's lady of course."

"I do not have a lady." Gilles hoped the layers of his shirt, cravat, and waistcoat muffled the rapid cadence in his chest.

"So you say."

Max cackled, clapping loudly. "You are mad, Émile. You're not suggesting Gilles has besotted himself with Caroline. Not after the thorough chastising she gave him."

Émile blew into his coffee. Though his eyes shone, he did not join in Maxence's laughter. "*La patrie* needs us to sacrifice our love for a better world, *mon frère*. It will be worth it in the end. I promise. Besides, as a Roman poet once said, 'Always toward absent lovers does love's tide stronger flow.'"

Gilles bolted to his feet. He tossed his coin to the table. "Your ridicule will not persuade me to change my conviction any more than your accusations."

"I've never seen you so severe," Émile said, grabbing Gilles's arm. "What happened to the merry Gilles who did not care whether we stayed or went, so long as he had a drink and a pretty face to gawk at?"

"He realized the seriousness of our situation." Gilles shoved the chair in, then removed his jacket from the back and shrugged into it. "And he decided to leave the gawking to you."

Max pointed to the empty seat. "We aren't finished."

"Then you must carry on without me." Gilles made for the doorway, following the path the servant girl cut on her way to take Marie-Caroline her refreshment. Maxence's and Émile's protests drowned in the babel of the coffee house, but they would not leave his head.

He would not go. He was right not to go. But a part of him insisted he really was the coward they accused him of being.

25 June 1792
Maison Valentin, Marseille

Ma chère *Sylvie,*

There is a strange energy in Marseille. I am sitting in our carriage, waiting as my brother meets with his friends in the café, and I sense it everywhere—in the set of the men's mouths as they pass in the street, in the anxious scurrying of mothers with children going home from the market.

What I wouldn't give for a dance. It's silly, isn't it? Our country is at war with itself, at war with foreign powers, and all I wish to do is dance. Throw cares to the wind, dress up in a new silk gown, and dance until my shoes are in shreds. I think mostly I wish for a way to dispel this tension mounting in my chest. My one comfort in leaving Fontainebleau and Paris was the hope of finding a little more quiet in Provence. But Marseille is ablaze with its own revolutionary fires, and home is no shelter from them.

Our priest, Père Franchicourt, has been at his ease these past few weeks. His nephew has gone to recruit for the Jacobins and is therefore not actively pursuing him. He smiles more readily, and Sunday I even met him in the back garden. Under a cloak, of course. The absence of his révolutionnaire kin has cheered him, or perhaps it is the fact that I have not had to confess my lying ways to him for some weeks.

Speaking of révolutionnaires leaving, I am shocked to hear of one who is not. Two days ago, Gilles Étienne walked home with me from le Panier, practically bursting with Jacobin pride. He told me that of course he was going, as though he did not know how I could think otherwise. But just this morning, Émile stormed into the dining room at breakfast grumbling that Gilles was suddenly doubting whether he would go.

Gilles. Who always follows his brother in everything—giving up life at sea, pursuing medical school, joining the Jacobins, playing their kissing games. I can hardly believe it. I am glad I had to witness only Émile's display of disgust and not Maxence's. He has so foul a temper. Émile and Maxence are in the coffee house as I write, attempting to convince him to join, and I do not envy Gilles.

I do wonder what has changed his mind. He was so determined. Not that I care whether he stays in Marseille or goes to Paris, bien sûr. But a passion such as his . . .

Gilles held the door of the carriage open while the serving girl deposited her tray of coffee. He helped her down before ascending the step and leaning his head into the coach. Mademoiselle Daubin's humming, always the same *Sur le Pont d'Avignon*, made him hesitate before he spoke. "May I come in?"

She sat with a little desk across her lap, a page before her and pencil in hand. Her eyes narrowed as they rested on him, but only for a moment. "Gilles? I thought Émile was having a word with you."

"Yes, he had several. And wasn't finished when I walked out." He and Max wouldn't hurry out of the café. He had a few moments.

Her brows lifted as she nodded. "Yes, Émile would. Come in. Would you like coffee? She brought two cups." She set her writing things aside.

Gilles pulled himself in and settled on the bench opposite Mademoiselle Daubin. "*Non, merci.* I had my fill inside." The cabin was warm, though a draft from the open windows kept the air fresh. "I am sorry to interrupt your writing."

She nimbly poured herself a cup and returned the coffee pot to its tray. Steam wafted up from the cooling liquid, swirling about her face. She inhaled it in much the same way as her father tested the scent of a new batch of perfume—eyes closed, faint smile. "It is of little importance. I am writing to my cousin in Fontainebleau, and I write to her several times per week."

"She is the one you lived with the last two years."

Mademoiselle Daubin sighed. "Yes. My youngest brother is still with them. I shouldn't envy a seventeen-year-old boy, but I do. I suppose another thing to conf—" She pursed her lips, then took a drink.

Gilles waited for her to finish her thought. She had almost admitted to something.

"I thought you had decided to join the *fédérés.*"

She had changed the subject. Gilles shifted in his seat. A carriage passed a little too closely, its aged occupants sitting prim and silent. "I do not think it best that I go."

She nodded, then sipped once more at her cup.

"I will still do my part at home," he said quickly. "My loyalties have not changed. It's only that my mother and sister-in-law need my help. And with so many already going, it seemed best to do my duty to my family. What's more—"

"You don't have to defend your decision to me."

Gilles's mouth snapped closed. She must think less of him for taking the apparent coward's route. Or perhaps she was satisfied, since one fewer militant *révolutionnaire* would march to her beloved Paris. "If only our brothers took the news as you have," he said.

"Are you aware, Gilles, that you do not always have to follow Émile and Maxence wherever they go? Nor are you obliged to do everything as they do."

Gilles leaned forward, elbows on his knees. "I am more aware that you have called me by my given name twice since I arrived at your carriage."

The young lady's face flamed. "I beg your pardon. Émile always calls you that, and it must have stuck in my head that way. Forgive my forwardness. I did not wish to imply anything by it."

"I do not mind." Gilles shrugged. "So long as I may finally call us friends, you may call me whatever you like." Though he did like the sound of his name from her particular lips.

She laughed, setting down her cup and picking up her pencil. Her fingers, free of gloves, turned it over again and again. "You know my misgivings with that, Monsieur Étienne."

"You have yet to give me a good excuse. In fact, you have given me many good excuses for us *to be* friends. If I am already simply Gilles in your mind, are you not fighting the inevitable?"

"It would seem that is all I do these days."

"Then why not give in on this little thing, so you may have greater energy to put toward more important things?"

The pencil dropped to her lap. "Such as opposing the revolution?" A fire snapped in her eyes that made it difficult for Gilles not to grin. He enjoyed watching that flame come to life when something animated her.

"Whatever you wish."

She swung her head back and forth. "I do not understand you, Gilles Étienne."

Gilles motioned with his head back toward the café. "Clearly you do better than those two."

"That isn't difficult."

He ducked to better see the sky through the window. "I should get home. My mother will have dinner ready, and I must fetch my nieces." Though he dearly wanted to stay. Not an angry word had passed between them, at least not directed at each other. Had that happened in any conversation they'd had yet? He nodded his head in a bow. "*Bonne soirée*, Mademoiselle Daubin." He pushed the door, still opened slightly for propriety's sake, wide. His brother and Émile had not exited the coffee house yet. Good. It was better to make an escape before they confronted him again.

"Marie-Caroline."

Gilles paused on the carriage step. "Pardon?"

She pulled the writing desk back onto her lap. "If I am to call you Gilles, it is only fair that you should call me by my given name."

A grin spread across his face that he could not hold back if he tried. "*Bonne soirée*, Marie-Caroline, then."

She bid him farewell as he climbed out, and when he glanced back over his shoulder, she was writing furiously. The tune returned, as though she did not realize she was humming.

Gilles stopped when his feet hit the road. "Have you ever been to Avignon?"

Her head lifted. "Yes. Why do you ask?"

He rested against the door. "You know that one cannot actually dance on the bridge of Avignon, as it says in the song. It's too narrow."

"I know that."

He was stalling. He shouldn't be stalling. And yet the rich scent of her drink, the ease of her stature, the hint of a smile, the camaraderie pulled him back in. Who knew what he would find at home, especially after Max returned? "Why do you like that old song so much?"

Marie-Caroline cocked her head. The pencil tapped against her smooth cheek. "I suppose because I love to dance. And it gives me hope that someday dancing will return to France."

"There is dancing still in France." At *révolutionnaire* gatherings, participants engaged in several different dances. Though they weren't the genteel society dances she likely missed. Some dances went in rather dark, violent directions.

"The *sans-culottes'* dances are barbaric. I meant pleasant dancing. With friends."

His heart skipped at the thought of dancing with her. He'd never attended any sort of social function. The revolution had brought an end to most parties outside of Jacobin meetings and rallies before he'd left his father's ship. But surely it wasn't antirevolutionary to desire the return of such things.

"I hope someday you get your wish," he said. And he truly meant it, for his own sake as much as for hers.

Sylvie, I have just had the most bizarre encounter, and you must tell me what to make of it. Gilles just left our carriage. Through the

whole of our conversation, we exchanged neither arguing word nor rebuke. He did tease, of course, but that is his nature as much as it is Émile's to flirt. And we parted as friends, something I would not have imagined after our first encounter.

He said he would not join the fédérés so that he might help his mother and other family. I suppose not all Jacobins are as heartless as I imagine. So many care first for their new France and second for anything else in their lives. Now, seeing this Jacobin give up the glory and honor a march to Paris would have given him, I wonder if I shouldn't give him more credit. Gilles does care for his family more than this revolution. There was something in his manner of speaking that hinted at another reason for his staying behind, but I did not press him.

I wish to amend my statement in an earlier letter to you. I said that Gilles did not have the same attraction as Maxence. And while Gilles does not have the same height or sharp features as the middle Étienne brother, there is a rugged sort of allure in the gentleness of his eyes when combined with his sturdy mariner build. The way he moves, it is as though he sways to the rocking of an invisible ship. And while Émile spends time and effort to arrange his hair in a look of disarray, Gilles achieves the nonchalance without the practiced air. Like he just stepped off a boat. I find it rather refreshing. And pray that you are not reading this aloud to your mother.

I will end, as Émile should shortly return, along with the serving girl to retrieve my tray. My brother will not be in high spirits when he takes me on to the Lamy family. How droll that one person and his actions can cause such opposite responses in my brother and me.

All my love to you, to your parents, and to dear Guillaume. I hope these fédérés do not inhibit our meeting again very soon.

Affectueusement,
Marie-Caroline

CHAPTER 13

2 July 1792
Marseille

Ma chère *Sylvie,*

Very soon you will have two members of my family in your vicinity, though I hope you do not face the elder. Tonight Émile sets off with the battalion of fédérés *to secure the liberty of* la patrie. *But I fear if you should meet him, it would mean quite the opposite of liberty for you and your family. I doubt he will try to make any contact, given how seriously he takes his duty to the revolution, but if he does, it will be to see Guillaume. I beg your family not to let this happen, for Guillaume is so easily swayed by the rhetoric of his brother. Though Guillaume has been more or less supportive of our cause and has helped in your work of sheltering holy men, I think Émile easily could win him over, just as François Mireur won over half of this city with his song of war.*

Maman has wept all morning. Papa went early to the office and has not been seen since. I nearly went with him to avoid the display, but Maman needed someone at home. As I'm certain you are thinking it—knowing your romantic nature and having read the ridiculous ideas expressed in your letter a couple weeks ago—I was not tempted to go to the savonnerie because of a certain swarthy clerk.

Émile has hardly mentioned Gilles's name since that evening at Valentin's coffee house. Each time he does, his face twists in disgust. I can only imagine how Maxence must treat Gilles at home, and I can only hope that he mostly ignores his younger brother. While Émile has more eloquence, Maxence has the raw and unbridled rage that drives the revolutionary zeal. Sometimes I wonder, if Émile and Maxence were not friends, would Émile have joined the fédérés? Perhaps he would have all the same, or perhaps my mother would not be sobbing on the settee as I write.

I do hope to see Gilles at the ceremony tonight. I only wish to assure him of his decision, mind you. He is still a Jacobin, even if he does not march to Paris, but I believe that making his own choice rather than following the example of his brother is a thing to be applauded. One less militant révolutionnaire marching on Paris will not make very much of a difference, but it is good to know that at least one friend will be out of harm's way.

I should say that sort of harm's way. Marseille is not a safe city. Fights break out daily, and there have been several murders of royalistes or nonjuring priests in the streets. I have been forced to keep the news from Maman. Papa and I agree it is for the best, especially with Émile diving into the thick of the révolutionnaire violence.

Will we ever dance again, Sylvie? Hide behind fans in a crowded ballroom, fluttering our eyelashes at boys across the room? We are too old for that, though I feel our time to do so was cut unfairly short. What I wouldn't give for one more dance.

Hélas, I was hoping to write an entire letter without the mention of either Étienne boy, and I have failed. The next time I write, I will not mention Gilles at all, simply to prove to you that there is nothing

to your claims. We are too far apart in conviction for there to be any-
thing more than friendship between us. But I do hope that this small
friendship, fragile as it is, might be one step on the road to healing
all that is wrong with our beloved France. If each Frenchman from
Calais to Toulon took such a step, do you not think that we could
find a path to understanding and truth in this jumble of competing
thought? That it would lead to eventual peace and prosperity for all?

I like to think it would.

No one would be able to hear once the ceremony began. Gilles's
ears rang as he followed Maxence back through the crowd to where
Maman waited. They'd loaded Maxence's contribution of supplies
onto one of the three wagons in preparation for their departure. Now
all they had left to do was wait for the ceremony to begin, and then
Maxence would be off for Paris.

Gilles kept his head ducked while they wove between the masses
of family and friends who had come to see their battalion off. His
family members had been all over the world, from the North Sea
to the Indian Ocean. But no one in his immediate family had ever
entered Paris. Maxence was traveling new territory, and Gilles hated
the regret pooling in his gut at the thought of missing the chance at
experiencing a new city. Unfamiliar sights and intriguing people had
been some of the redeeming things about life on *le Rossignol*.

A table had been erected at one end of the boulevard, which was
lined with liberty trees, planted in honor of the revolution. Maman
waited for them under the branches of one of the trees, just in view of
the table. She eyed the strap across Maxence's chest that held his musket onto his back. He'd sold most of his medical books to purchase

supplies, something Gilles silently lamented, even if he saw the necessity.

Gilles pulled at his already loose cravat. Though evening, the day's heat had strangely hung around the port city. He hadn't bothered with a jacket tonight and had rolled up his shirtsleeves to his elbows soon after arriving. How Max survived wearing a knit cap and his pack, he did not know.

"Maxence!"

His brother grinned as Émile came into view. When the tawny haired student arrived, they shook hands enthusiastically.

"Today we march for death and the glory of France," Émile cried over the buzz of the crowd.

Maman watched them with a guarded eye. Gilles could only guess what thoughts filtered through her mind, sending a son to war. Every time she saw them off at the docks, she knew battle was possible on the high seas. But the violence wasn't certain, as with nearly everything at sea. Today her son left on purpose to fight.

A few moments later, Marie-Caroline slipped out from the masses, followed by Monsieur Daubin supporting his pale wife. They greeted the Étienne family before the *monsieur* and *madame* withdrew a few paces away from the rest of the crush.

Marie-Caroline stayed nearby and sent Gilles a questioning glance.

"What do you mean by that?" he asked, dipping his head closer to hers so as to be heard.

"I see you have not been bullied into joining at the last minute."

He chuckled without much enthusiasm. "No, I made my decision." The right decision? He could not say. But his decision, nonetheless.

"The volunteers are assembling," Émile said, pointing to a group of red-capped and musketed men toward the front of the crowd. "Shall we join them?"

Maxence gave a firm nod.

"You won't stay through the ceremony?" Maman asked, her voice pinched.

"We leave as soon as it ends, so we need to be ready." Maxence embraced her lightly, but her arms clutched him close, not letting go for several moments.

Gilles looked away from her stiff form and his brother's indifference. His brother had better be thanking her for all the work she put into gathering his supplies, though he couldn't hear Maxence saying anything. Only the hum of their mother's voice, too soft to distinguish her words.

They could hear Madame Daubin's distress from the edge of the boulevard. It took Émile and his father's efforts to pry her off of her oldest son. When she'd collapsed into the *monsieur*'s arms, Émile turned to Marie-Caroline. A few words were exchanged, then a tentative hug, and Émile was free.

He stalked over to Maxence and Gilles, walking taller than usual. "*Mon ami*, our time has come." Émile nudged Gilles. "Do you not wish you were coming?"

To march for death and the glory of France. Gilles smiled weakly. Some part of him did.

"There will be more battalions," Émile said. "More ways to support the cause. We will see you in arms yet. Every citizen of France will stand to defend the birth of a new nation and liberty, or they will be trampled underfoot." He held out his hand. "But I wish to depart with no ill will to a brother and Jacobin."

Gilles shook hands. "I wish you the best of fortune."

"And if I do not return, I wish you to take my place at Montpellier," Émile said, a twinkle in his eye. "No doubt you would be a better student than I. I have written to my professor, who is saving our places until the time that we may return. He will contact you with the information if I meet that glorious end."

Gilles opened his mouth to speak but could muster nothing more than mumbled gratitude.

Maxence did not offer the same olive branch. The brothers stood unmoving, regarding each other.

Then stay and hide behind the women's skirts. And may your impure blood water the fields with that of every other enemy of France. Maxence's words from a week ago rattled in Gilles's skull. Was his brother thinking the same? Max gave no indication of regret. His jaw remained tight as he gave Gilles a nod of farewell, and the two friends departed to the sound of Madame Daubin's wails.

Frigid claws of loneliness cut off Gilles's breath. Maxence lost himself in the gathering, blending in with the other volunteers and *sans-culottes* wearing the same crimson cap. As a boy, he'd watched Maxence depart on his first voyage aboard their father's ship, leaving Gilles alone with Maman for the first time. Gilles had been old enough to not want to cry, especially in front of others, so he'd swallowed back tears.

Now the familiar lump returned to his throat. Not because his brother had left. That happened too frequently in their lives. An emptiness gaped in his chest, which should have been filled with the heartfelt farewell of brothers possibly parting for the last time. Would he see Maxence's face again? Could he live with himself after that farewell if he didn't? Even Marie-Caroline and Émile had put aside their extreme differences for a moment.

Beside him, Maman's chest rose and fell. She blinked rapidly, eyes fixed on the *fédérés*. Gilles put an arm around her and pulled her against his side. One of her hands seized his, holding to it like a ship too close to shore clung to its anchors in a storm.

The crowd parted for a line of men marching toward the front of the gathering—members of the Club that met on the *rue du* Thubaneau. It made sense they would lead this sending-off ceremony, as their feast for Mireur, combined with Barbaroux's letter, had launched this rising. The leader jumped up onto the table, and a cry of excitement erupted from the crowd, with the loudest shouts coming from the volunteers.

"Citizen soldiers!" More applause. "What a wonderful moment for the Friends of the Constitution!"

A hand slipped through the crook of Gilles's arm, smooth kid leather against his skin. A tingling galloped up his arm as Marie-Caroline appeared beside him. She watched the Jacobin's animated display at the front but kept her face void of emotion.

Was there a tremor in her hand? She held tighter to his arm and stood closer than she had on their walk back to the Belsunce district.

"How could we not come to see off our great volunteers and countrymen, who are pulling themselves from the embrace of wives, children, and family to march to the aid of *la patrie* and freedom?"

"They will come back," Marie-Caroline murmured—whether to herself or to him, Gilles could not say. Indeed he could not say much of anything. The hem of her airy skirts ruffled about his ankles, she stood so close. A hint of lavender perfume tickled the air, whispering of open fields and soothing silence.

"Of course they will." He would have squeezed her hand if he had not been supporting Maman as well. How comforting was the feel of the two women pressed to either side of him, even though both had come to him for solace.

A flag of blue, white, and red snapped above the gathering, which consisted of all ages and statuses. The Jacobin leader presented a liberty cap to the leader of the *fédérés* to a chorus of cheers. "We await your glorious return, as the heroes of old, stained with the blood of France's enemies."

Max was lost in the sea of red caps, but Gilles could still feel his disapproving stare, the one he had seen each time they'd met since Gilles decided not to go.

"Remember your brothers and sisters of Marseille, the ones you leave behind."

Gilles dropped his gaze. Heat rose to his face, and it wasn't from Marie-Caroline's touch.

"As we strive to uphold the cause of liberty and overthrow the tyrants of despotism, we will keep you always in our thoughts, our courageous *fédérés*!"

Marie-Caroline's other hand slowly wrapped around his arm. "You are not failing your cause," she whispered, so softly it was nearly lost in the clamor of enthusiastic *révolutionnaires*.

A signal was given, and the crowd parted for the volunteers.

"That is comforting, coming from a *royaliste*." He backed up to avoid getting stepped on in the shifting masses. Maman released him, stepping forward on her toes to catch a final glimpse of her second son. But the young lady did not let go of his arm.

"I thought you wanted us to be friends," she said. "Friends do not have to agree, only to support."

Her even tone eased the tightness in his chest. "I suppose you can also be happy I have not left you to clean up my mess, even if other men have."

Those full lips pressed into a line, and her eyes dimmed for the briefest of moments. He wished he could see the memory that seemed to pass across her mind like the last brief rays of a dying sunset. "In my observation, you seem more the type of man to clean up your own messes." She tipped her head. "Or at least attempt to do so, even if you are not always successful."

Gilles leaned in. "When have I not been able to clean up my own mess?" Her dark eyes filled his vision. Vivid. Rich. Flecked with the warmth of evening light. He'd never examined Marie-Caroline's eyes this closely.

"I do not wish to kiss you," she said slowly, carefully.

Her words slapped him out of his lavender-clouded stupor. He pulled back instantly, grateful the line of marching men held the attention of all around them. A series of deep breaths did little to calm his racing pulse. Not with her hands still encircling his arm. "Have we not moved on from the kissing game?" he asked.

At the end of the line of volunteers, two cannons rolled into place. Only two. *Le Rossignol* alone, though a brig, had a dozen six pounders. These looked pathetic in comparison. But then, he knew little about warfare on land. Perhaps he wouldn't have been the asset Max had claimed. He kept the guns at the forefront of his mind. It helped prevent thoughts of her from consuming him.

"Just ensuring you have not forgotten," she said. "We are friends, after all, not . . . anything else."

A fair reminder. He didn't really need it, though from her perspective it must have seemed so. Her hands slid away, lingering just enough to turn his skin to gooseflesh. On second thought, he might have needed that reminder today.

"I should help Papa with Maman," she said. "*Bonne soirée, monsieur.*"

He wasn't really falling for a *royaliste*, as Émile had suggested at the café. Marie-Caroline was not his lady. She was the older sister of a good friend and daughter of his employer. Their families were connected, so a friendship was logical.

Too late, he turned to bid her farewell. She'd moved to the edge of the boulevard with her parents. The noise of the crowd stayed elevated long after the volunteers had rolled out. Gilles's ears pulsed.

They should leave since the walk home would already take much longer than usual. He tapped his mother's shoulder and motioned toward one of the side streets.

Maman wiped at her eyes and took his arm. "I am glad you stayed."

He forced a smile. He could protect his family better from Marseille than from Paris. If only he could feel in his heart that he'd made the right decision.

CHAPTER 14

Gilles stepped through the door of the *savonnerie* into the bright evening sun and pulled on his bright red cap. If he'd bought it a few days earlier, would Maxence have given him such a glare at their parting? He brushed at the curls the knitted cap had pushed into his eyes. Four days of wearing it, and he still didn't know how to adjust his wild hair beneath it. He might need to settle for shorter hair.

A thin young man swept past him, forcing him back against the door of the office. The man wore a similar liberty cap. Never mind. Ill-mannered people could be found among all beliefs. Though something about the figure's lanky gait seemed familiar.

"Martel?"

The young man whirled. He blinked, jaw slack, before marching back to the door of the *savonnerie*. "Gilles! What are you doing here?"

"I just finished work." On time, for once. *Monsieur* had gone home early with features taut and a mind that seemed too preoccupied for anything useful.

Martel threw up his arms. "The volunteers! They all left."

Gilles straightened the brim of his cap. "I—I decided I was of better use to the revolution here." He braced himself for a rage that would exceed Maxence's.

Martel let his hands drop. His head tilted to one side. "You said you were looking for another opportunity to serve. Why did you not take that? You are not married, not attached. What kept you here?"

Gilles drew in a breath to give his practiced answer.

"If I had been here," Martel blazed on, "I would have been the first to sign my name to their list. The first in line to march toward Paris. The first to die."

With his level of fighting experience, that final statement could very well have come to pass. "Dying is not the only way to serve the nation," Gilles said.

Martel shook his head. "You call yourself a Jacobin. I beg you, do not turn into a Lafayette. I would not hesitate to shoot my own friend for the cause of liberty."

That Gilles didn't doubt. The comparison to Lafayette, who had denounced the Jacobins and fled Paris, made his shoulders stiffen. "Abandoning everything is not the only way to serve *la patrie*. Who would keep the economy in motion if we gave up everything? People would starve."

Martel snorted. "Not from the lack of luxury soaps and perfumes." He closed his eyes, as though contemplating how to explain something to an uneducated child. "There will be other ways to serve. But do not pass every opportunity, my friend. I am off to meet an acquaintance on the subject of a refractory priest."

"A priest?"

"My uncle. He has disappeared, and I suspect he has not left the city. It is my duty as kin to bring him to justice." He lifted a shoulder. "If I find satisfactory information, you might help me search for him. Another opportunity to step forward to help *la patrie*." Martel's brow raised in challenge.

"How was your journey?" Gilles asked quickly. "Did you have much success?"

"Not what I wished, but any growth is progress." He held up a hand. "I must go to meet this man. I will talk to you at the meeting."

Yes. Tomorrow night. Gilles needed to come up with a script for all the questions he would be asked. At the meeting just before the Jacobins' departure, he had not mentioned to anyone his decision not to go. He would be met with stares, if not scowls and whispering, by appearing after the *fédérés'* departure. For a moment, he considered conjuring an excuse not to attend. But that would only start more rumors.

"Until then." Martel stormed off, face set with concentration as if he'd already forgotten his disappointing friend.

How different this friend was from the new friend Gilles had found in Marie-Caroline. He turned down the street toward home. The one, a fellow Jacobin supposedly of the same mind, would shoot him for a disagreement. The other, of a completely opposite mind, supported him in his convictions.

What was he to make of that?

Bowls clanked and skirts whipped about as Gilles entered the kitchen, his mind still full of Martel's rebuke. He paused at the door to observe the clockwork chaos.

"No need to add water. Rosalie won't be joining us tonight," Maman told Florence. "We'll have plenty. Did you dress the salad?"

Florence swore under her breath and dove for another bowl.

"Is someone coming to dinner?" Gilles asked tentatively. A dozen aromas clouded the air, though the sharpest scent was ocean brine.

"Someone is here!" Florence hissed.

He scowled. "Who?" It wasn't polite to come early. The sitting room wasn't visible from his position. *Please, let it not be someone important.*

Maman tapped his arm with her elbow in greeting as she passed on her way to the door with a bowl of dirty water from washing vegetables. "I thought I told them six o'clock, planning to eat at seven, but I must have told them five o'clock."

Odd that she would tell them later. They ate that late only on Saturdays because of his Jacobin meeting.

She tossed the water out the door, then hurried back into the kitchen. "Gilles, stir that compote. Thank heavens your great-uncle sent over a basket of figs and summer pears today."

Gilles obediently went to the hearth to stir a small pot of sticky, sweet compote. He'd never seen Maman so flustered before serving dinner to friends. Unlike *bourgeoise* families such as the Daubins, they rarely tried to impress guests. Good food and good company was his mother's rule, even if the food were simple and the guests humble. Why she felt the need to impress these friends was beyond him.

He eyed a cloth-covered bowl that sat to warm beside the hearth. With a glance over his shoulder at his mother and Florence, who were counting dishes on their fingers, he lifted the corner of the cloth. The ridged surfaces gleamed in the firelight, and Gilles's mouth watered. Just as he'd suspected—*gaufres*. He contemplated snatching one of the buttery waffles sprinkled in sugar before Maman's cry made him drop the covering and straighten.

"The table! Gilles, take the compote off the fire and go set the dishes around the table. *Dépêche-toi.*"

"Who is here?" He seized the iron to pull the pot off, then scanned the kitchen for a place to set it, the pot wildly swinging from its handle. Maman came to his rescue and took the pot from him with a towel around the handle.

"Use Grandmère's china. But pay attention as you set it around."

Had she not heard him? They rarely used his *grandmère*'s dishes, mostly because each time they did, one of the sons found a way to chip or break a piece. "What are we eating?" he asked, rushing toward the dining room. He needed to keep his jacket on for the guests, but with the bead of sweat already trickling down the back of his neck, he wished he could remove it.

"*Bouillabaisse*," Florence chimed.

Ah, he should have guessed from the brine scent. "Who is here?" he asked, nearly shouting to be heard.

"The Daubins. Just the mother and daughter."

Gilles jerked to a halt in the doorway. "The Daubins?" His mother had invited his employer's family? He pivoted. "*Bouillabaisse*? For the Daubins?"

His mother's shoulders lifted as she emptied the compote into a dish. "There was rockfish at the market."

"You could not have waited for another night to invite my employer's wife and daughter? One when we were not eating *bouillabaisse*?"

Maman huffed. "I met them in Noailles today, and the madame still looked so distraught over the boys' departure."

They'd look like paupers. Gilles rubbed his brow. What would Marie-Caroline think? When he'd dined with them in May, the Daubins had served their guests four elegant courses of delicacies. And his family was returning the favor by serving a medley of leftover fish in broth.

"You love *bouillabaisse*," Maman chided. "Go set the table."

Yes, but he'd never served it to a lady before. Especially not a lady whose good opinion he wanted to keep. Gilles trudged to the dining room, stomping down the urge to peek into the sitting room. He opened the great chest, with a rope-and-knot decoration carved onto it by his great-grandfather, and carefully removed the gold-rimmed dishes from their wrappings.

Really, a Jacobin should not care that he was serving a modest meal to a wealthy family. A strange energy pulsed through his hands as he laid the dishes with as much care as he could manage. If Marie-Caroline were his lady, as Émile suggested, then he would be justified in feeling this offering inadequate. But she wasn't. And she never would be, as she had no trouble reminding him.

"I do not wish to kiss you."

Gilles startled at the voice that seemed to materialize from his thoughts. Marie-Caroline leaned against the doorframe of the dining room in a deep-blue round gown. That color did look well on her. "Will you ever tire of that greeting?" He went for the nicer utensils in their corner of the chest. It was hard to imagine her changing her mind on that point, but a boy could dream.

"I have found from recent experience that if I do not lay out the reminder at the beginning of our interactions, that my desires on those regards are forgotten."

"I would not have kissed you in front of half of Marseille. And your father especially." Though he'd certainly come close without realizing it. If Monsieur Daubin hadn't been preoccupied with his wife's hysterics, Gilles might not have been welcomed back at the *savonnerie* Wednesday morning.

Marie-Caroline folded her arms. "I would not have believed that. You were certainly admiring my lips at a close range."

"Eyes!" Gilles threw up his arms, still clutching a table knife. "I was admiring your eyes."

She raised a brow.

"I speak the truth. You have very fine ones." *Imbecile.* He could hear Max's and Émile's snickers in his mind.

Something played at the corners of Marie-Caroline's mouth. A smile, a laugh, a sneer—Gilles could not tell. But the heat creeping up his neck gave him no doubt she clearly saw his humiliation. What was the matter with him? He'd told plenty of girls they were pretty. All he had told this one was that she had nice eyes. He could appreciate a friend's eyes.

"Thank you." She watched him as he finished setting the table, the sensation of those nice eyes on him making Gilles fumble with the dishes.

"I think you might find our dinner very simple," he stammered to cut the silence. "We are having *bouillabaisse* as our main dish."

"I have no problem with simplicity. Nor does my mother."

He made a pointed glance at her attire. "I find that difficult to believe."

"We are not *aristos*, Monsieur Gilles," she said, drawing herself up to her full height, which nearly matched his. "My father worked hard to build up his *savonnerie* and *parfumerie* with his father. Just as your father's uncle has done with his ships." A little white rosette clung to the soft fichu about her neck. She should not have been wearing that in *le Panier*. The Étiennes' house was too close to the Hôtel de Ville, where several counterrevolutionaries had been quickly tried and executed.

"And yet your mother's family is made up of *aristos*. And you miss the life you lived in their company until a couple of months ago." He adjusted the plate sitting on the table before him. "I do not think your aunt would serve *bouillabaisse* at her table. So you can understand my worry."

"If fish stew is offered by a friend and eaten in good company, who am I to complain?"

Gilles tilted his head to one side. Perhaps he had overestimated her love of the fine, expensive things. Of course, that idea had been planted and encouraged by her brother.

His mother hustled in with a chorus of apologies and a steaming tureen that trailed the aroma of garlic and saffron. A flurry of motion brought Madame Daubin to the dining room at the same moment that Florence covered the table in a full course of vegetable dishes and crusty bread.

Madame Daubin did not turn up her nose at the simple fare, which contained far fewer dishes than she usually served. Did she know there was only one course and then dessert? Florence served the broth and fish, and still neither of their guests gave questioning glances.

"You are too kind to ask us to dine with you," Madame Daubin said between sips of the savory broth. "My husband has worked so many late hours in recent weeks. He does not even come to dinner most nights."

Late hours? The monsieur hadn't stayed at the office much longer than normal. Gilles had seen him off in the carriage on several occasions at the end of busy days. He must have been tending to work at home. But what tasks, Gilles could not fathom. The *monsieur* hadn't mentioned them to any of the clerks.

"It has been so lonely, with only the two of us at dinner." The woman dipped her head, lower lip trembling. To her right, Marie-Caroline's chest rose and fell in a sigh.

But before the daughter could speak, Maman touched Madame Daubin's arm. "It is so difficult to send family members away," Maman said, offering an encouraging smile. "I find the company of friends one of the best remedies to the melancholy that comes from times such as these."

The quivering lip stilled. "Yes, I think you are quite right."

"Madame Étienne, this stew is positively delicious," Marie-Caroline said. She avoided Gilles's gaze and took another spoonful of the *bouillabaisse*. Either she was attempting to prove a point to him, or she wished to return the favor his mother had paid to hers. Whatever the reason, Gilles could not help a grin.

The conversation among the women continued in an easy fashion, far smoother than Gilles would have guessed. Florence cleared the dinner dishes away to the Daubins' praises, then brought out the bowl of waffles and pots of jam and compote.

Gilles generously spread a helping of fig compote over a piece of waffle. Not a month ago he'd been eating figs in his uncle's orchard when Marie-Caroline passed by. He would not have thought they'd have that young lady sitting at their table so soon.

The honey and figs sat thick and sweet on his tongue as he chewed the crisp waffle. Across the table Marie-Caroline daintily nibbled on a section of fresh pear as she listened to Maman talk about the busyness that came with being a sea captain's wife. His friend did not look uncomfortable. The thought sent a homey warmth through his chest he could not attribute to the comfort of the much-loved dessert.

"I am grateful Gilles was able to be here tonight," Maman said, and he perked up. Why wouldn't he have been at dinner? He rarely ate at the cafés these days. "He usually has his club meetings Saturday evenings."

The buttery, sweet waffle turned to dust in his mouth. Today was Saturday. Not Friday. *Parbleu* . . . his meeting! He choked down his bite of waffle and whirled to look at the clock on the mantle behind him. Eight o'clock. The meeting had already finished.

He lowered the rest of his *gaufre* to his plate. He couldn't claim work after seeing Martel in the street. Gilles feigned a laugh and took a drink that he hoped would cover his panic.

Good excuse or no, Martel would have his head.

Do you remember balls? The thick air, the dripping candles, the merry hum about the room? Everyone dressed to be seen and admired. And when you caught the eye of a handsome young man across the room—and you knew you'd truly caught his interest, not just a fleeting glance—the glow of the room seemed to come from inside your chest. All you wished was to discreetly find a way across the dance floor in order to speak to him. For though you may not have known him well, in that moment he was the most desirable man.

I remember when Nicolas was the man across the room. It feels like a lifetime ago. So distant, I convinced myself I would never feel that flicker again. Do you think—in the midst of chaos and confusion, murder in the streets and war in the East, families separated by distance and conviction—that there could be room for such a little spark of happiness? I despair at ever being a young hopeful at a ball again, but perhaps there is a place in this maelstrom for the moments that make life worth living.

Tonight we dined with Madame Étienne and Gilles. Though the fare was unpretentious, I think it was one of the best meals I have had since leaving Paris. I can imagine you reading this now, devouring every word as I did every last drop of Madame Étienne's stew. You read too much into things, dear Sylvie, but tonight I will give you a little morsel I know you will find tantalizingly delicious. Before dinner, I met Gilles in the dining room, and he said—

CHAPTER 15

I finish in haste and say only this—I am grateful to have worked with you in sheltering so many from the injustice of so-called liberation.

Give my love to the family. And an extra embrace to Guillaume.

M. C.

Martel didn't bother to wait for Gilles outside after work on Monday. He paced the foyer like an injured wolf unable to sit still.

Gilles paused for a fortifying breath before descending the stairs from the upper floor. "Good evening, my friend."

"Where were you Saturday?

The truth was his greatest ally. Jacobins thrived on truth. "I thought it was Friday. My mother invited friends to dine, and by the time I realized my mistake, it was too late."

Martel's face remained scrunched in its scowl as Gilles made his way to the bottom of the staircase. "We signed a petition, Étienne. To remove the king. Of all the days to miss."

Gilles had heard talk of petitions circulating through the Club of Marseille. But the king's recent veto of a measure outlawing refractory priests had thrown the Jacobins and *sans-culottes* into an uproar. "I will sign it this week. I would not have missed if I hadn't miscalculated the days." Although an evening with Marie-Caroline would have tempted him more than he liked to admit. Something within chided him. Would he really have given up that evening with her?

"Will you?" Martel jutted his face into Gilles's. "Or is this just another excuse because you've found your courage and conviction failing, *mon ami*?" He spat out the familiar term with such force that Gilles wondered if he really considered them friends anymore.

Gilles sidestepped him and inched toward the door. "If you had the paper, I would sign it now. I have no love for Louis Capet. Only for France."

That seemed to ease some of the seething. "Then you will have no qualms in assisting me in duties to the country."

So long as it did not mean marching to distant corners of *la patrie*. "Of course. I live to serve the nation." Gilles held back a wince. What a Jacobin thing to say.

Martel nodded thoughtfully, though Gilles could not decipher if he believed the words or was pleased that Gilles knew the proper thing to say to get himself out of trouble. "Come, let's be off."

"Now?"

Martel swept open the door and waited for Gilles to pass through. "The nation needs us. If we are not to defend her on the front lines of Paris, we must defend her in the streets of Marseille."

Gilles nodded once. A little warning would have been nice, but when had *révolutionnaires* done anything with sufficient warning? He strode through the door and followed Martel down the street to a tavern, where a group of men waited around the front door.

He knew only a few faces from the Jacobins, who dressed in neat jackets and cravats. More of the gathering wore the patched garb of laborers and sported red caps. Gilles hastily pulled his hat from his pocket and pulled it over his hair. Best to try to fit in with this lot.

"Are we ready?" Martel asked.

"The sooner we serve justice, the better," mumbled one of the *sans-culottes*. Had they pulled these men from the tavern? This one seemed already intoxicated. A few carried sticks. One even had a hatchet. Precautionary weapons, certainly.

"Where are we going?" Gilles asked Martel as the group moved off in the direction of the factory. They weren't going to harass Monsieur Daubin, were they? Gilles tried to swallow down the tightness that leaped into his throat. Daubin had done nothing to incite Jacobin censure. He kept his ideologies mostly to himself. Besides, he had a son who marched to Paris. Did that not protect him in some measure?

Martel grinned. "I found my priest."

The *savonnerie*'s sign swayed like blooming lavender in the evening breeze ahead. Sweat beaded across Gilles's brow. Daubin was hardly a religious man. He wouldn't be keeping a refractory priest hidden in the factory, would he? Not with *sans-culottes* in his employ.

One of the laborers walking just ahead of Gilles spat at the door of the *savonnerie* as they passed, then glanced back at Gilles.

Luc Hamon? Gilles resisted the urge to wipe the spittle off the green paint. What gratitude. Daubin had saved the job while Luc and his family were sick, something most employers would not have done. Gilles's blood simmered. Not to mention Marie-Caroline had risked her safety taking the family a basket of provisions. And this was how Luc thanked them.

Gilles looked away quickly. No real harm had been committed. If Luc wished to be angry, he could carry it on his own conscience.

It took several minutes after passing the soap factory for Gilles's pulse to slow. The Daubins were not in danger. Thank the skies.

But as they moved out of town and into the orchards that cloaked the eastern edge, the tightness returned to his gut. Farther down this road lay his great-uncle's orchards, the ones Gilles had been reading in when he spied Marie-Caroline last month. His uncle, though wealthy from the success of his shipping company, had aligned himself with the Jacobins, at least in word. He wouldn't harbor a priest. Not with the worldly lifestyle he followed.

The familiar road was not so sleepy tonight as it had been that Sunday morning. Carriages passed and workers trudged home from long days in the fields. Most gave the group of *révolutionnaires* a wide berth. Some shouted, "*Vivre la France! Vivre la nation!*"

They did not stop at the orchards. Another relief. Martel led them down a different street and called for a halt. A few old, but well-cared-for houses extended down the road, and a church's steeple rose up behind them.

Martel motioned to a few men. "Our target is the third house on the street. You men circle around the back to prevent any escape. The rest of us will break down the front door."

Gilles nearly asked whether they should knock before barging in, but held back. Of course, someone running from the law should not be alerted to his arrest. Never mind that the law had been vetoed by the king. Under the current government, the veto was invalid. Wasn't it? The people of France wanted the law. Most of them.

The smaller division went ahead and climbed over the gate that protected the house's gardens. The shutters on the house had an odd look to them with their dull-brown coloring and irregular finish. They didn't match the elegant hues of the neighboring houses.

Martel swore and ran ahead. He threw himself at the locked gate, scrambling over with the grace of a flopping fish. The rest of the group hustled to catch up to him.

On closer examination, the strange shutters revealed themselves to be boards secured across the windows. Martel charged up the front steps and pounded on the door. Gruff murmuring rumbled through the group.

Gilles pulled himself up the iron gate and easily vaulted over. Shrubs and trees in the front garden looked well kept. Someone had swept debris from the path.

"Traitors," Martel hissed. "Filthy renegades. *Emigrés.*" He whirled toward the group. "Break down this door."

The man with the hatchet and a few of his mates ran up to hack at the neatly painted wood. Martel stood back, coming to Gilles's side.

"They were here Saturday night. I saw the blasted priest with my own eyes," Martel said through clenched teeth.

"Your relative?"

The young man nodded. "I should have acted then." He turned away, pulling at his hair.

Men pulled at the boards over the windows. One by one they clattered to the paved walkways. Someone took up a scathing revolutionary tune.

"Come help, Étienne." Martel shoved past him to get to the nearest window. The song increased in volume as many joined in.

Gilles pulled the boards out from under the feet of the other men and gathered them in a heap by a flowering rosebush. No need for someone to get a nail through their shoe in the mounting rage. In the last two years since Gilles had returned to land, he had avoided getting involved in riots. The lack of control in a frenzied crowd led to too many undesirable events. The newspaper headlines from the massacre at Avignon earlier that year wavered through his mind. Perhaps it was a good thing the inhabitants of this house had left.

The hatchet thwacks quieted. A large crack echoed across the garden as the man destroying the door kicked it in. Grey shadows lay beyond it.

Crash.

Gilles flinched as glass panes crumpled from their perches, the jagged pieces shattering on the ground. Martel swung again with his nail-studded board, then relinquished it to another and sprinted up the steps. Shards of window glittered on the ground in the opening notes of a sunset.

Ducking out of the way of the flying daggers, Gilles pulled more boards into his pile. His stomach jolted at each crash. It wasn't the blast of cannon reverberating across the deck of *le Rossignol*, but still his ears strained for the pop of a blast. The urge to crouch like a powder monkey scurrying between the guns threatened to make a fool of him.

With the windows properly disposed of, the men swarmed the house and grounds. Bumps and clangs echoed through the gaping holes left by the windows. Outside the gate, workers stopped to watch. Some scaled the fence to join, including a few young women. Max and Émile would have gone for the girls, rather than ruining the house.

Gilles wanted to melt into the crowd, but he couldn't leave Martel thinking he'd abandoned the task. With a board, he started smacking the rosebush. Yellow and pink petals exploded around him, spreading the summery aroma through the garden.

Did Marie-Caroline like roses?

The unexpected thought stopped him midswing. That morning he'd stopped her on the road, had she passed this very house and admired its gardens? Perhaps then the roses were just opening. He hit with the board again. It was just a bush. He ground his teeth. At least he wasn't dismantling the house like the rest.

Martel reappeared, mouth grimly set. He tramped through the carpet of rose petals and leaves to get to Gilles. "He was here. I am sure of it. They had a makeshift church set up in the attic." He shook his head. "But everyone is gone. The kitchen hearth is cold. Everything locked."

"I am sorry to hear it." Gilles's head ached, and his arms whined at their treatment. He hadn't used them with such force since his days at sea.

"Mariner!" someone called. A pair of Jacobins rushed over with several coils of rope. One shoved a length into Gilles's hands. "Tie us some knots."

"Knots?" What could they need knotted rope for?

The older of the two clapped him good-naturedly on the back of the head. "Nooses, boy."

Heat drained from Gilles's face. "Have we found someone?"

"If only we had," Martel muttered.

"For a warning." The older Jacobin sniffed. "If any of the priest's friends come back, we'll show them what happens to cowards who care more about a greedy clergyman than the laws of their own free government."

Gilles lowered his eyes to the rope in his hands. Of course he could tie a noose. What young sailor hadn't practiced that while indulging in sick jokes with his messmates? Now he wished he could have feigned ignorance. He twisted the rope around itself and secured it.

"Another! We'll hang them from all the windows!"

The pit in Gilles's stomach widened. It nearly engulfed him when the men took the ropes he'd tied and nailed them above the front windows of the house. A gentle breeze touched his face, bringing with it the scent of horse dung the mob had found in the stables and splattered across the home's façade. The looped ropes brushed back and forth against the ragged teeth of the demolished windows.

Dark stole in from the east, a rising tide cautious yet eager to flood the skies. But it had already settled into Gilles's core and threatened to cut off his breath.

10 July 1792
Marseille

Sylvie,

Papa said I must be careful with my correspondence. Please excuse the ridiculous nonsense I wrote above.

The couple sheltering Père Franchicourt was discovered. How, we cannot say. But they have fled Marseille. Papa says the priest cannot stay with us for long, but I do not know where to look for a better situation. Three days he has hidden in the cellar, and no one has come for him. All we can do is pray they do not catch our scent.

For now, Maman is happy to have the opportunity to attend services in the comfort of her home. She was never brave enough to venture out to the other meetings. I have not told her what happened to the house where Père Franchicourt previously stayed. Last night the Jacobins had their way with it. Papa drove past on his way to the lavender fields, and the chilling details make me physically ill. Everything was ruined short of burning the house to the ground. They even destroyed the roses.

I wish I could tell Gilles of my dilemma. Perhaps his father could steal Père Franchicourt away on his ship. Gilles is not like the others. He thinks before blindly following the leaders of the pack. But in the end he is still a Jacobin, and Père Franchicourt does not wish to leave this hopeless disaster of a city.

I hope your family and holy guests are safe. With how much closer our neighbors reside here, I am in constant paranoia.

Much love to all.

M. C.

CHAPTER 16

Gilles's fingers drifted over the vials of perfume at the shop in the Noailles district. He didn't often work at Maison Daubin, but the inventory needed to be checked regularly.

The tinkling of the vials sent a chill down his spine. It sounded like the glass debris from the house he had helped ravage three nights ago. The image of the vandalized house lying weary and beaten in the dusk would not let him be. He made a note in a ledger and moved to the next row of vials. The next time Martel caught the scent of Franchicourt, Gilles would make himself scarce. Standing up for the freedom of France did not have to mean destruction. If he'd wanted violence, he would have stayed at sea.

"Ah, Étienne. There you are."

Gilles straightened at his employer's voice coming through the door of the storeroom. "I have nearly finished here, *monsieur*. I need perhaps an hour tomorrow to finalize the numbers and—"

"Yes, yes. Never mind." Daubin waved a hand. "I have a more pressing matter."

Gilles blew on the ink, then closed the ledger and set it on a shelf.

"What do I need to do?" Another task would make him late for dinner. He hoped Maman would understand.

Monsieur Daubin sighed and closed his eyes. "It is my daughter." The older man kneaded his temples for a moment before casting a sharp gaze at Gilles. "Never have daughters if you can help it. Or sons, for that matter. They will send you to an early grave."

Gilles nodded slowly.

"She was to wait here while I met with Delacroix, but she insists on visiting the *navette* shop near the docks. A terrible time to be in that quarter." Daubin shook his head. "But she is adamant, and I cannot convince her otherwise. Not even the threat of telling her mother would dissuade her."

Gilles nearly protested that Marie-Caroline was no child to be making silly threats to, but he held his tongue.

"Not that doing so would help me," Monsieur Daubin said. "Then we would both have to deal with the hysterics."

"And you would like me to accompany her?" Gilles's heart lifted for the first time in days.

"Please. Then at least I can say I've done my best when her mother goes to pieces. The streets are more crowded today after that effigy business."

Gilles nodded. He hadn't participated, but everyone in the city had heard about the stuffed likeness of Lafayette hanging from the Hôtel de Ville.

"Thank you, Étienne."

Gilles wasted no time gathering his things and heading for the coach waiting just outside the shop. Like a ray of sunlight breaking through the clouds after a storm at sea, Gilles snatched the spark of light that flashed into his heart and grasped it tightly.

He needed this.

Gilles held out the paper wrapping, and Marie-Caroline selected one of the skinny, boat-shaped biscuits from the offering. They sat on an old, low wall looking out into the harbor. A forest of masts stretched before them. The dockworkers had cleared from most of the area, and Gilles had found a rare quiet corner.

Marie-Caroline nibbled the end off her biscuit. "We used to buy treats from La Petite Navette when I was younger. I haven't had one in years." Her gloves sat in her lap so as to keep them unspoiled. Her long, tapered fingers held the biscuit like a musician holding a flute.

"Your father could not fathom why you wanted a *navette* today, of all days." Gilles laughed. "I don't think he knows what to do with you."

"He does not have to do anything with me," Marie-Caroline said. "I should be married by now and mistress of my own home." She tilted her head so that the brim of her straw hat partially hid her face.

Gilles leaned forward to see past the brim. "But you are not."

"I am not." Her voice, usually so steady, wavered with a tone of . . . regret? Wistfulness? Perhaps she had left someone behind in Paris. His chest tensed. Was that why she did not want to come home to Marseille?

He laid his hand on the rough stone between them. "Did you—"

"Will you not have one?" She nodded to the treats in his other hand. "You bought them, after all." Her eyes stayed on the gloves in her lap.

So she did not want to speak of suitors. Gilles pretended to study the sand-colored *navettes* in their wrapping. "I do not enjoy them as you do."

"And yet you agreed to escort me to the shop."

He shrugged. "My employer asked me to."

Her mouth pursed. A crumb clung to her upper lip, and Gilles resisted the urge to brush it away. With how serious Marie-Caroline always took everything, the little unnoticed crumb made him want to chuckle. Not that it was very noticeable unless one was examining her lips.

"I also wanted to see you," he said quickly. "It's been a long time since we spoke."

Her lips curled upward. An itch tingled the tips of his fingers. They wouldn't mind stroking those full lips. In fact, they would enjoy it a little too much. His own lips might follow them. "It has only been a week, Gilles."

He tore his gaze away, clearing his throat. Idiot. He had sworn never to kiss her. *Friends.* They were simply friends. "I was also curious why you wanted *navettes* this evening."

She took another bite. The crumb on her lips tumbled onto her skirts as she chewed. Only then did she notice it and wipe it away. "I admit I had wished to see the effigy."

Gilles scowled. "Of Lafayette?" While he hadn't seen it, he had seen plenty of effigies in the streets of Marseille. Clothing stuffed with straw and a rudely painted face that only sometimes resembled the real person. *Marseillais* loved to abuse the likenesses. When effigies weren't immediately burned, they were hung from nooses in the public square and usually met their final fate in the gutters and sewers. "Why would you want to see it?"

Memories of the roughness of the rope as he had tied nooses Monday evening replaced the pleasant tingling in his fingertips. He set the biscuits in his lap and rubbed his hands together. He could still feel the tiny fibers biting into his skin. Scratching, unlike the smoother, treated ropes on *le Rossignol.*

"Everyone was speaking of it yesterday," she said. "I do not believe the man deserved such abuse, and I wanted to witness the injustice myself." She popped the last bite of the *navette* into her mouth and reached for another. Her arm grazed his as she pulled back her prize.

"Lafayette is a traitor to the revolution."

"Did your Jacobin friends tell you to say that, or do you truly believe it?"

Gilles scowled. "I can come to my own conclusions, *merci*." Well, that had cleared all desire to kiss her. Did she think him a simpleton, pulled along by the convictions of others? He'd decided on his own not to follow the *fédérés*, hadn't he? He pulled back the hand that had rested on the wall between them, but a touch made him pause. Her hand lay lightly on his, the golden hue of her skin bright in the gleam of evening sun.

Her chest rose and fell. "I'm sorry. That was unkind."

Gilles remained frozen despite the warm Mediterranean air. Even though he'd been away from the sea for years, his skin was tan compared to hers. Rough. The hands of a mariner, even though he didn't want to admit to his sailing heritage. Hers were the hands of a lady of class and prominence, unmarred by scars and callouses. Never mind that their fathers were both technically *bourgeois*. The Jacobins strove to break down these barriers, but could they ever truly erase the differences? Surely Marie-Caroline would never see him as someone worthy of consideration for . . .

She slid her fingers back, until they sat on the wall rather than his hand. "Why did you join the Jacobins?"

"Because I wished for a world where one could choose the course of his life, not have it chosen for him based on his father's occupation or the size of his inheritance."

"Men did that under the old government."

"Not easily." Gilles plucked up a *navette* and bit off a piece of the crumbly biscuit. A hint of orange flower tiptoed across his tongue.

The navette was sweeter than he remembered, but just as dry. It wanted a hearty mug of Maman's chocolate for dipping.

"Easier than it still is for a woman to do the same."

Gilles laughed. "You have stated yourself that women have played a great role in this conflict so far."

"For which they are hardly recognized."

He pointed his half-eaten *navette* in her direction. "Sometimes you sound very much like a *révolutionnaire*, Marie-Caroline. Why do you still want the old ways? Women have a greater possibility of changing society under a new government than under the king's regime." He popped the rest of the biscuit into his mouth.

"Not under the Jacobins," she muttered. "Since the gathering of the Estates General, everything has been in an uproar. Three years of warring with ourselves, changing opinions, making accusations, encouraging violence. Is it wrong to want the peace the traditions of the old system brought?"

Gilles took another *navette*. Late sun sparkled across the surface of the harbor. Calling to him, as it always did. That was why he avoided the port at all costs. The past did hold a certain allure. But progress meant leaving that behind. "There was not peace before 1789. People were starving."

"Famine is not the government's fault."

"How they deal with the problem is."

Her nostrils flared. "People wanted a fast solution to a problem that had been mounting for years. So they overthrew the government and expected the new one to bring a different result. We've had better harvests, but the Jacobins can hardly take credit for making the weather favorable. Little has been done in preparation for another bad year." She straightened, drawing in a breath. "Why not work to reform the system we have, rather than throwing it all to the wind?"

Marie-Caroline had turned toward him, rather than retreating. Her eyes sparked as she spoke.

"It worked for the Americans." Was it wrong to enjoy their arguing? He kept one corner of his lip clamped between his teeth to prevent any indication of his amusement from spreading across his face.

"What worked for a handful of colonies will not necessarily work for a kingdom like France."

He couldn't help it. Someday he would learn when to stop before he pushed too far. "Perhaps that is why Lafayette has failed and abandoned Paris and why his effigy is now being dragged through the streets."

"Lafayette has failed because the same people who followed his ideals have changed their minds in the light of the Jacobins' supreme wisdom." Her eyebrows lifted haughtily as she spoke the last two words. "Many of whom wanted a constitutional monarchy at the beginning and are now calling for the king's removal."

"And this is why you thought we could not be friends," Gilles said. He pulled out a third *navette*.

"This is precisely why."

"And yet, we are." At least, he hoped he hadn't offended her to the point she would retract their friendship.

She regarded him with a careful eye. The sea breeze teased a curl across her forehead and played with the ribbons of her hat. "Somehow."

He extended the biscuits to her with an uncertain grin, and her lips twitched as she took one.

"But we both know the real reason you want things to go back to how they were. You miss the dancing."

"That is not fair." The smile finally broke across her face. "You mustn't tease about dancing. I do miss it. More than you can imagine."

Gilles wrapped the biscuits and shoved the rest in his pocket.

How had he eaten so many of those? He didn't even like them, though they weren't as terrible as he'd remembered. "We dance these days. It is just different."

"That is not what I mean by—"

Gilles hopped down from the wall. "Come, let us dance a *farandole*." He snatched her hand, the feel of her skin sending a little thrill through his limbs.

"By ourselves. In front of the entire port."

"Why not? Spontaneous *farandoles* start frequently." He tossed his head to get a lock of hair out of his eyes. It would be difficult to perform the line dance with only two, it was true. And without music. But the rigidity in her jaw had eased.

She slipped to the ground and faced him. "And usually precede a beating, or worse, of some questionably guilty person." The words came out tired and small.

Gilles's shoulders fell. Yes, that did seem to happen more frequently lately.

"Or the destruction of other property," she added.

His ears warmed. Surely she could not know. He hadn't told anyone he'd been a part of that. Not even his mother. The nooses he'd tied Monday swung across his mind's eye, slow and limp across the vacant windows. Never again.

Marie-Caroline watched the harbor, still holding onto his hand. Ships' bells tolled across the water. The merry chimes mocked his guilt. She would recoil if she knew what he'd done. He recoiled each time he remembered the uncontrolled rage of his peers. While he couldn't agree with restoring the old system, perhaps she wasn't wrong in longing for the peace it had once granted.

"We should return to the shop. Papa will wonder where we are." She squeezed his hand, and then let it go. "Thank you for accompanying me. Perhaps . . . perhaps if dancing—the sort that I am used to—ever returns to France, we might try again."

Gilles could only nod. There was too large a gap between them. They could build a shaky bridge of friendship across it, but there would not be enough of a common foundation on either side for anything stronger or more lasting.

He cursed himself for allowing the seedlings of hope to begin their growth in his heart.

Hearts are funny things, aren't they, Sylvie? One moment they are sealed in a crypt of stone, and the next they are peeking through the hedge rows wondering if their turn has come again. And regardless which way you attempt to steer them, they are content to blaze their own trail through the underbrush of impossible dreams, no matter the difficulty of the path.

I suppose what I am getting to is that I enjoy navettes, but I enjoy good company more.

It will be a year on Tuesday since Champ de Mars. How has so much time passed? It comes at an opportune moment. I need the reminder that hearts are not to be trusted.

Be careful, and remind the others to do the same. I could not bear to lose another person so dear to me.

Affectueusement,

Marie-Caroline

CHAPTER 17

At least they weren't here with a mob this time.

Gilles stared through the iron gate at the house they'd ruined just a week before while Martel wriggled over into the garden. One of the nooses over the windows had frayed and fallen, but the other three hung limply in the lilac shadows of morning. Gilles hauled himself over the gate and followed his friend up to the battered door.

Flies already swarmed over the horse dung–covered walls, despite the early hour. The July heat had dried the long, brown streaks. Gilles wrinkled his nose at the stench.

"You start in the servants' quarters above, and I will start in the cellar," Martel said over his shoulder. "We will meet on the middle floor. Surely there is something here that will aid us. Franchicourt cannot run forever."

Gilles didn't respond as he ducked through the splintered door after Martel. He wasn't participating in any more destruction. Just trying to find the priest. This shouldn't weigh on his conscience. He glanced back. Through the shard-wreathed hole in the door, the decimated rosebush stared back at him with its brown and papery petals strewn about the pathway. He looked away quickly. They had a task to perform.

He paused at the top of the stairs. The mob's fury hadn't touched the servants' quarters as strongly as the rest of the house. The lack of finery had deterred them from doing more than breaking in the doors and scratching the word *Émigrés* onto one of the walls.

Gilles started at the far end of the hall and worked his way through storage and bedrooms. Few things had been left beyond old furniture and bed linens. He checked under each mattress in order to give Martel an honest report of a thorough examination.

Gilles lowered a mattress back to its frame, then knelt to check underneath the bed. A haggard comb lay forgotten in one corner, but nothing else. It was clear no one had returned to clean up the wreckage of the home. Or if they had returned, they'd quickly run away again.

If only Martel would give this up. True, the priest was his kinsman. Gilles could understand the responsibility one felt for the actions of a family member. How often had he agonized over his father's treatment of Dr. Savatier, feeling guilty over Père's decision to pursue that English merchantman instead of continuing into port and finding help? But this priest could be miles from Marseille by now. He could be on a ship to Italy or Spain. That was what the Assembly wanted nonjuring priests to do, wasn't it? So long as he was out of France and no longer imposing his influence on Frenchmen, they'd done their duty.

Gilles adjusted the haversack's strap over his shoulder. A ledger inside, which he'd brought home to straighten out after work yesterday, tapped against his leg. Something wasn't aligning in Monsieur Daubin's finances. Either the *savonnerie* was losing money somewhere, or it had not been bringing in as much profit as Monsieur Daubin claimed.

Gilles pushed himself off the rough floor and scratched his head. This was a fruitless search, much as his sifting through the ledger had been last night. But he'd do both to appease his friend and his employer. Well, he wasn't actually appeasing his employer, since the *monsieur* hadn't asked him to look into it. Of course Gilles worried over his job. He needed only until the end of the year to save enough to apply to the university at Montpellier, and the soap factory closing could delay that.

It wouldn't be a mere a delay for Marie-Caroline, however. Where would the family go if the soap factory could not be saved? To their relatives' home in Paris?

The feel of her cool hand smoothed over his fingers. Soft skin. Firm grip. No hesitation. She hadn't pulled away from him that day near the docks, even after their disagreement. The trust in her eyes made him want to believe that given time they could overcome their differences in conviction and find something more than friendship. But if she returned to Paris, with all its society and *révolutionnaire* conflict . . . Gilles shook his head as he moved to the next room. A little money lost could be recovered. The Daubins were hardly in dire straits. He worried over nothing.

This room was larger than the rest, no doubt belonging to the housekeeper or cook because of its size and proximity to the stairs. Hazy light poured through the window. He had less than an hour to finish this search with Martel before he was needed at the *savonnerie*.

He stopped just inside the door of the room and peered about. This couldn't be the housekeeper's quarters. It had no bed and only a few chairs piled haphazardly in one corner. An open trunk lay on its side near the window. Another storage room, it seemed, though it was odd to use the nearest room to the stairs as a storage room. Why would the family reserve the best room of the topmost floor for keeping things of little importance?

Gilles pulled a few chairs off each other, scanning the floor for signs of anything suspicious. Something grey shot past his feet, and he flinched, nearly dropping a chair. The little streak disappeared through the doorway. A mouse. He chuckled, as much to slow his racing pulse as anything. Scared of a little mouse. He'd rather meet a mouse than a ship's rat any day. He *had* gone soft, as Père loved to tease him about.

Gilles lowered the chair he was holding. On to the trunk, which looked empty anyway. Would Martel give up this obsession if they found no clues in the house? He couldn't hear anything on the floor below. Martel must still be in the cellar.

A white cloth, a tablecloth or bedsheet, lay caught beneath the trunk which, as he suspected, was empty but for fresh mouse droppings. That creature must have had plans to make this place his home in the absence of its previous occupants. Gilles lifted the trunk back to an upright position. It creaked and settled to the floor with a thud. He grabbed the cloth to fold and return to the trunk before closing the lid. The material was of a fine weave and weight, almost like an altar cloth. It would be a shame to leave it in a heap on the floor.

Something slipped from the cloth. Gilles cried out as a hard corner pounded into the top of his foot, driving the buckle atop his shoe into his bone. Pain shot across his foot, and he dropped the cloth. A book flopped to the ground. It must have been folded into the sheet. Groaning, Gilles pulled off his shoe and let it fall. He hopped, trying to keep his balance while massaging the stockinged foot. The force had been blunt and would probably only leave a bruise. He muttered a chain of curses under his breath. Who wrapped a book in a cloth that large?

After sufficient rubbing, he gingerly slid his foot back into his shoe and took a tentative step. The action caused little additional pain. No lingering harm. That didn't stop him from winding up to kick the stupid leather book across the room.

Gilles halted, stumbling to the side as his injured foot throbbed. Black leather. Etched cover. It couldn't be.

He stooped. Thousands of books just like this must exist through-out the nation, or at least they had before the start of the revolution. He picked it up, and the book fell open to the center. Several of the middle pages had been crumpled and smoothed out.

Just like the missal from Saint-Cannat.

Prickling crept up his back, as though a cold draft had swept in through the doorway. What was this doing here? Marie-Caroline had stolen this. It should be in her house in Belsunce. Gilles slowly straightened. When he'd stopped her in the road that Sunday morn-ing, she'd been walking in this direction. He snapped the book closed and swallowed against the bitterness that had seeped into his mouth.

She'd been here, no question. And regularly since she'd appar-ently risked her safety to fetch a book from a confiscated church, only to give it away. Gilles tangled his fingers in his hair. The stacks of chairs. The chest in front of them with a sheet. He should have seen it before. They were holding secret mass. His head throbbed as the implications fell into place. Even if she hadn't physically harbored this priest, she'd be counted as guilty for helping. He could be accused for not reporting it. His family could be harassed—or worse—for association. The most heartless of the Jacobins had beaten the wives and children of their enemies before.

A shout from below jolted Gilles from thought. He shoved the missal into his haversack. She was religious. He'd known that. But he didn't think she was insane. No one should have been able to trace the book back to her, and still it felt unwise to just leave it. If anyone could make the incriminating connection, it would be Martel.

He rushed from the room and down the stairs to answer Martel's call. The missal thumped against his hip with each step he descended, and the whirling in his gut intensified to a full-blown gale.

Condemn her or condemn himself. Neither option sounded appealing.

Gilles blinked and dipped his pen again. How long had he been trying to write this notice? He rubbed his eyes, which had blurred in his distraction.

For two days that missal lay buried in his bedroom, taunting him from across the city as he sat at his desk in the *savonnerie*. He hadn't seen Marie-Caroline since their *navette* outing. Thank the skies for that.

"Étienne, come with me to check the batch." Monsieur Daubin's voice rattled through the room, making Gilles drop his pen.

"Yes, *monsieur*. Of course." He wiped up the dots of ink that had splattered over his desk and rose.

"What are your plans for tomorrow afternoon?"

Gilles kept his face impassive, but he felt the eyes of his fellow clerks. "They are cutting soap tomorrow. I plan to inventory the stock, as usual."

Daubin waved a hand. "The others can mind that for a few hours. I wish you to come to a *boules* match at my residence."

"*Boules?*" He knew the game but hadn't played very much. It was a favorite of older men in Marseille, though he rarely saw it in the streets since the revolution. "To keep score?"

"No, to play."

Gilles shifted his feet. Why would the *monsieur* wish his employee to play? "I shall make arrangements to be there."

"Very good." Monsieur Daubin turned into the hall, and Gilles glanced over his shoulder as he followed. The other clerks studied the papers on their desks with more care than they had before their employer arrived.

Gilles trailed the *monsieur* to the factory. He should feel honored by the apparent preference, as he'd worked hard to earn his employer's respect. But the blatant favoritism in front of his fellow clerks left him itching to take back his acceptance of Daubin's invitation. Not that it was much of an invitation.

They descended the stairs before exiting the back door, and Gilles heard his name called from the opposite end of the corridor. He paused in the doorway. The eagerness in the feminine voice set his heart fluttering in ways he would have enjoyed two days ago.

He could pretend he didn't hear it. The door was nearly shut. His gut tightened. Eventually he would have to face her, and more importantly he would have to decide what to do with the information he knew. He might as well get one of them done with.

"I have forgotten something," he called to his employer, who was already halfway between the office and the workhouse door.

Monsieur Daubin grumbled something Gilles couldn't make out. "Don't let her keep you too long," he said over his shoulder.

Gilles's face heated as he slunk back into the office building. Words. He needed words. Speeches were Émile's strength, not his. Fancy, passionate words that made people listen. Growing into adulthood on a brig had not given Gilles a mastery of words.

"There you are. Were you going to run off without greeting me?" Marie-Caroline walked briskly toward him through the grey hall. Sunlight from the window by the door touched her face as she approached, and a grin appeared on her features.

A grin.

Gilles dared not breathe, lest he drink in her perfume and get lost in the dream of her presence. "*Bonjour, mademoiselle.*" He nodded his head in a bow.

"What greeting is this?" Her hands went to her waist.

"A respectful one."

She slowly folded her arms. "Though appreciated, it will not earn you a kiss." Those probing eyes traced his face.

"I did not think that was available for earning." He could put this off a few more days, until he figured out a plan. A little banter, and she wouldn't think twice of it.

"What is it, Gilles?" She reached for his arm, stopping just before her fingers grazed his sleeve. He didn't need the physical pressure to feel their touch. They were friends. Friends spoke to each other. Discussed their differences.

"I was at the house on the *rue de la Paix*," he said, fumbling with the cuff of his jacket. The movement put more space between her hand and his arm.

Her eyes narrowed, almost imperceptibly.

"I found that book you stole from Saint-Cannat." A thread had pulled loose from one of the buttons. He pinched it between his fingers. "Why have you involved yourself with one of them, Marie-Caroline?"

She retreated a step. "What right have you to question my faith?"

"This is not a matter of faith." He tugged on the thread to attempt tightening the button. Instead, a length of thread unraveled. *Ciel.* "It is a matter of safety. You could be hurt for even associating with a . . ." He dropped his voice. "Priest," he hissed through his teeth, hoping the sound didn't carry up the stairs. "The city is crawling with rumors of an imminent attack on Jacobins. Everyone is suspicious. Why give them a good excuse to accuse you?"

"You Jacobins and your professions of freedom." She backed up until the window's light left her face. "What my family does is not your concern."

Her whole family was attending secret mass. Gilles groaned. "It becomes my concern when my safety and that of my family is threatened by not informing authorities about what I know." If anyone found out he'd kept this secret . . .

"You wouldn't dare."

His confidence sagged at the rigidity of her stance. He'd worked so hard to gain her trust. The button on his cuff swung back and forth as he tried to wrap the loose thread around it in an attempt to salvage it.

"No, I wouldn't." He released the button thread and let his arms fall limp at his sides. "I should go help your father."

This time when he slipped through the door, she didn't call for him. And the silence that filled the gap between them rang in Gilles's ears.

I don't know what to do, Sylvie. It could be that he only knows I went to mass there, but what if he suspects more? Will that be the final push for him to report me to the Jacobins? My heart wants to believe he values our friendship more than that, but why should I believe my heart when it has been wrong about men before?

He has all the evidence he needs to bring harm to my family. Révolutionnaire *mobs have executed* royalistes *with charges based solely on rumors, and Gilles has physical evidence in the book.*

His face when we spoke—I've never seen him so wary, even after Émile's stupid trick when we first met. He wouldn't meet my eyes, and he moved so stiffly I would have taken him for someone else entirely. He must feel betrayed. Or confused.

The best outcome I can hope for is that he will remain silent and we will let this fledgling friendship slip through our fingers to be carried away on the wind like gold dust. A happy memory of what might have been.

I have not yet told Maman or Papa. My father has continued to retreat into himself, though over what I cannot say. Perhaps he worries for Émile's safety or regrets not mending their relationship before the fédérés' departure. And it would only worry Maman more to know of our danger. Père Franchicourt's presence, though soothing to her when immediately in our company, has set her pacing whenever I cannot occupy her thoughts with a game of cards or a book.

I've lost friendships before. Many I had before coming to live with you have dissolved due to Papa's unwillingness to zealously support the revolution. Several friends have left Marseille under the threat of violence. And, of course, there was Nicolas, but you know all about those dissolved relations. What I don't understand is why I feel so hollow inside knowing I will lose this one, regardless of the outcome. I've denied it for some time, but deep in my heart I wished—

It's back. He brought it back.

The footman brought in a parcel left on the doorstep. My name is across the front in a neat, masculine hand. Caroline, not Mademoiselle Daubin or even Marie-Caroline. Just Caroline. Call me a dunce, but my heart faltered at the sight of that one word. He cannot be so angry with me if he refers to me in such an intimate manner, can he?

And under the paper and string, which was tied in a knot one would only find on a ship, lay the missal. He included no note, no telling of his thoughts, and he left the parcel before anyone knew of his presence.

I wish I had seen his face and could know for certain what he meant by it. Does he wish to continue our friendship? Or was this a final token of goodwill?

Oh, Sylvie, why are you not here to help me sort through these frenzied thoughts? You always knew what to say or what to think with Nicolas. Not that the friendship between Gilles and me is in any way similar to what I had with Nicolas. I think it has been made very clear that friendship is the only logical relationship in our situation, but why does it feel so wrong to say it?

Forgive me for bringing up Monsieur Joubert so much. It has been a year, but I cannot chase him from my mind today.

Affectueusement,

Caroline

CHAPTER 18

Gilles glanced behind him as he followed his employer into the Daubins' house. None of his Jacobin acquaintances appeared to know about Marie-Caroline attending secret mass or his ties to the secret, but this sort of familiar visit would make it seem Gilles had a closer tie to the family than just that of a clerk. Most people in the area at this time of day were servants or *bourgeois*. While there was a split between *révolutionnaires* and *royalistes* in both groups, no red caps flashed among the passersby on this street, which signaled the absence of *sans-culottes*.

Still, the tightness in Gilles's shoulders did not loosen as he shuffled through the door. This event would help keep him in good standing with the *monsieur*, but he wished he could have excused himself. The footman shut the door behind him, and Gilles nodded his appreciation automatically, though Daubin continued into the front hall without a glance at the servant. In the Étienne house, Florence was as much a part of the family as he was. How different the Daubins and Étiennes treated their servants. Technically both families were of the merchant class, but the *bourgeoisie* comprised individuals of a vast array of fortunes and circumstances.

Gilles glanced at the stairs. The sun hadn't reached its zenith yet, and the western windows that flanked the door let in little light. But he could see the entrance was empty of everyone except the servant, his employer, and himself. Just as well.

Daubin whirled and motioned for the footman to quit the room, which the young man did obediently. Gilles fought the urge to step back as his employer advanced until they were toe to toe.

"I have a problem."

Gilles cleared his throat. "How may I be of service, *monsieur*?"

The whites of Monsieur Daubin's eyes shone, despite the dimness of the front hall. His employer's hands wrung. Gilles had never seen the man so agitated. "The *savonnerie*. It is in trouble."

Gilles nodded slowly. His examination of the ledgers and efforts to tally the expenses had made him fear as much.

Monsieur Daubin brought his hands together, as though in prayer. But instead of invoking deity, he tapped his fingers against his mouth. "I thought the *révolutionnaire* fervor would die down. That business would return. I let myself anticipate a renewed time of prosperity. Next year, things will be better. Next year. For three years."

No one knew at the onset of the revolution what the future would hold. Gilles studied the toes of his shoes. He could hardly blame Daubin for hoping. Didn't they all hope for a quick resolution?

"But our customers are fleeing," Daubin went on. "Merchants are not paying for luxuries. I still have crates of soap from two years ago."

Gilles's head jerked up. "Two years?" One of the ledgers had noted a large sale at the beginning of last year—almost impossibly large compared to their normal orders. "Did you . . ."

"I bought the lot." Monsieur Daubin kneaded his temples. "It's all in a warehouse."

A groan escaped Gilles before he could rein it in. "Have you bought any more?"

The man's head bobbed up and down. "Several batches here and there. But I cannot do it again. I have barely enough to support my family's current living through the end of the year."

He'd used all his family's funds to keep the *savonnerie* afloat. And not just afloat. He'd kept it steadily producing its normal output in hopes that the market would right itself. He was practically paying his employees from his family's purse.

Gilles closed his eyes. His earlier fears had more founding than he realized. Would the Daubins leave Marseille? His throat constricted, though it shouldn't have. If they left, the problem of their involvement in secret mass would be solved. "Do you have a plan? Ideas?"

"No plans. But I had hoped perhaps your father might help."

Père? Not likely without some incentive. He found preying on foreign merchantmen more profitable than his own trading these days.

"I would strike him a good bargain. He could make a fine profit in Naples, or perhaps Tuscany."

Daubin had sold to Père before, but then the profit had come from northern France. Most other Mediterranean countries made their own soaps.

"Or the Americas. They have little by way of European luxury there." Daubin's voice was pinched. "Surely there is some place that will take my inventory and make him a fortune. And I can—"

Gilles held up his hands to stop the man's musing. "I will inquire when he returns." Each word he spoke made his gut sink. Asking Père for a favor. His father would love that. "Until then, we should form a plan. Cut expenses. Decrease prices." Let workers go. Gilles's heart pounded, and he couldn't say it. Given the current circumstances, letting go of employees could incite a riot. "We will work carefully. Surely there's something to be done."

Daubin's hand settled on Gilles's shoulder. "Thank you, Étienne. I knew I could rely on your help. You've been a trusted clerk these two years."

Gilles forced a smile. He had planned to leave the *savonnerie* at the end of this year. Would he leave just as Monsieur Daubin's luck ran out?

Rushed footsteps across the floor and whispers above them caused his employer to step back. Had he told the *madame* yet? Or Caroline? Gilles held his breath in anticipation of a pair of fine shoes, a delicate dress, and a cautious stare striding down the steps, but no one materialized. His breath released slowly. He wouldn't face her today, which was for the best. If only he believed that.

"Come, the others will be outside, I believe."

Gilles followed Monsieur Daubin through the house and out the back door into the bright sun. Four other men in well-made jackets mingled before a rectangular *terrain* marked out on the packed dirt at the back of the garden with stakes and string. Daubin introduced them, and Gilles recognized Martel's employer among the players.

"This is my clerk, Étienne. He will play with us this afternoon."

A few brows raised, and Gilles forced himself not to duck his head. He had every right to play with the others. What did wealth and standing have to do with his playing the game? They lived in a new, free France, where social hierarchy was a thing of the past. And if his employer wasn't exaggerating, the Daubins and Étiennes were much closer in regards to wealth than appearances manifested.

And Caroline didn't know.

While Daubin divided them into teams, Gilles peeked at the house over his shoulder. He shouldn't want to see her. The book had been delivered, and it was safer for them not to associate. The more he discovered, the more danger she was in. What if she knew the whereabouts of Franchicourt?

A woman sat fanning herself on a balcony on the side of the house. Most likely Madame Daubin, concealed under the shade of a parasol, watching her husband play. Gilles turned to accept a drink from his employer. *Monsieur* should tell his family. That much he knew. His wife would not take it well, but she and Caroline deserved to know the truth.

"Has anyone been invited to attend the planting of the liberty trees?" Daubin asked. He picked up a wooden ball and lined up to throw it at the marker.

"Irritable business," the oldest of the group muttered.

Martel's employer, on the opposing team, selected a ball and tossed it lightly in his hand. "How can you say such a thing? It should be an honor to prove your loyalty to the revolution by participating in the ceremony. It's a small act. Or are you afraid to get your breeches dirty?" He tossed the ball. It landed with a crack, pushing Daubin's ball farther away from the jack, the smaller target ball.

It was a sly remark, one that everyone recognized as an accusation. Indeed, everyone but Martel's employer and Gilles wore the decidedly upper-class breeches instead of trousers.

"They only issued invitations to men they believe to be *royalistes*. They assume we are all for the monarchy," another merchant said. "Think of how poorly it will reflect on us and our business to be included in that party."

The rest of the men nodded gravely. They swirled their drinks and muttered in their fine waistcoats and gleaming shoes. Gilles chewed his tongue. Martel's employer was the only one who hadn't received an invitation due to his outspoken support. Would the summons knock some reason into them? The Jacobins were done with games.

France needed unity, or she would not rise above the infighting and brutality.

Martel's employer made room for the next man to throw and retrieved his glass from the small table nearby. "Those with nothing to hide have nothing to fear."

Monsieur Daubin shifted, glancing back at the house. Gilles followed his gaze to the woman in white on the balcony. Had the *madame* also gone to the secret masses? The *monsieur* was hardly religious, at least not outwardly. And when Gilles had stopped Marie-Caroline that Sunday morning, she had been alone with their cook.

Gilles narrowed his eyes. That wasn't Madame Daubin sitting on the balcony. The lady sat too regally to be the soap maker's wife. He hadn't noticed the dark curls sweeping down one side of her neck. Heat flew to his face, and he snapped his head back around. Caroline was watching them play.

"Your turn, Étienne."

Gilles shakily put down his glass, which he hadn't drunk from yet. How ridiculous. It should not matter to him whether she watched or not. They were only friends, and even that was doubtful now. Still, her brown eyes on his back as he lifted the wood ball and prepared to throw sent a thrill down his spine that made it difficult to concentrate.

It was all a game, wasn't it? The Jacobins trying to push and persuade the rest of France to see the light of liberty. The *royalistes* attempting to conceal their hand, play the right cards, and secure at least a constitutional monarchy. These merchants putting on a face to keep their businesses intact despite violence in the city. He and Caroline carefully stepping around each others' convictions to protect a friendship that had been shaky from the start.

Gilles fixed his eye on the other team's balls, which sat a mere length from the jack. He swung his arm back, drawing in a breath.

One wrong move could upend everything.

He stepped forward, releasing the ball. It flew through the air in a dizzying whirl and met its target with a satisfying crack.

23 July 1792
Marseille

They murdered them, Sylvie. Then strung them up like pigs in a butcher's shop. And dragged them through the street.

You'll forgive me. I hardly know how to write. I haven't been able to sit more than two minutes together since Cook arrived from the market this morning with word that two monks had been beaten to death. The mobs pulled them from the Hôtel de Ville itself, and no amount of begging, even from the revolutionary bishop, could spare them.

Maman fainted onto the sofa at the news. I could not help her. Père Franchicourt went pale, and Cook was sobbing at the door to the salon. Even now, my head pounds enough to burst. If we had not offered shelter to Père Franchicourt two weeks ago, he might have been the third clergyman slaughtered.

Some justice. Some liberty. Some equality these révolutionnaires have given us. They have offered the highest reaches of societal bliss but bestowed terror and discord from the depths of purgatory. That people may not believe as they please, without the worry of turning the mob indignation against themselves and their families, is an iron thorn on their rose of freedom. And one day it will turn against the very men who wield its barbed edge.

These murders come on the heels of four others only the day before, all condemned of conspiracy by crowds in the streets rather than a judge.

It will never end, will it, Sylvie? Just when I think that France cannot accept another ounce of lunacy, the people of this land push her one step closer to irreversible chaos.

Père Franchicourt has of course offered to leave. Not for himself, as he will certainly be caught if he attempts to leave the city, but for the safety of our family. I do not know what Papa will say when he returns from the savonnerie, but I insisted Père Franchicourt remain. If only until the riots over the conspiracy die down and we can secure him a safe passage to Spain.

The thought to beg Gilles for help crossed my mind, but I cannot turn to him. Just as Émile would have been, he was horrified at my participating in mass. He knew me to be religious, and yet he assumed I would not practice. If he knew about Père Franchicourt, he would have no choice but to report me.

Why then do I want nothing more than to go to him right now? Is it because the last time something so unnerved me, the strong arms I had come to rely on were the ones lying lifeless in the streets? The anniversary of the massacre on the Champ de Mars last week has no doubt made me more sensitive to this news about the clergymen, but I should not be so weak as to want the comfort of a révolutionnaire who cannot disentangle himself from the grasp of the Jacobins. Did I not learn my lesson with Nicolas? Loving a Jacobin only leads to heartache, whether he is left for dead or he leaves you for dead.

I hope you can read these words; I've written them so poorly. I pray for you, your family, and those you shelter every hour. Only a miracle can see all of us through this wretchedness alive, and we will not come out unscathed.

M. C.

How many pieces of soap did Monsieur Daubin have sitting in his storehouse? Gilles ran his fingers over the smooth, green blocks that sat in the back of the shop in the Noailles district. The sharp scent of freshly cut and stamped soap covered the scent of perfumes and colognes on the opposite side of the room. Only a little light reached into the storage room through the open door. Motes of dust drifted in the faint beam, but nothing else moved. Even the commotion of the streets outside was muted by the walls of silent goods.

Gilles should have been working. But the image of the limp form in the gutter he'd passed on his way to the shop filled his mind's eye, making it difficult to focus on numbers. He'd regularly seen death at sea, and as a physician he would see plenty more of it throughout his life. But that lonely corpse in the road, getting spit on by passing workers . . .

He swiped curls from his eyes and returned to pulling blocks of soap from the crate at his feet. He'd volunteered to stock inventory at the shop today. No one wanted to go out in the streets, especially in the well-to-do districts of Marseille, where many of the recent murders had occurred or been displayed.

The crate grated on the floor as he pulled it toward the next shelf. Gilles stiffened at a click. Was that a door opening? When no sound repeated, he went back to his task. The front door was locked since Daubin had decided not to open the shop given the events of the last three days. And Gilles had made sure the back door was secure after he let himself in. The only person coming in through the door would be his employer, or perhaps another clerk. But they would have announced themselves.

Gilles rolled a block of soap around in his hand, examining the *Savonnerie Daubin* mark with its outlines of lavender encircling the words. Soap residue created a fragrant film across his skin. Would he miss this, when the soap factory was gone? For all Daubin's hopes and plans, Gilles could not shake the nagging thought that attempts to salvage the business were futile in the current society.

"Gilles?"

He startled at the muffled voice coming from down the hall. Soft footsteps pattered across the wood floor. Gilles set the block of soap on the shelf and waited for Caroline's shadow to fall across the beam of light.

"What are you doing here?" he asked.

The greyness of the empty shop veiled her face. She clutched both arms, looking smaller than she ever had since they met. "Someday this will end."

"What will?"

She motioned in the direction of the streets. "The deaths. The fear."

Would it? Even *révolutionnaire* leaders hadn't been able to dissuade the crowds from breaking into the prisons and exacting their own justice on *royalistes*. If the leaders of the Jacobins had no control, would the mobs ever be restrained in the wake of threat, perceived or real? "Yes," he simply said. But it did not sound convincing.

"Each time this happens, I think it must be the last. Surely in the face of so much death and destruction, hearts will be softened to the horror of it all." She huddled in the doorway like a beggar in the depths of a fierce winter without a coat.

"The people of this country have endured a great deal. They have had enough." He picked up a few more blocks of soap and set them on the shelf.

"And that is a reasonable excuse?"

Gilles paused, then slowly swung his head back and forth. Angry crowds all over the nation were taking the law into their own hands, but none so frequently or violently as the people of Paris and

Marseille. If all the mobs rose up and banded together, would it hasten a new France, or send *la patrie* up in flames?

"You should not be here, *mademoiselle*." He pushed more blocks into place, then reached for the quill and ledger on a lower shelf to take note. "It is not safe."

Her hands dropped to her sides, the defiant stance he knew so well returning. "We came through the back streets."

His heart quivered with each tap of her heel against the floor as she traveled closer. It was fortunate he could not smell her perfume over the scent of the soap. Here they were, alone in the shop. No father or fellow clerk to barge in. If he wanted to, he could turn around and kiss those lips he'd been craving since May. Finally taste their sweetness. Would she let him? He drew in a breath. These thoughts would undo them both. "Your mother would be worried if she knew you had risked it." He straightened, setting the pen back in the inkwell. "But I'm not only speaking of braving the streets. It is dangerous for us to talk anymore, Caroline. You know that."

"As I recall, you insisted on our friendship." That edge in her voice had returned.

"That was before I knew." He turned one of the blocks of soap around so the whole line displayed *Savonnerie Daubin* on the front. Not that it mattered, as these would be transferred to the front of the shop when needed.

"Knew I practiced my religion? That I was a wicked Catholic who defied the truth of Jacobinism?"

"You know that isn't how I think," he said through a cringe.

"No, Gilles. I don't. You have never told me."

He kept his eyes trained on the olive-green cubes before him, avoiding the fire in her eyes that always sent his pulse galloping. He needed a clear head, or his will would falter. "I do not think you are evil. I think you are playing with fire by the powder magazine in a storm, but it is your life to do with what you wish."

Her soft laugh finally drew a brief glance from him. Had he said something amusing?

"I am being entirely serious, Caroline. You were right. A Jacobin and a *royaliste* make for a dangerous friendship. And I think we have reached the breaking point. If I knew more about your priest friend, it could endanger us both. If I let slip that I knew anything, my family would be at risk. It is better for both of us."

"That is not why I laughed." She trailed her fingers along the line of soaps as she widened the gap between them. "I love when your seamanship slides into conversation."

Gilles's ears grew hot. Blast his training and his heritage. He could not escape them. "And the rest of what I said? Have you any response to that?" He pulled down his shirt sleeves and buttoned them about his wrists. If she wouldn't leave, he should. Where was his jacket? He'd finish stacking this row and return to the factory.

Caroline stopped walking. She chewed her bottom lip for a time. "It has been a year since the massacre on the Champ de Mars."

Gilles halted with his hand resting atop the soaps. His eyes narrowed. That was not a *révolutionnaire* massacre. It had come at the hand of Lafayette's national guard against Parisians rallying a petition to end the monarchy. *Royalistes* killing *révolutionnaires*.

"I had a . . ." Her chest rose and fell. "Friend among the casualties."

"She was a *révolutionnaire*?" Why had Caroline been so against their friendship, then?

"He was a follower of Danton."

Oh. *He.* Gilles crouched for more soap, trying to ignore the twinge in his chest. A Danton follower. Danton was a zealous supporter of liberty and a clean break from the monarchy, someone the

Jacobin leadership observed with wariness because of his skills in inciting the Paris crowds. "Was he a dear friend?" *Stop it, Gilles. You do not wish to know that answer.*

Caroline pulled a block of soap from the neat lines and held it to her nose. Her eyes fluttered closed. She inhaled deeply once, twice, three times. "We were engaged for nine months."

Bien sûr. Gilles snatched up the ledger and busied himself with the numbers. Idiot. He had asked. All that wondering about whether she had left her heart in Paris. She had. Although, now he was dead. He glanced at her over the pages of the book. Those moments, such as on the stairs after the dinner party, when she could not hide the pain from her eyes, had she been thinking of that man?

"Nicolas broke off the engagement a month before the massacre. He could not reconcile himself with being tied to a monarchist."

"Ah." He lowered the book. "It is no wonder you were so against our friendship, then."

A sad smile graced her lips. She pushed the cube of soap back into place. "You proved me wrong."

Had he? Or had he proved her former intended correct, that it couldn't work? Gilles scratched the back of his head. "What did your father think of the engagement?"

"He did not know. No one knew. My sweet cousin Sylvainne was our only confidante."

A secret engagement. It didn't surprise him that she would attach herself without the knowledge of her parents. He closed the ledger and put it back beside the inkwell.

"When I found out about his death, I was furious," she went on, staring unseeing at the shelves before them. "I felt betrayed, though without an engagement, I had no reason to. I suppose I hoped he would change his mind and return to me." She shook her head, the pale light from the door playing over her curls. "And with those spoiled dreams came an increased resolve. I wanted to stay as far as I could from those seeking to upend life as we knew it."

Caroline drifted closer to him but did not meet his gaze. The pull to cut the distance between them nearly knocked Gilles from his feet. Here in Marseille, she had no one. Surely she could not lean on her mother for comfort, not when the woman struggled so much with her own fears. Monsieur Daubin was occupied with the dire straits of his business. Émile was gone, though he did not think the brother and sister were very close. The youngest brother was back in Paris, the oldest sister married and gone. And though he could not count himself a confidante . . . How could he pull away if he was one of the few supports she had left?

"When we heard about the beatings and hangings yesterday, I don't know why, but it felt like Champ de Mars all over again." Her fingers twisted together in front her. "I did not know those monks or the alleged conspirators. And yet, they may as well have been Nicolas Joubert." Her voice wavered.

Gilles reached out and took her arm. There had to be a way. He cared for her at least as much as he cared for Florence, and he wouldn't let anything destroy that friendship, no matter the danger. Though his insides didn't ignite when around Florence the way they did when Caroline stepped into the room.

"Another life taken. Another future gone." She shook her head. "Does it matter what they believed?" Her arm trembled beneath his fingers. She finally turned to him. Was it the dim light, or were there tears clinging to her lashes?

Before he knew it, Gilles pulled her against him and wound his arms around her shoulders. A soft gasp escaped her. For a moment, she stood rigid, though she didn't retreat. Of all the witless things for him to do. If he'd intended to drive her away, this would do the job. Just when he thought perhaps they could find a way.

Her head sank onto his shoulder. The tremor running through her frame was gone. Or had he imagined it?

"I don't wish to kiss you," she murmured. The tension in her body eased, and she relaxed against him.

He rested his head against the soft cap on her head, her curls tickling his skin. "I know."

The rich amber of her perfume spiced the air with the warmth of a Mediterranean sunrise. If Daubin walked in at that moment, Gilles's life was forfeit. If Martel happened upon them, Gilles wouldn't make it home. But drinking in her scent as he held her clouded those worries in a mist of oblivion he'd never experienced until now.

"I'm sorry," he said. "For what happened, and all the memories you have to carry. And I apologize for being a wretched oaf."

She laughed. Her back pressed against his arms, and he reluctantly let them slip from around her to hang empty at his sides.

Caroline stepped back and regarded him. "Are we to still be friends?"

"If you wish it." He sucked in a calming breath.

"What of the danger?"

What of it? He hardly knew what to say. Nothing had changed, except his resolve not to lose this friend who had become dearer to him than he realized. "We shall be careful. And not speak of anything regarding . . ." He waved a hand.

"Very well." She glanced around, as though expecting someone to appear. "I should return to the house. Maman will worry."

Or he might break his word not to kiss her. "Yes. Of course. That is wise."

"Thank you for listening, Gilles. And for proving me wrong."

His lips twitched. He hadn't proved her wrong many times since they met.

Caroline strode to the door, drawing the intoxicating amber scent with her. Soon the only smell touching his nose was the earthy soap once again. Just before quitting the room, she looked back at him and cocked her head.

"When we first met, I hadn't a clue how you'd managed to kiss any girls in Émile's games. I suppose I was wrong in my observations. You do have some charms to recommend you."

Gilles chuckled, grateful for the dimness of the storeroom to hide his reddening face. "Did you think I kissed only foolish flirts?"

"Oh, no. They most definitely were foolish flirts. But I cannot blame them so harshly as I always have, seeing what they were tempted with." She nodded toward him, then disappeared through the doorway.

He stayed still until he heard the back door close and a key twist in the lock. Then his shoulders slumped. He leaned against the shelf, face pressed against the wall of soap. He hardly knew what had happened, but in the time she had occupied the shop, he had gone from wanting to avoid her at all costs to longing to be back at her side the moment she withdrew.

It hit him like the broadside of an English first-rate ship connecting with a brig's hull—he had been terribly wrong in likening his relationship with Caroline to his friendship with Florence. In fact, he had rarely configured a grosser understatement.

CHAPTER 19

Nicolas Joubert. The name rolled in Gilles's mind to the rhythm of the carriage advancing toward the eastern fields. Late evening shone through the windows of the Daubins' coach. *Monsieur* dozed beside him, snores mixing with the rumble from the wheels.

Even with their relative privacy, Caroline remained silent on the other side of the carriage. Sometimes she watched Gilles, but mostly she stared out the window as the shops, factories, and houses turned into vineyards and fields.

Gilles couldn't say why the idea of Caroline's previous engagement stuck to his mind like a barnacle. And she'd engaged herself to a *révolutionnaire*, of all people. Then he'd been killed by Lafayette's men. The same Lafayette she'd defended when they discussed the effigy while eating *navettes* at the Old Port. On some occasions she had been plainly dressed, taking food to a sick family or stealing a contraband prayer book. Now here she sat, proud and proper as ever in her stylish straw hat and gaulle dress, nonchalantly fanning herself like an aristocratic Parisian belle. Would he ever understand this woman?

He looked away quickly as the memory of holding her at the shop sneaked into his mind. She'd stood so stiff and cold, then melted into his arms. The weight of her head on his shoulder and press of her body against his had loosened so many of the internal ropes holding him back.

This was dangerous, falling in love with someone who held beliefs so opposite his own. Gilles gave his head one sharp shake. In love. Ha! He was hardly in love with . . .

"Did you see something disagreeable?" Caroline's voice did little to wash away his unruly thoughts.

"Oh, no. I just . . ." Just thought about wanting to be more than friends. How impossible. He could hardly imagine Caroline playing the part of a physician's wife. Even as a successful doctor, he wouldn't have the means to satisfy her fashion and society needs. Though, if things continued to go poorly with the *savonnerie*, neither would her father before long.

"You haven't mentioned what I told you a few days ago to anyone, have you?" she asked in a softer tone.

"Not a soul." Outside, a billow of purple flowers filled the scene. They were nearing the Daubin fields.

"Thank you." She opened and closed her fan slowly in her lap, examining the scrolling pattern about the front. "And thank you for listening." The corner of her mouth lifted. "I do not have the opportunity to speak so candidly to a friend very often these days."

If she spoke too candidly they'd both be in trouble. But Gilles returned her smile. He did not mind being her confidante . . . So long as she didn't mention the priest. "I hope I may always be that friend to you," he said. "Whatever happens."

She nodded, face thoughtful. It was a bold statement, one he should not have committed to, and she knew it. Yet he could not deny that deep in his heart—perhaps the part that held his long-ignored yearning to return to the sea—he wanted to be the arms that held her each time the world seemed to close in.

Confound the danger. Some things were worth risking everything.

"Thank you, Gilles. If you'll take these back to the coach." Monsieur Daubin handed a pair of books to Gilles. The office at the lavender fields had darkened in the oncoming evening. "I must speak with Louis, and then I will join you there."

"Yes, *monsieur*." Gilles tucked the books under his arm and quit the small building, eyes instantly scanning the grounds for sight of Caroline. She hadn't joined them inside but had continued into the fields when they arrived.

Gilles had just deposited the ledgers in the carriage when he spied her not far away, winding through the rows. He quickly made his way to her, heart lifting. A few minutes alone and without her father's scrutiny would make this late trip to the fields worth it.

Caroline wandered toward the gold sunset, her back to him. Lavender stalks bobbed in the whispering breeze around her. The stems caught in her gossamer skirts, stark white against the blues and violets of the field. Her fingers wove through the soft blossoms as she walked and deftly avoided the fat bees getting their last sips of nectar before darkness set in.

Gilles halted where the small garden around the building met the edge of the field. That little tune she loved to hum in moments of solitude carried back to him over the uniform lines of flowers. She hadn't realized his presence. His eyes flicked to the stone bench resting under the garden's lone cedar tree. No need to disturb her meditation. He could watch without interrupting from there, and perhaps slow his ragged breathing brought on from the ethereal sight before him.

He settled down onto the coolness of the bench. Caroline continued her walk in the brilliance of the evening, still oblivious to his gaze. Would that sitting in her presence could always be this tranquil. Those sleepy yellow hills that cradled the Daubins' lavender fields kept back the turmoil of revolution in the city. The wind eased the intense heat of summer, and the aroma of lavender washed over him, only lending to the peaceful fairy tale. For a moment, he could almost pretend he wasn't a Jacobin and she a *royaliste*. Tonight he was just a man admiring the woman he'd given his heart to.

He closed his eyes. *The woman he'd given his heart to.* How had he let this happen? If tensions remained high, it could get them both into serious trouble. Though no more murders had occurred in Marseille since the monks' four days ago, anything could set off the mobs again. One wrong word to the wrong person at the wrong moment, and they'd lose it all. And Caroline clearly wasn't about to back down from her convictions, no matter the hazard.

His mouth twitched as the image of her determined face filled his mind—the way her eyes sparked with indignation and the feisty set of her jaw. Only his promise not to kiss her had held him back from doing the deed. That and the knowledge she'd probably never speak to him again if he tried.

"Is this one of your tactics?"

Gilles's eyes fluttered open. Caroline stood at the edge of the field, pulling the skirt of her gaulle dress from the last of the lavender blossoms.

"Tactics?"

"For getting those girls to kiss you. Do you sit with lips ready and waiting for the girl to fall into your lap?" She tilted her face to the sky, mimicking his pose.

Gilles instantly straightened. If only it were that easy. "You have been rather interested in the girls I've kissed lately." His voice wavered. *Get a hold of yourself, Gilles.* He'd been equally as interested in her former intended. No doubt Caroline held onto her senses better than he managed.

"The girls you've kissed lately?" Caroline cocked her head. "How many has that been?"

"I . . . no, I haven't—"

Her eyebrows rose as she meandered toward him. The ends of the azure sash tied at her waist rippled like a wave across a lazy sea. "When was the last time you 'made a conquest,' as Émile likes to say?"

"It was . . ." When *was* the last time? The baker's daughter, several weeks before Caroline showed up in Marseille? "It's been months."

"Months?" Her hand flew to her cheek in mock surprise. "Our brothers would tease you mercilessly for that."

Gilles gave an unsteady laugh. Yes, they would. But then he doubted they'd ever been overcome by disinterest in every other girl as he had since May.

Caroline paused in front of him, the hem of her skirt brushing against his shoes. The heat of the sunset glowed against the deep brown of her curls. Her short-brimmed hat did little to shield her hair from the breeze, and several ringlets swayed across her brow. She leaned down until her face leveled with his.

Gilles averted his gaze as she studied him, not daring to look at her lips—touched with the barest hint of rouge—for too long. The lavender's perfume had fogged his brain. She was close enough he could snatch her up in his arms without much effort. Far too close. If he weren't careful, he'd lose his resolve.

"Do you want to kiss me?" The sauciness in her voice should have made him laugh. She was toying with him. It served him right after all the kissing games he'd played. Caroline had always been inadvertent in her unfairness; she looked irresistible simply by being near him. This display, however, was unmistakable coyness.

He tried to swallow, but his throat had trouble complying. How was he supposed to respond to that? He ran a finger under the cravat he'd tied too snuggly that morning.

She stayed there, face hovering in line with his. Could she be testing his ability to keep his word? Gilles cleared his throat. It still didn't help him gulp down the dryness. He had to move carefully. Speak carefully.

"I gave you my word, so what does it matter if I wish to or not?" He shifted in his seat. If he slid across the bench and ducked around her to escape, she'd surely laugh. "You do not wish to. You never tire of reminding me."

"I am not like all those tavern girls you've made conquests of."

"No, I've found you very difficult to catch." Gilles mentally smacked himself. Don't give in to the blatant flirting. What she was trying to prove or disprove, he couldn't say. Was she determining whether he was just like his brother and hers? He didn't know how to meet this challenge. *You must learn to recognize which battles you can win and which you must flee.* He hated that words of wisdom so often came in Père's voice.

His collar tightened as her fingers curled around his lapel, sending a roll of thunder through his chest more rattling than any he'd felt during the long, dark storms at sea. He gripped the edge of the bench to keep himself anchored against the firmness of her grasp.

"I will not be caught, *monsieur.*"

He had little doubt of that. If only she wouldn't play with him. He should make an excuse. Return to the coach. Break off this dizzying—

In a flash her lips covered his.

Soft.

Warm.

Fierce.

He drew in a sharp breath, still as the stone beneath him. A thrill coursed up his spine. He had barely a moment to drink in the fullness of her lips against his skin before she broke away.

"I dare you to call that a conquest," she whispered in his ear. The pressure around his neck dissolved as she released his lapel and turned. She sauntered toward the carriage as though she hadn't just stopped time, stopped the rotation of the earth. Sunbeams danced through the garden, lavender rustled, bees mumbled their final harmonies.

And Gilles sat panting in the grandeur of the summery Provençal countryside, unable to fathom what had happened.

"Étienne!"

He blinked. Monsieur Daubin had finally appeared and was now assisting his daughter into the carriage. Gilles bolted to his feet and hurried over, eyes on the ground to keep from stumbling on shaky legs.

She'd kissed him. He hadn't even managed to kiss her back.

"Are you well?" Daubin asked, bringing a hand to Gilles's shoulder before he could enter the coach.

"Yes, *monsieur*. Perfectly." Perfectly confused. At least her father hadn't witnessed that scene.

His employer gave a nod, then motioned him inside where Caroline greeted him with an indifferent nod and beat of her fan.

Only the twinkle in her eye let on that she knew she'd utterly muddled his already confused mind.

Of all the foolish actions! This is what happens when you let your heart run wild for only a moment. To make it all worse, he did nothing to goad me. I have only myself to blame for this glorious

predicament. It would seem I am the same as all the other girls I like to look down on for being too generous with their favors. But he sat there so thoughtful and serene, the wind smoothing back his rebellious hair. I could almost imagine him at the rail of a ship, drinking in the invigorating breath of the sea. How was I to resist?

I told myself I wanted only to prove the difference, to show him what he missed in his ridiculous games with Maxence and Émile. I lied to myself. I really just wanted to kiss him.

And I did.

Oh, Sylvie, I've made such a disaster of this! What will happen between us now? What will happen now that I've let my heart take the reins? So many terrible things.

Yet, I cannot bring myself to regret it more than I enjoyed it, nor can I force myself to hope it never happens again.

Heaven help us.

Affectueusement,

Caroline

CHAPTER 20

Monsieur Daubin did not like to get his hands dirty, which made it very difficult for Gilles to keep his face impassive as they made their way through the crowded street of *la Canabière*. The day had arrived for the wealthy merchants of Marseille to plant liberty trees to demonstrate their loyalty to *la patrie*. The soap maker had nearly worn grooves into the floor of his office from pacing that morning. He'd insisted Gilles join him.

"Is your family coming to watch?" Gilles asked, walking half a step behind his employer. He pulled his red cap over his hair as they approached the celebration.

"If I locked her in the Hôtel de Ville, Caroline would still find a way to come." Monsieur Daubin removed his gloves and stowed them safely in his waistcoat pocket. At least the man had had the foresight to wear trousers instead of breeches today. "She'll be the death of her mother, that one."

Caroline. Gilles's stride quickened of its own accord.

Nearly two days had passed since Caroline kissed him. Thirty-nine hours staring at the wall remembering the sensation of her lips on his, dodging questioning looks from his mother, ignoring thinly veiled laughter from a knowing Florence, and plotting a hundred ways to accidentally meet her on a Sunday. None of the ideas had come to fruition. If only he knew where she now met for mass.

Which would only make matters more dangerous. If she'd found another meeting place for mass, he could not know. That realization was when he stopped trying to devise a meeting and instead held onto the hope that he would see her at today's planting.

Drums and fifes carried over the chatter of the crowd as the pair moved through the crimson-capped citizens of Marseille. They found a place to stand near a line of young trees, which lay on their sides with roots extended in preparation for planting. The merchants who had attended Daubin's game of *boules* trudged over when their comrade appeared and left Gilles free to scan the masses for Caroline.

On the opposite side of the street, a dark-haired woman turned the corner with a footman in tow. A grin he couldn't control broke across Gilles's face. Caroline wore her white dress again, but this time with no other color at her waist or on her hat. He faltered a step. Surely she wasn't trying to make a political statement in this crowd by wearing the white of the monarchy.

He sighed. Knowing Caroline, that was exactly her aim.

When he reached her, he held out an arm. A wry look tinted her features for a breath. Then she took his arm quickly, which swept away some of his worry. A woman on the arm of someone wearing a liberty cap would not be harassed. At least, he hoped she wouldn't. One could never know what would stir the *sans-culottes* into a fury.

"And how are you today, Caroline?" Just having her near again sent an electricity through his limbs which he'd craved since Saturday's outing to the lavender fields.

Her rosy lips pursed. Could he steal a kiss without drawing the eyes of the crowd? Or worse, of her father? She leaned in, the brim of her hat tickling his ear like it had the glorious moment she'd kissed him. *Ciel*, what he'd give to return it now. Suddenly he wished he'd left his jacket at home and only come in a waistcoat. Sweat already gathered around his collar.

"I do not wish to kiss you."

Gilles inclined his head. They were back to that greeting again? After all that had happened?

She straightened, head turning indifferently as she surveyed the festivities. Blue, white, and red swirled around them in a frenzy of cockades, caps, and banners.

Whatever game she had decided to play, he would not let her win this time. If she wanted to play coy, he would match her wit for wit. "That is not the impression I received Saturday."

"I am sorry to say that whatever observations led you to such an impression were incorrect."

How curious. He laid his free hand over hers, and she did not pull away, but neither did she meet his eyes. Was she embarrassed by her forwardness? She needed not be. It was received only too eagerly. He took a deep breath so as to quell the flush that threatened to overtake his cheeks. "While I hate to contradict a woman—"

"On the contrary, I think you enjoy it very much."

He paused their course, turning her to face him. "Please tell me, then, how I was supposed to interpret your actions in the garden." She couldn't be serious. After all the pious scolding about his kisses meaning nothing because of the games, she wanted to pretend like Saturday evening didn't happen.

Caroline scowled, glancing about. "Hush. That sounds terrible."

He took her elbows and pulled her closer, until she was practically in his arms again. "What did you mean by it?"

She pressed her mouth into a thin line. Revelers jostled them from all sides, but Gilles held her steady. She didn't kiss for the fun of it; she'd made that clear from the beginning of their acquaintance. Her head turned so the sparse hat hid her face.

"Caroline?" A chill ran across his skin, despite the July heat. Why wouldn't she talk to him? Fear of being heard? Perhaps the risks they were taking had pushed her into a panic, as they sometimes did to him. Whatever the reason, he had to know. The strange ache sprouting in his chest wouldn't let him back down.

"I do not know what you are talking about," she said.

"That's a lie."

She tugged against his grip, and all he could do was let her go. Her arms slipped from his hands.

"Wait," he said. "Please."

She bent in a rigid curtsy and raised her voice. "Monsieur Martel."

Sacrebleu, Martel! He always appeared at the worst of times. Gilles dropped his hands to his sides as Caroline darted away, giving his friend a wide berth. Her footman scrambled to catch up to her. She didn't look back once as she located her father near the waiting trees.

Martel watched her go with a sneer, brow arching when he turned back to Gilles. "You missed the Jacobin meeting again."

Gilles winced. "I had to finish work. I told you I might." The choice between an outing with Caroline and an evening with angry Jacobins had been an easy one.

"Someday employers will not have the power to force citizens to work whenever they fancy." That was the same thing Luc Hamon had said. While Gilles agreed, the menace in Martel's tone unsettled him. Martel grasped Gilles's arm and pulled him away from the front of the crowd and Caroline. "You have become rather intimate with the Daubins lately."

Gilles let his friend pull him forward, even though he had the muscle to break away without much resistance. "He's my employer. How do you suggest I avoid him?"

"It's one thing to work in his factory and another to attend social events at his home." Martel led him to a liberty tree planted the year before, which citizens had draped with the colors of the three Estates General. Gilles wondered if white would be removed from the trio of hues if the Jacobins had their way and disposed of the monarchy. "My employer mentioned you attended Daubin's game of *boules* a couple weeks ago."

"He had business to discuss with me." Business they'd made little progress on. They'd found a few ways to cut expenses, but they wouldn't be enough to save the *savonnerie*.

"And then I see you ogling the daughter like some besotted mongrel."

Gilles bristled. "I was hardly ogling her," he snapped. "Caroline is my friend's sister." Mongrel? The hypocrite.

Martel crossed his arms. "So it's 'Caroline' now?"

"The planting is about to start." Gilles pivoted, but Martel jumped to block his path.

"I have news on Franchicourt."

Gilles rubbed his brow. Caroline would not be safe from the risk of her secret meetings until Martel gave up. "Has he fled?"

"His co-conspirators have," Martel growled. "We traced them to a ship sailing for Spain. But my uncle was not with them."

Gilles ground his teeth, praying his face didn't register any panic. "So he left the city another way?"

"Of course not." Martel's head lolled back. "It means he didn't leave the city. He's still here, aiding in the fight against liberty."

"I see." Did Caroline . . . He wouldn't even travel that path of thought. Knowing anything, even guessing, could spell disaster.

"I have a few leads I wish to investigate. Will you come with me tomorrow evening?"

Gilles pasted on a smile. "I would do anything to rid *la patrie* of traitors."

"Sometimes I wonder. I will meet you outside of Daubin's after work." Martel slapped his arm in farewell and lost himself in the crowd.

Gilles pulled off the red cap, his curls bouncing into his face. He wiped at his forehead with his sleeve. Two days ago, he'd had the world at his feet. Now he found himself once again gasping for breath in the narrow alley between love and duty, wishing for the open, intoxicating air of lavender fields.

2 August 1792
Marseille

Émile,

Thank you for writing. With all the chaos in the city fueling Maman's fears, your words have given her reason to smile. We are grateful to hear of your safe arrival in Paris and continue to pray for peace in that quarter.

Maman has little to say, except that she loves you and hopes you will not see any action. She says to give Guillaume and the Valois family our love if you should see them, even though I assured her there was little chance of that.

Papa has even less to say, and I do not think it because of his feelings on your joining the fédérés. Before you left, did you have any inclination that things were not right at the savonnerie? Papa has not said anything, but he has taken to locking himself in his study at home when he is not working late at the office. I broached the subject with Gilles when last we met, but he would not answer my questions directly. I do not understand why Papa would keep something to himself that could drastically affect us all. I will write with more information if I uncover it. Please tell me if you know more than I.

I have wished to thank you for some time for making amends before your departure. We do not see this revolution in the same light, but I am grateful we could put away our differences for a moment to remember the greater importance of our family bonds.

Do you know if Maxence has written to his family? Gilles says he has not, and he usually changes the subject quickly afterward. They did not leave on good terms, those two, and I think Gilles regrets it. I can see it in the narrowing of his eyes whenever someone mentions the volunteers. What will it do to him if something happens and they have not made peace? I know the Étienne family is much more familiar with situations of death and the unknown. Still, it must be difficult. Would you ask Maxence to write? If only for his mother's sake?

May you be blessed with health and no need to fight, though I know you hope for it.

Marie-Caroline

CHAPTER 21

The growling coming from Monsieur Daubin's office made Gilles slow his pace in the corridor. That did not bode well. Though his employer had maintained an unusually foul temper since the liberty tree planting a week and a half before, he hadn't sounded this angry in some time.

Gilles scanned the room before entering. One of the other clerks cowered before the *monsieur*, a sheet of paper in hand. Their employer stood with fists pressed against his temples and face red as a *sans-culotte*'s cap.

"You needed me, *monsieur*?" Gilles said at the door.

"What kept you?" Daubin snatched the paper from the other clerk and shook it in Gilles's direction. Gilles kept still. Had he made a mistake on an order? "Why are you the only competent man in my employ? I'm needed at the *parfumerie* immediately."

So he wasn't at fault. Gilles refrained from slumping in relief. His poor comrade stood shaking in his shoes.

Daubin stalked toward the door, motioning for the other clerk to follow. The paper in his hand crackled. "Take Caroline directly home, Étienne. If the business still stands after this debacle . . ."

Gilles scurried out of the doorway to make way for Monsieur Daubin. Caroline! He hadn't noticed her in the room. She stood at the window with arms crossed.

"Who misplaces an entire shipment?" her father shouted as he turned the corner.

They lost a shipment? Daubin couldn't afford that. Gilles hoped for the clerk's sake it was recovered quickly, though an impish part of him was grateful for the moment alone with Caroline. Their last parting had left a strange taste in his mouth. One he'd like to get rid of.

"You needn't look so disgruntled at the prospect of being escorted home by one of your father's clerks," he said, moving to the window and leaning against the sill next to her. A door slammed across the shop, and they both winced.

Caroline did not pull away from him, as he'd half expected her to. But he could not read the look in her eyes. Wariness? Eagerness? Of course his heart had chosen the one woman he couldn't decipher. "The last time I was left alone in an office with one of the clerks, it led to his humiliation," she said. Her arms stayed stiffly across her middle. If only he could get her to loosen her posture. They were friends, after all. Or perhaps a little more.

"I would hope he's made amends by now." His shoulder brushed hers. No response to his touch. She stood as though he hadn't initiated anything. In the kissing games with his brother and Émile, Gilles would have taken her lack of response as an invitation. But Caroline had proved him wrong in such assessments on too many occasions for him to attempt anything now.

"Amends? I don't know I would say that."

He turned and planted a hand on the sill on either side of her so that she was caught between his arms. Warning bells blared in his mind. This was too forward. He could get dismissed if anyone passed that open door. But no more forward than her actions at the lavender fields. "How have I not made amends?"

Her lips pursed. He'd let her answer before he went in for the kiss. The pounding in his ears seemed to echo through the still room. She cocked her head. "For one, you are attempting the exact same venture you did that afternoon, as though you learned nothing from the debacle."

Gilles let a grin melt across his face, the boyish grin that had gained him ground on even the toughest of targets. "Come, that's hardly fair. You gave me no time to kiss you back Saturday."

Caroline averted her eyes and took interest with something in her pocket. Was that a blush on her cheek, or a flush of anger? He'd affected her somehow. "*Quel dommage*! A missed opportunity." Her voice carried a hint of forced flippancy.

For two months he'd dreamed about kissing Marie-Caroline Daubin. She'd teased him. Twice. The first time into thinking she wanted it, and the second into thinking she didn't. Her light breath whispered against his skin, matching pace with his own. He leaned in.

A flurry of wood and silk attacked his face. Gilles ducked away, his hand coming up to block Caroline's fan. In a moment, the broadside was over as she walked briskly out of his reach.

Gilles threw up his arms. "What is this? You were perfectly willing last week."

"Did you think that gave you permission to kiss me whenever you wished?" she asked, flouncing toward the door. "*Mais, non*. It was more to show you what you've been missing during your little games."

Gilles closed his eyes, dragging a hand through his hair. He willed his heart to slow its raging. "I told you I haven't played those games in months."

Her shoulder lifted and fell. The stupid fan beat before her, partially obscuring her face. "Now you have good evidence why you should not, in case you are ever tempted to indulge again."

"Caroline, what is this?" She was playing games just as terrible as any he'd played. Surely she could see that.

The waving of the fan slowed, and the mischievous sparkle dissipated from her eyes. "We should go. My mother is expecting my father and me soon. I hope she'll settle for just me."

Gilles's throat tightened as he spoke. "Very well." Perhaps it was best to just let the argument fall, to take her home and forget this longing that had taken root. As if that glorious evening had never happened.

They had just turned onto *la Canebière* when Caroline stopped and tugged Gilles's arm for him to do the same. "What is that?"

A crowd of *révolutionnaires* had gathered at the square, much like they had for the tree planting and the send-off of the *fédérés*. His stomach twisted. Unlike those rallies, the only music filling the air was the murmur of agitated voices. "We should get home." Not all the *révolutionnaire* gatherings led to violence, but enough did.

Caroline released his arm and hurried toward the large group. Gilles groaned. Her attire was neutral enough today. He had to hope that would suffice to keep her unnoticed by the grumbling masses.

Some sort of platform had been erected at one end of the square. A few men paced atop it, their heads a bit above the rest. Shouts punctuated the low conversations, and Gilles strained to decipher what they said. As Caroline moved closer to the platform, the people squeezed in tighter. He snatched her hand so he didn't lose her, and she let him keep hold of it.

She took them around the side of the crowd. Vertical beams towered over the men on the platform. Gilles had assumed them to be scaffolding from the building behind, but on closer examination they looked to be standing on their own.

Caroline pulled up short, and Gilles had to grab her shoulders to avoid knocking her over from behind. A cart with waist-high bars stood off to one side. Between the bars, a balding man in ragged clothing sat on the floor of the cart with his hands tied behind his back. That could signify only one thing.

Ciel. They needed to get out of here.

"Probably a nonjuring priest," someone muttered near them. Caroline stiffened.

Someone barked an order from the platform, and a man pulled on a rope connected to the two beams. The afternoon sun glinted off a sheet of metal that rose between the two sides of the wooden frame. The bottom edge was angled and sharp.

Hisses rippled through the crowd. Words for the device he'd read and heard about but never seen. *Louisette. Guillotine.*

Gilles back stepped, trying to pull Caroline with him. "Let's go. We need to—"

She pulled out of his grasp and approached the guard at the side of the cart. "What is happening?"

The guard reached up to open the gate on the back of the cart. "What do you think is happening, *mademoiselle*?" At the front of the cart, someone unhitched the horse. Unbalanced on its single axle, the cart flopped forward. Inside, the prisoner skidded against the rough floor. The guard hoisted himself up to drag the unfortunate man out while others steadied the wagon.

"What is he accused of?" Caroline demanded.

"Caroline, we should go." Gilles tried to take her arm again, but she shrugged him off. She marched forward, blocking the guard's way.

"Conspiring against the revolution. Stand aside."

"On what charges?"

The guard smirked. "Are you a judge, *mademoiselle*? This man has already been to trial."

Gilles couldn't see her face, but he didn't need to. He knew those dark eyes seethed. "I hardly trust he faced a fair one," she said.

A voice from the masses bellowed, "Death to the monarchists!" Others took up the call.

The guard elbowed Caroline out of the way as he stepped down. She shoved the gate of the cart into his arm, pinning it before he could pull out the prisoner. The man cursed and released his hold on the convict. He whirled on Caroline.

"Do you want to follow him, little *royaliste*?" He gestured toward the guillotine. Before Gilles could rush in to stop him, the man seized her arm.

"*Monsieur*, please." Gilles held up his hands, but neither glanced at him. Did he run in and cause more trouble? "Can we not—"

"I think *you* should follow him," Caroline shouted. "You and all the revolutionary swine, and leave the rest of us to live in peace." She spat in his face.

Gilles gaped. Heaven help them now.

The guard turned away, but not fast enough. The spittle ran down his reddening face. With a growl, the man hurled her against the cart. Too late Gilles dove to catch her, but she smashed against the corner—the cart creaking angrily—and rolled to the filthy street.

Gilles hit the cobblestones on hands and knees beside her. "Caroline? Are you hurt?"

She groaned, pushing herself up on one elbow. Her hat was skewed and dirt streaked one side of her face. But her eyes blazed.

"Take this one up," the guard barked. "I'll bring the wench."

"Run!" Gilles jerked Caroline to her feet and thrust her away from the cart. Someone pulled at his jacket sleeve, but he elbowed them off. Another of the guard's comrades came at Caroline from the side. Gilles lowered his shoulder and crashed into him, sending the man sprawling.

"Don't let them escape!"

Gilles snatched Caroline's wrist and bolted down an alley. Calls of their pursuers echoed against the buildings as they ran. They headed south, the opposite direction from the Daubins' house. Confound it.

Surprised citizens flattened themselves against the buildings as Gilles and Caroline passed, their protests mingling with that of the guards' friends.

Somewhere to hide. Somewhere to hide. If only Caroline had decided to make people mad in *le Panier* district. Or by the docks. He'd know plenty of places to disappear.

The docks. Gilles yanked Caroline around a corner. They weren't terribly far. Closer than the Daubins' house, at least.

A feral cheer rang from behind them, chilling and cruel. Caroline faltered beside him. He glanced back. The men hadn't given up.

"We can't stop."

Caroline matched his pace, not stumbling as he twisted their path down unfamiliar streets. When the inviting ocean air hit their sweat-drenched faces, Gilles veered toward the back door of a warehouse, darted inside, and slammed it shut.

As one, they dropped to the floor by the wall, sending out a cloud of dust and straw. Something squeaked and rushed by them. Rats. Gilles didn't have the energy to shiver.

They sat panting for several minutes. Nothing else moved in the darkened warehouse, one that Gilles's family often let for storing shipping goods. Voices came and went outside, but no one tried to open the door.

Gilles's shirt and waistcoat clung to him like a second skin. His curls plastered his forehead. He brushed them back to keep sweat from dripping into his eyes.

He startled as Caroline's arms circled his waist. They trembled. He shifted so she could scoot against his side. She pressed her face against his shoulder. Perhaps trying to get the image of the guillotine blade or the satisfied roar of the crowd out of her head. Even in the darkness, the memories rolled through Gilles's mind.

Caroline didn't cry. He shouldn't have expected her to. The hatred they'd witnessed didn't lend itself to tears.

It was the same hatred he'd seen in the faces of Martel's group when they ransacked the priest's hiding place. Gilles passed a dry tongue over drier lips. He wanted liberty for France. He believed in all that Maxence and Émile stood for. But how could he look on when his compatriots had lost all humanity? If the Jacobins couldn't keep control of this revolution, what hope did anyone have of surviving it?

They huddled silently in the heavy shadows until the light coming through the cracks around the door lengthened and bent, heralding the fall of evening.

CHAPTER 22

Gilles and Caroline walked silently through the crush milling about the harbor. Most of the ship loading was done for the day, but life never settled completely at the docks. Usually when forced to pass this area, Gilles couldn't help scanning the water in dread for signs of *le Rossignol*. Today he kept his head down and a hand on Caroline's elbow.

"We'll make a circle and come back to Belsunce from the north," he said softly as they neared the edge of the dockyards. It was doubtful anyone would recognize them with so many people about, and their pursuers had long since vanished, but they still had to take care. And no doubt her father would hire that guillotine for Gilles's neck when they finally made it back.

A trio of men hefting large sacks swept by, and Gilles tightened his grip on her arm to guide them out of the way. Caroline moaned and pulled back.

Gilles released her. "What is it?" He glanced down at her arm, which she pressed against her side as she continued walking.

Dried blood tipped the insides of his fingers and stained his nails. "Wait. You're injured." He hurried to catch up.

Caroline shook her head sharply. "It's nothing. I scratched it on the wagon."

Hardly nothing with that much blood. "Let me look at it."

"Gilles, it really is . . ."

He put a hand on the small of her back and guided her to the wall where they'd sat eating *navettes* weeks before. Where he'd first realized there could be a chance of them not always standing at odds. He turned over her arm. The delicate white muslin of her sleeve was shredded and brown, surrounding a deep gash. It wasn't quite the length of his hand but extended up most of her forearm. Dirt and dust flecked the sleeve, and fresh blood seeped from the wound. Not serious, but a far cry from "nothing." If they didn't get it cleaned, infection could set in. Gilles had seen too much of the life-altering effects of infection in his days at sea. "Send for a doctor when we get you home. You need this closed, or it will get worse."

Caroline retreated. "No. We cannot let my parents know what occurred. My mother is already struggling to stay composed with all that's happening." Her voice came out shrill, panicked. "Not a word to either of them. Do you understand?"

Gilles slid a hand down the side of his face. "And how do you plan to keep this from them? You have blood all over your dress." Something he should have spotted as they were leaving the warehouse, but he'd been preoccupied with making sure their pursuers had left.

She examined her arm and gave a helpless sigh. "Can you not do something about it?"

"I am not a doctor."

Her head fell to one side. "How many years did you practice under the ship's surgeon?"

Two, almost three. "I have not gone to school. I can't call myself a doctor."

"What does that matter?" She held her arm toward him. Yes, that would need attention. Sooner, rather than later. "You are trying to convince me that this is worse than anything you had to treat at sea."

Gilles let out a slow breath. Not by a long shot.

His house was only a few minutes away. If they hurried, perhaps . . . no, the Daubins would get suspicious no matter what happened. It was nearing five o'clock. Her mother had expected Caroline hours ago.

After one last glance around the harbor to be sure they weren't followed, Gilles led her to *le Panier* district. He let them in the front door to a silent and dark house. A large chest took up part of the front hall.

Père. Perfect.

Gilles called out to his parents, but no one answered. He could only hope they'd gone to Rosalie and Victor's, and that they wouldn't return any time soon.

The kitchen, golden in the evening sun that streamed through the windows, sat empty. They must have let Florence go home early, and Gilles thanked the heavens. One less person to explain things to.

"Sit here," he said, directing Caroline to the bench at the table while he removed his jacket. He located a candle and lit it, then brought it to Caroline's side. Shears, a knife, a strip of plaster, a bottle of wine, cloth. Perhaps a needle. He ticked off the things he'd need, bustling around the kitchen like Florence and Maman before a large meal. Get the grime off his hands. Boiling water would take too long. They'd have to use the warm water left in the kettle.

Caroline's eyes tracked him wherever he went, and he had to keep repeating his list of tasks to prevent distraction. The dirt, sweat, and blood that covered her did not deter the attraction swelling in his chest. *You already tried kissing her once today.* He practically threw himself down the ladder into the cellar for the bottle of wine. Best to not repeat that rejection.

When he'd assembled everything, he settled down beside her on the bench. Red lines tracked across the whites of her eyes. She'd removed her sullied gloves and bonnet, and stray curls rimmed her pallid face.

"Ready?"

She nodded.

Gilles gingerly lifted her sleeve, trying to maneuver it around the wound, but the slender shape did not give him much room to work. Eventually he had to resort to cutting the tiny stitches along the seam. Not that the sleeve would be easily salvageable where it had been torn. He rolled the excess fabric up around her elbow and set her exposed arm atop a cloth. That had been the easy part. "What will we tell your parents?" He unstopped the bottle and poured a trickle of wine over the cut.

Caroline gasped as the crimson liquid mingled with blood and ran into the cloth below. Bits of straw and dirt washed out, but tiny white fibers from the sleeve still clung inside. Blast. "We can tell them we got held up by the crowds, but they can't know what happened."

"That was a long time to get held up by crowds." Gilles took up a needle. Should he try to strap down her arm? It's what he would have done on the ship. Somehow the thought of tying her to the table, even for her own good, soured his stomach. "I don't think they'd believe it."

"We will have to think of a story."

He prodded a fiber in the cut. Caroline flinched, and he drew back the needle quickly. "You will need to hold very still."

She tensed, but as he went to continue his extraction, she twitched again. Gilles sat back, chewing on his lip. This wasn't going to work.

He'd only hurt her more, potentially pushing the debris farther into the wound, if she moved.

"I'm sorry," her small voice murmured.

"Not to worry." Gilles turned his back to her and straddled the bench. He pinned her elbow between his arm and side, then grasped her wrist with his free hand. An awkward arrangement, but they'd have to make do.

"I mean for everything. We should have kept walking."

Yes, they should have. "That wouldn't have been very like you." Gilles poked at the thread again. This time he managed to keep her arm relatively still, despite her reaction to the pain. What he wouldn't give for a set of pincers like Dr. Savatier's. This needle wasn't nearly as effective. Maman might have had some pincers, but he didn't know where to look. After a few attempts, he lifted the fiber enough to trap it between the needle and his thumb.

"Why are they so eager to kill?" she whispered. "What did that man do to any of them?"

Gilles pulled out the thread and laid it on the cloth covering the table. "These people have been oppressed for generations."

"So they should take innocent lives in revenge?"

He started on another piece, this one deeper in the center of the wound. "We don't know whether the man was innocent or not."

"They were too eager to see that machine in use." She sank against his back, her hair grazing his neck.

A tremor surged across his skin, lovely and strange all at once. Gilles froze. "Yes, the bloodlust is out of hand." He tried to breathe normally. There was a task to complete, but he wanted to sit and drink in her touch, her feel. Evenings cuddled together before a fire played across his hopelessly diverted mind. What would he give to make those visions a reality?

"I was stupid to think I could do anything about it," she said.

He blinked away the fantasies and lowered his head to his work. "You stood up to the injustice you saw. I think most would call that courage." The candle was making the kitchen too hot. Or perhaps it was his concentration, or the lingering warmth of the hearth. Or maybe it was the press of her, the way she curved so comfortably against him.

Love wasn't supposed to find him now. What was he to do? Make her wait the long years it would take for him to finish his schooling in order to provide for her? Take his father's offer and return to sea?

He dipped a rag into water and wrung it over the wound. Nothing else seemed foreign in the cut, but a few more rinses would help his confidence. The plaster bandage needed trimming and warming. He dabbed water and blood from the wound and reached for the shears. She'd relaxed, and her breathing had deepened. He didn't think she'd fallen asleep, but he moved slowly in case. Studying with Dr. Savatier on *le Rossignol* hadn't prepared him to work under such distractions.

"Thank you." Her low voice swept through him, a welcome breeze on a hot and motionless sea. "You did not have to help me like this."

"And leave you to confront that louse on your own?"

"He might have been a Jacobin," she said.

That distinction was growing less and less important to him. "A *sans-culotte*, more likely. Though they're really just names, aren't they?"

She nodded against his shoulder. "How one acts carries more weight than what he professes."

Gilles held the plaster over the candle's flame to loosen the adhesive. She had proven that, to be sure, and had proven she believed it. He licked his lips. "Your Nicolas. He was a Jacobin?"

In her following silence, Gilles kicked himself. But so many questions had circled his mind in the weeks since she first mentioned her former intended.

"He was a Cordelier," she finally said.

Ah, yes. She'd mentioned he was a devotee of Danton. Georges Danton and the Cordeliers had melded into the Jacobins in the last couple of years. "Is that why you were so against the idea of us?"

She lifted her head to rest her chin on his shoulder. Her soft eyelashes brushed the tip of his ear, sending bumps across his flesh. *Ah, Caroline.* Did she know how she undid him with her touch? "Of us being friends?"

Gilles tapped the plaster to check its stickiness. "Or . . . or more." Too much too soon. Idiot. If only his brain functioned just now.

"Yes. It frightened me. Even though I didn't expect . . . That is, even though you only asked for friendship."

He hadn't known then that, all too soon, friendship would not suffice. "Do you still love him?"

"Oh." She gave an unsteady laugh and straightened, breaking contact.

What a foolish thing to ask. Of course it would push her away. Gilles moved the plaster slowly back and forth over the candle. She wasn't responding. That had to be an affirmative. His stomach sank.

"I suppose there is a small part of me that still wishes things had worked out in a different manner." She spoke haltingly. "To have it end with such frustration, and then to learn of his death soon after, left me struggling to make sense of it."

A bead of tallow gathered under the flame. It swelled, reflecting the brightness beside it, until the weight sent it spilling over the edge. The melted whiteness streaked down the top of the candle's shaft but slowed as it cooled near the bottom. "That must have been a great burden," he murmured, "to be in the depths of grieving and not have the liberty to show it."

She sighed sadly. "It was. But do not think me the helpless maiden wasting away as she pines for lost love. I am not the sort to believe love strikes only once in a lifetime."

A slender strand of smoke twisted heavenward as Gilles singed the bandage on the flame. He pulled it out quickly, eyes flicking to hers. Candlelight bent and ebbed in their depths. He turned as best he could on the bench. She'd soundly rejected his advances hours before, yet here she sat, lips parted and face upturned.

Diantre.

The kitchen door snapped open. ". . . and there he stood like a rat in the storeroom, the pipe in his dirty hands." Père strolled into the kitchen, Maman on his arm.

Gilles bolted upright, and the plaster slipped from his fingers. It snuffed the candle as it plopped to the table. His parents halted. Maman's brow furrowed, and her eyes widened as they looked from Caroline, to Caroline's arm, to Gilles, and back again.

"I thought we wouldn't see you until much later," Père said easily, as though he regularly found his son binding the wounds of young ladies on his kitchen table. "Did the cafés not suit you this evening?" He nodded a bow to Caroline.

"We met some trouble." Gilles snatched up the plaster and straightened it out. "Monsieur and Madame Daubin cannot know."

Père nodded at the bandage. "Shall I help you with that? It seems you would do better seated in a more straightforward position."

Gilles reddened. How awkward it must look, him straddling the bench and Caroline so near. "Thank you," he stammered. "That would help."

Père took the bench on the opposite side of the table. "Claudine, perhaps you have something a little more suitable for Mademoiselle Daubin to wear. I think if the aim is to not alert the parents, her dress's current state might alarm them."

Maman agreed, giving Gilles a curious look as she poked the fire and put the kettle on before quitting the kitchen. There would be an interrogation later.

Gilles swung his leg back over and adjusted his position. "If you would hold her arm while I apply this."

"May I, *mademoiselle*?" Père asked with a debonair smile.

The cur.

She nodded, and Père took her by the wrist and elbow. The early rigidity returned to her body, but his father did not react. Gilles lined up the bandage over the wound. Best to get this done swiftly.

"Has Gilles told you about his first days at sea?" Père asked.

Gilles pinched the wound together. Caroline flinched.

"He hasn't spoken very much of it."

Gilles pressed the bandage over the top to seal the edges of flesh together, working carefully up her arm. Wherever Père was taking this, it couldn't be good.

"Practically ran up the gangplank, so eager to get on board. His two brothers of course had gone before him, and he had begged to go for years." Père went on as though he were enjoying banter in the local alehouse, rather than assisting his less-than-qualified son play at doctor. "We hadn't even unfurled the first sail before he was bent over the rail. Stayed that way for the next four days, poor fellow." He chuckled. "But any time I asked if he regretted coming, he would beam and say he loved the life of a sailor."

"I can see that," Caroline said. "He pretends to be a landsman, but the sea in his soul appears often enough to prove otherwise."

"Ah, yes. After those first few days, he took to sailing as though he'd been born on the gun deck. One of the best sailors I've had on my crew. It was a shame when he left us."

Was this his father trying to win him back in a new way? It wouldn't work.

"But I think he will make a fine physician," she said.

Halfway. Gilles hoped his cheeks weren't as flushed as they felt. Caroline's eyes narrowed each time he pulled the skin together.

"It was not always so. You should have seen his first glimpse of a wound. It could not have been much worse than what you have here, and not from battle either, and the poor lad nearly keeled over."

"That did not last long," Gilles grumbled. He'd taken to following the surgeons by his second voyage.

Père lifted a hand and ruffled Gilles's hair, like he used to years ago, making Gilles grind his teeth. "No, you overcame that one just as quickly. As you always do."

"You must be very proud of him."

Gilles kept his eyes on his work. How would Père respond to that? They had not been friends since Père's failure to make land to find help for Dr. Savatier. Both Savatier and Gilles had left the crew afterward. Père knew what Gilles thought of him.

"I am very proud. He is a fine man with a good heart and steady mind."

Gilles paused before laying the last length of the bandage. His father always praised Gilles's skills as a sailor, but he'd never said anything of his character. Proud? A strange sensation stirred within, the ghost of that starry-eyed boy who had idolized his father.

With care, Gilles laid the rest of the plaster over Caroline's wound. A few angry scratches from the rough wagon poked out from under it, but those had welted rather than releasing blood. "We should wrap it to be certain the plaster doesn't come off."

Maman returned after he'd finished the wrapping to the sound of Père's enthusiastic tales of the sea. Caroline smiled and laughed at his anecdotes, despite the dark circles beneath her eyes.

"I have a gaulle dress in a very similar style," his mother said as she came in. "It's laid out on my bed. Let's change you out of that, and I will try to clean and mend yours for you."

"A pity," Père said, "I do love that dress."

"It will return soon enough." Maman shook her head, lips twitching.

Gilles helped Caroline stand. She pulled at the rough ends of the sleeve he'd cut. "You are too kind, *madame*. But I don't think this one is salvageable."

Maman waved a hand. "I will see what can be done. I've sent the neighbor boy for a *cabriolet*, and Gilles and I will escort you home. After you eat something and drink tea. You look positively famished."

Gilles led Caroline to the door, following his mother back through the dining room into the hall. Caroline paused. "*Merci*, Gilles. For everything." She placed the barest kiss on his cheek. Then she hurried after Maman, white skirts fluttering behind her.

He stood immobile in the doorway. So that is how it would be? She would kiss him whenever she chose and knock him senseless, but if he ever attempted it, heaven help him. It hardly seemed fair.

"That was the moment you were supposed to take her in your arms and show her what a true mariner is made of." There was a laugh in Père's voice.

Gilles turned on his heel and strode back to the kitchen. "That is not how it is with us."

Père snickered as he rose from the table. "She has you caught like a fish in a net." He gathered the cloth and the dirty instruments and carried them to the washbasin.

"Hardly."

Completely.

8 August 1792
Marseille

Dearest Sylvie,

I have been so stupid. Gilles was walking me home from the shop when we came across an execution. By guillotine. I had hoped that vile thing would not make it out of Paris, that it would remain the morbid toy of the insane elitists. But it is here. Do you remember seeing the aftermath of its first trial in April? You must, as I cannot get those images from my head. And when I saw the beams standing above the crowd, I had to see it.

The poor man they were sending to his death. They said he was conspiring against the revolution, but I doubt it was so serious as that. Just as in Paris, the people of this city need little excuse to exe-cute perceived justice. I could not be silent, and I nearly succeeded in getting myself and Gilles dragged up to the guillotine with him. I was wounded as we ran, and Gilles had to tend to it before I could show my face at home.

Papa hardly noticed I'd been gone for hours longer than I should have. Someone had lost a shipment of supplies at the factory, and they still haven't located it. He will not tell me the implications, but I fear we are on the brink of disaster. Maman was easily pacified by Madame Étienne's apologies claiming she'd invited us in to wait out the crowds in the streets. That woman is a saint, to be sure, though with an incorrigible husband and three strong-willed sons, I should have guessed as much. All is set to rights, except one very alarming thing.

Sylvie, I think I'm in love with Gilles Étienne. As though I've learned nothing from a year ago with Nicolas. Perhaps I have al-lowed myself to fall into love's trap again because this feels so different from the love before. It is more natural somehow. Not a fiery passion that consumes us both, but a mutual respect and unspoken attraction.

But in the end, he is a Jacobin. How can this last? If he knew I harbored a priest, he would cut off all contact. As he should. As I should now, before this gets too far.

What have I done? I fear there is no painless way out for either of us. And the selfish part of me will let it continue until it is too late.

M. C.

CHAPTER 23

Gilles flicked the string of the little package in his lap. One of the older members of his club droned on about the injustices they'd experienced at the hand of the king. Around him, men sat on the edge of the pews, the revolutionary fire alive in their veins. Brassy light streaming through the high windows of Saint-Cannat punctuated the fervor.

It wasn't as though Gilles didn't believe in what was being said. France did not need a king, especially not one who would abandon the country at a moment's notice to save his own neck. But they'd already said all of this last week when they passed around the petition once more. Ranting and raving with practically the same speech meeting after meeting did little to move the revolution forward. Everyone in earshot already believed in the Jacobins' cause and did not need convincing.

He slipped out his pocket watch. This had gone on for an hour. He suppressed a groan. It was nearly impossible to slip out of the church without notice. And Martel would track him down if he tried to leave early. The sorry face of a desecrated saint stared down from its perch on the wall beside him. Were he the praying sort, he might have offered a plea for intervention.

Of course, it didn't help that he planned to call on Caroline after the meeting. As he'd asked, his mother had met him at the church with a package of fresh *navettes* and a knowing smile. Bringing Caroline a treat would not look too forward, would it? Three days had passed since the run-in with the guard, and he wanted to inspect the wound on her arm, though how he'd do it in her parents' presence remained a question. What would they think about a clerk calling on their daughter, and at this hour? He twirled Grandmère's ring around his finger. The more important unknown was what they would think when he declared his intentions.

Which would not be for some time. He ran a hand over his brow. No need to start that anxious spiral in his mind again. He didn't have competition, after all. Only with a memory.

The man seated in front of him stood, and Gilles lifted his head. Jacobins meandered into groups about the nave, the orator having closed the meeting. Martel appeared at his elbow.

"Your head is in the clouds this evening."

The lavender fields, rather, but Gilles did not correct him. He rose swiftly, heart rate rising as well. "Work has been distracting lately." They'd found places to economize in the *savonnerie*'s budget. But not enough.

His friend's eyes fell on the little package. "Your mother brought you food?"

"I have to meet with Monsieur Daubin after this." Gilles laughed uneasily. "She didn't want me to go hungry." Though she would have brought something besides *navettes* if that were truly her worry.

"You are going to the Belsunce Quarter, then. I will walk with you. I have business there as well."

"Oh, but I must go quickly." Gilles nodded toward those

congregating around the church. "I do not want to pull you from important conversations." Such a companion would damper the excitement of the walk.

"My errand is more pressing than socializing."

It wouldn't do to make Martel suspicious, so Gilles shrugged and left the church with his comrade. Martel spit at the saint statue as they descended the steps, then moved closer to Gilles with a lowered voice.

"I have another lead on Franchicourt."

Please don't let it have anything to do with Caroline. "What have you found?"

"Someone who met a frazzled man of his description a few weeks ago." The wolfish grin on Martel's face sent a chill down Gilles's back, even though he was not connected to the situation. "It was in the Belsunce neighborhood. They agreed to questioning. I always appreciate your perspective. Perhaps I can wait while you speak with Daubin and you could join me for the interview."

Gilles's stomach leaped into his throat. "Oh, no. It will be a long meeting. We have much to discuss."

"Employers." Martel wagged his head back and forth.

"I agreed to it." And Daubin had no knowledge of the impending visit. "What's more, my mother wished me home as soon as possible. My father is in town for only a few days before he sails with a shipment for Corsica."

"I did not think you gave your father such priority."

Gilles put the *navettes* in his pocket to keep from crushing them completely. The paper was already crinkled from how much he'd handled them. "It is for my mother, not for him."

"Have you read the reports from Paris? There is unrest with the volunteers. We might have some interesting news shortly." Martel rubbed his hands together, as though anticipating a rich postdinner *gâteau*.

"I should hope not. Violence in Paris does the rest of the country little good." He kept his eyes on the road beneath them.

"It will allow Marseille's best to prove their courage." Martel went on as though he'd heard nothing. "And there is talk of forming another battalion very soon. We might be on our way north in a few weeks."

Gilles kicked a rock in his path. He'd never join the *fédérés*. Not after forming this attachment to Caroline.

"Have you heard from your brother?"

"Not a word. He is apparently very busy."

Martel nodded gravely. "Yes, of course. The cause of liberty keeps one always on the move."

Martel's rapid pace suited Gilles just fine that evening, more so when the young man stopped talking and focused on walking. They reached the Daubins' house faster than Gilles would have on his own. It was not until his lanky friend turned the corner, leaving Gilles alone before the front steps, that he realized he had not come up with an excuse to give the Daubins for his visit.

He ran up the steps and knocked before he lost his nerve. What could he ask Monsieur Daubin? The newest batch of soap had started today, though he wouldn't usually make a house call to ask after it.

The cook answered the door instead of the footman. For a moment, the middle-aged woman stared at him. Her face paled. "Yes?"

"Good evening. Is—is the family at dinner?" He shuffled his feet under her owl-like stare.

"They are not."

"Is the *mademoiselle* at home? I wished to speak with her." He toyed with the *navettes* in his pocket. If he got them out, the cook might insist on taking them to Caroline herself and turn him away. "It is a matter of importance." His smile did not feel convincing.

"You are Gilles Étienne."

"Yes, *madame*."

The cook's eyes narrowed as she looked him up and down, then glanced over her shoulder. "If you'll follow me to the salon."

Praise the heavens. She allowed him to step through and slammed the door behind him. Gilles flinched at the crash. Then she marched him down the corridor, past the small front parlor where the Daubins usually entertained callers. The woman practically shoved him into the large salon where they'd gathered after dinner all those months ago. A fire burned in the hearth, but no one occupied the room.

"If you will please wait here." The strain in the woman's voice put Gilles on edge.

Voices sounded in the front hall. The cook ran from the room and pulled the door shut behind her. Gilles stood in the middle of the salon, unsure if he should sit since he had not been invited to. He removed his hat before taking the package of *navettes* from his pocket. An eerie silence permeated the chamber. He couldn't even make out the ticking of the clock on the mantel.

Gilles wandered over to the writing desk in one corner, where Caroline had sat much of the evening he'd come to dinner. A page sat on top with a quill in the inkwell. The date, address, and *"Chère Sylvainne"* topped the paper in confident, flowing penmanship. He set down the packet of *navettes* to trace a finger over the lines of writing.

Sylvainne. That would be her cousin in Fontainebleau. He wished she'd finished more of the letter. What he wouldn't give to know the thoughts running through her head once in a while.

The door opened. Gilles straightened and stepped back from the desk, lest anyone think him encroaching on her privacy. He left the *navettes* for her to find when she went back to her writing.

A slender, balding man stepped in and closed the door softly behind him. He wore a simple black robe that reached to the floor, with tabs of cloth about the collar.

"*Madame* wishes to . . ." The man's eyes locked on Gilles.

Gilles's mouth went dry.

"*Aie pitié de moi*," the man breathed, backing up and fumbling for the door handle. "Lord have mercy."

A priest. Here, in Caroline's home.

The man darted out the door, rapid footsteps echoing down the corridor. Gilles's nails dug into the brim of his hat. That wasn't . . . Couldn't have been . . . Surely . . .

Light purple cotton drifted into the room. "Gilles. This is unexpected." Caroline's tense smile did not reach her eyes.

Gilles dropped his hat. He crossed the distance between them and snatched her by the shoulders. "*Que diable,* Caroline! Have you lost your mind?"

Her face hardened, and she shook off his hands. "I am not the one shouting. Don't accuse me of losing my mind."

"A priest, Caroline? You're harboring one of them?" He clapped a hand over his face and retreated until he hit the sofa. Martel was in this neighborhood sniffing about like a foxhound. His insides clenched as a thought dawned. "That was Franchicourt, wasn't it?"

Caroline stood with hands calmly folded. "We agreed not to speak of him again."

"I didn't know you were housing him." He grabbed fistfuls of hair as he leaned against the back of the sofa. There was a traitor in this house, and it was only a matter of time before Martel discovered him. What would happen to the Daubins? The guillotine blade flashed, sharp and ravenous. Nooses swung heavy on lampposts. Still forms lay in the streets. Blood seeped across her soft, olive skin. "How long has he been here?"

"Since his previous refuge was compromised."

More than a month. If that group who had ransacked the house knew the priest had come here, they would have swarmed. Gilles rubbed his eyes with the heels of his hands. What did he do now? Lie to protect a priest and save Caroline? And his own family was more at risk than ever. "My friend Martel is scouring this district looking for that priest. He will find him eventually. I don't understand why you would put yourselves in this danger."

Caroline folded her arms. "And I do not understand why you still call that rat a friend."

In truth, neither did he. Gilles turned his back on her. It took little effort to imagine the *sans-culottes* descending on this parlor and tearing its brocade sofas and gauzy curtains to shreds. Soot and muck would stain the imported rugs. Furniture would splinter under an ax or a club. Martel would oversee it with glinting eyes, especially if he caught the priest this time. The same glinting eyes that had raked over Caroline when he visited the *savonnerie* and that would relish the opportunity to do it again, and more, if she were captured as a traitor to the revolution.

He planted his hands on the back of the sofa as his stomach threatened to heave. "What am I to do?" Gilles hadn't meant to say it aloud. "Martel frequently pulls me into his search."

"I don't know." Her voice was soft, devoid of its defensiveness. "Why did you come here unannounced?"

"I wished to check on your arm." He thought he'd earn the suspicion of her parents with this visit. Now he'd kicked open an anthill.

"Do you still wish to?"

Gilles pushed off the sofa and swept the hair from his face. He might as well finish his task.

Caroline pulled off the green jacket that covered her dress's half sleeves. "You won't have to cut my sleeve this time."

Unable to muster a smile, he took her forearm in his hands. He rolled the white bandage off to reveal the plaster, which still stuck well. The skin around the plaster had lost its redness. He slid a finger down her arm. No swelling. "In a few more days, you may remove the plaster, but do not force it. Keep it covered with a clean bandage, and it should heal well."

"Our cook has been helping me with it." That would explain the cook's willingness to let him in at such an odd hour.

He paused to drink in one more moment, cradling her arm in his hands, and then released her.

"That is all?" she asked.

Did she long for more, as he did? Another touch, another moment pretending this revolution couldn't reach their little haven of something between friendship and love? Gilles bent to collect his hat from the floor as she twisted the bandage back around her arm. "I will take one more assurance that you do not want to kiss me, and then I shall be on my way. You are on the mend and have no more need of a former surgeon's apprentice."

Her eyes searched his, though he did not let her search for long. She didn't repeat her well-used reminder.

"What are you thinking?" she asked, pulling the sleeve of her jacket over the rewrapped bandage.

Gilles sighed. Too many things. "That perhaps your Nicolas was right, and it is foolish for a Jacobin and a *royaliste* to hope for something beyond just passing friendship."

Caroline's fingers paused as they worked over the buttons up the front. "Did you hope for more?"

He rubbed at the back of his neck, which had gone hot. "I should go." He sidestepped and made for the door, keeping his eyes on the ground.

"Is this *adieu*?"

Adieu. A final goodbye. Did her voice tremble, or did he imagine it? Yearn for it? "I must think on everything." He nudged the door open. Beyond it, the front hall sat dark. What were the odds that Martel's business finished the same time as his? His comrade would likely take the same route back to the Panier Quarter. He could not, under any circumstances, let Martel catch him so soon after this revelation. "The last thing I want is to endanger you. Martel will continue his hunt until Franchicourt is found."

"He's a good man, Gilles." No emotion leaked through Caroline's defenses. She stood calmly, as though speaking of the weather. "As are you."

To the Jacobins, both sentiments could not be true. Most among the monarchists would also disagree with the comparison. The other side was always wrong. Truth could not come from both extreme sets of belief. "I don't know what that means anymore." He exited the room, not looking back and not sure whether he could trust himself to see that determined face again.

. . . At least he left navettes. *You'll excuse any crumbs.*
Will anything beautiful, anything rich, anything that makes life worth living survive this abominable revolution?

"How is your girl?"

Gilles blinked. He paused on the threshold into the house, pinning himself between the doorframe and the door. Père lounged on the sofa just inside the sitting room, seaman's cap covering his head. The corner of a sheet of paper poked out around his shoulder.

"Oh. Very well. *Elle va bien.*" Gilles swept the door shut and pulled off his hat. The aroma of roasted vegetables lingered in the foyer, but rather than make his mouth water, it caused his stomach to protest. He didn't need food. Just time to think.

Père turned. The shortness of his hair under the cap made his thick, raised brow more prominent. A pair of eyeglasses perched on his nose. When had Père started wearing those? "Your words say one thing, and your voice says another."

Gilles had attempted nonchalance. But the sight of the shocked priest standing at the entrance to the salon would not leave his mind. Caroline was harboring a priest. It shouldn't have surprised him. Deep down, he'd known the good probability of her at least knowing the man's whereabouts.

"Perhaps you should sit." Père inclined his head toward the opposite couch.

Talking with Père was the last thing he needed tonight, and yet Gilles shuffled obediently into the room. Daubin still wished him to talk to his father about an arrangement. Business would be a distraction. He sank into the sofa. Its soft familiarity did not cradle him as usual. He planted his elbows on his knees and buried his face in his hands.

"Did she refuse you?"

Gilles's head shot up. "Refuse me? I did not make her an offer."

"Why not? What are you waiting for?"

One of them to change their beliefs. A peaceful end to the violence. Stability in France. A miracle. The impossible. "Caroline and I are not marrying."

Père's spectacled eyes returned to the paper in his hands. A small stack of documents sat beside him. The next contract, no doubt. "Is that an unspoken agreement, or did she make that clear this evening?"

Gilles flopped against the back of the couch. This man was intolerable.

"Tell me she appreciated the *navettes* at the very least. I wouldn't want you to have to force them down your own throat." He picked up another page. "Though I would offer to help you dispose of them, if you haven't already."

"I left them on her desk, and she did not say anything about marriage, to refuse or to accept, this evening."

Père went back to the first page he'd studied, then swapped them again. "Despite your political alliances, the two of you are closer in your beliefs than it sometimes appears."

"I never took you for a matchmaker." Gilles spun his grandmother's ring around his little finger.

"Not many opportunities to practice at sea," Père said. "Though I try to stay far away from that business. Too dangerous."

"Then you'll excuse me if I don't appreciate you trying to meddle in my affairs."

Père lifted his shoulders, unaffected by the remark. "I do not think the solutions to what this country needs are as obvious as your Jacobins seem to think. I hope you have not been blinded by their fancy words and lofty dreams."

"The people of France want leaders who will create change," Gilles growled. Somehow his father had turned traitor in his time away.

"And it may be that this country needs a new government." Père nodded as he read. "It also may be that the government currently forming is not the one France needs. In that case, you and your *mademoiselle* would both be right and both be wrong."

"Caroline wants a return to the old ways. She wants to be able to dance again and carry on in her high society." Gilles dismissed the ridiculousness with a flutter of his hand, but then let it drop to his lap. That generalization was hardly fair. Yes, Caroline missed the old days, but their disagreements carried deeper. She clung to the old religion with the same fierceness Danton and Robespierre and Marat held to their ideals of liberty and equality. It wasn't as though she didn't know the possible consequences of her actions. Behind the fashionable gowns and lofty airs stood a woman unafraid to face the injustice she saw.

"Can you blame her for missing her friends and diversions?"

A small part of Gilles wished he could see her dance. She'd be graceful and steady, with a firm command of all the steps. Her eyes would sparkle in the candlelight. He could almost hear the swish of her silk gown, elegantly understated but striking. The fantasy sent a tingle over his arms.

"One quickly loses his sense of humanity without the opportunity to gather with others for a moment of frivolity," Père went on. "That is why I support my men congregating so often in the evenings. But I find it severely lacking here at home."

Gilles pursed his lips. There were still some opportunities for society, but they had become wrapped up tightly in revolutionary propaganda. Someone of a different belief would not find much diversion from them. And there were the gatherings in cafés, though women could rarely join and the meetings, again, centered on revolutionary ideals. Dancing had turned into calls for violence. So had most of the singing.

"What sort of government do you think we need, if you don't think the current attempt is working?" Gilles rested his chin on his interlocked fingers. Perhaps the Jacobins had gone too far in their attempts to put off the old regime. Caroline certainly believed so. Did the situation really necessitate such overstepping, rationalizing actions that were against their purported beliefs?

Père shrugged. "I do not care who is in power, so long as the import taxes stay low. Though, come to think of it, I would not mind a return to smuggling. That brought a fine income."

Gilles snorted. "You never left smuggling. You sneak in your piracy prizes as much as you did your smuggled goods before the revolution."

"I beg your pardon." Père dramatically threw down his papers on the stack. "Privateering. I have a letter of marque."

They'd never see eye to eye on this. Gilles bit back a reluctant chuckle. Some things would never be resolved, and maybe it wasn't of great importance that they were.

His father cracked a grin. "I just don't have a letter recognized by the current government."

Gilles stared at the man sitting across from him. Père had never admitted to that.

"Your mother doesn't much like the term *piracy*. *Privateering* sounds more acceptable, so I use that." Père sank back against the sofa and rested a foot on his knee. "Sometimes you have to make allowances for those you love, even if you disagree."

"Such as allowing your sons to pursue careers contrary to your wishes?" Strangely Père hadn't yet turned to lamenting Gilles's absence on *le Rossignol*. He rarely missed an opportunity for that.

Père tapped his chin as he nodded. "Even if the son makes a better mariner than he realizes." He slipped a hand into his waistcoat and withdrew a folded piece of paper. "I heard from Dr. Savatier on my return."

Gilles tensed. He thought Dr. Savatier had distanced himself from the Étienne family forever.

"He asked after you. He mentioned he was looking for an apprentice."

As much as he admired the surgeon, studying at Montpellier would open more doors for Gilles. Still, the offer stirred up an urge to leave Marseille and all its frustrations behind. Saint-Malo in the north, where Dr. Savatier resided, as everywhere, had been hit with the plague of unrest, but it was a place that did not mind so much if a person's fortune was made legally or not and was largely free of the stifling expectations of the Jacobins. For now.

"Did he say anything of the last voyage?" Gilles couldn't help the question.

Père ran a finger over the folded edges of the letter. "He wished to put past offenses behind us. Though we did not see things in the same light, and though one of us made a terrible mistake, he said the friendship held more importance."

Gilles studied the man he'd scorned, avoided, practically hated for so long, remembering the betrayal in the doctor's pale, damp face when he'd learned Père had put prizes ahead of the life of a dear friend. The rift between the doctor and his father had seemed irreparable. Years of justified anger, and then Savatier just forgave him? The iron fist around Gilles's heart slackened ever so slightly. Père had admitted to being wrong, after years of denial.

"I'm glad of it." Gilles mimicked his father, nestling into the warmth of the sofa. He still had to decide what he would do with this new revelation about Caroline and Père Franchicourt's whereabouts. Martel loomed in the background of his thoughts. But as he sat in the first comfortable silence he'd enjoyed with his father in years, watching the sunlight from the window dim, a solution to this latest issue with the woman he couldn't hope to forget did not seem so far away.

CHAPTER 24

Martel occupied the same couch where Père had sat Friday evening, but instead of Père's thoughtful conversation, excited chatter rattled the windowpanes. A few other acquaintances lounged about the sitting room with copies of newspapers clutched in their hands. The pages circled through the room retelling the daring fortitude of the *fédérés* in Paris.

"Thank you for letting us meet here," Martel said, slapping Gilles's shoulder. "The noise makes my mother nervous."

"*C'est mon plaisir.*" Gilles hadn't anticipated Martel's meeting to be so rambunctious when he'd agreed to it. He'd reluctantly allowed his friend to gather those helping him with the search for Franchicourt, only to keep up the appearance that Gilles had no connection to the refractory priest. But when news arrived from Paris, the meeting had turned into chaos.

"Here, have you read this from the *Journal*?" Martel pushed a news sheet into Gilles's hands.

Yes, he'd read it. To read one article was to read all of them, but he obediently scanned the type. Twenty thousand of the national guard and *Marseillais fédérés* had stormed the Tuileries Palace on August 10, carrying off the king and his family to prison. Four days ago France had been a constitutional monarchy. Now she marched toward becoming a true republic. While Gilles found the prospect thrilling, the casualty numbers jumped off the page with such force he could not ignore them. At least two hundred *révolutionnaires* had died. More than five hundred of the king's Swiss Guard. And in the mix, somewhere between sixty and eighty men from Marseille.

He wasn't having to lie about Franchicourt at the moment, but the sinking in his gut dampened his ability to celebrate with the others. How many of those men did he know? What was Maxence and Émile's role? Had they . . .

Gilles returned the sheet. "An exciting moment for France."

"To be certain." Martel hungrily read the article again. "To think we are finally rid of that despot and his greedy household."

"This calls for wine," one young man shouted.

"Indeed!" Martel nudged Gilles. "Let us raid the cellar. Surely your father has some prime offerings from his voyages."

None that Gilles would give this crowd. He leaned toward his friend, lowering his voice. "If we are in the business of humoring our mothers, I do not wish to upset my own with a riot. Would it not be better to seek out a café or an alehouse?"

Martel glowered, his first unhappy gesture of the evening. "We all must sacrifice for the cause of liberty."

Celebrating a slaughter was hardly worthy of that sort of sacrifice. Gilles swallowed. When had Caroline's sentiments seeped into his thoughts?

A knock on the door brought Gilles around but did little to disrupt the revelry in the parlor. He excused himself. Another friend of Martel's, no doubt, to add to the clamor. He took a deep breath before pulling the handle.

"Étienne, come quickly."

He stepped back at the sight of the well-made, if wrinkled, coat and breeches. The man before him was the last person he expected to see at such a party. "Monsieur Daubin?" Gilles darted through the door and shut it behind him. "What is this? Has something happened with the new batch of soap?"

"No, not that. It's about the . . ." Monsieur Daubin glanced toward the window. The drawn-back curtains revealed Martel and his friends in their excitement.

"About *him*? The . . ." Had Martel followed him to the door? The young man seemed distracted by the August-tenth business.

"Yes, about him. Caroline insisted we send for you."

Confound this onset of fluttering in his chest. Knowing she wanted him despite it all nearly erased what had happened the last time he'd seen her.

"In truth, she meant to come herself. I somehow convinced her to allow me." The *monsieur* shifted. "We need a doctor."

Gilles straightened, a sudden cold stilling the fluttering inside. "*Monsieur*, I have only had a little training in surgery on board a ship. I am not qualified—"

"We cannot go to our normal physician. It is for him." Monsieur Daubin's eyes flicked about, checking their privacy. "He has been ill for several days now. We thought it due to remorse about your encounter Friday evening, but he has not been able to eat since. Even when he tries, he can keep nothing in his stomach. He needs help."

Gilles stood immobile on the front step. Aiding a refractory priest. Not just keeping the secret but actively helping him.

Did it matter? He wanted to be a doctor to help others, to have the means to aid them in their suffering instead of standing back helpless, as he'd done with Dr. Savatier. Why did he pause at helping a clergyman?

Gilles nodded once. "Tell your driver to turn the corner and follow the street halfway down. I need to clear these Jacobins from the house before I leave so my mother does not have to."

Monsieur Daubin hurried back to his coach. Twilight blanketed the street, enough to conceal the identity of those passing the rows of town houses. Every figure seemed an informant ready to report back to the Club. Gilles closed his eyes. If Martel caught wind of this, he would see it as treason. Perhaps it was. But as Gilles had learned from three years of revolution, sometimes treason was right.

He came. Oh, Sylvie, he came. I thought it impossible after the look of betrayal in his eyes when he left Friday evening after discovering Père Franchicourt. The whole while Papa was gone, I ran to the balcony at the sound of every passing carriage. When Gilles walked through the front door, I nearly kissed him in front of Cook and Papa.

Père Franchicourt has not improved since my previous letter. The cook and I have been at his side constantly the last few days. Nothing she could think of giving him has helped. When even Papa grew worried, we debated for an hour what to do.

As I write, Gilles and Papa are transferring Père Franchicourt to one of the upper bedrooms. Gilles could not say whether bad air from being so frequently in the cellar has contributed to his ailment. He has suggested small sips of ginger tisane as often as we can coax Père Franchicourt to drink and has given us instructions for a draught to help him sleep. He does not think it a putrid fever, which is a relief to all.

This scare with Père Franchicourt has left so little time for thought of the insurrection in Paris, but I pray for you and Guillaume and your family every passing hour. The city must be a disaster. So much death. So much waste.

Maman has been in or near hysterics since this morning and has largely kept to her room. I know it will be difficult, but if there is any way for you to find Émile and beg him to write, please do. He warned us his letters might come less frequently, and it has only been a week since last we received something, but Maman always fears the worst.

And if it is not too much trouble, ask Émile to send word of Maxence Étienne. While I would hate to bear any bad news to that family, they deserve more information on their son and brother than they have received.

Gilles closed the door to the small bedroom in the Daubins' attic. Faint light from a distant window tinted the corridor blue. He'd loved the twilight hours at sea, just before the ship came alive in the morning or just after it had drifted to sleep at night. Closing his eyes, he imagined for a moment the serenity of those solitary moments and let the calm filter into his soul.

He'd done the right thing. Jacobin or not, his duty as a physician would be to help. He'd face the consequences. The priest's weak but humble gratitude before Gilles's departure only confirmed the decision. Despite not complying with the new laws on religion, Père Franchicourt didn't deserve to be hunted through the city by his zealot nephew.

Look what she'd done to him. Gilles didn't care one wit for Caroline's politics—France had no use for a monarch after centuries of abusing the power—but in one thing she was correct. Right or wrong, the people of France deserved to choose what they believed and not face persecution over it.

Creaking on the stairs brought Gilles's head up. A little glow appeared, haloing Caroline's face. "Gilles?"

What was this smile that split his face, as though the very real danger she'd drawn him into were nothing but a fleeting nightmare?

She hurried toward him, making the flame of the candle in her hands flicker. "He'll be all right?"

Gilles nodded. "I think the likeliest cause is bad food. Your cook said he received some provisions from a parishioner. That might have been the cause." He kept his voice low so as not to be heard by the cook and priest in the nearby room.

"A parishioner." Caroline's gaze dropped to the floor. "As though there is a real parish anymore. Sometimes I wonder if this is all in vain. Why would a person try to stand for their beliefs, when legions stand ready to storm all safe places and murder any who oppose?"

The weight of Grandmère's ring pressed into his little finger. *Jamais en vain.* Never in vain. "Perhaps someday we will find a solution to which both sides can agree. But that can't happen if you give up."

Her brow furrowed. "You want me to fight?"

"I love it when you fight."

A thrill raced up his arm as her fingers closed around his. She didn't meet his eye, just stared at their joined hands. "I'm sorry for everything. I know you wouldn't have chosen to be involved in this. But thank you for coming."

He smoothed his thumb across her cool skin. "Life throws us more things we don't choose than things we do." Such as falling in love with the woman before him. He wouldn't have chosen it before their humiliating meeting, but he also wouldn't trade this affection for the richest prize a mariner could imagine.

"I suppose this is goodbye?" She gave a mirthless laugh. "I thought Friday evening would be the last I'd see of you. I should be grateful."

Gilles tilted his head, but she still would not match his gaze. "Do you want it to be?"

"I do not particularly enjoy goodbyes." A curl came unwound and fell across her face, but she didn't release her hold on him to push it aside.

Would she go on? Breath caught in his chest as he waited.

"I do not want to say goodbye to you." She squeezed his hand, and his heart pounded like a row of twelve-pounder guns unloading their shot. His tongue sat paralyzed in his mouth. It took several attempts at swallowing before he could call up words.

"I will gladly take that over an insistence that you do not want to kiss me." He caught the wayward curl gently between his fingers and lifted it out of her face, which she'd turned up to him with an unconvincing scowl. "I do not want to say goodbye to you, either." He swept the lock into the rest of her curls, using light tucks to secure it. "Not tonight. And not forever."

Her eyes fluttered closed as he worked. One corner of her full lips tugged upward.

Kiss her. Ciel, how he wanted to. Would she pull away again? The curl was secure, but he let his fingertips linger in her soft tresses.

"There is only one way to ensure that never happens," she murmured. In the candlelight her lashes cast feathery shadows which wavered as he trailed across the line of her hair.

Only one way—to marry her, to look past their disagreements, and to find common ground. Lashing a slipshod privateer to a sleek frigate would look comical at best, but perhaps he could offer the protection her father's once prestigious position had. Safety could be worth the price of living poorly through his schooling, though he could not say if she would see it the same. Gilles brought her hand to his mouth and placed a tender kiss on her knuckles. A hint of lavender touched his nose, drawing up the sensation of her lips moving fiercely against his in the midst of the blossoming fields.

"You gave your word," she whispered, but no accusation tainted her voice. Yes, he'd promised not to kiss her, but so much had happened since that Sunday on the road by the vineyards.

"Do you wish me to keep it?" His lips still grazed the back of her hand, which had warmed under his touch. He didn't move. She would have pulled away if she wanted him to keep the promise. At least the Caroline he knew would have.

"Not anymore."

He tugged her hand, easing her closer. "Truly?"

"I'm not certain why you're waiting."

Neither was he. He slipped his hand along the side of her neck, pulling her face toward his. Her stolen kiss in the lavender fields had only made him want it more. Heat surged through his veins as though he'd swallowed a Mediterranean sunset.

Hinges creaked down the hallway. They jumped away from each other, whirling to meet the intruder. The cook, carrying a teacup. Gilles fought to still his panting.

"He's finished this." The woman's lips pursed as she glanced between the two of them. "I think the *madame* would do well with some tea. Would you like to take it to her, *mademoiselle?*" The woman hurried to them, throwing an expectant look at Caroline.

"Of course." Caroline took a nonchalant façade. How, given the circumstances, Gilles would never guess.

"Thank you for your help, *monsieur,*" the cook said, dipping into a brisk curtsy. "Shall I show you out?"

"Oh, no." It had been in his reach. And he'd lost the opportunity to kiss her. Again. "I have business with Monsieur Daubin."

The cook nodded. "He is in his study." She motioned for him to precede them down the stairs.

With one fleeting glance at a stone-faced Caroline, Gilles shuffled past. The stark disappointment would have to wait to be satisfied. But he swore it would not wait long.

He only had to face her father first.

CHAPTER 25

18 August 1792
Marseille

Chère *Sylvie,*

Maman was at the pianoforte this morning. I don't remember the last time she sat at the instrument. And of all things, she played Sur le pont d'Avignon, *the song I've had circling in my head since returning to Provence. I hadn't heard it played in ages until I came down for breakfast. It was so curious to see her plucking away at the merry tune. A few days ago, when Papa went for Gilles, she was near to hysterics, and she hasn't been at ease since Père Franchicourt entered the house. But this morning she was as close to relaxed as I have seen her since my return, and I cannot understand why. I asked if she had heard from Émile, and she said that she hadn't. I thought the reminder would turn her mood, but it dampened it only slightly. She also hadn't heard from Guillaume, and despite this happy episode, I ask that you have the little knave write to his mother so she may worry less about at least one of her sons.*

The last three or four days Papa also has had an odd manner at breakfast, which he has taken sitting at table with the rest of us instead of in his study or rushing off to the savonnerie. He even spoke throughout the meal! Of all the shocking occurrences. When he finished this morning, he bid me a good day before he left. After the tension of a few nights ago, I cannot think what has entered my parents' heads. I hardly know them from who they were a few days ago. I've half a mind to find a way to the savonnerie to ask Gilles if he has noticed anything strange, though I doubt he would have much insight. I would not mind seeing him this morning.

Oh, who am I fooling? I am aching to see him this morning. And every morning. Not to mention every evening. And all through the day. Was I this terrible with Nicolas? Tell me truthfully.

Père Franchicourt has improved a small amount each day. He has been able to eat a little gruel and the ginger tisane Gilles suggested. He sleeps for several hours, which gives me hope that he is on the mend, as he hardly slept from Saturday to Tuesday. Perhaps it is as Gilles told the cook, that he would have turned the corner that night regardless of Gilles's help, but just having him there seems to have affected all in the house for the better.

Praise the heavens none of your clerical guests have needed a doctor's care. I'm certain it is harder to find anyone to trust so close to Paris. I am very fortunate, since one of the only people I trust has gone through much training as a surgeon's mate at sea, continues to learn through extensive reading on the subject, and is more handsome than a savonnerie clerk has any right to be.

So much danger surrounds us in these troubling times, and yet I cannot be weighed down. Where has the fear and frustration gone? They are swallowed up in a mischievous grin and pair of warm brown *eyes. I am a hopeless cause, and yet more full of hope than I have been in more than a year.*

Affectueusement,

Marie-Caroline

Gilles pulled out his watch and held it up to the light coming through the Daubins' salon window at the back of the house. Three minutes to nine o'clock. He took a fortifying breath and ran a hand through his hair. Maman had offered to cut it that evening. He should have let her, instead of pacing his room for two hours after dinner.

In the darkness, the street before the Daubins' house was nearly empty, for which he was grateful. Unnecessary attention from over the low garden wall would make him lose his nerve.

"Marie-Caroline, you look lovely this evening." Madame Daubin's chipper voice carried through the slightly open window.

"I haven't changed a thing since dinner." Caroline's level tone sent a wave like that of a warm southern sea through him. Though he couldn't see her, the image of her seated by the hearth, brow raised in that knowing way of hers, flashed across his mind's eye and nearly drew a chuckle. He shouldn't have expected the mother to act normal. And even more, he should have known the daughter would get suspicious. "Maman, really. Is something wrong? You have been acting so strange today. Shall I help you to your room?"

"Of course not. I feel wonderful. In fact . . ."

Was it time? Gilles pushed off the wall. The balmy night air rang with the harmony of crickets and a distant nightingale cheering him on.

"How would you like some music, *ma fille*?" Footsteps crossed the salon floor.

"You have been suddenly musical today." Of course Caroline suspected something. Gilles pulled at his waistcoat. The cloth was thin and perfectly suited to the evening, and still it stifled him. He skirted around the light that painted the soft grass outside the salon. "I think I shall go check on Père Franchicourt."

Gilles froze. No, she couldn't leave. He hazarded a glance toward the window but couldn't see anything more than a fold of Caroline's lilac skirt as she stood.

"I will send the cook in a moment. What I'd really like is a few heads of hortensia from the garden. Would you cut some for me? I think they would look very nice arranged on the pianoforte."

The blue rounds of hortensia blossoms swayed not far from him, bobbing their heads encouragingly. This was it.

"Now?" Caroline asked.

"Yes. Here, I have some shears."

He turned toward the double doors that led out of the salon into the garden and forced his hands down to his sides.

Caroline's voice floated out into the garden. "You came rather prepared this evening, Maman."

Gilles twirled Grandmère's ring around his little finger. He knew she'd accept, but the pessimistic pieces of his mind insisted she had too many reasons to decline. He was a clerk. A privateer's son. A Jacobin. His heart leaped into his throat when a small crack of light appeared between the doors and then widened. The smooth lines of her silhouette darkened the entrance before disappearing into the dimness of evening as she closed the door.

She paused for a moment. "Ah, there you are, Gilles. I thought I'd find you out here."

"Was it very obvious?" He itched to knead the tightness from his shoulders.

Caroline glided toward him, her pale gown turning from azure hues in the moonlight to soft purple as she crossed the patch of candlelight on the lawn. Madame Daubin had positioned nearly every candle in the room by the window, making matters more conspicuous. "I suppose I hoped you would be out here."

A smile spread across his face as he met her in the middle of the grass. How wonderful to see her under calm conditions. That hadn't been the case in weeks. "Then I am glad to satisfy your hopes."

The tips of his fingers longed to slide around her waist and pull her against him. He could almost feel the glossy silk of her gown on his palms. Finally, finally, he would press his lips to hers. Relish the moment. And for the first time in his life put all his heart and feeling into a kiss.

But not yet.

A quick glance at the house showed a shadow cross an upper-floor window. The form should not have frightened him, not after speaking with Monsieur Daubin on this subject several times over the last few days, but still Gilles straightened. He must follow the proper order.

Caroline watched him, the hint of a wry grin on her lips. She saw straight through him, as always. Gilles gulped and tried to match her ease in posture. Madame Daubin was to give them a few minutes before she began, but Gilles's mind had gone blank. Perhaps he should have prepared a script for tonight.

"What brings you here this evening?" Caroline prompted. "Are you here to ask after the invalid?"

"Your father said he was on the mend." Of all things to discuss, the priest.

"Then you are here to see my father on business?" Had she leaned in closer? The brilliant moonlight reflected in her eyes, while the night breeze sent a puff of lavender perfume across his senses.

Breathe, Gilles. "Dancing."

She cocked her head, and a thick curl bounced against her neck. "Dancing? Here?"

Gilles cleared his throat. "Of course. Why not?"

"Are you teaching me one of your revolutionary *farandoles*?" The lift of her brow told him exactly what she thought of that.

"In fact, I was considering an *Allemande*." He had practiced with Maman and Florence for the past three nights, and he'd mastered the intricate figures. Mostly.

Her eyes sparkled, but this time not from the moonlight. "We have no music. Are you to serenade me as well?"

As though she'd been listening, Madame Daubin struck the opening chords on her pianoforte. The cheery melody of *Sur le pont d'Avignon* skipped through the open window to fill the garden. Caroline's face softened, the teasing attitude dissolving.

"Will this do?" Gilles extended his hand. The thrill raced up his arm even before her hand settled into his. He hadn't worn gloves. He knew she wouldn't have them, just coming from the house. "I apologize it isn't as elegant as it should be. Our ballroom has a bit of a draft, and I could not think of any other guests to join us." Nor did it have a decent dance floor, refreshment, orchestra, lighting—

Caroline squeezed his hand. "It's perfect."

He twirled her to start the dance. Her skirt swished, and a tiny laugh, almost a giggle, escaped her. Then he turned under their joined arms as they moved in a wide circle about the lawn.

Should he ask now? No, let her have her moment to dance. Would asking during the dance make it all the better? Where was Max when he needed advice? He should have asked Maman before leaving.

He turned, then she turned, again and again while the dizzying melody guided them across the lawn. Almost of its own will, his hand started to linger at her waist as their arms wove through intertwining figures. After a moment, she returned the gesture. Her fingers trailed across the small of his back, and suddenly his pulse thundered in his ears. That mischievous grin of hers flashed in and out of the candlelight's caress.

Heavens above.

He stumbled out of the steps, catching her in his arms. She kept spinning, laughing as they nearly toppled to the grass. Enough. The swelling in his chest was about to drive him to insanity. "Caroline," he said breathlessly, "I must—"

"Monsieur Gilles!" A voice from the street broke through the merry tune as the gate clattered open.

Caroline spun toward the sound, breaking their grasp. Gilles blinked, the cool left by her sudden distance awakening him like a plunge into a frigid sea. Someone barreled toward them in a dress and cap. The woman waved something in her hand.

"Florence?" He fought to keep irritation from his tone. She knew what he'd planned for the evening.

"I'm such a fool," the young woman wailed as she approached, shoving a folded paper at him. "I put the letter in my pocket this morning, and I meant to give it to Madame, but I forgot until I returned home, and when I found it this evening I ran straight back, and—" He couldn't tell if she was gasping or sobbing.

"Calm yourself, Florence." He held up a hand as he took the letter. The crescendo of anticipation in his center, now without an outlet, itched to turn into anger at this interruption. A letter? How could this not have waited?

"I gave it to Madame," she continued, as though she hadn't heard him, "and she read it and told me to come straight here."

An eerie prickling tiptoed up his neck. Had Père's ship gone down? Thirty years his mother had fought the constant worry her husband would never return. He glanced down at the folded page. The sealing wafer and its waffled stamp mark faced him with the direction side toward the ground. A ragged tear around the circle of paste marked Maman's haste to open it.

But Père hadn't left long ago. It was too soon to hear about a sunken or taken ship. That could only mean one thing.

"Monsieur Maxence!" Florence cried. Her fists flew up to hide her mouth.

Gilles traced his thumb over the sealing mark, mouth suddenly dry. After a moment, he slipped a finger under the edge of the paper and slowly unfolded the letter. Maxence's bold script marched across the top of the page, and a smaller folded sheet nearly fell out. It read only "Mère" across the back and didn't seem to have been opened.

A last letter?

His eyes tracked back to the date. The thirteenth of August. His pulse quickened. This was after the *fédérés'* assault on the Tuileries Palace. Max had survived it, then. Or had he survived it by only a few days?

Gilles turned toward the light from the salon. The merry tune Madame Daubin played seemed to come from a great distance, circling the silence of the garden but not penetrating the abrupt stillness.

Mère,

I write to tell you I am well. We marched on the palace three days ago and brought down the tyrant, just as we said we would. Monarchy is no more. Despotism is no more. And to their places surge the power of liberty and equality.

We paid no small price to bring down the king's Swiss guard. Many worthy patriots gave their lives. I was wounded by bayonet, and while I have recovered my strength enough to write, you must forgive my brevity.

Gilles's grip loosened on the page. He was not a victim, then. No doubt wounded worse than he let on, based on the vague language. But if he was well enough to write, that was a good sign.

Only a few lines remained. Was he to be sent home? Did Maman wish Gilles to go to meet him? Wonderful as this news was, he could not say why she had made Florence run across the city to deliver it tonight, of all nights.

> *Enclosed is a letter I wish my brother to deliver to the Daubin family.*

The air cut off in his throat.

"What is it?" Caroline's hand covered one of his.

He couldn't bring himself to raise his eyes. They remained locked on the last sentence he'd read, unwilling to go on, unwilling to meet her gaze. Continuing could change the world forever, though less for him than . . . Gilles clenched his jaw. This was to have been a night he'd remember all of his days. For joy, not pain. How could he read on?

There was little choice. He had to know. More importantly, they had to know. Stomach burning like a batch of soap left too long over the fires, he went on.

> *I lost my dearest friend and brother, Émile, to one of the Swiss dogs.*

Caroline. His heart twisted tighter than a cable in the rope yard.

> *I missed my shot, and the blackguard fired back. It passed me by but hit a target of far more worth. I saw to it he was given a burial fitting a true Frenchman and friend of liberty.*
> Vivre la France.
> *Maxence*

Gilles drew a breath that rattled in his lungs.

Both of Caroline's hands grasped his. "Gilles, tell me." She leaned in, her face blocking out Maxence's awful words.

Beside them, Florence covered her face with the hem of her apron and turned away. Poor woman, running through the streets at night to deliver this. "Thank you, Florence. I can walk you to your house if you will give us a few moments."

Caroline's grip tightened.

Florence shook her head. "My husband came with me. I'm so very sorry, *monsieur*."

Gilles nodded as she turned and hustled back through the gate. Words. He needed words. But the cogs in his mind had ground to a halt.

"Why will you not answer me?" Caroline whispered. "Is it your brother?"

Ciel. His eyes burned as he slipped the still-folded page from Max's letter. "It is not my brother. It's . . ." He held it out to her.

Caroline stared at the square of paper. Her hands fell to her sides. Gilles waited for tears, for a sob. None came.

"What did your brother say?" she asked. Her voice wavered.

"He said that . . ." The words scratched against his throat as he spoke. "Émile did not survive the fighting at the Tuileries."

Her face went blank, and her eyes glazed, as though her mind had fled. Silence blared in his ears. He waited, tensed. *Say something.*

She snatched Maxence's letter from his hands and turned away to scan the page. Gilles hung his head. She needed her moment to understand. Then the hollowness would take over as it had for him.

"Curse this revolution."

Gilles bit his lip and reached toward her. She stood rigidly, her back perfectly straight. He took her by the arms and gently pulled to bring her into an embrace. She would not suffer this alone.

But Caroline did not budge, and his hands slipped against her silk sleeves.

Please. Let me help you.

"Curse the Jacobins and their foolish ideals." It flew from her mouth with greater force. "Curse them and all they stand for." She whirled, eyes blazing. "Curse Émile for believing their lies, and curse your brother for convincing him."

Now she was shouting. Gilles held up his hands in an attempt to calm her. "We should go inside. Your parents should know." Much as she needed this moment, cursing the Jacobins in the open could bring down the wrath of the Club on this house. "Please, *chérie*."

Caroline tore Émile's letter from his fingers and shook it in his face. "Curse this land. Curse this so-called freedom. Curse every man who ever contemplated this revolution." Her voice had gone shrill.

Gilles tried to take her in his arms again, but she shoved him away. "And curse you for making me believe it could ever come to rights."

Maxence's letter crumpled in her hand, and she threw it to the grass. The ache in his chest threatened to choke him. "There is always hope for better days to come." He kept his arms close to him, though they screamed to reach for her again. What pain had rent her heart, he could not fully fathom. But he would do anything to take it from her. As much of it as he could.

"Curse your hope. It was all in vain."

Gilles took a step back. He'd anticipated sorrow, not anger. "What can I do?"

She pulled in her chin, the candlelight glinting across her gaze. "Leave."

He blinked. "Caroline, please. Let me help you. I love—"

"Leave!" She turned on her heel. "Do not come back." Her pale purple skirts fluttered as she stormed toward the salon doors. "We were fools." Her voice dropped so that he barely heard it against the rustling of the hortensia bushes.

She moaned, or perhaps it was simply the hinge of the door as she slammed it shut. Gilles flinched. She didn't really mean that. Couldn't mean that. Grief had overcome her.

The music of the pianoforte cut off abruptly, replaced by hysteric shrieks. Wetness gathered below his eyes, and he dropped his head to his hands. He'd seen derision on Caroline's face and incredulity. But he'd never seen a fire so like hatred on her countenance. Not directed at him. The look she'd thrown him when he tried to kiss her that first evening paled in comparison.

Gilles backed away from the house, which seemed to tremble with the horrid realization coming to light for all within. Fatigue suddenly weighed down his limbs. He did not retrieve Maxence's letter but trudged to the gate. Caroline wanted him gone. He would obey her wishes tonight. Anything to lessen the unthinkable anguish.

Gilles glanced over his shoulder before he shut the gate. He ran his tongue over his dry lips, then whispered the phrase he had never muttered aloud, and which she had cut off before he could finish.

"I love you."

Would she ever give him another chance to say it?

CHAPTER 26

He's gone, Sylvie. Just writing the words, I can hardly believe them. Everything familiar suddenly feels strange. How dare the world keep on existing as before, when all our light has been snatched away? Three days has done little to dull the confusion. Or the ache.

I let myself hope that the deaths would end. Perhaps someday they will, but not soon enough for our family. Just now it seems this purgatory of twisted thought and patriotic fervor will only continue to swarm, like an infestation no one can exterminate. And though I may further call down His wrath for such thoughts, I have begun to wonder whether even God Himself can interfere.

Maman weeps herself into fitful sleeps. Papa has hardly spoken a word since Saturday evening. And I wander the corridors gazing at phantoms of former times, before Émile took up his wild ideas. I see his face at every turn, mostly the ecstatic grin he wore as he marched off to Paris. What more could I have done to beg him to stay? Did I push him away with my arguments? Should I have agreed more with his révolutionnaire reasoning and made certain he felt as much at ease here as he did in his cafés and club meetings?

The Lord only knows. We've passed the point of reconciliation forever.

The Étiennes' servant brought the news, sent by Gilles's brother. Perhaps I only imagined seeing hints because I so wished it, but I thought Gilles was about to propose. He set the evening up so wonderfully. I was nearly ready to throw myself into his arms despite both my parents watching from the windows. How I thought I wanted those words. How I held to every sound that escaped his lips, anxious for the question. What was I thinking, believing in such a fantasy? It took the stroke of death to bring me back to my senses.

I've prayed so many hours for Émile's safety. For Guillaume's. For my whole family's. I believed He would hear. What have we done to deserve this? What has any French man or woman done to deserve their loved ones being ripped from their arms by distrust and hatred and war? Why is it our lot to walk the path of martyrs?

Things that held such weight this morning—the fate of the savonnerie, the turmoil in Marseille, Maman's fits of nerves—now seem insignificant. But there is one thing that I wish would fade like the rest. In the midst of so much sorrow over my dear brother, why is there a hollow place inside that laments those impossible dreams of Gilles?

Gilles grasped a lower branch of the tree and planted his foot part way up the trunk. It felt sturdy enough to bear his weight. Moonlight guided his path as he climbed. Twigs and leaves scratched against the side of the balcony as he positioned himself as close as he dared.

His heart galloped, and not just from the climb, though he hadn't scaled something this tall since *le Rossignol*'s mast two years ago. But then he hadn't had the added worry of being discovered at a young lady's bedroom window by her parents.

Though nothing had changed about the façade, the Daubins' house seemed to hunch in the night, bowed down by the weight of what had transpired. Windows reflected a weepy moon in their rippled glass, the rooms behind them empty and black. Most were tightly shut, but those just above the balcony had been opened. Specter-like curtains fluttered on the midnight breeze, which exhaled across the balcony. The wind lifted his curls, drying the sweat on his brow.

She'd listen. That was the only thing he knew for certain. Grandmère's ring weighed heavy on his finger, and he pulled it off. It shone softly as he stroked the gold letters across its surface with his thumb. *Jamais en vain*. Never in vain.

"Caroline?" It came out too hesitant, so he tried again. "Caroline, are you there?"

He held his breath, listening. Was that a creak? Were those footsteps? He called again, as loud as he dared.

The door handle shifted, and a face appeared shrouded in shadow. "What are you doing here, Gilles?"

A tremor swept through him at the sound of her voice. It had been only three days, and yet it felt as though he'd waited an age to hear that sound once more. "Were you asleep?"

"No." She sighed, then stepped through the doorway and onto the balcony. "You shouldn't be here."

For a moment Gilles stared, his mission forgotten. Her long hair hung over one shoulder in a satiny plait. The breeze played with the hem of her gauzy dressing gown, which she held tightly across her front with folded arms. He'd only ever seen her in a state of high fashion and immaculate dress. This unpretentious vision served a sharp pang to his chest. "How are you?"

"Well enough."

He squeezed the ring against his palm. "Truthfully."

She pursed her lips. "How do you think I am?"

Exhausted. Confused. Angry. In despair. "I can imagine it, but I wanted to hear it from you."

Caroline looked away. "It will take time, but we will recover. You needn't worry yourself."

Needn't worry himself? "I cannot help but worry over you. I love—"

"Don't say it."

His throat tightened. "Please. I wish to help."

"There is nothing that you can do." She squared her shoulders. "I thank you for your concern. Now I should get my rest."

"Wait." Gilles's gaze dropped to the circle of gold in his hand. The ring sat warm against his skin. "I came to give you something." He held it out to her.

She hesitated, then crept forward to see. Her chest rose and fell before she recoiled. "No, I cannot accept that."

"Why not?" The refusal didn't surprise him, but he hadn't anticipated so sharp a sting.

Backing away, Caroline shook her head. "I think we should have listened to our own reason from the beginning. We knew it couldn't work. Why torment ourselves needlessly any further?"

Jamais en vain. The words on the ring clasped tightly in his fingers pulsed through his frame. "I will never look on our time together as needless."

A humorless laugh escaped her. "Nothing will come of it."

"But something already has." He extended his arm, pushing the ring closer to her. "I am a better man having known you these few months. Nothing will take away the effect you've had."

Her mouth curled reluctantly at the corners. "You were already a better man. You just didn't know it."

"Then you helped me discover it. And showed me there was more beyond my limited vision."

"I can hardly take credit." Her stance had relaxed, and she finally looked at him. "We should not be discovered here."

Of course not. Monsieur Daubin had been sullen and easily provoked since the news of Émile's death. Gilles hardly blamed him but did not want to excite any greater anger. "Please take this."

When she pulled back again, he hastily added, "I mean nothing by it. I only wish you to remember me when you see it. And remember that despite all that has passed, our . . ." He swallowed against the tightness in his throat. "Our friendship was never in vain."

Seconds ticked past before Caroline finally raised a hand toward him. Rough bark bit into his skin as he reached. Her fingertips grazed his as the ring lifted from his grasp. The sparks at her touch raced over him one last time, the whisper of wind across a stagnant sea. If only it would carry him through the void forming in his middle.

"Thank you." She turned her back on him and retreated to the door. "Now go. And I beg you not to return."

"*Bonne nuit, mon amour*," he whispered through the bitterness on his tongue.

She paused in the doorway. Her hand formed a fist around the ring as her shoulders lifted and fell under the white dressing gown. "Good night."

And then she was gone.

CHAPTER 27

29 August 1792
Marseille

Chère *Sylvie,*

*Why do you not write? The choking emptiness that has perme-
ated this house these past weeks is more than I can bear. I've longed
for the brightness of one of your letters. I only hope no ill has befallen
you. I must trust your silence is due to some matter of great importance, and I imagine pleasant possibilities, mostly involving a certain
dashing* monsieur.

*Everywhere I turn, I find memories. Émile and his grin striding
through the front door. His laugh over a glass of wine at the dinner
table. His quizzical brow in the corner of the salon while discussing
the revolution with the Étienne brothers.*

*I ventured into his room this morning. I don't think anyone has
been inside since we received his last letter through Maxence Étienne.
It felt as though nothing had changed. Surely he would be returning from Montpellier any day and retiring here to muse on the grand*

revolutionary ideas his Jacobin friends had planted in his head. How could it all look and feel the same when our entire world has changed?

I have not seen Gilles Étienne since that night on the balcony. I try not to think of him, but the hole inside me gapes open like a fresh wound. Can you mourn the loss of someone who has not died and who has not even really left? Especially when you are the cause of his absence. What ridiculousness. And yet I mourn as much as I did with Nicolas. Somehow knowing that Gilles is in this city, still going about his work, still planning for his future as a physician, still interacting with my father makes it just as difficult to bear. Is everything around me continuing on its normal path while my life has halted?

I hate this revolution. What a world it has forced on us.

Please write soon. Assure me that there is still happiness somewhere in this existence and that I was right to push him away. Tell me my remaining brother is watched over in the arms of our loving family. And also beg him write to his grieving mother. She direly needs some word from Guillaume.

Affectueusement,

Caroline

"So this is your soap factory."

Gilles glanced to the door, the familiar voice rattling his concentration. It was not a sound he had ever heard at the *savonnerie*. Père glanced around, hands in the pockets of his jacket. His loose neckcloth and slouched cap contrasted with the careful attire of Gilles's fellow clerks, who exchanged looks from their desks. Père was not the usual customer they received here.

"I did not expect you home so soon." Gilles capped his ink and rose quickly. How had Père entered without them hearing?

"We had good winds, and the sea favored us with none of her surprises." His wry grin did not rankle the way it usually did. Gilles could not tell if the fog of weariness dulled his usual annoyance or if their last conversation had settled some of the mistrust.

That had been back when there was still some hope with Caroline.

"Do you need something?" he asked.

Père finished his examination of the sparse room. "I have a proposition for Monsieur Daubin. You mentioned he might be interested in my business."

Most certainly. The other clerks resumed their tasks, and Gilles hurried to the door. The other clerks might suspect the dire situation at the *savonnerie*, but Daubin had not yet made them privy to how bad it was. Gilles motioned toward the *monsieur*'s office down the hall.

Père followed with an easy gait and hummed an old sea tune. Gilles might have joined in once, but he couldn't find the voice now. Who knew what he would find behind the door of that office? Perhaps a drunk employer, perhaps one fast asleep, or perhaps one who looked like he hadn't rested in weeks. Gilles had seen all three in the recent days.

Gilles knocked but could not decipher the answer. At least that meant Monsieur Daubin was awake. He opened the door a crack to spy the soap maker pacing in front of his desk, a paper clutched in his hands.

"*Monsieur?*"

Daubin clapped a hand to the side of his face. "They're gone."

Gilles swallowed. His employer's countenance had gone pale. Even paler than usual since receiving word of Émile. "*Monsieur*, is everything—"

Daubin whirled. His eyes popped, whites stark in the gloom

of the office, as though Gilles had slapped him from his solitude. "They're gone. They've fled."

Perhaps Père should return another time. Something had gone horribly wrong, in either Monsieur Daubin's mind or in reality, Gilles couldn't be sure. "My father has come on a matter of business. Shall I ask him to come again tomorrow?"

The *monsieur* dumbly held up the page he'd crumpled in his hands. "The Valois family. They've gone. And Guillaume . . ."

Valois. That was Madame Daubin's brother's family, the one Caroline and her younger brother lived with in Paris. "Gone? But where?" Gilles held up a hand to signal Père to wait, then stepped into the office. "How do you know?"

Monsieur Daubin handed him the letter. "They left just after the attack on the palace. Who knows where they went?" He rubbed his already bloodshot eyes and turned away. "What am I to tell Angelique? Caroline? My wife cannot take another loss."

Gilles's eyes fell to the paper. The writer hadn't tried to write legibly, and the person they'd entrusted to post the letter must have waited some time since it was dated the day after the attack on the Tuileries. Gilles squinted to make out the words saying they had fled the country after it was discovered they were harboring refractory priests. Just like the Daubins.

A shiver crept down his spine as he read the final words declaring that Guillaume was escaping with them. The Valois family had fled just in time. Would Caroline and her parents be so lucky if Martel uncovered their secret? The chill spread through his arms to the tips of his fingers.

"Perhaps they will write when they have reached safety." He tried to give the letter back, but Monsieur Daubin didn't take it. Was it too bleak to suspect that very soon Marie-Caroline Daubin would disappear completely? While she yet resided in Marseille, that maddening spark of hope, a guiding star on a midnight sea, kept him believing that someday the chaos would end and he might have a chance to reason with her. But if she fled France, all would be lost.

"They won't risk it for some time." Monsieur Daubin moaned. "What if they didn't make it out? Are we to ever know? *Ciel*, what am I to tell my wife?"

Gilles had never seen the proud, stern soap maker in such a state. The man rocked back and forth, floor squeaking beneath him. With disheveled clothing and pale countenance, he looked nothing like the employer who had hired Gilles and rejected Martel.

"I think all you can tell her is the truth, *monsieur*," Gilles said. They deserved to hear it. Caroline's wild grief, which she'd bridled behind those dark eyes the night they learned of Émile's death, haunted his mind. Something in his core knotted tighter than a hangman's noose. How could Caroline bear this? And alone, since her father would put all his efforts into comforting her mother.

He'd have run from the *savonnerie* straight to the house in the Belsunce Quarter that moment, but she did not want him to come to her. His eyes squeezed shut against the throbbing.

Gilles hadn't felt so helpless since *le Rossignol* sailed away from land in pursuit of a prize, while Dr. Savatier lay close to death in the murky darkness below deck. At least then he'd had someone to blame. Now the one organization he could condemn was the very group who could condemn them all for treason.

CHAPTER 28

4 September 1792
Panier Quarter
Marseille

Caroline,

I find myself with few words, all of which poorly express how I feel just now. I write simply to ask what I can do and to beg you to let me help you in this excruciating time. If all I can do is hide my adoration for the woman I love, hide the longing to once more hold you in my arms, so be it. I will do whatever you ask, no matter the sacrifice.

All my love,
Gilles

Gilles stared into his untouched coffee. The steam had dissipated several minutes ago while he pushed cool porridge around his bowl. Dishes clinked in the kitchen as Maman and Florence cleaned up from making breakfast.

"I'm surprised Daubin went for the offer," Père was saying as he bit into a slab of toast. "I meant to haggle with him before coming to an agreement."

Gilles lifted his spoon, letting thick clouds of porridge plop back into his bowl. Three weeks, and still that woman drove him to distraction. He should eat. He'd be needed at the *savonnerie* soon. Had she received his note from two days ago? He'd received no response. Which should have been response enough.

"Did you read the papers this morning?"

Gilles raised his head as Père nudged a page across the table. Neither of them usually bothered with the newspapers. Martel always told Gilles what he needed to know. The bold print across the top of the page read: "The Purging of Paris." He lowered his spoon. "What is this?"

The crafty twinkle that always resided in his father's eye had vanished. "The national guard and the *fédérés* executed more than a thousand prisoners around Paris."

A thousand. Gilles's stomach lurched. "Counterrevolutionaries?"

"Some." Père wrapped his fingers around his mug as though he needed to warm them. "There were priests, women, and children as well."

Women and children? Gilles scanned the text before him to push out the nightmarish image of Caroline being among that number. Not that she was anywhere near Paris, but as news spread through Marseille . . . The sinking in his belly increased as he read on. No wonder the Valois family tried to escape, if tensions around Paris were escalating to this.

"Marat is calling for the provinces to follow suit," Gilles mumbled as he read. "He wants the *royalistes* exterminated." The Jacobin politician Jean-Paul Marat had always taken the most severe approaches on how to deal with counterrevolutionaries. He regularly called for blood, but Gilles couldn't fathom an execution on this scale. Few, if any, of these people could have received a proper trial.

"Your brother would have been there."

Gilles nodded slowly. He'd almost gone as well. Now there were calls for a second battalion of *fédérés* to march for Paris. Martel would insist they go.

"There is always room for you on *le Rossignol*." Père stood, taking up his mug and empty plate.

For the first time in years, the call of the sea wrenched at Gilles's soul. A calm morning on empty waters cleared even the most troubled mind. The ocean had a way of making someone forget the cares waiting on land.

Gilles should have bristled at the tedious offer. Instead, he nodded without meeting Père's gaze. Even given the deal Père had made with Daubin to purchase soaps for his next voyage, the *savonnerie* did not have much promise past the end of the year. The *révolutionnaire* government had allowed the medical school at Montpellier to remain open because of its worth to society, but who knew how long that would last?

Père made for the kitchen, leaving Gilles in the stillness of the dining room. Gilles let the newspaper flutter to the table and dropped his head into his hand. Outside the window, a bird called to its friends, oblivious of the disasters unfolding on personal and public scales in the human world around it.

If he did return to the sea, he would not spend each day hoping Caroline would walk through the door. And that in itself could be worth the price.

Gilles picked at the cloth covering the table. For perhaps the first time, he couldn't see a clear path before him. Each way seemed clouded by the fog of doubt or strewn with the debris of broken plans. None of the roads called to him. If anything, they all attempted to dissuade him. Where was he to find that place of belonging? He'd never felt this uncertain before.

8 September 1792

I do not know why I continue to write to you each day. I sit here with eight folded letters displayed on my desk, all of them addressed to you, even though I know you will never read them. How I wish there were some way you could get word to us that you are safe, but I know that to be impossible for now. I don't allow myself much time to consider any other possibilities except that you, my brother, my aunt, and my uncle are safe and very far from this purgatory they still have the audacity to call France.

A letter from Gilles sits with the rest. It's more of a note, in truth. I wish desperately to answer it and wish to throw it in the hearth all at once. Gilles didn't put Émile up to joining the fédérés. I'm not so blinded by grief as to give in to mindless blaming. No, I hold the Jacobin Club fully responsible for the nonsense and lies they tell their worshipers. Gilles is one of them, even if he is more civil and understanding than the rest. In the end, he will not renounce his unfeeling comrades.

Oh, Sylvie, how did I allow myself into this mess again? Did I not learn with Nicolas? I did learn. I knew it would never work. And yet my heart pleaded that this time was different. Gilles is not so fiery as Nicolas in his defense of the revolution, but he has always believed in it.

The revolution took Émile from me forever. It has taken Guillaume, and who knows for how long? Not to mention you, my dearest friend and cousin. It is taking my family's livelihood, as Papa admitted to us this evening. My religion. My faith in human kindness.

Will I have anything left when the ash settles? Or will this strife re-duce our beloved France to blackened heaps of rubble on a barren wasteland?

I wear his ring more often than I should, and when others are near, I slip it into my pocket. "Never in vain." How can those words be true? My whole life seems to have been in vain. Yet the tiniest flicker somewhere in the depths of my soul reflects off those gold letters on the ring's surface as I stare at it. I cannot believe them, but how I long to.

Give my love to Guillaume, wherever you are. I pray you're safe. It's all I can do.

Marie-Caroline

Martel met Gilles on the steps of Saint-Cannat before the Jacobin meeting. Gilles tried to return his friend's satisfied smirk with a smile, but the stiff motion of his mouth could not have resulted in anything better than a grimace.

"I hear you'll soon be in search of work," Martel said, following him into the abandoned church.

Gilles fought the urge to swat the man away like a troublesome fly. How had word of that spread? Daubin had only spoken of it to a few. "That is not a certain thing."

"I have it on good authority it could be sooner, rather than later. *Will* be sooner, I should say."

The loosely disguised cackle in Martel's voice grated at Gilles's ears. Where had he heard that? His own employer's speculations? "I wouldn't be so certain." Of course Martel would exult in a business-man's misfortunes, especially those of Daubin.

Dark was closing in faster these days with the approach of au-tumn, and candles had been lit around them in the nave of the church. Gilles slid into a pew, hoping Martel would find a more en-thusiastic person to converse with.

His spindly friend squeezed in beside him. "You and I both know Daubin to be a *royaliste* and a tyrant. What a downfall to witness."

"He has never stood against the new government." Gilles inched farther down the bench to put space between them.

"If a man cannot declare himself a supporter of the new gov-ernment, surely he must be counted against it." Martel inspected his nails. "And if that man is engaging in anything contrary to revolu-tionary support, he should suffer the consequences."

Gilles ground his teeth. Martel had no proof. Perhaps he had come to a dead end in his search for Franchicourt and was now trying to occupy his thoughts with other matters. The president of their chapter still stood at the door greeting members. Wasn't it time to start?

Martel leaned toward Gilles, lowering his voice enough to create a sense of secrecy while still allowing his words to carry through the room. "I heard Daubin insisted his son destroy his *fédéré* uniform."

A man sitting in front of them turned his head. "Daubin did?"

"Let us not dishonor the dead with rumors and speculation," Gilles growled. Of all the ridiculous accusations. "Daubin sacrificed his son to remove the king from his palace. That merits respect."

Martel shrugged. "Émile Daubin deserves the respect, not his father, who only cares about selling his opulent soaps no one can afford."

"It is not so bad a thing to want to provide for one's family." Would his friend take a great deal of offense if he scooted to the opposite end of the row and out of this conversation?

"When it takes precedence to the good of France, it is a very bad thing," the man in the pew before them said. "France is our family now."

A dark, calculating shadow crossed Martel's face, and Gilles squirmed under the accusing stare.

"Of course, you will be too occupied to need work," Martel said.

Gilles's eyes narrowed. Occupied? He wouldn't begin his studies until January at the earliest. The desire for a wisp of ocean breeze in the heavy chapel air tugged at Gilles's soul. There were other options as well, if only he could find where he belonged.

"The battalion?" Martel draped his arm leisurely over the back of the pew. "Do not tell me your courage is still too weak to volunteer."

Blast. The new battalion, which the leaders in Marseille wished to send to strengthen the ranks of *fédérés* already serving in Paris. His insides twisted into knots as print from the newspapers flashed across his mind. A thousand dead. Women and children, cut down in prisons. He shivered despite the mugginess of the nave.

"I have already added your name to the list." Martel patted Gilles's shoulder as though encouraging him, but the edge in his voice dared Gilles to protest.

"Thank you." Gilles pretended to adjust his seat, putting himself out of Martel's reach. When was the battalion to leave? He had to fight to keep from choking on the dryness in his throat. *Ciel.* How could he stay out of it this time?

A thousand dead.

Women and children.

The president of their chapter strode to the front of the room, and conversations quieted. Gilles didn't hear his greeting. He stared at the back of the next pew, trying to slow his breath.

Martel leaned in so that he was nearly lying across the bench. "Daubin will get what he deserves. Count on it." Then he straightened and called out a cheerful answer to the president's question.

Gilles reached with his thumb to twirl Grandmère's ring around his little finger, despite its having been gone for two weeks.

Heaven help them all.

CHAPTER 29

Gilles sat in the dark kitchen and watched the hearth fire dim. Maman and Père had retired at least an hour ago. He'd stayed to douse the fire but hadn't yet pushed himself to accomplish the task.

The warning in Martel's sneer hadn't left him since last evening's meeting. Even now he could practically see his friend's beady eyes in the darkening flames. Martel knew something about Monsieur Daubin. Was he just crowing over the downfall of a successful man? He couldn't have discovered Franchicourt.

Gilles kneaded his brow. He should have gone to the Belsunce District to warn the Daubin family instead of mulling it over all Sunday long. Fool. Caroline wouldn't have begrudged him the visit if it were for her family's safety. He might not have even seen her. He'd go to the *savonnerie* early tomorrow to have a word with Daubin. Perhaps he could at least help his employer make plans in case things escalated.

He blew out a sigh and planted his elbows on the kitchen table. Not seeing her might have been as bad as seeing her.

Maman wouldn't have appreciated his venturing out. The

massacres in Paris had launched a series of attacks in Marseille against *royalistes*. Gilles had avoided such a gathering on his return from the Jacobin meeting last night. While he hadn't seen any victims, the torches and rope waving in the air to a chorus of angry shouts could have meant only one thing.

When had liberty meant only liberty for like-minded Frenchmen? Gilles pushed himself to his feet, his movements slow and stiff. Inside him, the revolutionary fervor that had once burned bright in the fuel of Max and Émile's words sputtered into dying embers and ash. France deserved better than what she'd been given. Louis XVI had been removed from his throne. Was that not enough?

He trudged to the hearth, stubbing his toe on the basin of dish water waiting to be thrown over the fire. Growling, he hopped back. Florence! Why must she—

Thump, thump, thump.

Gilles startled at the crack of a fist on the kitchen door. It was nearly midnight. Who could that be at this hour? Voices rumbled from outside as the knock came again. One voice was a man's, so it couldn't be his sister-in-law needing help. And Victor wasn't due back for another few weeks.

The protests he'd witnessed the night before came howling back to his mind. He reached for the poker beside the hearth. Père's pistols were in his room, but if someone had brought a mob, they'd do little good.

Knocking came again, more frantic this time. "Gilles!"

The cry made him drop the poker. His heart stumbled as he ran for the door, pushing the table's bench out of the way in his haste. He fumbled with the locks and jerked the door open.

A flash of white exploded through the doorway and barreled into his arms. He backed into the wall to keep from crashing to the ground.

"Caroline, what . . ." *Bonté divine.* She was still in her dressing gown. Not that he hadn't seen the frothy white robe, with its delicate lace circling her throat and wrists, when he'd met her on the balcony. The ensemble was perfectly decent, especially with the added cloak. But holding her like this set his wits abuzz.

Another figure in dark garb slammed the door behind them and leaned against it, covering his face in his hands. Franchicourt. The firelight from across the room reflected off his balding head.

"They've found us." Caroline's gasps were muffled in the shoulder of Gilles's waistcoat. Her braided hair had sprung from its tie. Beneath his arms, her whole body trembled.

The clergyman sank to the ground with his back against the locked door. "God have mercy," he murmured.

Breath caught in Gilles's chest as Martel's words from the meeting hit him. *Daubin will get what he deserves. Count on it.*

He'd said Daubin would fall sooner rather than later. He must have known.

"How did they find out?" Gilles glanced around the kitchen. If the *révolutionnaires* were on their tails, they had no time to stand in the entrance talking.

Caroline lifted her head, red-rimmed eyes glinting. "A footman betrayed us, and then had the decency to inform us when his conscience got the best of him."

"You cannot stay here." Where would he hide them? The cellar was too obvious, though the closest choice.

Her fingers dug into his shirtsleeves. "Gilles, we have nowhere else to go. Please, I beg you—"

He tightened his grip around her. How could she believe he'd turn her out? "I mean you cannot stay in the kitchen. We must find a place to hide you."

The horror on her face dissolved, and she let her head collapse against his shoulder. If only he could freeze this moment, relish the feel of her against him.

A shadow shifted across the doorway to the dining room. "What has happened?"

Caroline flinched away from Gilles at the voice. Père. A strange relief flooded over Gilles.

"Martel is after the Daubins." He took Caroline's arm and guided her toward the kitchen entrance, nodding for the priest to follow. "They've been harboring this priest, and Martel has discovered them."

The crooked grin ever-present on Père's face fled. "The *monsieur* and *madame*, where are they?"

"At home," Caroline said. "Maman and Papa are still at the house. Papa thinks he will be able to reason with the *sans-culottes*, especially when they see Père Franchicourt is not there. We escaped out the back gate and through the alley, but we could see people gathering farther down the street."

"Your mother will not be able to hold back her fear. She'll give it away." Gilles pulled at the back of his hair. Martel would see through any attempt to hide the truth.

"She was still asleep when I left. Papa was hoping to have done with it before she realized." Caroline spoke haltingly, as though she could see the hopelessness of the situation as she explained it.

Père stroked his chin. "After the riots in Paris, I have little confidence in that plan. Your skulking friend is too thorough not to turn over every item in that house."

Gilles nodded. Martel would find something. And then burn the house to the ground.

"I will go to Belsunce. You hide them here." Père moved back into the corridor toward his room.

Gilles caught his arm. "If Martel sees you, he will know we're involved and where to find them."

The sly smirk on his father's face should have rankled him. Instead, it mellowed the rising storm in Gilles's chest. "You have no confidence in my stealth? I've been pirating longer than you've been alive, boy."

"I thought you said it was privateering."

The waning firelight glimmered in Père's gaze. "They're all just words." With a shrug, he disappeared into the dark dining room.

Gilles closed the door to Maxence's room, making the candle in his hand flicker. Max would snarl like an injured wolf if he knew a Catholic priest was now hiding under his bed. Gilles wondered if he would ever tell his brother. Would he even see Max again to have the option?

Best not to think of that. He turned toward the stairs and nodded for Caroline to ascend before him. She clutched her cloak tightly around her, eyes on the floor. "I'm so sorry, Gilles. I didn't know where else to go."

"I wouldn't have wished you to go anywhere else." He rested the candlestick in her hand so she could light her path as they mounted the stairs to his room.

Maman was asleep below, and moments before, the back door had closed, signaling Père's departure. The priest was safe in his hiding place. Gilles pushed open the door of his room. Caroline paused on the threshold, peering into the shadows. They were practically alone in the darkness, the rich amber of her perfume filling the stairway. He clenched his fists and averted his eyes from the soft curls that brushed across her brow and neck. It was all he could do not to snatch her into his arms again and cover her lips with his. His whole being screamed to do it. What if this were his final chance? The heavens only knew what tomorrow would bring.

But Caroline would be gone, that much was certain.

He flinched at the sting in his chest. Likely he would not know where she went. The thought of living in a world without Marie-Caroline Daubin . . . He scrunched his eyes closed. Tomorrow. He'd think on it tomorrow.

"I was unkind," she said. "That night in the garden. I—"

"You were in pain. Confused. All is forgiven." He gently guided her into the room with a hand on her elbow. Medical books he hadn't been able to focus on for weeks lay open and scattered across the bed from his attempt at study earlier in the day. "I'm sorry I don't have a better place for you to hide. When we find your parents, perhaps we can find a better situation." He knelt and ran his hands under the bed, feeling for any boxes or books that might have been shoved beneath by accident.

Caroline lowered herself to the floor beside him to light his search with the candle. The floor looked so rough and unyielding in the dimness. "I would rather be safe than comfortable. You've done more than enough for me tonight." She set the candlestick on the floor and brushed her hair back, ready to crawl under the bed.

"Here, take this." Gilles snatched the pillow from his bed and stuffed it underneath. It might make her head too high off the ground to fit, but the thought of her lying for hours on the wood floor did not sit well.

"Oh, no. I couldn't." She paused, kneeling back on her heels.

He waited for her to speak. The room rested so silent, their breaths seemed to crash in his ears like waves lapping the shore.

"I thought it would work," she finally said, voice strained. She raised her head. "I wanted it to work more than I've wanted anything in my life. Even more than I wanted things to work with Nicolas."

Gilles nodded. She loved him, then. "I had hoped . . . That is, after all this was over, I thought perhaps . . ." Perhaps he could share his life, whatever it ended up being, with the one person whose fiery passion brought a light to his existence more brilliant than any he'd ever dreamed of.

"I don't think it will ever be over, Gilles."

He blew out sharply. "Not for a very long time." Years. Even decades.

"It's better this way." But the tightness in her words hinted she did not want to believe them any more than he did.

Gilles took her hand and cupped it in both of his. His fingers slid over the cool metal of a ring about her thumb. Its gold lettering shimmered. Grandmère's ring.

He brought her hand to his lips and kissed the smooth, amber-scented skin. Père needed his help. Maman needed to be warned. The house needed to be set at rights in case someone arrived. But he would have given anything to stay just as they were all night. If the horrible letter from Max had not come, would they have been spending this night together on the happiest of terms and in the comfort of each other's arms rather than crouching in fear on the hard floor?

"Caroline, I—"

Pounding on the front door echoed through the house. Their gazes locked.

Caroline scrambled under the bed as the knock came again. Gilles caught up the candlestick and ran for the door. He glanced behind to make certain she couldn't be seen, then dashed into the stairway.

Slow. He needed to pretend he'd been awakened. His clothes were too neat to have just come from bed. With one hand he yanked off his cravat, then unbuttoned his waistcoat. Shoes and stockings, too, confound it. The knocking continued and a voice, indiscernible from upstairs, came through the door. Gilles left his discarded accessories in a hcap at his door and hurried down the top flight of stairs to Max's room. He pulled the button that closed the neck of his shirt free.

"Gilles, what is it?" His mother's scratchy voice carried from her room as he arrived on the ground floor. "Is your father still asleep?

"I'll see to it." He pulled at his curls with his free hand, hoping his dishevelment was convincing. Because if the man behind that door was who he thought it was, Gilles would need the skills of the greatest actor the *Comédie-Française* had to offer to fool him.

He steeled himself and offered a prayer to whatever deity would take pity on him. Then he opened the door to Martel's crooked grin.

CHAPTER 30

"I have spies on every street in Belsunce," Martel said as the hired coach flew down the cobbled streets. "When I give the signal, we pounce. My uncle will not get away this time."

"Let us hope not," Gilles said. How would he have responded before knowing about the priest? It seemed a lifetime ago, though he'd known about the Daubins' involvement only for a month. He had to fight through the cold that seeped into his core to focus on their conversation.

Torches dotted the way as the coach pulled onto the Daubins' street. A few dozen citizens mingled in small groups that thickened the closer they got to the house. Gilles craned his head but could not pick out Père from the crowd. Had he made it in time? Lights in the windows suggested the family was in the home, but perhaps it was a ruse.

Martel leaped from the coach when it stopped and strode toward the front steps. He signaled to a man, one of the *sans-culottes* Gilles recognized from their previous night of destruction, with an ax.

Gilles threw himself out of the carriage, tripping into the streets and nearly falling. "No! Martel, wait." No one reached out a hand to steady him. Murmurs and satisfied smiles swept across their faces as they watched tonight's leader advance on his prey. Starved hounds licking their chops at a scent of meat.

Gilles pushed through the throngs to catch up to his friend. "We cannot just break in without warning."

"Traitors don't deserve that sort of respect." Martel nodded to the *sans-culotte*, whose hat seemed to burn a furious crimson in the torchlight. "Look at the light through the windows. They're clearly expecting us. I intend to give them a knock worthy of their crime."

The man lifted his ax, and Gilles retreated from range. Martel remained where he was, face dripping in satisfaction as the blade bit into the door's handsome finish with a crack.

Gilles looked away. *Please let the Daubins be gone.* Most of the men gathered wore liberty caps. Gilles scanned for Père's tan mariner cap. Another crack.

The door flew open, revealing a fully dressed Monsieur Daubin. He raised his hands at the sight of the big man lifting his ax for another strike. "What is the meaning of this?"

Gilles coiled to spring at the big man, who looked ready to bring the ax down on Daubin. He opened his mouth to shout. They couldn't execute justice this way.

The man finally lowered the ax to his side.

"I think you know very well what this is," Martel growled.

Daubin's eyes flashed to Gilles. "Certainly not."

He gave his employer the slightest nod. Would Daubin understand his daughter was safe?

"You are harboring a refractory priest, Monsieur Daubin."

"A priest? You are mistaken, young man." The soap maker's gruff countenance would have convinced Gilles.

Martel advanced a step, putting himself nose-to-nose with Daubin. "I have the word of your servant."

"A servant, Martel?" Gilles said. "Surely that cannot be taken as condemning evidence. Servants—"

His friend whirled. "You will hold your tongue, Étienne."

Gilles took his arm. "I know you wish to find Franchicourt, but can we not go about this in a more peaceful manner?"

Martel shrugged him off, shooting daggers with his eyes. "This has gone on long enough, and I intend to bring to justice any man fighting against the revolution."

"I am hardly fighting against the revolution," Daubin said.

A shrill voice sounded from within the house, and the soap maker turned to answer it. Gilles wiped his hands against his trousers. He had no faith in Madame Daubin's abilities to cover their secret.

"Take him and everyone else from the house while we search," Martel barked to the big *sans-culotte.*

Daubin heard too late, giving him no time to resist as the man hauled him out the front door. *Madame* shrieked from inside. Red-capped men stepped up, some of them shoving others aside in their eagerness to lay hands on the captive.

"Bring out the *madame* and the daughter." Martel threw Gilles a sneer. "I know a few of us who would like to have a little fun with that one."

Gilles seethed. He bit down on the inside of his cheek to keep from shouting. Marie-Caroline was safe under his bed at home, but the lust in Martel's eyes urged him to show the spindle-legged bilge rat the wrong end of a twelve-gun broadside.

"My daughter has returned to Paris," Daubin growled. He did not fight his captors as Gilles would have expected.

On order, men surged through the front door, and shrieks followed.

Martel cocked his head. "You lie, *monsieur*. I saw her on her balcony just this morning."

The older man's face flamed.

"And I do not think that is the only lie you've told tonight."

The *sans-culottes* dragged a hysterical Madame Daubin through the door, bedgown rumpled and cap falling over her eyes. Gilles couldn't discern her blubbering exclamations. They pushed her toward her husband, and she nearly collapsed to the paved walkway.

"I will keep watch of the prisoners," Gilles said. There had to be a way to get them out of this undiscovered.

"Of course not." Martel gripped his shoulder. "I want you searching with me."

He couldn't let the Daubins out of his sight. The horrific stories from the newspaper about the Paris massacres glued his feet to the floor. If he entered the house, there was no knowing if he'd ever see Caroline's parents alive again.

"Come, Étienne."

One of the men holding the Daubins caught Gilles's gaze and urged him forward with a nod. His liberty cap hung low over his eyes. Between the high collar of his waistcoat and the brim of his hat, a little gold hoop caught the torchlight. Gilles narrowed his eyes. Père?

"Turn over every piece of furniture," Martel cried. "Leave no door unopened."

Praise the skies. Père was here.

Gilles ducked inside after Martel and made for the stairs. He passed the spot where Caroline had sat that night after dinner, lilac petticoat shimmering about her, when the weight of *révolutionnaire* arguments had driven her to distraction. So much had changed since that night. He bolted for her bedroom. The door had already been kicked in.

"She's not here," one of the three searchers said when Gilles entered.

"Check the other bedrooms. She must be hiding." Her wardrobe had been opened, and clothing lay strewn about the floor. The man who spoke immediately jumped to follow Gilles's command, but the other two glanced at the gowns.

"If we shove a few in the corner, they won't be found," one of them mumbled. "We can come back later."

Some patriotic fervor. They were here to pillage. Gilles turned on his heel and strode to the desk as though to look through her papers. What could he salvage? Very little, unless he stayed to the very end of this when the rioters had dispersed. What would Martel do when he didn't find Franchicourt inside? Ransack the house, no doubt, as he had done before. Gilles had to find something for her. She came to him with nothing. These filthy thieves were raking their fingers through everything she had.

A stack of letters sat on her writing desk, and he picked them up as though investigating them for clues. All were addressed to Sylvainne, her cousin, though no directions were listed. All except . . .

Blood drained from Gilles's face. His note. He shoved the page into his pocket, ignoring the sting as one edge sliced across his finger. That would lead them right to his house in the Panier district.

He turned an ear toward the others. The men behind him were still discussing the dresses—which would make the most when sold and which to bring home to their wives. Gilles ran his thumb down the stack of letters. How many of them mentioned him? Perhaps none of them, but he couldn't know unless he broke the seals. He didn't have room in his pocket to smuggle all of these out.

Gilles pulled open a drawer. He prayed no one else would come upon these until he could return for them. A sheet of paper filled with Caroline's writing sat atop the items in the drawer. The first line read, "*Cher* Gilles."

His heart leaped to his throat. She'd written to him. He snatched it up and crammed it down his waistcoat. *Sacrebleu*, how many more things in this house linked her to him in a more intimate way than as just her father's employee? He pushed the cousin's letters to the back of the drawer. The gowns would only remain a distraction if he didn't make a scene.

But she'd written to him. And he hardly knew whether to float into the clouds or cower in the shadows.

Cher *Gilles*

I've been writing so many letters my loved ones will never read. Letters to Sylvie, letters to Émile, letters to Guillaume. I have not as yet written to you, though I've longed to since receiving your note weeks ago. I don't know why I picked up the pen tonight. Clearly I do not know what is good for me.

Sometimes when the long, dark nights press in and sleep evades my sincerest efforts, I let you wander into my mind. Your easy grin brings a sense of comfort I cannot find in other sources. To be with you is to feel warmth and light. It is little wonder, then, that you taught me to hope in ways I did not think possible when I first re-turned to Marseille.

There are nights when I am back in the garden with you, with the hortensia in full bloom and Maman's buoyant rendition of Sur le Pont d'Avignon *drifting through the open window. Your servant does not arrive. No letter is delivered. And when we've worn down the grass dancing the Allemande again and again, you take me in your arms and ask me to be your wife. I say yes, of course, because I* cannot refuse the thought of waking each morning to the sunlight in your smile.

But wishful thinking and silly dreams only bring more tears when I recall all that has been lost—lives and opportunities and love and happiness.

Other nights I imagine you at the prow of a ship and envy the wind as it plays through your hair. I cannot say why, as I have yet to see you on a ship, but ever since that first day in Papa's office, I have found it most natural to picture you at sea. You will hate me for saying it, I know, but you seem born for that life. Not sitting in a cramped office doing my father's bidding. I'd hoped someday to see you there, in so natural an element, but it is one more thing not meant to be.

There are times I wish with all my being that I had not fallen in love with you. I have already seen that a romance could not work between a royaliste and a révolutionnaire. You hardly gave me a chance to resist, despite your silly games and rakish air when we first met. I think I sensed, even then, that there was more to Gilles Étienne than the mask you wore around Émile and Maxence.

Then I look at this ring you gave me that night on the balcony. I think I would rather have loved you and felt the magic of your love than to never have felt its fire. Jamais en vain. Truly this spark of heaven was not in vain, and wherever our roiling world pushes our paths, I will look back on this as a sweet mercy of God rather than a curse of the revolution.

Someday the memories will not tear at my heart.

I nearly let you kiss me that night on the balcony, as you've wanted to do for so many months. I needed it so badly. My reason won over, but now I wonder if I will always regret not taking the chance.

Caroline

Furniture crashed around him. Glass shattered. Shouts and jeering shook the house. But Gilles stood silent and unmoving by the attic window, where faint light from the street illuminated Caroline's letter. He should have put it away before someone returned, but he let it fall to his side.

What a disaster, all of it. He leaned his head back against the wall and closed his eyes. When this year began, he'd been a new Jacobin, on fire with patriotic passion and eager to follow in his brother's devoted ideals. Only a year more of work, and he would have enough to pay his way into medical school at Montpellier, finally closing the door on all possibilities of going back to his father's ship. Times were difficult for France as 1792 dawned, as they had been since the start of the revolution three years previous. Peace hadn't looked impossible, however.

Then he'd met Marie-Caroline Daubin, and all the world changed. Now that future, so certain a few months ago, was swathed in uncertainty. He'd even allowed himself for a moment to consider returning to sea.

A mirthless grin cracked his face. That alone proved the instability of his current state.

Thundering footsteps rang through the corridor, and Gilles hid the letter in his waistcoat once again.

Martel appeared, murder in his eyes. "He's gone." The man let out a string of curses more vulgar than Gilles had heard since stepping off *le Rossignol.* "Gone, with no hints to his whereabouts." Martel kicked a trunk, sending it toppling and its contents clanging. He stormed to the window. "Look at them. They're only here for the loot."

Indeed, some of the crowd had already dispersed. Bickering carried from below, squabbling over the Daubins' possessions. Gilles swallowed bile that rose at the mob's greed. How were these people any different from the *aristos* whose avarice kept the peasant class in poverty?

"We head to the *savonnerie*. Now." Martel pushed off the window.

He was going to leave the house to be dismantled by plunderers in the middle of the night to continue his crusade? "I will stay and question the Daubins," Gilles volunteered. "And be certain the crowd disperses. We don't want a riot among the *sans-culottes*."

"A riot is the least of my worries. The Daubins are coming with us. We will question them on the way."

Blast. Would Martel recognize Père? Gilles followed him out, Caroline's letter crinkling softly against his chest. At all costs, he must keep Martel from discovering his true loyalties. Caroline was safe so long as his responses remained neutral. Her parents, on the other hand . . . He did not know what the night would bring for them.

Downstairs, *sans-culottes* scuttled out of Martel's way as he strode toward the front door. Men and women, some severely inebriated, filled the house. One man stabbed at a family portrait with a dull blade, uttering oaths. A pair of women pulled at the fine curtains over one window until the rod broke and it tumbled down to gleeful exclamations. Still others ran from the house with arms full of bundled clothes and valuables. The heat of torches and candles, which had been lit in every room as though mocking the extravagance, sent sweat running down the back of Gilles's collar.

When they burst outside, Martel made for the spot where they'd detained Monsieur Daubin. Gilles searched the gathering for Père's face, but he'd melted into the crowd.

"What is this? Where are they?" Martel snapped, halting.

Gilles crashed into his back and was shaken off. They were gone?

Bumps washed over his skin despite his sweat. They couldn't be gone. Where was Père?

Martel seized a man by the sleeve. "The Daubins. Where are they?"

The man shrugged. "Dragged off. No doubt they're getting what they deserve."

"How long ago? What direction did they take?" Gilles cried. Was Père with them? He wouldn't let them come to harm, but what if he'd been overpowered? Monsieur and Madame Daubin could be dead in the street by now.

Martel cursed again. "I haven't time for this." He rested his hands on his hips, surveying the chaos. "Does anyone in this city have a functioning mind?"

A stocky man appeared a few paces away. He was dressed the same as most of the other men in the mob, in simple, worn clothes and a red hat. His unwavering stare caught Gilles's notice.

Gilles knew that face. It was Père's bosun on *le Rossingol*. The bosun raised one brow and dipped his head.

A signal?

The man turned his back and extracted himself from the gathering. Gilles soon lost him in the dark.

It had to be a sign. Père was telling him the Daubins were safe. Gilles wouldn't allow himself to believe anything else.

"I will look for them." He tapped Martel's shoulder. "You go on to the factory. I'll meet you there with the Daubins when I've located them."

His friend snarled. "Good luck finding them in one piece." After a moment, Martel nodded slowly. "You go, and I will see you at the *savonnerie* in sixty minutes. They need to be questioned. Imbeciles. Who takes off with prisoners before they've been questioned?"

A rabid crowd fueled by zeal and alcohol. "I'll do my best." There were a dozen streets that led back to the Panier district, if that's where Père was taking them.

"I don't want your best," Martel growled. He snatched up a torch from someone beside him and whirled on the house. Noise billowed from the home like smoke, as though the lust for all the riches of a hard-working *bourgeoise* family had ignited. "I want it done."

His friend marched toward the house, and before Gilles could shout, Martel threw the torch at the white-painted exterior of the Daubin home.

"What are you doing?" Gilles's voice rang shrill in his ears.

Flames leaped up from the toppled torch. They flew over the grass and licked their orange tongues up the well-maintained walls. Martel fixed him with a glare, but Gilles could only watch with eyes the size of capstan wheels as the fire spread.

"*Que diable*, are you insane?"

"Sixty minutes, Étienne." The young man turned his back and stomped off.

Gilles didn't wait for Martel to leave. He sprinted for the house. The fire, fueled by some accelerant in the paint, had streaked up the wall. He stomped at it to no avail as it rose. How many people remained inside?

Martel was no patriot. He was hardly a Jacobin. Some irrepressible monster had taken up his mind, urged on by a hate Gilles would never understand.

He bolted for the front door. "Everyone out. Fire! Get out." Shrieks sounded as the acrid smoke stung his nose. Men and women who a moment before had rejoiced in their destruction now scrambled for the doors and windows. Like rats scurrying from a disturbed nest. Some brought what they could carry. Others dropped everything to run.

Gilles swerved to avoid them as he made for the stairs to warn those left inside. Whatever dream Martel and the other Jacobins had for a new France, if it included this sort of mindless waste, he wanted no part of it. Candelabras were knocked over in peoples' flights, and tiny new blazes erupted up and down the house.

"Get out! Fire!"

The hellish glow soon permeated the interior of the house, and smoke thickened the air. Though Caroline was safely sheltered beneath his bed at home, he saw her livid face everywhere he turned. This was what she'd always feared and criticized about the *révolutionnaires*.

France was pressed between the anarchy of Jacobin mobs and the tyranny of Bourbon kings. He continued to shout for people to run to safety as he flew up the stairs. Did they truly have no other option? Unless they found one, France, Marseille, his family, everything and everyone he loved would be swallowed in the flames of grand ideas.

Dawn fizzled through the curtains on the other side of the bedroom as Gilles hauled himself through the door. Soot stained his white shirtsleeves. He'd lost his jacket somewhere. A *sans-culotte* most likely took it.

He dropped to his hands and knees to check under the bed. Caroline lay curled up with his pillow, her back to him. Though his bed called to him with a siren's song and his limbs ached from a night of combatting arson, he dared not lie down on it. He couldn't remember how long it had been since they had tightened the bed ropes. No need to wake Caroline by squishing her into the floor.

Splinters, burns, and scrapes on his hands protested as he crawled to the wall. Nothing serious. The physical hurting paled to the pain and confusion that rattled his core. The Daubins' house was gone.

The *savonnerie* was gone in a similar fire, its smoke blanketing the city. And heaven only knew where its owners had gone.

Père hadn't returned. Maman paced downstairs waiting for him, though she claimed to be waiting for Florence to start their wash day. Gilles had never seen so many lines about her eyes, despite twenty-two years of watching her wait for her mariner's safe return.

Gilles sat against the wall, letting his head fall back until it rested on the bare wood. His hands slid useless from his lap to the floor, and he could not keep his eyelids from drooping. He allowed sleep's enchantment to overcome him, if only for a moment. With the growing light slowly illuminating the room, Caroline was sure to wake soon.

When she did, he would have to tell her how her entire world was no more.

CHAPTER 31

11 September 1782
Panier Quarter
Marseille

Gilles,

You'll forgive my use of your writing materials and my pretending to sleep as I wait for you to go downstairs. I had to take this moment to thank you, and I doubt my ability to adequately speak my feelings.

You did not deserve to get wrapped up in any of this. I cannot comprehend why your family would do this for me and mine, especially when we believe so differently. Your compassion at such a time is not only humbling, but fills me with a measure of hope I cannot seem to chase away no matter how hard I try.

I do not like to say farewell. Is there a person on earth who really does? And yet I think this farewell will be more difficult than the rest. So many things have been torn from me of late. My mind still reels at the thought that our beautiful home is no more. The life I once took for granted is no more, but there is one thing I must leave that will hurt far greater than the loss of the others. To think I will walk out your front door in a matter of hours, never to find joy in the sight of your smile or feel comfort in the strength of your arms around me again, makes what has been a dull and constant ache in my chest grow to unbearable intensity. All that could have been between us lies shattered on the ground, and I wish with all my being we could have the time to see if the pieces might fit back together.

I should not have pulled away that night at the lavender fields. I was still clinging to my stupid vanity from our meeting in Papa's office. I thought I was so much better than those girls you played games with. I had more sense, more passion, more wit, more style. I didn't want you to see, and even more so, I didn't want to see that I was no more capable of resisting you than the greatest flirt among the café maids of Marseille. The only consolation I keep is that I knew a much different Gilles Étienne than they, and I count myself blessed that I was allowed a glimpse into the benevolent soul despite my harsh rejection.

I love you, Gilles. I should have swallowed my foolish pride and showed it much earlier than I did. Now it is too late. I should not ask more of you, as you have already given so much, but I would rest much easier in my despair of all we lost knowing you remembered me without regret.

Jamais en vain.

Marie-Caroline Daubin

Caroline entered the dining room, a blanket clinging to her shoulders, and it was all Gilles could do not to rise from his seat to embrace her. Père glanced at him as if expecting it, but Gilles locked his attention on his porridge.

"Your parents are anxious to see you," Père said as Caroline sat.

Maman appeared from the kitchen with a bowl of porridge topped with a dollop of fig jam. Caroline smiled tightly as Maman set the bowl before her. The whispered thanks barely reached the other end of the table. "I am anxious to see them as well. Has my mother improved?"

Père's mouth twitched, and if Gilles had been in any mood for it, he would have grimaced. Madame Daubin had not taken well to the motion of the brig ever since Père and his crew had hidden them on *le Rossignol* the night before last. If she could not stand the boat at dock, she'd be in for an unpleasant surprise when they put out to sea.

"She was better last evening than she was in the morning." Père finished his coffee with a swift gulp. "But we must discuss how to get you and the priest there without detection." He set the cup down, nodding toward Gilles. "Your little friend has spies at the docks."

Gilles dropped his head to his hand. "And at every road out of the city. He told me." Martel had summoned him to a tavern last night for a drink to discuss the next plan, and Gilles had only gone to gather what the man knew. In fact, not long into the evening, he had left Martel, practically drowned in beer and snoring, to pay for the bill and find his own way home. If Gilles had taken more than a sip, he might have felt sorry.

No. He wouldn't have.

Hot, orange columns racing up the sides of the well-kept home and the factory crackled in his mind. He would never feel sorry for anything that happened to Honoré Martel again. Let him wallow in self-pity for not catching his quarry. If only it would give them time to remove the Daubins from Marseille.

"He unfortunately knows exactly what to look for this time." Gilles sighed. "Franchicourt's last shelterers were not familiar to Martel, but he knows the Daubins."

"What can we do?" Caroline's soft voice sounded as though it came from someone else. The strength he'd seen through all the summer's struggles had wilted. The defeated sound tugged at his heart, but he dared not look at her.

Père shrugged. "It is perhaps too obvious, but I can move my sea chest back to *le Rossignol* today. One of you would fit in there."

Not comfortably. But it was an idea. "What about your equipment?"

"We will find a way to smuggle it out. I've had a little experience with such activities." Père grinned wickedly.

Gilles sat back. It could work, especially if they went during the busiest hours and could lose themselves among other hired coaches hauling bulky chests. "But we need two." Two chests wouldn't fit inconspicuously on the back of most hired coaches.

"You still have a sea chest."

Gilles nodded. Filled with medical books now.

Père stood, gathering his cup and bowl. "I'll go with the priest as soon as possible. He's in the most danger. You come as soon as you can with Mademoiselle Daubin."

Gilles finally looked at her. She did not cower in her corner of the dining room, but a vacancy in her once brilliant eyes cut him through the core.

"Where is the priest?" Père asked as he headed for the kitchen.

"Upstairs. Praying." Caroline pulled the blanket tighter around her. She still hadn't touched her porridge.

Père laughed, though there was no derision in the sound. "Something we should all be doing right now if we want to see tomorrow."

Gilles squeezed into the stairway with his trunk in arms. All the books once inside now stood in orderly rows at the foot of his bed. With measured steps, he descended the narrow staircase, his shoes clunking ungracefully on the floor as he focused on keeping his balance. The handrail pressed into his back, aiding his progress.

Caroline and Maman stood in the front hall below, his mother fussing with the front closure of the old dress she'd given to Caroline. It wouldn't fit perfectly, but Maman rarely gave up until the last moment.

"I have never been to Saint-Malo, but my sons always enjoy themselves there." Maman slid another pin into place and stepped back. She sighed, then adjusted the white fichu to cross in front before moving around to tie the ends behind Caroline. "This will have to do. Roger has a needle and thread that you may use to take in the front to lay correctly. You'll have plenty of time on the voyage, of course."

The grey-blue linen looked so plain compared to Caroline's usual attire. Gilles made it to the last stair and paused to catch his breath. Even with the humble dress, he couldn't think of a more wonderful sight. Morning rays lit the white cap that covered her thick, dark curls, which were brushed back into a knot.

"Are you ready?" he asked, passing her and setting the heavy trunk beside the door.

She didn't respond but turned to Maman and took her hands. "Thank you for everything. You have put your family at great risk to help us."

Maman squeezed her hands. "*C'est naturel.* We wouldn't think of doing anything less for our friends."

Gilles had to look away. Seeing his mother and the woman he loved together caused that cursed throbbing in his heart to start up again. He'd been pretending it was gone as he busied himself with preparations all morning.

After her goodbyes, Maman quit the front hall to return to Florence and the kitchen. Gilles swallowed. How could he say his own farewell?

Caroline stuck her hand into her pocket and withdrew a letter. "I wished to give you this. And to thank you."

"No thanks are needed." He took the paper, hoping the shaking in his hand wasn't as noticeable as it felt. "You know I would have done anything needed."

Her eyes narrowed, and she ducked her head as a tear escaped her lashes. "You are the best of people, Gilles Étienne."

He couldn't speak through the lump in his throat, so he lifted the lid of the trunk and pulled out the stacks of old clothing from his sea days that he'd thrown inside. When he straightened, he noticed she'd moved closer.

His pulse raged as she took him by the sleeves. Her lips, soft as a brush of summer lavender on an evening breeze, caressed his cheek. She started to pull away, but he caught her by the waist and held her there. The sun caught the moisture glistening under her eyes.

"I don't know how I'll rise tomorrow. When I wake and find you missing from me," he whispered.

"You could come to the dock and see us off."

Would it be so wrong to pull her into his arms, as though she weren't readying to leave forever? To destroy his mother's handiwork by running his fingers through Caroline's neat hair? To kiss her trembling lips and to pass to her what little strength he had left with every longing touch?

Would they always regret this last taste of what might have been?

"I'll be there," he said hoarsely. "Though you should stay hidden below until *le Rossignol* has put out to sea."

"Just knowing you're there . . ." She stepped back, and he let her go, the emptiness within him screaming through the silence of the front hall.

Gilles offered her his hand and helped her into the trunk. She had to curl up into a tight ball to fit. Together they tucked in her skirts. Then he set about arranging his clothes and some blankets around her to pad the hard wood and obscure her if anyone decided to quickly peruse the contents of the chest. He made sure she still had air through the layers of linen and wool, which rose and fell under her tight breaths. He would urge the driver to hurry so she wouldn't have to suffer for long.

When the coach arrived, he and the driver dragged the trunk out and secured it on the back. Gilles winced every time the driver callously knocked the chest against something. He tugged at the driver's hasty knots around the trunk. The man was obviously not a mariner, but the knots would hold.

A figure stumbled toward him as he went to get into the carriage. Instantly Gilles's palms went slick with sweat at the sight of the thin young man.

"Martel? I did not think I'd see you this morning. Should you not be at work?"

Martel observed him with sharp eyes, as though he were reading everything in Gilles's head. Stubble covered his cheeks, and he still wore the same clothes from his night of drinking at the café, though now they hung rumpled and stained. "When did you leave last night?"

When Gilles had had enough. "You'd finished talking, and I needed to help my parents."

Martel rested a hand on the sea chest. "Where are you off to?"

Keep breathing. "The dockyards. I've taken a clerical position with my family's business for now."

"For a week?" Martel squinted at the sun, as though condemning it for shining at nine o'clock in the morning. Though he seemed lucid, he couldn't be in his right mind yet. Not after how much Gilles saw him drink.

The itching to leave grew. Caroline needed to get out of that blasted chest. "Until I have saved enough for Montpellier."

His friend straightened. "The battalion leaves in a week."

"I . . ." Gilles chewed his lip. What would happen if he stated directly that he had no intention to go? Martel was a formidable enemy, but they needed to leave for the Old Port without further delay. Talking around the issues and making uncommitted promises would only keep them here longer.

"What's this?" Martel tapped the lid of the trunk. Even in the open air, he still reeked of alcohol.

"My father's trunk. He leaves again tomorrow." A trickle of sweat trailed down his neck from under his cravat. Though September, the heat had returned in full force this morning. "I must get this to him quickly." Gilles fumbled for the door handle, only to realize the driver had opened the coach already. "Shall I see you tomorrow at the café?"

His friend continued to drum his fingers on the lid. "Your father already left with his trunk a couple of hours ago."

Ciel. How long had Martel been on this street? "That was his chest of equipment, of course." Gilles tried for a laugh. "My mother hadn't finished packing his personal effects."

Martel pulled at the lid, and Gilles's insides lurched. The lock held. The key's weight in his pocket did little to comfort him. This man had pushed himself into impossible situations to find the information he sought. Somehow a simple lock didn't seem enough to protect Caroline from Martel's crazed hunt.

Gilles motioned into the carriage. "I can have the driver take us to your house before I go to the docks, if you'd like." Caroline would have to stay inside longer, but it was better to get Martel away.

"You're going to sea, Gilles," his friend growled.

"Pardon?" Gilles blinked.

Martel advanced like a wild cat on a vole. "You have no intention of going with the battalion to Paris. You think to hide on your father's ship."

Gilles squared his shoulders. "I have no intention of leaving Marseille. But I think we would do better building up our piece of France against the attacks of tyranny than giving all of our strength to Paris." Let that tyranny be from a king or from a mob.

Martel spat. "You are a pathetic excuse for a Jacobin. And not worthy to be called Maxence Étienne's brother or Émile Daubin's friend."

"Yours is not the only way to fight for liberty, my friend."

"You think that peace and compassion are going to win this war?" Martel snorted. "You are a simpleton. Just as I thought. I imagined your lackluster dedication to the cause was from an unfamiliarity to the Jacobin ways. Now I see it for what it is—an unquenchable cowardice that has no place among the friends of France."

A swell of words surged from somewhere inside, and Gilles could not keep them back. "If France falls, it is because her so-called friends have turned into the very despots they claim to despise. If the upholders of liberty only protect liberty for those who think as they do, can they really call themselves champions of freedom? Or are they no better than the tyrants who reigned before?"

Martel's fingers wound around a knot in the cords holding the trunk to the coach. His face took on a shade to rival a *sans-culotte*'s cap. "You are very close to speaking treason, Étienne."

Gilles caught the man's wrist and pulled it firmly away from the ropes. "It is not treason to want equality for all, not just one faction. And if the ruling party has made that a law, then I want no part of it."

Martel jerked his hand away. "You'll regret this." He retreated as he spoke, punctuating each word and pointing an accusatory finger at Gilles. "When we've purged the land of tyranny and reclaimed glory for France, you'll regret the weakness that drove you to flee. France wants men, not children. You will have no place here."

"So be it."

Martel turned on his heel and stalked away without another look back. With slumping shoulders, Gilles pulled himself into the small, rackety coach, wishing Caroline had still been inside the house for that exchange instead of in the discomfort of the trunk. He'd just made an enemy of every member of his Jacobin club. Martel would not keep quiet. But perhaps it was now time to take the stand he'd been too afraid to take.

If only he had found the courage to stand in time to help Caroline.

CHAPTER 32

The coach slowed to turn a corner before reaching the dock. At a knock on the roof, Gilles pried his hands from their white-knuckled grip on the hard seat to stick his head out the window. The driver in front leaned his head around the corner.

"Pardon, *monsieur*, but there is another carriage that has been following us for some time. I have slowed to let him pass, but he slows and quickens as I do."

Gilles swiveled his head. The other carriage made to turn the corner, and he could just make out Martel's prominent nose through the window before it pulled around.

Que diable. Gilles ran a hand over his face. That man really was sent from the devil himself.

"Do you wish to lose him? Another *livre* and I would not mind taking the risk."

A little more money added to the fare was worth losing that rat. "As quickly as you can." He immediately rued the request as the coach took off, darting around another corner. Even with a strong stomach, Caroline would no doubt be ill after this ride.

Hold on, my love. He winced as the force of the carriage threw him against the opposite wall. The driver shouted outside and cracked his whip. Terrified citizens sped by through the windows. The coach jostled in the other direction, and Gilles's breakfast threatened to re-appear. Two years on land, and he'd gone softer than he realized. Even the breeze from the open window didn't calm his stomach.

He had to go to the docks. That's where he'd told Martel he was headed, so he couldn't change his destination to lead the other coach away. What if the Daubins happened to be above deck when he found *le Rossignol*, or one of the crew mentioned the priest hidden below?

Gilles swiped at his brow with a sleeve. He had to hope the Daubins would be hidden away and the crew would hold their tongues. They were smugglers as well as privateers. He had no reason to worry.

His head snapped forward as the carriage hit something in the road. The coach careened on two wheels, shoving him to the floor. Gilles dragged himself back upright but froze at a sickening crash from behind. The back of the coach jumped lightly as though sud-denly freed from a burden.

The trunk.

"Stop the coach!" Rocking nearly drove Gilles to his knees again while he fought to unlatch the door. The coach finally righted, and Gilles threw the door open. "Stop the coach!" The trunk lay on its side in the gutter several yards behind them. Martel's coach swerved around it, nearly hitting a wagon going the opposite direction.

The carriage swayed, slowing slightly as it turned toward the docks. The driver continued cracking his whip. He hadn't heard. Let the carriage go on to the docks. Lead Martel away. Gilles had to get to Caroline.

He threw himself through the door and twisted so his back hit the ground first. Screams echoed around him as pain flared up the length of his back. Something popped along his side, sending a stabbing sensation through his ribs and up his spine. He let himself roll over the packed dirt, curling his arms against his chest to protect his already aching side. When he came to a stop on the filthy street, he gasped for breath.

"*Monsieur*! Are you hurt?" Someone hauled him up. For a moment he stared at the faces around him.

"Idiot! Why would you do that?"

"Jumping from a moving coach!"

He held up his hands while trying to shake the fog from his head. "I am well, *merci*." His voice wheezed. He waved them off and slipped through their ranks. He had to get to the trunk.

One figure did not back away. "Monsieur Étienne, that was quite the jump." Light hair. Large eyes. One of the baker's daughters. She leaned in, fluttering her long eyelashes as she followed him to the sea chest. Gilles stiffened his arm to keep her from pushing against his injured ribs.

"It was nothing." He attempted a laugh. What was she doing here?

"Quite the fuss for a trunk," she said sweetly. "Why did you not ask the driver to stop?"

"He—he wouldn't stop. I couldn't have my things stolen." He discreetly felt along his ribs under his coat. They didn't seem broken, only displaced. But he couldn't tell for certain.

The girl raised a brow and cocked her head. "Monsieur Martel didn't tell me you'd be throwing yourself at my feet."

Gilles halted. "Martel?"

She clasped her hands behind her, as though hiding something. Her cheeks turned rosy. Did she practice this perfect coyness? "He gave me a few coins and a kiss to tell him if you came by the docks."

How long had he suspected Gilles would run off? "It is fortunate you were unoccupied this morning." They reached the trunk, and Gilles carefully righted it. He couldn't tell if the soft moan came from the trunk or from inside it. It was all he could do to keep from tearing open the lid in front of one of Martel's agents.

The girl slipped between him and sat on the trunk before he could block her. She lifted her face toward him. "Are you really going to sea, as Monsieur Martel said?"

Best to keep him guessing until *le Rossignol* was safely out of Marseille's harbor. If he played along with this distraction, Martel wouldn't have as much time to focus on his search for the Daubins. "I have not yet decided."

"It must be thrilling to go to sea," she said with an airy sigh. "Always in motion. Seeing new lands and meeting interesting people."

"In truth, most days are rather dull." He had to get her off the trunk. But then what? His shoulder throbbed from his landing, and too much movement agitated his ribs. He couldn't very well drag the trunk to the ship himself, nor could he get Caroline out of it with passersby watching. Any Jacobin-minded citizen would run for reinforcements at the sight of a woman climbing out of a trunk on the side of the street.

"Will you tell me about it?"

Gilles glanced over his shoulder. Any moment Martel could double back. "Perhaps another time." Could he drag the trunk to the alley a few shops away? They'd have to cover Caroline in his clothes and run for *le Rossignol*.

The baker's daughter stood, putting her so close she was nearly pressed against him. "You are leaving, then." Her wide eyes locked on his face. "A kiss and a few coins, and I'll tell Monsieur Martel I didn't see you." As though she could keep a secret from that monster.

"He already knows I'm headed for the docks. He followed me." Once he would have welcomed her proximity as an easy conquest, but now her closeness made his insides writhe uncomfortably. He stiffened, intensifying the ache in his bones. Dragging the trunk any distance by himself was out of the question.

"But does he know there is a person in your sea chest?" She said it with such innocence.

His body went cold.

"So there is a person." Her lips curled. "I wondered what was shifting beneath me."

Blast it. She was baiting him. Gilles scanned the street behind him. If he grabbed Caroline from the trunk in the middle of the street, how much of a stir would he cause? If this girl sounded the alarm—or worse, followed them—they wouldn't stand a chance. She couldn't be Martel's only lackey in the area.

"I won't tell, *monsieur.*" Her brows lifted, but he caught the uncertain tremor in her voice. How old was she? Eighteen? And clearly desperate to prove herself beautiful enough to catch a young man's eye.

Gilles drew in a breath. He could do it. Buy her silence long enough for them to get away. A few months ago he wouldn't have blinked at the suggestion, especially not with the girl mere inches away and begging. For the Daubins, for Caroline, he could kiss this young woman and send her on her way.

When had he become so choosy? Perhaps when he'd walked into that office on a warm April evening and unknowingly lost his heart to a dark-eyed enchantress. She'd changed him in ways he'd never imagined, and he didn't think he would ever recover.

Caroline. She needed to get out. She needed to get to the docks.

Maxence would guffaw at how long Gilles was taking on this girl in front of him. A simple kiss. He needn't linger. She would try to draw out the kiss, as she had the last time he'd kissed her on

Maxence's challenge, but he'd pull away. Fulfill the bargain and be done.

But how could he do this with Caroline lying so close? How could he not, if it meant saving her from Martel's vengeance?

The girl lifted onto her toes, tilting toward him. Just a kiss. *One* kiss. He could give someone a silly, meaningless kiss. For Caroline. Her breath brushed across his lips. He hardly had to do anything; she'd done all the work for him.

"No." He took a step backward, jarring his ribs.

The girl's face fell. "You . . . you want me to tell him?"

"You don't deserve to be used for pleasure by someone who doesn't mean anything by it."

She retreated until her heels hit the trunk. "That is not what you said the last time."

Gilles looked away, running a hand through his hair. He was endangering them all. "I was a disrespectful fool. But I will not make that mistake again."

Tears pooled under the girl's eyes. "You lie. You think I'm not worthy of your notice."

He caught her hand. "I think you're far too good for the attention of men like me." He bowed over her hand. "And I hope someday you will find a man who will stop at nothing to prove it."

"Gilles!"

They both turned. Père hurried down the street toward them. Praise the heavens.

"Do you truly believe that?" the girl asked.

Gilles caught her gaze and nodded. "You can't measure your worth by how many halfwits you get to look your way."

Despite his run, Père breathed easily as he approached. "*Mademoiselle*, it is good to see you have found our trunk."

She gave an uncertain smile. "My sister is on the next street. You must be careful." She stepped away from the trunk as Père readied to lift one side. Gilles's brain blurred in the flood of relief. They could make it.

Gilles nodded to her. "Thank you."

"The coach was empty when it arrived," Père mumbled. "The driver was beside himself with confusion."

Gilles grunted against the pain that swept up his side and back as he and his father picked up the chest and started up the street. Just before they turned the corner, he glanced back to see the baker's daughter still standing where the trunk had been, staring after them.

Gilles groaned as they started up the gangplank and the weight of the trunk rested more heavily on him.

"Put it down, put it down," Père hissed. "Don't injure yourself more." They eased the chest to the ground. "Moreau! Laurent!"

Gilles passed his sleeve across his brow as two men appeared from *le Rossignol* and clambered down to help his father. What a weakling. His knees knocked together from hauling the trunk so far. They'd had to change directions and take a longer route to avoid the baker's other daughter.

Père cleared his throat and gave a sharp nod. "The Jacobin."

Gilles didn't look for Martel. "Has he seen me?"

"He's headed this way, but he isn't looking at you."

Gilles darted around Laurent and Moreau and hurried up the gangplank. The crewmen's footsteps ascended behind him. He should have warned them to take care.

Martel's nasally voice sounded from the dock as Gilles dragged himself toward the hatch. He was out of eyesight of the people below, but the sound made his skin crawl. Would Caroline be safe here with

Martel sniffing about? They should have had Père come back for the other trunk. Gilles had led the rat straight to the prize.

"My son will be down shortly," Père's voice rumbled through the noise of the harbor. "You may wait here."

Gilles halted and waved on the crewmen carrying the trunk. "Hurry!" He couldn't make out Martel's words, only his father's responses, but he could only imagine the Jacobin's fury at being denied. Gilles pointed to others of the crew. "Come help. Take it down right side first."

"I do not want you getting in the way of my crew. Of course you will understand." Père's voice held such calm, almost to the point of being patronizing.

Gilles's limbs threatened to give out as he hurled himself down the ladder after the trunk. He didn't have much time, but he had to see her.

They made their way to the belly of the ship, and the conversation on the dock faded. Gilles blinked as his eyes adjusted to the blackness. A small lantern sat in one corner behind a row of crates with three forms surrounding it. "Over there," he said. "Gently."

Madame Daubin started weeping before the trunk touched the deck. The crew backed away, and Gilles dropped to his knees. Bruises he hadn't remembered collecting protested the action. He fished in his pocket for the key, still panting from the effort to get to the brig.

Gilles shoved the key into the lock and twisted, his heart wrenching with it. He threw open the lid.

Inside, clothes had shifted. Gilles tore them away, revealing Caroline curled up with her arms covering her head. "Caroline?" She wasn't moving. *Pitié.* He reached for her. "Caroline!"

She moaned. Her arms slowly pulled away. Even in the dim light he could see the redness around her eyes. She stiffly lifted her head, and Gilles helped her sit up inside the trunk before crushing her to him. A dozen pains flared through his body, but none so sharp as the one in his chest.

"Are you hurt?" With that fall, she'd have to at least be bruised.

She clutched his coat, her entire frame shaking, and buried her face in his shoulder. "My head, my side, but nothing terrible." Even as she tried to brush it aside, her voice quivered.

"I'm so sorry," he choked, eyes burning. "I should have tied those knots."

Madame Daubin cried her daughter's name, but she was quickly hushed by her husband. "A moment, Angelique. Wait."

"Are we safe?" Caroline whispered, arms encircling his waist.

Gilles squeezed her tighter. This moment of wholeness with her pressed against him. He had only moments left. For her to be safe, he had to go. "You will be," he murmured, lips grazing her neck. "I promise."

They sat in the darkness holding onto each other until her shaking stilled. He felt down her arms. She didn't flinch. Then he ran his hands down her sides, praying nothing was broken, but he couldn't feel anything amiss through her stays. "Can you stand?" He stumbled to his feet, gritting his teeth, and bent to help her up.

"I think I fared better than you did." She grasped his hands and let him guide her out of the trunk. "What happened?"

"Monsieur Gilles." Laurent's voice carried down the ladder. "That man will not leave. He is starting to make threats."

Always ruining his moments with Caroline. He would curse Martel until his dying day. "I'll be above shortly," Gilles said.

Caroline's eyes widened. "Who?"

"Our favorite Jacobin." Gilles closed his eyes. Another farewell. How many of these would he have with Caroline?

"We owe you our lives, Étienne," Monsieur Daubin said from his seat. "I don't know how we will ever repay you for helping a family who believes so differently from you."

Gilles tightened his grip on Caroline's hands. "Doing what is right is more important than who is right, I think."

No one spoke for a moment. At least this would be the final goodbye. After tomorrow morning, he knew for certain he would not have to do this again. He turned to go.

She stopped him by taking his face in her hands. Her thumbs smoothed over his cheeks, and he realized they were wet. She brushed back the unruly curls he could never hope to tame, her touch burning in beautiful, longing ways.

"Until we meet again," she said. The faint light reflected in her fierce eyes and played along those full lips. How he wanted kiss them one last time.

Gilles smiled weakly. If only he could hope to meet her again. *"Adieu."* He pulled away, meaning to race up the stairs but barely succeeding to hobble. He paused on the ladder before clearing the hatch. A moment to catch his breath, to clear his mind of all the ache—both in his heart and body—and he was ready to disembark. Martel would spring at the slightest hint of weakness.

"That man is persistent." Père stood at the rail, looking down the gangplank.

Gilles moved to his side. On the dock below, Martel paced like a hound who'd cornered his prey but could not get to it. "Thank you for your help," Gilles said softly. He owed his father more than that but had no more words.

"You seem a bit depressed, *mon fils.*"

Gilles cleared his throat. "How can anyone not be, with this disaster we've made?" He waved a hand toward the city. He'd have to go straight to his great-uncle's office and make a show of throwing himself into his work. And he couldn't let on that his limbs felt ready to fall off.

Père stroked his chin. "It is a magnificent mess, isn't it?"

People moved about on the dock, jostling Martel as they went. "It can't end well."

"Oh, I wouldn't say that."

Gilles sighed and kneaded his brow. "I tried to hope. I tried to inspire hope in others. But it came to nothing."

"Do you remember when you were young and you went to my uncle's vineyard to plant fig saplings?" Père asked.

Gilles laughed, despite himself. "I remember."

"You were so angry when there wasn't fruit on the trees the next week." His father chuckled. "Maman tried over and over to explain that trees take time to grow and produce fruit. It boggled your little mind."

"We're not talking about fruit now," Gilles said, straightening. "We're talking about people and lives being lost to hatred no one can curb." He made for the gangplank. The longer he left Martel down there, the angrier he would be.

"Don't give up hope because the tree you planted doesn't have fruit yet."

Gilles paused, one foot on the plank.

"You have to believe there will be peace again. Water that tree with your best efforts, and someday you'll see it."

Gilles didn't know how to trust those sentiments. "I hope so."

"My offer still stands." A mischievous grin crossed his father's face. "You can't tell me this voyage would be as bad as previous ones." He threw a pointed look toward the lower decks.

Gilles almost smiled. A voyage with Caroline seemed near to paradise just now. But even if his father believed Maman and the girls would be safe, Gilles had to keep an eye on his former friend.

He grew weary just thinking of the false clues he'd need to plant and hours of dissuading he'd have to manage. "You know I can't."

Père nodded, threading his fingers together on top of the bulwark. "Your mother said you would say that. But you should know that for once she is on my side with this." That playful glimmer in his eye returned.

"Safe voyage, Père." The sea breeze tickled Gilles's face, calling to mind warm days on clear waters. If only. He plunged down the gangplank before he could falter and put them all in danger.

Gilles sat down gingerly on the back step in the dying twilight. He refolded Caroline's last letter, which he'd finally had a moment to read on the walk home from the shipping company's office. The blasted tears didn't come. Only the reality of being watched by Martel's spies kept them at bay. He'd seen Luc Hamon sitting across the street in the shadows of an alley watching the house a moment ago.

He arched his back, then rounded forward, trying to get his ribs back into place. He'd sleep well tonight, so long as his thoughts didn't get the better of him. After all that had happened the last few days, a sound sleep was perhaps too much to hope for.

A deep laugh coming through the kitchen door made him pause. Père was at the docks. He'd already bidden Maman farewell. They'd sail with the tide before the sun rose. And that most certainly wasn't Max.

Gilles shoved the letter back in his pocket. The dream of Caroline was over. He'd do well to move forward. He had work with his great-uncle and university to anticipate. People to help and family to protect. Martel to prove wrong, at least until the man left with the battalion.

Now there was a happy thought.

He pushed himself up slowly and mounted the steps. Hardly in the mood for company, his curiosity over the voice forced him to move. Perhaps it was only Florence's husband. He'd greet them all and then retire.

As he entered, his eyes fell on a pair of stocky shoulders and head of short curls mostly covered by a mariner's cap across the table from Maman. Gilles dropped his hands to his sides. "Victor?"

His oldest brother lifted a mug toward him. "How are you Gilles?"

"I've been better." No sense hiding the truth. "What are you doing here? I thought you wouldn't be back for several weeks."

"We avoided storms and made good time." The oldest Etienne brother finished off his drink. Victor was a man of few words, something Gilles and Max used to laugh at. Now Gilles appreciated it. He wouldn't get flowery sermons on the revolution tonight.

"Come sit," Maman said, pointing to the bench across from Victor. "I'll make you some chocolate." She got up and went to the hearth.

Gilles didn't have the energy to protest and obediently sat. What was Caroline doing now? Sleeping off the jarring escape, he hoped. "*Félicitations* on the—"

Maman whirled on him, shaking her head frantically.

"—safe arrival," Gilles finished, staring at their mother.

"Victor has come straight from the docks on his way to surprise Rosalie. That was very kind of him, was it not?" she said sweetly.

Oh. Victor didn't know about the baby yet. Gilles's face warmed. Rosalie was a very patient woman, but she might not be so patient with Gilles if he spoiled her secret.

Victor nodded. "I should go, but I wanted to tell you I'd arrived safely." He rose from the table. He and Gilles were built in the same design—stocky and dark haired like their mother's family. But Victor had received all the luck and gained a little more of their father's height than Gilles. "I'd hoped to catch Père before he left. He should make good time to Barcelona. I hope the weather holds the rest of their journey."

Gilles nodded. They were to make land in Spain and leave Père Franchicourt in a place that still accepted his religion. Then they'd take the Daubins to the port city of Saint-Malo, a favorite of privateers and those at odds with the law. Somewhere they could blend into the patchwork of residents without being asked too many questions. Would Père meet Dr. Savatier? If Gilles ever did abandon his plans for Montpellier, it would be to apprentice himself to Savatier rather than to sail with Père.

And Caroline would be there.

The oldest brother fixed his eyes on Gilles. "I'm surprised you're still here."

Gilles rubbed his chin. Was that only a day's worth of stubble that scratched his hand? He couldn't remember the last time he'd shaved. He must look a sight. "I won't have the funds to leave for Montpellier for some time. But I hope by next summer I'll have saved enough."

"What I meant was, I'm surprised you aren't on *le Rossignol*."

"I . . ." Maman avoided Gilles's gaze. Of course she'd told Victor everything. He listened better than any of her boys. "I need to be here. To protect Maman. And your family."

Victor raised an eyebrow. "I won't be leaving again for some time."

"And I must keep Martel from sniffing out the Daubins. If he discovers they're in Saint-Malo, he'll raise his own battalion to track them down."

Maman held up the spoon she was using to stir the chocolate. "I thought he was leaving with the new battalion soon."

Gilles arched his back again. She had a point. But until then, Martel had to be watched. "He has spies. He would be furious if he found out I had joined Père's crew instead of the *fédérés*."

Victor retrieved his mug and took it to the washbasin. Instead of simply sinking it into the water for someone else to wash, he crouched and began rinsing it. "Working is not against the revolution. He'd have no sound reason to retaliate."

Gilles rounded his shoulders. His ribs had to go back in sometime. "I'm so close to reaching my goal of studying at Montpellier. I do not wish to give that up." It wasn't like Victor to argue. He'd been away from home too long.

"Hm." Maman briskly stirred the chocolate, the spoon clattering against the sides. "It seems to me you would get much more useful experience under the tutelage of a surgeon as good as Savatier than by sitting in a hall listening to some physician's lectures."

There was truth to that. Gilles pushed harder into the stretch. A powerful pop reverberated up his back. Ease flooded the area, and he sagged against the table. He twisted his torso back and forth carefully. He hadn't put every rib back in place, but it was a relieving start. "I committed to working for Great-uncle." His excuses were becoming less pressing.

Maman put a chocolate-stained hand against her hip. "If you do not wish to go, then simply say, 'I do not wish to go.'"

"Gilles can't say that, because it isn't true." Victor straightened and set his clean mug to dry on the table. There was a twinkle in his eye. "Gilles has never made a good liar."

A flutter disrupted the determination that had settled in Gilles's chest. Why could he not go? What did staying truly serve him? "But Martel. He has spies waiting for me to set foot outside of this house."

"You avoided them once," Victor said with a shrug.

Gilles twisted his back more. His heart thrummed. Pop. Pop, pop. He sighed as the day's pain finally let up. His back and side were still sore, but when he stretched, everything seemed back in its normal place. If only he could fix the rest of his life in the same manner. "I appreciate your concern, *mon frère*. I did not realize how much my family enjoys making matches."

Victor folded his arms. Maman tilted her head, dripping chocolate onto the floor from the spoon, which she must have thought was still in the pot.

Gilles held up his hands. It was too much. After all that had happened, it couldn't really work so easily. "In the end, she is a *royaliste*. I am . . ." He swallowed. He wasn't much of a Jacobin anymore. "I am for the revolution. How can we possibly make it work?" They'd proved their relationship would fail time and again over the course of the summer.

"She's a woman and you're a man who love each other," Victor said. "The labels don't matter. If you are both committed to making this work, how can you fail?"

Gilles chewed the inside of his cheek. Stepping on that ship was giving up his entire world. His dreams, his plans, his life in Marseille. His family. "I'd be leaving you. Perhaps forever." His eyes fell on the table. No more late conversations with Maman over chocolate or quiet nights studying in his room. No fiery sunsets spent walking through lavender fields. Caroline couldn't return to this place, and if he married her, neither could he.

Maman drifted over and sat beside him on the bench. She threaded her arm through his. "My dear boy. This war in France will not last forever. You will always have your family, no matter how far you wander from home." Her voice wavered, but she smiled bravely.

"But . . . I don't even know if she's still committed to making it work." His throat tightened.

Victor swept his cap off his head and threw it at Gilles's face. Gilles caught it before it fell to his lap. "What is this?"

Victor gestured toward the Old Port with his head. "So you can pass as me and fool the spy in this light. There's only one way to find out if she is committed, and you have only a few hours."

Gilles settled the cap down over his hair. It wasn't as tight as his liberty cap, only snug enough to be comfortable. A path free of deterring brambles lay at his feet. It meant sacrificing everything he thought he wanted. But as he looked down the road before him, the light of an unknown and exciting future beamed in the distance. Gilles glanced between his brother and his mother and grinned.

CHAPTER 33

12 September 1792
Marseille

Cher *Gilles,*

Our first night aboard was not terrible, but your father in his usual teasing way assures us it only gets worse from here. I believe him but cling to the hope that we will get used to the simple quarters. It will make us stronger for our new life in Saint-Malo.

It is hard to think that in a few hours, we will leave Marseille behind us forever. In May, I hated returning to this place. Now I am loath to leave. Isn't it funny how your entire perspective of something can change just because of one person?

I want so badly to go above for one last look at the city. But mostly I wish for one last glimpse of you. Last night I dreamed you stowed away with us. I suppose I will have to content myself with that happy dream.

Affectueusement,
Marie-Caroline

A bright-eyed boy bounded up to Gilles, an awed grin on his face. How he had the energy to prance like that when they'd all been awake at such an abominable hour, Gilles would never know. Though he had probably been the same at twelve.

"Course is set, sir. Captain says you're free to go below."

Gilles nodded and winked, and the boy's smile nearly split his face. He scampered off to his duties, leaving Gilles alone at the stern. Marseille's port lay in the distance, painted in blue as it waited for the sun to come over the hill. He closed his eyes and could almost smell the earthiness of his great-uncle's dewy vineyards and the sharp scent of a batch of soap ready to be stirred at the *savonnerie*. He'd miss mornings in Marseille.

Faint footsteps pattered up to the quarterdeck and stopped at the stern rail near him. Gilles expected the fawning cabin boy, back to relay a message from the captain. Teasing words halted on his tongue when he saw his companion.

Caroline stared out across the bay, fingers gripping the rail tightly. She'd tied her hair back in a simple knot. Strands of it had already pulled loose in the brisk wind carrying them out to sea. She hadn't looked at him yet. She must have thought him another crew member. He'd quickly gone to the hold after boarding last night, but all the Daubins had been asleep.

"You should still be below," he said. "We haven't cleared the bay." Though the chance was slim, if someone on a nearby ship was looking for the Daubins and pointed their telescope at *le Rossignol*, they could recognize her.

"I know I should," she said, turning to him. "I only wanted one last . . ." Her mouth went slack. "Gilles?"

He threw her a grin to rival the new cabin boy's. In a moment, she'd thrown her arms around his neck. "When they said the captain's son had come aboard, I thought they meant your oldest brother." He could barely make out her breathless voice.

"Victor captains his own boat these days." That look of pure joy on her face made all the trouble of sneaking onto the ship under Martel's nose worth it. He couldn't recall the last time she'd really smiled.

She pulled back to look him in the eye. "But what are you doing here? What of your family? Montpellier?"

What a fool he'd been to think of letting her go. He tightened his arms around her. "My mother is a strong woman. I've recently learned not to cross strong women when they've set their minds to something."

"I thought you swore never to return to sea."

A ridiculous vow. Père was right—he was born for the wind's caress and waves' embrace. But perhaps more accurately . . . for Caroline's. "I have a friend who is a surgeon in Saint-Malo. He has asked me to be his apprentice."

Caroline grasped his arms. The little white cockade she'd pinned to her jacket's bodice rose and fell with her rapid breaths. "You're coming with us to Saint-Malo?" She rested her forehead against his shoulder. "I'm still dreaming."

Gilles chuckled. "It feels that way." The ocean swished past the brig's sides, quieting the crew's chatter on the main deck behind them. This was as alone as they would get for weeks. "I thought your father could use help adjusting to his new employment." As a clerk for Père's brother, oddly enough. "And finding lodging for himself and your mother, since I know the city." The words were tumbling from his mouth but not the ones he wished to say.

Caroline tilted her head. "No lodging for me?"

Gilles gulped. With all the wind rushing past, how was he short of air? "I had hoped . . . That is to say, I wished to ask . . ." *Ciel*, he was making a mess of things again. "My friend offered me lodging with the apprenticeship, and . . ." Well, that was unromantic. Heat flared across his skin.

Caroline watched him, the corners of her lips creeping upward. "You wish me to live there with you."

"I-I thought it might be nice," he said with a shrug.

"Exactly what sort of arrangement are you proposing?"

Her alluring coyness, which he'd desperately missed the last weeks, had returned. Now he'd never be able to redirect the course of this conversation. "The sort of arrangement where I come home from a long day of work—"

"To a fine meal that I've cooked? I should warn you, I am worthless in the kitchen."

"No, I come home and you tell me about all of the people you've helped in our hours apart." His fingers ran over the hem of the little jacket she wore, which fell just below her waist. *Oh, spit it out, Gilles.* "We discuss the news of the day, more often than not arguing about the direction of our government—"

"Which argument I win more often than not."

How he loved this stubborn woman, who would not even allow him to ask for her hand without asserting herself. "Naturally. But instead of retiring angry, we acknowledge the points on which we do agree, and then I kiss you, because I cannot imagine how I was blessed with so wonderful a . . . wife."

Gilles searched her impassive face for any clue to her thoughts. Perhaps in time he would get better at reading her expressions.

"What do you say to that arrangement?" he asked after a moment.

She cocked her head. "I think you will need to kiss me first. I still don't know if you can do the job properly."

A thrill raced down his arms as he cupped her face in his hands. Her soft lips beckoned. "In all fairness, you've never given me the chance."

Her brow arched. "I thought you would jump at the suggestion, rather than standing there complaining about—"

Gilles pressed his lips to hers. Gently at first. But then her arms stole around him, pulling him against her. She kissed him back with the fierceness he'd dreamed of for weeks, and for a moment the sea and *le Rossignol* faded. Once again they were in the endless lavender fields, the ocean wind replaced by the fire of a golden sunset.

He let her take the lead, and as her lips moved fervently over his, the kisses melted into each other. He couldn't tell where one started and the next began, his head buzzing with the rush of this moment he'd believed would never come. The warmth of their breath mingled in the cool sea air. She didn't relent, and he didn't want her to.

So this was what she had meant when she said her kisses weren't sweet.

A whistle and a chuckle wrenched his mouth away from hers, and he spied his father retreating from the quarterdeck. Caroline's grip on Gilles's jacket did not let him get far.

"I'm sorry. This is hardly a good place." His face warmed, and he pulled at his neckcloth. That was a fine way to set tongues wagging. They wouldn't have a moment's peace the rest of the voyage with all the teasing.

Caroline looked away, back toward Marseille and the rising sun. "We'll never see it again, will we?" She spoke with a steady voice, while Gilles could barely think through the pounding in his chest. How did she do it?

"Not as it was. All of France will be a very different place." He took her by the shoulders. "But we'll change it for good. Together."

A small smile touched her lips. She wrapped her fingers around his and squeezed. "Yes, together."

He rested his forehead against hers. "Does that mean the kiss will suffice?"

"I found it lacking in one thing, which I'm sure is only a sad consequence of your little games."

Gilles pulled back. "Lacking?" His dizzy mind had yet to settle from the taste of her lips.

"Yes." Her fingers crept along his neck and buried themselves in his hair. "I found it entirely too short."

Short? "The crew," he gasped as she leaned in.

"What of them?" Her words brushed across his lips.

Well, if she wasn't worried . . .

She swept him back into a kiss, her slender hands refusing to let him escape. And as their lips moved in time to the beating waves, he was happy to comply as long as she wished. No matter what the tides of revolution threw across their path, they would weather it so long as he had this woman to hold.

EPILOGUE

September 1793
Saint-Malo, Brittany, France

Young men marched down the street heading south toward Paris. Citizens of Saint-Malo lined the path around them, waving and singing the stirring anthem so popular in Marseille. Some cried. Others cheered. But Gilles and Caroline watched in silence until the battalion moved out of sight.

"You should be grateful," she said as they turned toward the door of their little apartment. Gilles couldn't help his grin as he followed her back inside the cramped home. Her presence spread light to every dark corner.

"Why should I be grateful?" He closed the door and leaned against it to watch her make her way to the kitchen. Cloudy light illuminated her features as she took a bowl of resting dough from its place near the hearth.

"If you hadn't married me, you'd be marching off with them."

She uncovered the bowl and tipped it upside down. The dough slowly tumbled onto the small table they'd squeezed into the kitchen.

Gilles sauntered through the makeshift sitting room. "I suppose you're looking for thanks, then." On the lone, broken-down sofa sat an old pair of stays. Caroline had started picking apart the garment's side seams last night to add more lacing. She insisted she needed the extra room already, though she didn't look much bigger to Gilles.

Caroline shrugged, then batted at a loose curl with the back of a well-floured hand. "You know I always welcome gratitude." She said it impishly, but he could hear the worry hidden beneath. Someday the government might require husbands to join the fight against foreign invaders. For now, they counted their lucky stars it was limited to single young men.

Gilles caught the curl and gently brushed it back under her cap. "*Merci*, my Caroline, for marrying me so that I do not have to go to war."

She gave him a satisfied nod as she kneaded the dough. Biting back a mischievous smile, he sat on the edge of the table.

"Gilles!" She swatted at him. "You are getting flour all over your trousers."

"And thank you for marrying me so that I do not have to scavenge for food."

She put her hands on her hips, careful to keep her sticky fingers off of her clothes. The movement pulled her apron tight across her growing belly. Perhaps she did need more room in those stays. But they'd been married long enough for him to have learned not to say that aloud. "You are far better at cooking than I."

"But you insist on taking care of the kitchen, for which I am grateful." He leaned back on his elbows, blocking her from her work. "And thank you for marrying me so I do not have to retire to bed alone each night."

"Now you're being ridiculous. I need to form this bread, or we'll have none for dinner tonight." She tried to nudge him out of the way with her elbow.

He shouldn't . . . But he couldn't resist. Gilles collapsed onto the table. The dough squished under his back like a lumpy pillow.

"*Gilles!*"

He chuckled as her fists pounded his chest. Little globs stuck to his waistcoat. Her squeals of protest dissolved into exasperated laughter. "You horrible oaf! I worked hard to make that." She crossed her arms and rested them on his chest. "Now what are we to have with our dinner?"

He attempted a sheepish look. "I'll fetch a baguette from the bakery."

Her full lips pursed. "We've had to do that too often in the last year."

"It's worth it if it makes you happy." That earned him a smile. "But I wasn't finished thanking you."

She lifted an eyebrow.

He slid his arms around her, and his heart quickened its pace. "I also wanted to thank you for making this life more brilliant than I ever imagined it could be. *Je t'aime, mon amour.*"

Those deep brown eyes softened. She leaned down, placing a kiss on his forehead. "I love you, too." Her lips found his, and he lost himself in an immortal summer evening.

Too soon she pulled back with a sigh and furrowed brow. She'd started taking on the more of the weight of the world as her pregnancy progressed.

"What is it?" Gilles came up on one elbow and reached for her hand. The dough pulled at his jacket before plopping onto the table behind him.

Caroline held up her hand, wiggling the ring on her finger so the lettering glimmered. "You love to repeat 'Never in vain' when something goes wrong. And most of the time I believe you." She huffed. "But even you must admit that all the work I put into making that dough was in vain."

Gilles winced. "My apologies. But surely it was worth it for the kiss."

"The lengths you'll go to just for a kiss. Shameless flirt indeed." She shook her head. And then she kissed him again.

ACKNOWLEDGMENTS

This novel could not have been written without the help of a few very dear friends and critique partners. Jennie Goutet was an invaluable help to me as someone with whom I could discuss French history, culture, and language in order to make the best decisions for this book. Megan Walker was the support I needed through the highs and lows of the writing process. Deborah Hathaway believed in this story from the start, despite reading it chapter by chapter as a very messy first draft. Joanna Barker (to whom I dedicate all ten semicolons in this book) also gave me incredible feedback as one of my alpha readers, and Heidi Kimball cheered me on through all the growth this novel took. You ladies are wonderful.

A huge thank you to the staff at Shadow Mountain, especially Heidi Gordon for her enthusiasm and Alison Palmer for all the work she has put into making my stories shine. I so appreciate all the hours spent planning, editing, designing, promoting, and marketing.

Thank you to my friends and family members who have been so supportive of my writing dream. There are too many of you to name, but I appreciate each of the texts, social media posts, beta reads, child care offers, and everything else. A special shoutout to Madame McFarland and the Devarenne family for instilling in me a love of France, its language, its culture, and its history.

To Jeff and our children, thanks for giving me this space to grow and create. I appreciate each time you step in to keep our home intact while I'm in absent-minded professor mode. The knowledge that you're behind me every step of the way is one of the greatest comforts.

And to my Heavenly Father, thank you for giving me this gift and the opportunity to share it.

DISCUSSION QUESTIONS

1. Gilles and Marie-Caroline have different political views, yet still are drawn to one another. Have you ever differed with someone close to you on politics or religion? How would you address those differences? Are there character traits that are more important than political opinions?

2. At one point, Gilles is pressured into participating in destroying someone's house. Do you think the revolutionaries' actions were warranted? Have you ever been pressured to do something you were uncomfortable with?

3. Marie-Caroline steals a church book and publicly stands up to revolutionaries, even though doing so endangers her life. Do you think her actions are wise? Have you ever felt the need to stand up for what you believed was right, despite possible consequences?

4. Gilles decides not to join his brother and friends to march on Paris, despite intense pressure to do so. Have you ever had to make a difficult choice, unsure at the time if the decision you were making was right or wrong?

5. Gilles and his friends have a game of trying lure women into kissing

them. Why is this game unkind? What does it imply about both women and men? Are there similar attitudes in today's society?

6. During the French Revolution, violence was used to overthrow an oppressive monarchy, which eventually led to a freer society. Do you think the ends justified the means in this case? Do you think other methods of bringing about change would have been more or less effective?